IN FIRE FORGED

FORGED

WORLDS OF HONOR #5

DAVID WEBER

In Fire Forged

This is a work of fiction. All the characters and events portrayed in this book are fictional, and any resemblance to real people or incidents is purely coincidental.

A Baen Books Original

Baen Publishing Enterprises
P.O. Box 1403
Riverdale, NY 10471
www.baen.com

ISBN: 978-1-4391-3414-6

Cover art by David Mattingly
Interior schematics by Thomas Marrone, Thomas Pope and William H. Edwards

First printing, February 2011

Distributed by Simon & Schuster
1230 Avenue of the Americas
New York, NY 10020

Library of Congress Cataloging-in-Publication Data

In fire forged / [edited by] David Weber.
    p. cm. — (Worlds of honor ; no. 5)
  "A Baen Books original"—T.p. verso.
  ISBN 978-1-4391-3414-6 (hc : alk. paper)
  1. Science fiction, American. 2. Harrington, Honor (Fictitious character)—Fiction.
I. Weber, David, 1952– II. Title. III. Series.

  PS648.S3I52 2011
  813'.0876608—dc22

                                                             2010052024

10   9   8   7   6   5   4   3   2   1

Pages by Joy Freeman (www.pagesbyjoy.com)
Printed in the United States of America

To Sharon, Megan, Morgan, and Mikey.
For putting up with Daddy.

Contents

Ruthless

Jane Lindskold

Gone. Her child was gone.

Frantically, Judith Newland searched the small apartment she shared with her two-year-old daughter, Ruth.

Bedroom. Bathroom. Living area.

When she started opening cabinet doors and bending double so that she could look all the way to the back, Judith admitted to herself what she had known all along.

Somehow, during the short time she had stepped out into the hall to talk to that new woman from Human Services, little Ruth had completely and utterly disappeared.

A momentary urge to scream, to panic, filled Judith's heart. For all that her nineteen years had included kidnapping, rape, murder, piracy, and countless other horrific experiences, these last two years had been relatively peaceful. Almost without her noticing, Judith had allowed herself to be lulled into accepting peace—rather than all the rest—as normal.

Now the steel at the core of Judith's soul, the quality that had permitted her not only to survive her long captivity on Masada, but to prosper and grow, met the urge to panic and pushed it back.

Judith closed her eyes and took a deep breath.

Ruth wasn't in the apartment. Very well. Where might she be? The apartment had only one exit, but there was a safety escape outside the bedroom window. There had been a drill just a few days before. Ruth had been fascinated by how the grav tube had

1

appeared at the touch of a button concealed in the programmable nanotech "wallpaper."

Judith didn't think Ruth could have reached the button and activated it, but then again, Judith was the last person to underestimate someone merely on the basis of age. If her former husband had not underestimated Judith…

But, no. She wasn't going to think about that. That, at least, was done.

Already Judith's feet were hurrying her down the hall to the bedroom. A quick glance was all she needed to see that the grav tube remained undeployed. Ruth hadn't left that way.

Panic was trying to rise again, but Judith ignored it. Grabbing her apartment keys, she hurried out to check if any of her neighbors had seen anything.

The residential tower where Judith and Ruth lived was unique even among Manticore's eclectic society, for it housed most of the four hundred or so refugees who had fled in a body from the planet Masada something over two and a half years before. This alone would have made the complex peculiar, but since those refugees had been nearly all female—the males had been small children, usually under five years of age—the dynamic was skewed again. Add to this that most of the women had been accustomed to life in communal harems. They continued to find privacy, rather than the lack thereof, unsettling. Therefore, the three floors of the tower they occupied more resembled a beehive than a modern residential community.

Judith herself was one of the few who treasured privacy and hadn't chosen to reside in a larger apartment with two or more adults and any associated children. But then Judith was different from her fellow Sisters of Barbara in many ways, including her birthplace, level of education, and complete lack of the faith that—although modified—continued to be a dominant influence in the spiritual lives of her associates.

However, Judith still felt closer to her fellow refugees than she did to almost any Manticoran. She was especially attached to the woman to whom she now fled with her problem.

"Dinah!" Judith said, rushing in past Dinah and closing the door behind her. "Ruth is gone from our apartment, vanished completely."

The tale poured from Judith's lips, how the doorbell had rung, how the new woman from Human Services had asked if she could speak to Judith. How Ruth had been napping, so they had stepped out into the hallway.

Dinah listened without interrupting, her gray eyes hardening to steel as the import of what Judith was telling her went home. Too old to be given the Manticorans' anti-aging prolong therapies, nonetheless, Dinah had benefitted from the Manticorans' advanced medical science. The heart condition that had nearly killed her during the escape from Masada had been completely reversed. Without a weak heart subtly undermining her strength, Dinah now appeared a decade or more younger—a gray-haired, gray-eyed, round-figured dove rather than the haggard old woman her thirty-eight years of marriage to Ephraim Templeton had created.

"I wasn't gone more than five minutes," Judith concluded. "When I went back in, something seemed a little off. I went to see if Ruth had climbed out of her crib—she's getting better and better at that—and she wasn't there."

"You checked everywhere." Dinah's words were a comment, not a question. She knew Judith better than most, and knew she was thorough, often to the point of obsession. It was a trait that had served them both well in the past.

"I did."

"But you wouldn't be offended if I checked again?"

"No."

"Good. I'll do that. You go and speak with our neighbors. Ask if they saw Ruth. Ask about that woman from Human Services, too."

Judith was thrusting her keys into Dinah's hands when the oddity of that last statement caught her.

"Her? Why?"

"From what you told me about the questions she was asking you, I find it peculiar that she didn't come and speak with me. I have been home for the last several hours, preparing texts for tomorrow's service."

Judith frowned. That omission was odd. Although Judith's skills had made the escape from Masada possible, there was no doubt who was the leader of their community—and who had been the head of the Sisterhood of Barbara before they had ever left Masada. The new woman should at least have introduced herself to Dinah.

"I'll ask," Judith promised. She hadn't thought she could be any more afraid, but Dinah's words had crystalized a fear that had been budding in her heart.

She didn't wait for the lift, but ran for the stairs.

❊   ❊   ❊

"Oh, Michael!"

The speaker's voice was feminine, high pitched yet musical. It held a distinctly lilting note of welcome and invitation. Even so, rather than slowing at the sound, Michael Winton, lieutenant, senior grade, serving in Her Majesty's ship *Diadem,* picked up his pace.

Michael tried to act as if the call might be meant for another Michael, not him, but although the name and its variants were very common in the Star Kingdom, his appearance was not. Michael's skin was the dark brown of the Wintons, rather than one of the more ethnically blended mixes common in the realm. Although Michael had been away from home over the last two years, there was no reason for him to believe his slight increase in height, and slightly more mature muscular development, was adequate disguise. For one thing, he looked far too much like his father—and the late Roger Winton's portrait still hung in many a public place, never mind that the king had been dead for over nine T-years.

Michael's companion, a young man with dark blond hair and laughing, light brown eyes, hissed under his breath.

"Michael, what's your problem? She's waving at you! Since when did you start running away from pretty girls?"

Square-jawed and handsome, Todd Liatt, one of Michael's closest friends, was always trying to get his more retiring friend to join him in his leave-time pursuit of the fair.

Michael glanced side to side, looking for a route of escape, but although he knew both the public and private areas of Mount Royal Palace as well as he knew his own cubby aboard the *Diadem,* he knew he couldn't get away without being obviously rude—and pure rudeness was a tactic denied to him.

He slowed his pace and swallowed a sigh. Then he schooled his dark, boyishly handsome features into a polite smile as he turned to face the young lady who was hurrying down the wide corridor toward him.

She had skin the color of coffee with lots of cream. The freckles Michael remembered from when they had been children had faded, but she still wore her dark honey-colored hair loose, the thick, tightly curled mass falling past her shoulders to the middle of her back. She'd been cute as a child, but now Michael had to admit Todd was right, she was decidedly pretty, maybe even almost beautiful.

"Alice! What a surprise to find you here."

"Daddy's attending a meeting of some committee or other," Alice said, clasping the hand Michael politely offered to her between two of her own. Her amber-flecked golden eyes danced with mischief. "His secretary is on holiday, and I'm filling in. What luck he told me he didn't need me just when you were going by!"

Alice released Michael's hand and stepped back a pace, looking up at Michael admiringly. "I thought it was you, but I wasn't sure. You're so much taller, and that uniform is so dignified."

Given that they hadn't seen much of each other since Michael had switched his study program at the age of thirteen T-years, when he began seriously preparing to attend the Naval Academy, Michael thought Alice's comment about his height idiotic. However, his training in not saying what he thought pre-dated his Academy education by many years.

"I would have known you," he said. "You still wear your hair the same way."

Alice laughed delightedly. "And you used to love to pull it. I remember you saying you liked how the curls bounced like springs."

She shook her head just a little, as if inviting Michael to take a tug, but he felt no such temptation. A slight motion at his side reminded Michael that his social duties were not concluded.

"Alice, let me present my friend, Todd Liatt. Todd was my roommate at the Academy, and now we're bunking together in *Diadem*. Lieutenant Liatt, this is Alice Ramsbottom. As you must have gathered, we went to school together."

Alice offered Todd a slim hand and a polite smile. Todd was generally thought the more attractive of the two men, but Alice's attention didn't stray from Michael. She gave a light laugh.

"Ah, good old school days," she said in a deliberately affected manner. "You were Mikey, then, but someone told me that you go by 'Michael' now."

Alice paused, and Michael observed with slow horror that she was actually simpering at him.

"Of course," Alice went on, "I realize I should have addressed you as Crown Prince Michael or Your Highness, but I was so thrilled when I saw you, I didn't think. I hope you don't mind..."

She fluttered long lashes at him, and Michael felt relieved—not for the first time—that his dark skin prevented anyone from seeing him blush.

"No. Sure. I mean, we've known each other since we were kids. Anyhow," Michael realized that he was babbling, but the combination of Alice's flirtatious manner and Todd's poorly concealed amusement were too much. "I mean, the 'Crown' bit is really a formality now that my nephew Roger is showing himself such a promising young man."

"Prince Roger is a darling boy," Alice agreed. "I've seen him at all sorts of receptions, so straight and manly in his formalwear, escorting little Princess Joanna so seriously. The prince is how old now?"

"Six T-years," Michael responded promptly. "In fact, he's almost seven now. In less than four more T-years, he'll take his qualifying tests and be formally named heir apparent. Princess Joanna will second him in just a few years more, and the 'Prince' in front of my name will become in truth what it really is now—a mere courtesy title."

"You're so modest," Alice said, "as if anyone could ever forget you're Queen Elizabeth's only brother, and a scion of the House of Winton."

"I wish they would," Michael muttered.

Alice's amber-flecked golden eyes widened in surprise, but like him she had had training from the cradle on that kept her from saying the first thing that came to mind.

"Well, it's awfully nice that you gave me permission to call you by your first name," Alice said. "I don't suppose you—and Lieutenant Liatt, of course—have time to go grab coffee or something?"

Michael saw Todd starting to nod agreement and cut in quickly.

"Perhaps another time. We have someplace we need to be."

"Sure." Alice looked disappointed, but Michael thought he caught a flicker of another emotion—relief? It was gone before he could be sure. "Anyhow, I probably should be checking in with Daddy. You're on leave for a while?"

"A while," Michael agreed, deliberately vague, lest he be pressed into setting up another meeting.

"Well, I'm off to Gryphon this afternoon to take care of some business for Daddy, but I'm sure we'll see each other again. 'Bye now, Michael. A pleasure to meet you, Lieutenant Liatt."

The two young men echoed her farewells, and turned away. As they walked down the corridor, Michael heard the soft whisper of following footsteps.

He didn't need to turn and look to know they belonged to Lieutenant Vincent Valless, Palace Security, the crown prince's bodyguard.

For Michael, accustomed as he had become during his time in the Navy to going where he pleased without needing to be trailed—the logic being that the entire ship's company could be considered the crown prince's bodyguard—Valless's presence was disquieting.

Michael knew that most of his shipmates were looking forward to this holiday as a relief from the formalities and rituals of military service.

Why am I the only one, Michael thought with a flare of an anger he had thought long buried, *who doesn't get a holiday?*

❋   ❋   ❋

Todd held back the questions Michael knew he was aching to ask until they were in the air car Michael had been issued to use as his own during his leave and the flier had been cleared for departure from the palace grounds. The assigned sting ship followed it off the field, hovering discreetly in the background.

"Michael, why did you turn tail and run like that? You were almost rude."

"And I'm never rude," Michael replied seriously. "I know."

"That isn't an answer. We have hours before we're due to meet up with that friend of yours. We could have had coffee or something. I thought that Alice was cute, and she clearly was glad to see you."

"Me?" Michael retorted, feeling that familiar anger again, fighting to keep it from touching his voice. "Me or 'Crown Prince Michael'? When I'm shipboard, I almost forget what court is like. Ever since the Masadan affair when I was a middie, most of the Navy accepts me for what I can do, not for who I was born."

"Alice called you 'Michael,'" Todd reminded him.

"Yeah. I would have felt that was more genuine if she'd called me 'Mikey,' like when we were kids."

"You weren't crown prince then, were you?"

"Nope. Elizabeth stood between me and responsibility," Michael said, trying to keep his tone light. "Then our dad died, and she was queen at eighteen T-years, and I was crown prince. I'd never expected to be, you know. Dad was young enough that he'd been eligible for Prolong. I was just a kid, still trying to figure out what I wanted to be when I grew up, and suddenly I was next in line for the throne of the Star Kingdom of Manticore."

Todd knew this, of course, but oddly enough, they'd never really talked about it. Todd's easy acceptance that Michael Winton wanted to be treated as nothing more, nothing less, than another student at the Naval Academy had cemented their friendship, a friendship that had not weakened over the years they had been separated for their different middie cruises and junior officer assignments.

Todd heard Michael out, then said softly, "That had to have been rough. Still, you're never going to escape that you're Queen Elizabeth's little brother, no matter how many others come to stand between you and the throne. Isn't it about time you came to terms with it?"

"I thought I had," Michael said, and Todd—who hadn't specialized in tactics without learning a thing or two about choosing his battles—had the sense to change the subject.

"Tell me about this friend of yours we're going to visit. You met her during that Masadan affair you mentioned, right?"

Michael nodded. "Judith was one of the ringleaders, only sixteen, about three months pregnant, and fierce as hell."

"Wildcat?"

"No. The reverse. Calm. Controlled, but with fire in her soul. Impossible as it may seem, Judith taught herself to pilot a spaceship with nothing but virtual sims—no tutoring, no practice flights. She did so despite the likelihood that she'd be beaten or even killed if anyone found her out."

"Those Masadans are savages," Todd said. "I'm glad the government has decided to throw in their lot with the Graysons. Your friend wasn't the only one who escaped Masada at that time, was she? I seem to remember there was a whole shipload."

Michael grinned at the memory, although he'd felt like anything but smiling at the time.

"Somewhere around four hundred women and children. Only a few of them had skills beyond borderline literacy or maybe some simple mathematics. Even those who had learned some technical skills found them antiquated by our standards."

"So, what did they do?" Todd asked.

"They were given asylum by the Star Kingdom, and when the ship they'd made their get-away on was sold..."

"I bet that was one ship that didn't go to a scrapper," Todd said, "bet Intelligence couldn't wait to get their hands on it."

"For more reasons than one," Michael agreed, relaxed now and cheerful. "Turns out Judith's kidnapper—I refuse to call him her husband—was a pirate as well as a merchant. That ship and its computers solved more than a few 'missing vessel' reports."

"So what do Judith and her associates do now?" Todd asked.

"They were settled in a nice community here on Manticore. A lot of people don't realize that Human Services has an entire division that specializes in integrating refugees into the population, but Dad organized it very quietly when we started getting so many of them from worlds the Peeps had conquered. HS has had a lot of experience dealing with culture shock, and they recommended we find a place far enough from the big cities that the Masadans wouldn't be overwhelmed—Masadan society is highly anti-tech, remember. Of course, even one of our 'small-town' towers was pretty overwhelming anyway, when they first saw it, but at least Friedman's Valley is a lot slower-paced and more laid-back than someplace in downtown Landing.

"Since then, Judith and her associates have been getting educated and more integrated into our society. A few of them continue as consultants for Intelligence. They're not a burden on the taxpayer, in case you're wondering. The money from their ship, even when split, gave them all a stake. After what they did to escape Masada, they're eager not to be dependent."

"I'd guess not," Todd said. "After all, if they wanted to stay barefoot and pregnant, they would never have left Masada. You know, I'm looking forward to meeting this Judith of yours."

"Not mine," Michael said, maybe a little too quickly. "Very much her own. If she belongs to anyone, it's to her daughter, Ruth. You'll like Ruth, cute as a button, and smart..."

Michael glanced at the air car's chronometer and shrugged.

"We'll be a little early, but not too much. Why don't we go on ahead?" He glanced back at Valless. "Any problem with that, Vincent?"

"None, sir."

"Todd?"

"If you think we'll be welcome," Todd said. "Absolutely. Like I said, I'm looking forward to meeting this Judith."

✳   ✳   ✳

As outsiders saw them, George and Babette Ramsbottom were a highly unlikely couple.

George was a staunch Conservative. Babette was an outspoken Liberal. Although neither was a noble, both were something more important—rich and influential members at the most active and important levels of the Star Kingdom's society.

George spent all his free time—when he was not serving in one senior ministry post or another or appearing before Parliament as an "expert witness" in favor of some bit of legislation—focusing on his many and lucrative business interests.

Babette, on the other hand, had run for office several times with the support of her party. She'd won against her husband's favored candidate more than once, and, like him, she had also served in appointed posts that had somewhat less public visibility, but no less opportunity for influence. When she was not involved in politics, Babette was a highly visible socialite, seemingly as devoted to spending her husband's money as he was to making it.

They had been witnessed arguing both in public and when they believed themselves in private. Enemies wondered why they didn't simply get divorced. Friends of one or the other—they shared few in common—had other theories.

George and Babette stayed together because neither wished to risk losing contact with their children. George didn't want to settle any money on Babette. Babette didn't want to lose access to the money George made with such seeming lack of effort. Another popular theory was that neither would budge on who received custody of the sizeable and historic Ramsbottom estate—an estate where both, despite their apparent acrimony, continued to reside.

Oddly enough, for the amount of gossip and outright snooping expended on the effort, none of these speculations was correct, for all of those doing the speculating lacked a key piece of information.

Far from being each other's most violent adversaries, George and Babette Ramsbottom were each other's nearest and dearest friend and ally. They managed to hide this even from their three children—largely by sending the children away to boarding schools and expensive educational camps, and making their frequent and attentive parental visits separately.

The Ramsbottom estate did have servants, but George and Babette took care to maintain their charade even in front of these. And if the estate—and most especially the private offices and conjugal suites—were as heavily shielded as the most secure areas of Mount Royal Palace, what of it? George had been heard to say frequently and loudly that he wasn't going to let Babette snoop on his business, and she to retort that she certainly didn't trust him with her private matters.

If everyone overlooked that the same shielding protected George and Babette from being detected in their private conferences, that could certainly be excused. No one knew better than George and Babette Ramsbottom that people love a flamboyantly fighting couple. Moreover, no one ever looks for what could not possibly be there.

"When do we place the call?" Babette asked.

"Three more minutes," George replied.

"And if Judith Newland isn't there?"

"She'll have a comlink with her."

George spoke with the confidence that had closed many a business deal, but when three minutes had passed and they placed their call, there was no answer.

"So she didn't take her comlink," Babette said with just a touch of the acid she used so well in public. "Remember, she's a primitive, probably never thought of it."

George scowled. He took *his* comlink with him even into the shower. The idea that someone—especially someone in a crisis—wouldn't take her link was alien to him.

Babette softened. "Don't worry. She'll think of checking her phone before long."

"But I want her to get the call before Prince Michael arrives..."

"Don't worry."

The next time George placed the call, a female voice, quite familiar to them from the surveillance tapes they'd viewed, answered. A moment later, an image appeared on their screen.

It was of a young woman, slim and graceful, her thick, dark auburn hair pulled back from her face. Even if her features had not been tight and stern from worry, no one would have thought

Judith Newland pretty, but hers was a face that many would turn to look at twice, and then a third time, after prettier faces had been forgotten.

The eyes were what would bring a person back—green eyes, ringed with brown, not blended as with more traditional hazel. Their expression was as fierce and focused as that of a bird of prey.

Babette found herself pulling back when that gaze was directed to the screen, even though she knew the dummy program George had set up displayed a crowd of sexless, featureless wraiths. Their shadowed forms overlapped, creating an image far more ominous than a mere blacked out screen could ever have been.

"Yes?"

"Are you alone?"

Babette heard George's words twice: once as spoken, once in the whispery voices supplied by the avatar program.

"I am. Is this call to do with my missing daughter?"

Despite the research that had told them Judith Newland was a tough young woman, Babette was surprised by this composure. That same research had told them that if there was one person in this universe that Judith loved without reserve it was her young daughter, Ruth. Babette had expected crying and wailing, at least those green eyes flooding with tears, not this iron control.

But George had permitted himself a chuckle. Without speaking, he pointed to a line of figures streaming across the bottom of the screen. Using infrared scanners and some very sensitive analysis programs, the computer gave lie to Judith's apparent calm. Her pulse rate was elevated, and George tapped an overlay where green and black patterns showed hot spots beneath Judith's skin, hot spots that revealed just how upset that composed young woman really was.

Babette relaxed. George spoke.

"We are. Here are our terms. Ruth is alive and intact—for now."

At that cue, a picture of Ruth, the date/time stamp showing it was concurrent with the transmission (although that stamp was a forgery) appeared on the screen for a tantalizing half-second. The little girl was curled on her side, wrapped in a pale pink blanket, sound asleep. Her balled fist was snuggled close to the rosebud of her cupid's bow lips.

Even Babette, who normally preferred almost anything to small children, had to admit that Ruth looked adorable.

George continued to speak.

"If you wish Ruth returned in that state, you must convince your friend Michael Winton to publicly and openly behave in a fashion unbecoming to his rank and station. Public lewdness would be an admirable choice. If he is asked about his behavior..."

As we will make certain he is, Babette thought smugly. She already had the newsie picked out and primed.

"...then he is to comment that he is a Winton, and that the Wintons have always done what they desired—and that nothing, especially not the reaction of a bunch of superstitious, prudish primitives, even if they are the residents of a newly allied world makes the least difference to him."

For a moment, the wooden expression on Judith's face changed to one of confusion.

"Why do you think he'd listen to me?"

"Just do it," George said sternly, his avatar voices hissing and echoing in a truly frightening fashion. "And remember, mentioning to anyone that Ruth is missing would do at least as much damage as anything Prince Michael might say. After all, if the Wintons cannot protect those who live on their own home world, what can they do to protect those who live in distant systems?"

Judith's face again became carved wood. "And if I do as you wish?"

"Within a day of Prince Michael's announcement, you will be told where Ruth can be found."

"And if I refuse?"

"Then Ruth will be returned to someone who wants her very, very much—her father, Ephraim Templeton."

This time Judith's composure broke completely.

"You wouldn't!"

"Return a daughter to the father who has never had the privilege of holding her in his arms, of stroking her soft, fair hair... Why, I think that would be a wonderful thing. Don't take too long, Mrs. Templeton. I get teary at the thought of such a wonderful family reunion."

Judith was stammering something incoherent when George cut the transmission.

"There," he said with satisfaction. "Message delivered. I was a bit concerned by Judith's reaction when I indicated that she could influence Prince Michael to behave in a fashion so out of character—and so contrary to his sister's policies. We couldn't possibly be wrong..."

"About how close she and Prince Michael are?" Babette concluded. She shook her head decisively. "Not in the least. Remember, this whole idea came to me when I happened to see them together a year ago. He tried to hide it, but it was very apparent to me that the sun and moon rose and set in that unattractive primitive's green eyes."

Babette stretched catlike, and continued, "And I've done quite a bit of research since. They write each other regularly. He sends little presents. She sends photos of the kid. I managed some rather adroit questioning of the social secretary who handles Prince Michael's appointments those rare times when he's in-system and off-duty. She was quite amused that the first—and only—thing Prince Michael always insists on is time to visit with Judith Newland.

"More importantly, although there was every evidence before he met Judith Newland that Prince Michael was a perfectly active heterosexual young male. Since he met her, he has had no serious relationships—not even flirtations. I couldn't even get any solid evidence that he has frequented pleasure parlors—and what sailor on leave does not?"

"One," said George, who truly was more conservative and straightlaced than his wife, "who values his reputation, and that of his family."

"True, true," Babette said, leaning forward to kiss George on the tip of his nose. "All the more reason why Prince Michael's lack of public restraint will be such a shock. He's always been such a good boy..."

"But what if he refuses?"

"He won't," Babette said with certainty. "He loves Judith—and the brat, too. Even if Prince Michael doesn't react as I've calculated, we still have the child. Then our assistants hand little Ruthie over to Ephraim Templeton and record the exchange on video. It should be quite ugly. Templeton hates the mother. Why, I wouldn't be surprised if he gives the kid a wallop or two as soon as he has her in his hands..."

"And that behavior," George said, "can certainly be turned to our advantage. Not only will the Star Kingdom's residents see once again what brutes the Masadans are, but the Graysons can be made to understand that a Star Kingdom that cannot protect a single child is a weak ally indeed."

"And then," Babette concluded, her face suddenly serious, her eyes shining with the fervor of a reformer, "we can get the Star Kingdom back on track, stop concentrating on making alliances with foreign powers, stop exhausting our resources propping up their primitive technology."

"That's right," George said. "For the price of a little nasty gossip little Ruth will be home with her mama, and the Star Kingdom's policy will be refocused on our domestic needs."

✳   ✳   ✳

Until the air car settled on the tower landing and Michael got out, Judith had been so overwhelmed by the events of the past hour or so that she had completely forgotten that her first and best Manticoran friend was scheduled to visit that day.

For a moment Judith marveled at the coincidence. Then something hard and cold whispered ice through her soul. They'd known. The kidnappers had known, and they'd timed both Ruth's kidnapping and that horrible call to take advantage of Michael's visit.

Judith glanced at her chronometer. Michael was at least half an hour early. Depending on just how much information the kidnappers possessed, his early arrival might spoke their wheels.

Judith advanced toward the air car, not bothering to hide her eagerness, hoping her desperation didn't show. She slowed slightly when a second young man got out of the passenger side. She recognized him from pictures Michael had sent her as Todd Liatt, one of Michael's best friends. She wondered what Todd would think when she asked Michael to betray his queen and her interstellar policy to save one small girl.

And why do the kidnappers think Michael would do such a thing? He's a military man. There must have been dozens of times when he or his commanders have had to make the decision to let some die so others might live. If we lose our alliance with Grayson, it tears a hole in a critical part of our coverage against the People's Republic.

Judith actually stopped walking forward as the significance of that "we" hit her. The Star Kingdom wasn't just Michael's responsibility. It was hers as well, hers as a citizen. She might not command starships or gun batteries or hold political office, but she felt a responsibility nonetheless.

I can't ask Michael to betray his people—our people. Not even for Ruth. But I can't let Ruth be returned to Ephraim.

Michael Winton had come up to Judith as she stood caught in this revelation. Todd Liatt stood to one side about a pace back. A thickset, dark-haired man with "bodyguard" so written into his watchful posture that his Palace Security uniform was hardly necessary stood three paces behind the crown prince.

Crown Prince, Judith thought, glancing away from the security man to the small dot of the sting ship hovering overhead even now. *Not just Lieutenant Michael Winton.*

She reached out one hand and took Michael's dark one in her own.

"Michael, I can't say how glad I am to see you." Judith was relieved that her voice didn't quaver. "This must be Todd—excuse me, Lieutenant Liatt. I feel as if I know you from Michael's correspondence."

Todd grinned and politely shook the hand she now extended to him. " 'Todd' is fine. Just don't call me 'Toad Breath' as our mutual friend has been known to do."

Michael turned to indicate the bodyguard, "And this is Lieutenant Vincent Valless."

Judith did not offer Valless her hand—she still found associating with strange men took a real effort—but she forced herself to give him a warm smile.

"Won't you all come to my apartment? I have some refreshments."

Michael looked around. "Where's Ruth? You wrote that she's gone from toddling to running. I expected to get tackled."

"I'm sure we'll find her," Judith said, and hoped the words would be prophetic.

❊   ❊   ❊

Michael didn't bother to hide his surprise when Dinah—with no trace of Ruth in sight—greeted them at the door to Judith's apartment. The older woman's face was seamed with worry, and Michael sensed some unspoken communication between the two.

Judith drew Michael to one side.

"I need to speak with you," she said. "Can I do so without him," she glanced over at Vincent Valless, "listening to every word?"

Michael's heart skipped a beat. "I'm not sure. If we were at Mount Royal Palace, but this is an unsecured area..."

Judith gave a deep sigh, not of exasperation, but of despair. She glanced at her chronometer.

"We can't wait. I can't wait. I'm just going to have to trust... Michael, can you at least ask him and Todd not to interfere?"

"If you're not planning to overthrow the government," Michael replied, trying to make his voice light.

To his utter astonishment, Judith's eyes flooded with tears. He'd been present when she'd been interrogated about the deaths of her parents, about her own capture by the Masadans, about the brutal treatment she had received while in Ephraim Templeton's custody. She'd never shed a tear. In fact, as far as he could remember, the only time he'd ever seen Judith cry was when she believed Dinah was dying.

Michael didn't reach to brush away the tear that now trickled down her check, knowing that even now Judith found all but the most impersonal physical contact distasteful, but he moved to shield her from view while she got herself under control.

It didn't take long. In three deep breaths, the tears had vanished, and Judith, with another glance at her chronometer, turned to face the other three.

Todd and Dinah had been exchanging awkward introductions, pretending they were not aware of the tension between the other two. Vincent Valless was outwardly impassive—a benefit of his extensive training—but Michael had no doubt that the bodyguard was also puzzled by this strange turn of events.

Judith motioned toward the round table that stood to one side of the immaculate, if sparsely furnished, apartment.

"Please, be seated. I did get some refreshments, but while I pull them out, I'm going to start talking. I have a feeling that time may matter."

Dinah, Todd, and Michael moved to the seats indicated. Valless stood where he could watch both window and door. Judith stepped into the small kitchen, and while she got out a plate of little sandwiches and some sweets, she started talking.

"Ruth has been kidnapped," she began, then held up one hand to still the gasps of protest. "Yes. I'm certain. I had just come up from asking my downstairs neighbors if they'd seen her, when I was called by the kidnappers."

Dinah nodded. "Judith is not hysterical. I was here when the com chimed the first time, but didn't pick up. When Judith returned and took the call, they asked if she was alone."

"I lied," Judith said. "I wanted someone else present in case there was any detail I forgot."

"Odd that they'd trust such a call to a public com," Michael said, "and asking you if there were witnesses and then trusting you..."

Despair filled Judith's green eyes. "Actually, I don't think they really would have minded witnesses. I think they would have preferred them. I think you'll see why when I tell you what they said."

She reported the call in clinical detail, but her cheeks blushed dark rose as she stated the conditions for Ruth's return.

"I'll do it," Michael said, instantly.

Two voices overrode his words before he could clarify.

Todd said, his voice alive with horror. "Michael, you can't!"

And Judith said even more firmly, "I won't let you."

Michael stared at her.

"I won't," Judith repeated. "I have no idea why they think they can use me to manipulate you, but I'm not going to let someone destroy both a key alliance and your reputation."

Michael thought. *You have no idea, do you? I do. Looking at Todd, he does. Dinah does. I bet even Vincent has a pretty good guess. I guess I've been better at hiding my feelings, at least from you, than I thought.*

But he didn't say this. Instead, he said incredulously, "You're not going to let them hand Ruth over to Ephraim Templeton, are you?"

Judith shook her head, the dark auburn hair cascading around her shoulders in a silken fall.

"I am not. I'm going to find her and I'm going to get her back. Then when I have her back, I'm going to blow them all so high that they'll never do anything like that again."

Michael wasn't in the least surprised, but he doubted that Judith had the skill necessary to find Ruth, and he wasn't about to let her destroy herself and her child when he could help. He could also tell that arguing further would be a waste of valuable time.

"If you're going after her, I'm helping." Michael turned and looked at his bodyguard. "And you're going to have to trust me, Vincent. There's a little girl's life at stake, and from the demands Judith says they're making, this has 'political motives' written all over it. But we don't know a damned thing—yet—about who these people are. Until we know more about the situation we can't risk any communication outside of this immediate group."

"The entire Masadan exile community here may suspect Miss Ruth is missing," Vincent reminded the prince delicately.

"I know," Michael said, "but other than Judith and Dinah, no one knows Ruth has been kidnapped."

"Actually," Judith said, "Dinah was suspicious before I was. Something she said made me very careful when I went down to check with my neighbors. When they said Ruth wasn't with them, I said that I guessed that Ruth must have gone across to Dinah's apartment, and I'd check there. When I came back up here to report to Dinah, that's when the call came."

Dinah smiled and pushed herself back from the table. "But I'll wander downstairs with the excuse that you forgot to get milk for the tea. While I'm there, I'll mention how excited Ruth was to see her 'Uncle Michael.'"

When Dinah had left, Judith motioned everyone to seats around the round table that dominated one end of the room.

Michael returned his attention to Vincent Valless.

"Vincent, I know your job is to keep me out of physical danger. If I promise to duck if you say duck, retreat if you say retreat, will you work with me on this?"

"If I have your word," Vincent said. "I would be more comfortable, however, if I could report the changed situation—especially one so charged with political implications—to my superiors."

"I know," Michael said. "So would I. There's just one problem. Until we know who took Ruth, no avenue of communication is safe. For example, while I'm certain Elizabeth isn't involved—"

"I should hope you would be certain, sir!" Vincent looked shocked at even the implication that the Queen might be so accused.

"Right. But I don't know if someone close to her might be involved. Someone might have a tap on Mount Royal communications. Or it might be something simpler, someone near at hand, nearly omnipresent—a servant, say—paid to report if certain matters are discussed or even if I call Elizabeth within the next few hours."

"I understand," Vincent admitted. "I don't like the implications, but I understand."

"I thought you would," Michael said. "I wouldn't need you to be my second skin if people were honest and the world was a safe place. Very well. You have my word that I won't put myself in physical danger or go against your direct command if you decide I'm in such danger."

Todd, whose alert silence had reminded Michael that his friend was training in Tactics with every intention of winning a command of his own someday, now spoke directly to Judith. "Count me in. I've been security checked this way and that, I'll bet, since I've been Michael's roommate not once, but twice. You can trust me."

"I do," Michael said. "Even without the checks."

"And I will," Judith said, "if Michael says so."

Vincent Valless cleared his throat and said, "I have seen those reports. You are wise where you trust."

Todd flushed in pleased embarrassment, but Michael had returned his attention to Judith. "Thanks for your patience. I realize you must be aching to get a move on."

"I would be," she replied, "except that we don't have the least idea where to make that move. Running about aimlessly would do neither Ruth nor our cause any good."

Michael saw Vincent shake his head in admiration for this display of self-control.

You should see her on the bridge of a starship under fire, Michael thought.

Judith, apparently unaware of these reactions, had continued speaking. "Obviously, the place to start is that woman from Human Services who came to talk to me. She gave me a name: Dulcis McKinley."

"Probably an alias," Todd said. "Still, it's something."

"What did this Dulcis McKinley look like?" Michael asked.

"She was about a handspan taller than I am," Judith said, gesturing, "and very slim. Fair hair, pale skin, light eyes—blue or gray, I think. She wore her hair short, almost shaved at the back of her neck. In spite of this, there was nothing at all mannish about her appearance. Her lips were full, and I remember admiring her cheekbones. Very high and elegant."

"Short hair isn't exactly in fashion right now," Todd said with the air of one who had been using his leave to make a detailed examination of women who were not Navy personnel. "The one set of professions where short hair remains perennially popular are those where you regularly don a vac suit or related gear. Hair gets in the way."

Michael nodded, running a hand over his own tightly curled crop. "Okay. So possible space-side service."

He'd carried in his minicomp, since he'd been planning to show Judith and Ruth pictures of some of the places he'd been since he sent his last letter. Now he pulled it out. "I'm going to check on that name," he said.

"Is that wise?" Judith asked. "Someone might have set telltales to warn them of just such an inquiry."

"Actually," Michael said, "given the situation, it would make less sense if you didn't make just such a query. Let me use your comp. They may not bother to check registration numbers, but I would..."

The search did not lead them to their target, but it did turn up an interesting bit of trivia. Dulcis McKinley was the name of a secondary character in *Hearts Aloft,* a romantic comedy that had been popular about fifteen T-years before.

"That's why the name sounded familiar!" Todd said. "My sister had a crush on the male lead and for weeks she kept downloading the damn thing and watching it on the biggest display we had. I think I knew every line."

"Not useful now," Michael said, "but it might turn out to be. Now..."

He turned to Judith. "Why don't you and Todd see if you can generate a computer reconstruction of Dulcis McKinley?"

"And you?" Todd said.

"First, I'm going to set up some jamming fields so no one can tell what we're doing here."

"Won't someone notice?" Judith said anxiously.

"Not if I'm careful," Michael said. "The Navy has been training me to be extraordinarily good at getting information out of both people and machines without their being aware of my interest. The same goes for setting up diversions. If someone snoops here, they'll find about the right level of jamming. Beneath that they'll get traces of agitated talking, weeping, et cetera."

"Vincent, I want you to see what you can do about tracking vehicles," Michael went on, "the woman from Human Services got here somehow, and Ruth didn't leave here by magic. I know you have access to satellite records of traffic patterns. Can you make an excuse to look at those that surround this area?"

Vincent was looking almost animated. "I can do better than that. I can get records for this entire tower and both of its neighbors. This entire neighborhood is under full-time surveillance."

Michael cocked an eyebrow, and his bodyguard shook his head. "We didn't have anything to do with it, Your Highness. I only know because it's part of my job to check about things like that before I let you go somewhere, but they're there, all right."

Dinah was letting herself in as he spoke, a cup of milk in one hand. She shut the door carefully behind her and said, as if answering a question, "That's right. When we first came here, many of the women were nervous about predatory males. That was foolishness, but we did have some problems with a few curiosity seekers. The cameras were set up then, and they've stayed."

"Inertia," Michael said, "can be useful."

Vincent already had his minicomp out. "My request should go through without question. It's pretty standard to check traffic patterns in an area before and during a sensitive transit situation."

"Want to see who might have been hanging around for just a bit too long," Michael said. "Good. Get on it."

"What are you going to do when you're done with the jamming field?" Todd asked.

"I'm going to take a look at the chip Judith made," Michael said. "You recorded it, didn't you, Judith?"

"I did, but what good will viewing it do?" Judith asked. "I told you, they used some sort of avatar program."

"I know," Michael said. "Trust me. I won't be wasting our time."

His stomach did a funny flipflop when Judith looked at him, those brown-rimmed green eyes steady. "Never doubt it, Michael. I trust you."

❋   ❋   ❋

Judith jumped when Vincent Valless broke the intense silence that had filled the room as each had turned to their assignment. True, she and Todd Liatt had talked a little as he helped her access and set up the right graphics program, but once that was done, and Judith focused on building up an image of Dulcis McKinley from Human Services, talk had hardly been necessary.

"Sir," Vincent Valless said, "I have something I think you should inspect without further delay."

He projected the data from his minicomp so everyone could see. "This is the scene immediately around this tower shortly before Ruth was taken."

He zoomed in on a landing platform one floor below the Judith's apartment. "This is the vehicle from Human Services.

These..." He showed a line of mismatched air cars, "are all registered to residents of this complex. This one vehicle is the only anomalous one."

He indicated a neat van bearing the logo of Anywhere Anytime, a well-known delivery company—a type of vehicle so ubiquitous that no one would give it a second glance.

"The A.A. van," Valless went on, "arrived at approximately the same time as the air car from Human Services. The A.A. man went to a service entry. The woman from H.S. went to the public entry."

"Surveillance cameras don't extend beyond the entryways into the building," Valless continued, "but those on the exterior captured the following sequence."

The delivery man had entered the building carrying a bundle, easily recognizable as one of the unassembled shipping boxes A.A. supplied for their customer's convenience. When he exited just a few minutes later, he was carrying a similar box, but assembled. Judith imagined Ruth tucked inside, body bent in a fetal position. She pressed her fist to her lips to keep from screaming.

The man from A.A. loaded the box into the back of the van, made certain the back was locked, got into the driver's side, and a moment later, the vehicle pulled away from the building and left the complex.

"Judith," Michael asked, "is there another entry into this apartment?"

"Only the windows," she began, but Dinah interrupted.

"There is," she said. "There's a conduit from which pipes and other such things can be serviced without the need to cut holes in the walls. Technically, the conduit doesn't 'enter' the apartment as such, but if someone entered the conduit and knew the layout of the building, they could get into any apartment."

Todd was nodding. "They'd need to remove a couple of wall or ceiling panels, but if they had the right tools, it would be easy. I worked summers for a company that did repairs, and I always felt a bit like a burglar. Of course, entering that way without permission is highly illegal..."

"But so is kidnapping," Judith said sharply. "Lieutenant Valless, where did that A.A. van go?"

Valless snapped his head in a curt, military nod. "I tracked it, and I believe you'll find the following sequence quite informative."

In her impatience, Judith appreciated that Valless had set his record to run slightly faster than real-time, but seeing the van speed away made her heart beat faster, as if Valless was causing Ruth to vanish more quickly.

Valless had highlighted the A.A. van in pale turquoise, so it was quite easy to track. He pulled back the perspective, and directed their attention back to the tower.

"Less than thirty seconds later, the ostensible Human Services representative also took her leave."

This vehicle was highlighted in a bright violet. Although air traffic did not follow roads as such, traffic patterns created the illusion of them in the trackless sky. It became rapidly evident that the two vehicles were following the same route.

"Where do they end up, Vincent?" Michael said. "I'm assuming they end up at the same place?"

"Yes, sir. At the Colonial Memorial Spaceport."

"No!" Judith gasped, but she was already on her feet, heading for the door.

Dinah grabbed her. "Judith, this was twenty minutes ago. Nothing can be gained by blindly following them."

Reluctantly, Judith slowed. She looked at Michael. He was looking at Valless.

"Yes, sir," Valless said in answer to an unasked question. "I've accessed the records from the cameras inside the spaceport. However, no one matching our two alleged kidnappers has left the parking facility and entered the port."

"Aren't there cameras in the garage?" Todd asked indignantly.

"There are, Lieutenant Liatt," Valless said, "but they don't provide a hundred percent coverage. My assessment of the situation is that the kidnappers had located one or more of these blind spots in advance, and made their arrangements accordingly."

"Reasonable," Todd said, "but where did they go? Did they go into the port, or did they merely use the garage as somewhere to change vehicles?"

Judith felt that urge to scream again, to remind them all that this was no intellectual puzzle, but her living breathing daughter they were discussing. Dinah's hand tightened on her arm, and Judith nodded. Screaming would not help, any more than tears and protests had stopped Ephraim Templeton from raping his twelve-year-old "wife."

I must think, she thought. *I must put aside that this is Ruth, and think.*

"Lieutenant Valless," she said, "did you get a good image of the woman from Human Services?"

"Not a very good one," he admitted. "I believe she'd studied where the cameras were, and did her best to assure that her hand or hair would 'accidentally' block her face from view. You will note that the man from A.A. managed something similar between his uniform cap and the boxes he was carrying."

"Not a trick," Michael said, "that would work at Mount Royal, but perfectly fine for an apartment building. Still, Vincent, pull me what you can. Judith, how did your image come out?"

"Fairly well," she said. "I think."

"Feed it to me as well," Michael said, "and I'll combine it with what Vincent has. I have some video feed of Ruth in here already."

He made a few adjustments with his minicomp as the data came in, then nodded to Valless.

"All right, Vincent. Access images of the incoming traffic from the garage into the spaceport—foot traffic, arriving passengers, and the like. I've set up a program to search for any one of our three targets, separately or in combination. We'll see what comes up."

"Separately?" Dinah asked.

"That's right. We don't know that the same kidnappers will be operating at all stages. The woman from H.S. and the A.A. man might have handed Ruth over to someone else."

"You say 'Ruth,'" Todd said curiously. "Don't you mean the box?"

"I don't," Michael said. "You've been in the Navy too long, bud. Routine security scans quite likely would find a child in a packing crate. My guess is that they've done a few things to change her appearance, and will bring her through as a sleepy little girl. No bored security officer would look twice except to be grateful that she's not screaming or whining."

"Maybe," Judith said eagerly, "we should call the space port, ask..."

She stopped herself, shook her head. "I forgot. That would start questions, and while our enemies might like questions and the scandal they might generate, that's the last thing we want."

Michael nodded. His dark brown gaze was abstracted, watching the datafeed, but his voice was perfectly alert.

"Judith, I don't care about the scandal, neither will Elizabeth when she understands why I did it. Just let me . . ."

"No!" Judith said firmly. "I'm glad you and the Queen would be so willing to accept disgrace, but disgrace is the least of this. If the alliance with Grayson is disrupted, lives will be lost. How can I sacrifice someone else—many someone elses—for anyone, even my own daughter?"

And, she thought to herself, *how can I sacrifice you, who have been my friend? I know I should care more about Ruth, and I do care more about Ruth, but I care about you, too, Michael Winton. I care . . .*

"Judith," Michael said quietly, "if it comes down to a choice between letting them get away with Ruth and our calling in reinforcements, I'm calling in the reinforcements." He looked up from his display for a moment. "If we get her back, the scandal will be survivable, trust me, and I am *not* losing your daughter."

"Michael—" she began, then stopped herself.

What am I going to say to him? How noble can I be? This is my child. *The trigger for our entire escape was to save her from being aborted by Ephraim, murdered before she was even born! God only knows what he'll do to her now, if only to punish* me. *I can't* let her *be handed back over to him, but I can't hurt* Michael, *either, so—*

She forced her mind away from those uncomfortable thoughts and said aloud, "I'm tired of being used. Even if permitting someone to use you shamefully would get Ruth back, how could I ever feel safe again? No. I'll get her back. *We'll* get her back, without giving them *any* of the scandals they want, and then . . ."

The words trailed off into inarticulate fury, but Judith was saved from having to explain what one lone refugee could do against those who had orchestrated this kidnapping by a sharp beep from Michael's minicomp.

"Match!" he said. "I'll bring up the image."

He did. It showed a delightfully domestic unit. A man, a woman, and a sleepy little boy in a pram. The man was guiding along a trunk that hovered on anti-grav skids. The woman pushed the pram. Both looked peaceful as they turned to follow signs directing them to "private vessels."

"That woman doesn't look anything like the one Judith was designing," Todd said dubiously. "The H.S. lady looked like a Valkyrie turned executive secretary. This one is almost dumpy."

"Near perfect match," Michael said satisfied. "The program

ignores the things that have distracted you like hair color, weight, and attire. It focuses on subtleties like posture, shape of the eye, bone structure."

"Is that little boy..." Judith asked.

"Even a closer match," Michael said. "They've cut her hair and darkened it, changed her clothes. With her asleep, she's not going to be talking and giving anything away. And—" he smiled thinly "—they lost time doing it, too."

He shook his head to dissuade further conversation. "I want to track where they're headed."

No one spoke as the images zipped down corridors, through tubes, and down underpasses. The little family never paused, but they never hurried either. They acted like what they seemed: a moderately well-off family, heading back to their ship.

Perhaps the father worked for a company located on Sphinx or Gryphon, and had brought the family to the city with him for the day. A nice outing. Now they'd take the company ship back home.

Or perhaps they were wealthy enough to own a ship of their own. Interplanetary vessels were not as expensive as hyper capable. As the Star Kingdom became more prosperous, such "commuter ships" didn't turn a head, and could even be considered economical if the time savings aspects were computed into the equation.

Michael was slowing down the image. "Shuttle pad twenty-seven. And the shuttle on it was registered to *Banshee* out of Sphinx. Vincent can—"

"I'm already on it, sir."

The words were polite as ever, but Judith was pleased by the thrill of excitement that underlay them. Vincent Valless was completely committed to their mission.

"It's registered to Highland Mining Associates of Gryphon. They have interests all over the binary system, sir, including corporate offices and subsidiaries on all three planets. I fear we won't be able to use that to anticipate *Banshee*'s ultimate destination. The flight plan they filed with Astro Control doesn't state more than Sphinx as a destination."

Michael nodded, but he was now pushing himself to his feet.

"Right. That's at least a four-hour trip, and that shuttle only left the pad three minutes ago. Time for us to get moving. My air car will hold all of us."

He looked at Dinah, but the older woman only shook her head.

"No. I'm not coming. I'll remain here and defuse any interest that arises. No one will be surprised if Judith goes off with her friends."

"Even if she goes without her daughter?" Valless asked. "We don't want to trigger any alerts, and I know local law enforcement does keep an eye on this area."

Dinah shook her head, and it seemed to Judith that the older woman was trying to conceal what—given the circumstances—seemed like a wholly inappropriate smile.

"No, I don't think anyone will think it strange if Judith goes out without Ruth, especially if I lead them to believe the child is with me. Go with God, my friends, and bring back our lost lamb safe and sound. I will pray for you."

Michael Winton gave the older woman a slight bow. "Thank you, Dinah. We'll need every prayer you can spare. I'm going to leave you with two very important things. One is a priority code that will enable you to contact us if there are any difficulties. The other is a short report I've dictated explaining to my sister why I've made the choices I did. If anything happens so that I'm not in a position to explain, I want you to get this to her."

Dinah accepted the information, shooing them out of Judith's apartment as if they were wayward schoolchildren.

"I'll take care of it. Now, go. And hurry."

❊   ❊   ❊

Michael was glad Judith hadn't broken down. He thought she'd been close, but she'd managed to collect herself. That was a relief, because if she'd started crying, then he wasn't sure he'd have been able to keep from gathering her up in his arms, and that would almost certainly have made matters worse.

Even though Michael had started falling in love with Judith on the bridge of her embattled ship, he had never spoken of his feelings—not only refusing to speak to her of his love, but to anyone else. He wanted no pressure, no matter how subtle or well-meaning, put on her. These last two and a half years had been the closest Judith had ever had to a life of her own, and he wanted her to have a sense of her own self before he tried to convince her to join her life with his.

Michael thought Todd knew how he felt about Judith, and he was beginning to think Dinah did as well. He wondered how many other people had read significance into what he thought was his very guarded, very proper behavior around the lady.

Certainly at least one person has, Michael thought grimly as he settled himself into the back seat of the air car and let Todd handle the driving. *Or they wouldn't have thought they could use Judith to manipulate me.*

After giving Todd instructions and warning air-traffic control that he intended to exercise the royal family's priority clearance, Michael pulled out his minicomp. The ride wouldn't be overly long at the speed his clearance would permit, but he had an idea or two. Hopefully, before long, he'd have narrowed the field regarding precisely who the kidnappers might be.

❊   ❊   ❊

"Mount Royal spaceport," Judith repeated when Michael announced their destination. "We are going after them."

"That's right," Michael reassured her, his fingers still busy with the minicomp balanced between his hands. "I've already requested flight clearance for one of the ships that was set aside for me when I came home on holiday."

Judith now understood the flurry of activity that had held Vincent Valless since they had entered the air car. Without ever losing his attitude of quiet alertness, Valless's fingers had been skittering over his own minicomp, doubtless handling the security arrangements that would make the crown prince's arrival and departure so fluid as to almost create the impression Michael Winton was an ordinary person, who could come and go as he chose.

Michael touched a send icon on his minicomp and looked up at her, his dark brown eyes holding an expression both serious and reassuring.

"*Banshee,*" he explained, "is a *Pryderi*-class ship. It's a nice little runabout—bigger than a standard cargo shuttle, but not a lot—and it's got some fairly comfortable passenger accommodations. But it's an off-the-shelf civilian design, and it's way too small to be hyper-capable. That means they aren't getting out of the system without our being able to track them. And anything we can track, we can chase.

"And, speaking of chasing," he smiled that thin smile again, "*Ogapoge,* the ship I've arranged for us to take, is an *Arrow*-class. The *Pryderis* aren't bad, but they use standard civilian components because they were designed for economic maintenance and extended service life. The *Arrows,* on the other hand, use *Navy* components. BuShips designed them as high-speed intrasystem VIP transports, and they're a little smaller than the *Pryderis,* which gives them a higher acceleration rate. And *Ogapoge*'s one of the *Arrow-Alphas.* That means she's armed."

Ruth's eyes widened, and he shook his head.

"Don't be thinking they're any sort of warship, Ruth. They've basically got the same weapons fit as a standard assault shuttle, but they were intended from the beginning for really *important* VIPs." This time, his smile was more than a little crooked. "Vincent's people will actually let me fly around in one of these without insisting that an entire destroyer follow me around 'just in case.'"

Judith nodded in understanding, and he shrugged.

"*Banshee*'s acceleration rate is going to be somewhere around four or five percent lower than ours, but their particle screening is just as good, so we won't be any faster than they are once we're both up to maximum safe cruising speed. Still, we'll *reach* max speed faster than they will, and we'll decelerate faster, too, so it's probable we'll make up time in pursuit. But," he looked at Judith, offering her the honesty she deserved, "it won't be a lot, I'm afraid."

"How long will it take us to get there?" Judith asked.

"If they're going to Sphinx?" Michael replied. "I've run the numbers, and a *Pryderi* should do it in roughly four hours and fifty minutes. We can only shave about seven or eight minutes off of their time, and they'll have a good twenty-minute head start. That means we aren't going to catch them short of the planet, but we'll be right on their heels, certainly close enough to see where they go. I can com ahead to have a shuttle waiting for us when we make orbit. I expect we'll have just a few advantages when it comes to getting Astro Control to clear us to planet, too. We may actually be on the ground before they are—assuming they're headed for the surface, and not one of the orbital habitats. If we don't beat them down, it'll be neck-and-neck, at the very worst."

"And *Ogapoge* is large enough to fit us all?" Judith asked.

"More than," Michael said. "I'd hoped..."

A funny note came into his voice and he cleared his throat and started over again.

"I'd hoped to take some friends out to see more of the other planets in-system, but I wasn't sure just how large our party might end up being."

Judith blinked. *He means me. I'm sure he means he wanted to take me and Ruth out. And he prepared from the start not only for the two of us, but whoever I might want with us so I wouldn't think the worst of him... And bodyguards. Always bodyguards.*

She sat mulling over this, thinking that the only time a young man worries about a young woman thinking the worst of him is when he thinks of her as more than a friend.

Or maybe when he doesn't want her to get any ideas that he thinks of her as more than a friend?

She lowered her face into her hands and rubbed her forehead and temples, trying to clear the confusing maelstrom of thoughts before they overwhelmed her. Her muddled thoughts wove and interwove with her worry for Ruth until Todd gently brought the air car to rest at the berth that had been reserved for it.

Vincent Valless was first out, and he spoke with the several security types who immediately bustled over. Their expressions were relaxed and easy beneath the formality that came from their all too great awareness that the young man swinging his legs out of the back seat of the air car was the current crown prince and their reigning queen's only brother.

Judith guessed that Valless had used Michael's original explanation as to why he had reserved *Ogapoge* for his own use. Prince Michael was taking a few friends on an outing. That was all.

I wish, Judith thought as she hurried after the others to the pad where the shuttle waited to ferry them up to the *Ogapoge, that this truly was all, that Ruth and I were going out with Uncle Michael, perhaps to visit the treecat preserves on Sphinx or go snow skiing at one of the resorts on Gryphon. God willing, this will be so, someday. Someday soon.*

When the shuttle reached *Ogapoge,* Judith realized that the little vessel's armament was almost as well concealed as the guns of Ephraim Templeton's privateers had been. Then she shook herself. Of course Security wouldn't want to casually advertise the fact that the crown prince's runabout was armed. Or, for that matter, draw any untoward attention to it in the first place. After all, concealment and surprise were weapons in their own right, and often decisive ones. That sleek hull probably concealed a deceptive amount of armor as well.

For related reasons, the ship was not adorned with the Winton colors. The shining ice blue of the hull was attractive and expensive, but told nothing of the ship's occupant.

As soon as they cleared the boarding tube from the shuttle, they discovered that the ship was already occupied. A woman and two men sat in the seats closest to the back of the vessel. They wore the uniforms of Palace Security and the very neutral expressions of people who know their presence may cause someone important to lose his temper.

Indeed, Judith saw the storm that swept across Michael's dark features when he saw the three additional security operatives. She also saw the sigh he swallowed as he turned to Vincent Valless.

"I called ahead, Prince Michael," Valless said without waiting to be asked. "My duty requires that you be properly protected. Since we're leaving the planet, and in pursuit of potentially dangerous people, I couldn't take the responsibility for your safety wholly upon myself."

"Understood, Vincent," Michael said. "Do they know of our mission?"

"I haven't told them," Valless replied. "They're part of the detail already assigned to your protection, so I could alert them without any need for explanations."

"Fine. Explain now, making clear—very clear—why we're not giving advance notice for what we're doing."

"Yes, Prince Michael. As I'm the senior member of this detail, they'll obey my decision."

And that means, Judith thought, *that Vincent Valless is taking a lot on his own head. If something goes wrong, he could find himself being tried or court-martialed or whatever they do to security officers who let their subjects put themselves at risk.*

Well, she thought, taking the seat Michael indicated was hers and strapping herself in, *I'll just have to do my best to make sure that no one has anything to regret.*

An eighth person, this one a regular Navy master chief, stepped into the passenger cabin through a small hatch, then paused, raising one eyebrow as he saw Judith and Todd.

"Your Highness," he said in an admirably calm tone, and Michael grimaced.

"Master Chief," he replied, then looked at the others. "Master Chief Lawrence is *Ogapoge*'s flight engineer. He's been my keeper on these little jaunts for the last year or so. Master Chief, Lieutenant Liatt and Ms. Judith Newland. I believe you know the rest of our little crew?"

"Yes, Sir," Lawrence replied, nodding respectfully to Todd and Judith.

"We're going on a slightly different excursion, Chief," Michael continued. "And I'm going to want everything the compensator can give us." His eyes met Lawrence's levelly. "And I *do* mean everything, Chief. We're going to redline her."

"Your Highness," Lawrence began, "I—"

He paused, looking into the prince's eyes, then glanced once at Lieutenant Valles and the other Palace Security personnel.

"Yes, Sir," he said instead, and Michael gave him a tight nod before turning back to Todd.

"Todd, you take the helm. You always scored higher than I did when it came to piloting small craft."

"In any sort of piloting," Todd cheerfully reminded him.

"Whatever," Michael said, a small smile quirking one corner of his mouth. "I've got some research I want to take care of while we're in transit. I can't do that and handle the ship."

Todd nodded, solemn for a moment as Ruth's predicament once again came to the fore. Then his usual high spirits surfaced and he grinned with pleasure.

"I'll be happy to take her up, Michael. Besides, this is the only way I'm likely to fly one of these darlings."

"Good," Michael said. "Now, hurry up and get acquainted with your own true love, will you, Toad Breath? We need to break orbit the instant Astro Control clears us."

"I'll be ready for it," Todd said, turning to head for the fleet little vessel's compact flight deck. "You just figure out where we're supposed to be going once we get to Sphinx."

"That," Michael said, settling in to the seat next to Judith and pulling out his minicomp, "is precisely what I'm hoping to do."

❋   ❋   ❋

"They're not," Babette said, mild disbelief in her voice, "going to give in to our demands."

George grunted reluctant agreement as he examined the information feed they had pulled in from various satellites.

"I thought," he said, "when they stayed in that Judith's apartment for so long, that they were going to knuckle under, that they were waiting for a reasonable hour for the prince to go clubbing."

Babette nodded. "I know. When they headed toward Mount Royal, I wasn't worried. After all, there are many more highly visible night spots near the palace than there are out in the sticks where Human Services settled those Masadans."

George pushed his chair back. The holofeed showed *Ogapoge* already heading out of orbit. Despite their surprise, neither of them really doubted where the fleet little runabout was headed.

"Dulcis McKinley and Wallace Ward have two definite advantages. They have a solid lead, and they have the child. There is another factor in our advantage."

"Which is?"

"Prince Michael may suspect they are being observed," George said, "but he cannot be certain."

"How can we take advantage of that?"

"I think we should switch to our second plan," George said.

"So soon? Before they have a chance to come through?" Babette frowned. "Manticoran reactions to turning the child over to her Masadan father have always been harder to calculate."

"As far as Manticoran reactions go, yes," George agreed. "But we can be certain how the Graysons will react. There is a high probability that proof of how little the Star Kingdom could do to protect one child—and having that child turned over to their hated enemies—will tilt the balance of public opinion so far that the Grayson government will be forced by an angry public to renounce their alliance with the Star Kingdom."

"True," Babette said. "After all the treaty nearly didn't happen. If the Navy hadn't interfered in what was a purely local political situation, I think it's likely the Grayson government would have decided against the alliance. You're right. First goal has always been to achieve a termination of that treaty. Discrediting the Royal family has always been a bonus."

George hadn't waited for his wife's agreement. He'd already reached for his com unit and was coding in a call for *Banshee*. The call took somewhat longer than usual to place because of the numerous layers of security screening he had in place, not to mention the fact that *Banshee* had been underway and accelerating at 5.491 KPS^2 for almost thirty-six minutes. She was already over

12.8 million kilometers away from Manticore, moving at 11,860 kilometers per second. At only three percent of light-speed, the time dilation effect wasn't noticeable, but the forty-two-second light-speed communications lag certainly was.

As with the call to Judith, neither George's face nor his voice would be in the final feed. Anonymity was everything, after all. When he'd established initial contact with Dulcis McKinley and Wallace Ward, the professional criminals who were the Ramsbottoms' hands and feet for this job, George had represented himself as a revolutionary fanatic.

Precisely what he—or she, for George had chosen to represent himself as an androgynous creature, rather like a winged angel in his contact with the criminals—was fanatical about had been left deliberately unclear. A liberal scattering of phrases such as "The Will of God" and "Divine Revelation" had been included to give the impression that the fanatic was not a mainstream member of the Star Kingdom, most of whom were pragmatic rather than otherwise in their political dealings, no matter how religious they might be in private.

"We are switching to Plan B," George announced without preamble. "Instead of delivering the child to Choire Ghlais, make rendezvous with *Kwahe'e*."

He waited patiently for the transmission to catch *Banshee* and *Banshee*'s reply to reach him. Eighty-four seconds later, it did.

"Rendezvous with *Kwahe'e*?" Wallace Ward's voice said. "Why?"

He sounded both unhappy and suspicious, George noted. It wasn't a surprise. The man was a professional, and he didn't like unexpected changes.

"It was always a possibility," George reminded him. "That's why we set up the rendezvous in advance. Now the good Lord wills that we use it. And you should know that it is possible you are being pursued."

"Unlikely," Ward said hotly, a minute and a half later.

"All things are possible," George rebuked sternly, "and only the Lord is infallible. As an added safeguard, you are to go to Aslan Station and exchange *Banshee* for *Cormorant* to change your transponder code. They are both *Pryderi* class ships, so you should have no difficulties. Take *Cormorant* for your rendezvous with *Kwahe'e*."

"We will do as you command," the other man said after the

unavoidable, lengthy, and very irritating transmission delay, "when our bank balance shows that the added deposit has been made."

"Done," George said. "The additional deposit has been made to your account. When you transfer the child to the custody of *Kwahe'e*'s captain, your final payment will be authorized. The crew of *Kwahe'e* will take over from that point."

George recited the coordinates where *Kwahe'e*, a hyper-capable ship belonging (through several shell corporations) to the Ramsbottoms, would be waiting. In order to not attract undue attention, *Kwahe'e* was in a distant parking orbit, listed with Astro Control as awaiting parts and supplies.

And so they are, Babette thought as George alerted *Kwahe'e* to expect *Cormorant* and to accept consignment of her rather unusual cargo.

One reason *Kwahe'e* was owned by a shell corporation was that it tended to be given jobs that fell rather into the legal gray areas. Returning a child to her father, and recording the reunion might be peculiar, but it was far more legitimate—at least superficially—than many other jobs *Kwahe'e*'s captain and crew had performed.

Neither George nor Babette expected any difficulty.

After George had signed off, Babette rose and stretched.

"I must be going," she said. "I've promised to go out with some of *my* friends tonight. I had hoped we would witness Prince Michael's disgrace, but it seems I shall have to settle for an evening of dancing and fine food instead."

George rose and embraced Babette with a fervor she returned. After Babette broke from his kiss she said thoughtfully, "I do have one regret that we were forced to go with our second plan. I had so looked forward to Michael Winton becoming disillusioned with his Masadan lady, then putting our Alice in his way. I really think she could have been the one to soothe his broken heart. I thought their meeting at Mount Royal earlier was very promising."

"I agree," George said. "I took some infrared readings, and his surface skin temperature rose quite a bit when he was talking with Alice. I don't believe he is at all indifferent to her."

"We don't need to give up," Babette said, reaching for her cosmetic case and touching up her lips. "After all, when this attempt to rescue Ruth fails, I doubt the relationship between Michael and Judith will survive."

George gave a deep sigh, as of one who sees a wonderful

banquet set up just out of reach. "That would be splendid. We have the Liberal and Conservative parties covered, but Alice could be our conduit into the inner workings of the Crown Loyalists. It would be lovely to have our daughter as the one who rehabilitates Prince Michael in the eyes of his peers."

"Who knows?" Babette said, turning to go with a swirl of her skirts, "we may yet hear our grandchildren call our reigning queen 'Auntie Liz.'"

❖   ❖   ❖

"Choire Ghlais." Michael looked up from his minicomp. "That's our destination," he said into the silence that had settled over the passenger compartment of *Ogapoge*.

Three hours and forty minutes had passed since they had cleared Manticore orbit, and they were just over fifty-five and a half million kilometers short of Sphinx, decelerating hard. *Banshee* was twenty million kilometers ahead of them, also decelerating. The other runabout would enter Sphinx orbit in another fifty-nine minutes; *Ogapoge* was fourteen minutes behind her.

"Choire Ghlais?" Judith said. "What is that? A city?"

"A private estate," Michael said. He heard the tension in his own voice and forced himself to calm as he explained. "There is a town associated with the estate, and some nice hotels. The area is owned by a wealthy businessman, a major landholder. They say he has aspirations toward a title."

"Who?" Judith asked, when Todd poked his head back into the passenger compartment from the flight deck.

"Sorry if I'm interrupting anything," he said, "but it's pretty obvious these people are going to make orbit before we do, and I don't really recall anyone explaining just what it is we're going to do when that happens."

He looked back and forth between Michael and Lieutenant Valles.

"They're only going to be fourteen minutes ahead of us," Michael pointed out, "and it's going to take at least a few minutes for them to get a shuttle up from the planet to meet them. So, for all intents and purposes, we'll actually be in a dead heat."

"And we're going to do precisely what after this 'dead heat' arrival?" Todd inquired politely.

"I've been thinking about that, Toad Breath," Michael replied. "I've pulled the stats on *Banshee* from her last safety inspection, and she's completely unarmed. So one possibility is to make orbit right behind her, then use *Ogapoge*'s guns to prevent the landing shuttle from docking with her. They may not even have realized we're back here, and even if they have, there wouldn't be a lot they could do about it."

"And then? Threaten to fire on *Banshee* if they don't surrender and hand Ruth over?"

"Tempting, Toad Breath. Very tempting. And it would *probably* work, assuming these people are as professional as I think they are. On the other hand, they'd know we were basically bluffing. There's no way we're going to fire on them when they've got Ruth on board."

"So once they know we've got them and their shuttle can't get to them, we call in the cops?"

"If we have to," Michael agreed. "I'd really rather not do that, though. If they really are professionals, they're probably smart enough to hand Ruth over unharmed when they realize they're trapped. Certainly no *professional* criminal is going to risk making things even worse by harming her at that point! But if we do it that way, the kidnapping, at least, comes out into the open, and I doubt we'll ever have any hard proof of who was really behind it."

"I know you, Michael," Todd said, watching him narrowly. "And I know that tone of voice. So since it's obvious you don't want to do it 'that way,' suppose you tell us just what you *do* have in mind?"

"What I'd really like to do is to let them land—with Ruth," Michael said, looking squarely at Judith. "I'm pretty sure I know where they're headed, and if I'm right, and if Vincent can whistle up a couple of sting ships from the Sphinx detachment, we could use them to cover the estate and prevent anyone from smuggling her out while I confront the estate's owners over the com." He smiled thinly. "Believe me. Once they know that we know who they are and can prove their involvement if we have to, they'll hand Ruth back so fast her head will spin! We may not want this to come out into the open, but neither will *they* . . . especially with the possibility of prison hovering in the background. But only if you trust me enough to do it that way, Judith. Otherwise, we hold them here in orbit, call the cops, and get Ruth back *now,* and the hell with the scandal or nailing the people behind it."

Judith looked back at him levelly. Her face looked thin and

pinched with worry, but his heart swelled at what he saw in her extraordinary eyes.

"I trust you," she said simply. "But I would like to know what makes you so confident that you know where they're heading and who's responsible for all this, Michael."

"Of course," he said. "Let me show you what I've been working on." He turned his minicomp so she could see the display, then started tapping keys.

"I was fascinated by the software the kidnappers used when they contacted you," he began. "Eventually, I want to go into research and design for the Navy. So while Todd has been reading spaceship 'zines, I've been keeping up with the latest in technology—especially electronics and communications."

Judith was nodding, her expression relaxing a touch. Michael couldn't help but remember how she hadn't drawn her hand back when he'd squeezed it, and he longed to reach out again.

But enough is enough, he cautioned himself, and returned to his explanation.

"What struck me right off was that the software being used to generate that particular avatar simulation was a very new design." Seeing a wrinkle of protest shaping around her mouth, he hastened to continue. "Really. I realize to you it probably didn't look any different from the programs kids use to play games, but I assure you, it was cutting edge. That particular program is very, very expensive, and so I figured that relatively few copies would have been sold at this point. I contacted the company and requested a list of purchasers—hinting I was interested in buying a copy myself, and wanted to check with others who were using the program."

Judith managed a smile—a very small one, but the bravery of it wrung Michael's heart.

"And the opportunity of being able to say 'as used by Crown Prince Michael' was such a tremendous temptation that I bet they overcame any qualms they had about customer confidentiality."

"That's right," Michael said. "But I wasn't pinning all my hopes on that one angle. I also put in a request for information about *Banshee.* Vincent helped there. Between his sources and mine, we came up with the owner of the ship."

Judith frowned. "Wouldn't that be a matter of public registration?"

"Oh, absolutely," Michael agreed, "and learning the ship was owned by Starflight Rentals told us less than nothing. However,

Starflight Rentals is a franchise, and this particular franchise is run by Timberlake Incorporated of Sphinx, and Timberlake Incorporated of Sphinx is owned by Mountain Holding Trust, and Mountain Holding Trust is wholly owned by one George Ramsbottom—who also happens to be on the very short list of people who bought the security software package in question."

"And *Banshee* is heading toward Sphinx," Judith said.

"Michael," Todd said, his voice puzzled, "wasn't the young lady—the one we met today—wasn't her name..."

"Alice Ramsbottom," Michael said with deep satisfaction. "Alice Ramsbottom who 'just happened' to show up when we were leaving Mount Royal today. I wonder if she was checking our timetable, making sure we would arrive at Judith's apartment at the right psychological moment."

"But," Todd protested, "Alice asked us if we could stop and have a coffee or something."

"I am willing to bet," Michael said, "that if we had accepted, she would have 'just happened' to be called back to work so we could make our timely departure. As it was, we were a little early, but that worked to our advantage."

"She seemed like such a nice girl," Todd said, disbelief and a mournful note coloring his words.

"I liked her, too, when we were kids," Michael admitted. "But a lot of years have passed. Alice said she was working as her father's secretary. George Ramsbottom is an outspoken Conservative. Like most Conservatives, he is adamantly against our alliance with Grayson. Come to think of it, Babette Ramsbottom, Alice's mother, has also spoken against it—but from the Liberal position. Isolationism's probably the only point where the Liberals and the Conservative Association actually agree. So Alice could have been scouting for either of her folks."

"And she seemed like such a nice girl," Todd repeated.

"Prisons are full of people who seemed like 'nice girls,' Lieutenant Liatt," Vincent observed sourly. "And I'd have to say, your Highness," he continued, turning to Michael, "that I think your reasoning is sound."

"And can the Sphinx detachment rustle up the sting ships for us?" Michael asked.

"There will probably be some questions asked," Vincent replied with what Michael recognized as massive understatement. "The fact that I'm assigned directly to *you* should mean that they only get asked afterward, however. In fact, I can probably arrange to have an entire company ready to move in on the ground to tighten the perimeter, if you wish."

"I wish," Michael said grimly, and Vincent bent his head in brief, formal acknowledgment of his prince's order.

"In that case, Your Highness, I should probably get busy on the com."

✳ ✳ ✳

"Michael, I don't think *Banshee* is heading for a standard orbit after all," Todd Liatt said. "Look at this."

Michael poked his head into the flight deck and frowned. Todd was right. Rather than settling into one of the low orbits small ships like *Banshee* and *Ogapoge* would normally use to rendezvous with passenger shuttles, the other runabout was obviously bound for a much higher orbit.

"They're headed for that freight platform," Todd said, indicating the transponder beacon. "Aslan Station," he added.

"Vincent," Michael called over his shoulder, "I think a new factor has been added."

"Were we wrong about the Ramsbottoms?" Judith asked, her voice tense, and Michael spared her a small smile. How many anxious mothers would have said "we" in a case like this instead of "you," he wondered.

"I don't think so," he replied. "Aslan Station is a freight and passenger transfer platform that just happens to be operated by Timberlake Incorporated under a long-term lease from Astro Control."

Her expression lightened, and he looked at Valles.

"I think we're going to need docking clearance, Vincent. Can you arrange it without bringing me into the equation? Just a nice, simple little civilian docking request?"

"I believe I can manage that, Your Highness," Vincent agreed, and bent over the com again while *Banshee* headed directly towards the platform. The other ship was obviously expected and precleared to dock, and Michael frowned as *Banshee* settled into the platform's docking arms and the personnel tube ran out to her.

"Problems, Vincent?" he asked quietly while Todd brought *Ogapoge* smoothly to rest relative to the platform. There seemed to be a *lot* of small craft and heavy-lift shuttles in the vicinity, but no one seemed in any hurry to insert *Ogapoge* into the approach pattern.

"I'm afraid so, Your Highness," Vincent admitted. "The station seems to be very busy at this time of day."

The lieutenant's eyes met Michael's and the prince frowned.

"You think they're really that busy?" he asked. "Or is it just a trick to keep us floating around out here?"

"I don't know," Vincent said slowly. "I'm inclined to think it's genuine, judging by the traffic we're observing. Of course, they knew where they were going before we did. If they also knew how busy Aslan was going to be, they may have deliberately factored that into their planning. Preclearing *Banshee* would be one way to let them get back a bit of their lead on any pursuers."

"Can we do anything to hold *Banshee*?"

"We could," Vincent hesitated. "I'm in touch with the platform Customs detachment, and I'm sure I could convince them to take a special interest in her. But interfering that openly might have severe ramifications for Miss Ruth."

"You're right," Michael said. "We're just going to have to get aboard ourselves."

Time passed with aching slowness as they waited to be cleared to approach the orbital station. Vincent had contnued his communication with the station's Customs and Astro Control detachments while they waited. Now he spoke with a degree of hesitation unusual for him.

"Prince Michael, I think we have a problem. *Banshee* has been docked for over forty minutes now, but according to the senior Customs officer, she's more or less sitting there abandoned. Her passengers apparently debarked immediately and headed for another ship, *Cormorant*, which arrived in from Manticore just a short time ago. Both of them boarded *Cormorant* and have already departed the station."

"Course?" Michael said.

"They requested clearance for out-system. That's all. Space is a big place. We could search for hours and not find them, even though they don't have a very big head start."

"Crew?" Judith interrupted before Michael could ask for more details. "Did they see Ruth?"

Vincent shook his head. "The pair had with them several pieces of luggage. I asked a few discreet questions, and there were two trunks of a size that could have held your daughter. I'm sorry, ma'am."

Michael slammed his fist into his palm. "Damn!"

"We've got clearance—finally," Todd put in from the flight deck. "Do you want me to go ahead and dock? Or do we track *Cormorant*?"

"Take us in," Michael said. "We're going to have to check to make sure they weren't just cutting their losses. They could have left Ruth behind on *Banshee.* Or they could have traded her to someone else and she could be on station. And maybe we can get some better information as to *Cormorant's* destination."

"Right," Todd said.

"Vincent," Michael said. "I want everything you can get me about *Cormorant.* There must be in-station cameras. Get us pictures of her crew. Bend rules. Go ahead and throw my name around with the people you're already talking to. I also want a full list of ships that leave that station after *Banshee's* arrival, their destinations, everything, just in case there was an exchange."

"Yes, sir."

Michael reached over and squeezed Judith's hand. "Let me see what I can learn about *Cormorant.* That's still our most likely target."

He took out his minicomp, logged into the Sphinx planetary data system, and started requesting information. Fortunately, he was requesting information on a civilian ship, so he did not run into any of the difficulties he might have had he been making the same requests about a military vessel.

The results came in just as Todd was bringing them into dock.

"I found out a few things," Michael said. He felt a vicious smile twist his face. "*Cormorant* arrived in dock only a few hours ago. She's also owned by Starflight Rentals. By odd coincidence she included among its incoming passengers someone I would very much like to speak with, someone who I believe is still on station."

"You don't mean . . ." Todd said, swinging around to look at Michael.

"That's right, Alice Ramsbottom."

❋ ❋ ❋

"Alice Ramsbottom," Judith repeated. "So we have confirmation of your suspicions that one of her parents is involved in Ruth's kidnapping. How can we use that? Kidnap her, perhaps? Arrange for an exchange?"

"Your Majesty..." Vincent Valless began, but Michael cut him off with a wave of one hand.

"Don't worry, Vincent. We're not going to do anything so very illegal."

Michael reached out and took one of Judith's hands, cradling it between his broad, brown hands.

"Judith, I can do a good many things, but I can't do that. I'd rather go to a nightclub and dance naked on a table while making outrageous pronouncements about the stupidity of my sister's public policy. That would only damage my reputation. Kidnapping, though, that's nasty stuff—not only illegal, but flat out wrong."

Despite her fear for Ruth, Judith felt herself smiling at the image of Michael dancing on a table. Instantly, she became serious again.

"Michael, I don't want you to do anything that would hurt you or Queen Elizabeth. But I want my baby back."

"So do I," Michael said. "Let's find Alice Ramsbottom. Let's talk to her."

"And then?" Judith asked.

"We improvise."

❈　　❈　　❈

They found Alice Ramsbottom over at *Banshee*'s berth.

The inboard end of the ship's boarding tube was open when they arrived, and so was the hatch at its outboard end. Vincent Valless insisted on boarding first, and Judith saw Michael's fist open and close in a gesture of concealed frustration, but he didn't protest.

Poor man. He may be a prince, but in some ways his life is as restricted as that of any Masadan wife. Unlike me, he can't run away and make a new life for himself without hurting those he loves and respects.

Michael boarded close behind Vincent. As they entered the vessel, Alice could be seen through the flight deck hatch, intent on the control panel, apparently running a pre-flight check. She was concentrating on her task too intently to notice their arrival until Michael spoke in a soft but firm voice.

"Alice, it's me. Michael Winton. I need to talk to you."

Judith was just a few paces behind Michael, almost treading on his heels, and she saw Alice's expression. There was surprise there, mild shock when she saw the pulser on which Vincent's hand rested, but no guilt.

What if she doesn't know anything? What if we're just wasting time? Oh, God—I'll believe in you again—just give me back my baby. Alive. Happy. Unhurt.

"Mikey?" Alice looked at the prince. Her hands remained on the control panel, but she didn't move. It wouldn't have mattered if she had. Before they had come to *Banshee*'s berth, Michael had done some tech wizardry that cut the ship off from outside contact while creating a data loop to hide the fact.

Judith didn't have the least idea how Michael had done it, but she took his word that for the moment at least Alice was isolated.

"Is anyone else aboard?" Michael asked.

The video images Vincent had been tracking even as they moved through the station had shown Alice alone, Judith knew, but it never hurt to check.

"No," Alice replied, her voice puzzled. "Mikey? What's going on? Who is that woman? Why does your guard have his hand on his weapon? What are you doing here?"

The three had all entered the ship's roomy cabin by now. *Banshee* was a bit larger than *Ogapoge,* but otherwise, the two little runabouts were much alike. A few rows of comfortable seats stretched back from the flight deck, sandwiched between its hatch and the equally cramped engineering section aft. There was a small cargo area between the passenger seats and engineering, but its hatch was open and it was obviously empty. Judith glanced around anyway, looking for any sign Ruth had been here. There was nothing.

"The woman is my good friend, Judith Newland," Michael said. "We're here because her daughter, Ruth, is missing, and we have reason to believe Ruth left Manticore on this ship."

"What? How..." Alice let her hands drop to her lap, and stared up at Michael, her momentary expression of incredulity fading, colored with something else. "Go on. Tell me. Fast."

Michael did. Judith knew he had various holo files ready to show if Alice demanded evidence, but the young woman only listened, her intelligent eyes narrowing.

"Search," she said, waving her hand back, "but you won't find anything."

"Do you believe me?" Michael asked.

Judith listened as she moved among the rows of seats.

"I do," Alice said. "My parents have been behaving strangely lately. My dad insisted that I come to Mount Royal with him today. He sent me into the corridor, flat out telling me he'd seen my old schoolmate the prince in the hall, and wouldn't it be nice if I made myself really friendly. He even reminded me you didn't go by 'Mikey' anymore. Then he sent me off in *Cormorant,* only to tell me to leave her in dock and get *Banshee* down to Choire Ghlais. No reason, no explanation—just do it. It was pretty obvious he was busy with some scheme, but I never expected something like this."

"So you believe he'd plan a kidnapping?"

"If he could make himself believe it was for the greater good, yes," Alice said. "Helping get the Star Kingdom back on track. Reuniting a daughter with her father. Yes, I do. It's obvious they've managed to misread the Grayson mindset badly, if they expect this to have the effect they obviously want, but that doesn't really surprise me. They're very good at maneuvering within their own political and power circles, but outside that, they both tend to see what they want to see. I don't doubt that they could convince themselves to believe this would all work out 'for the best,' and Daddy is particularly good at distancing himself from the human aspect... Look at his relationship with my mother."

Michael nodded. "Yes. Married enemies. That can't be easy on anyone, but..."

Alice shook her head. "There's more to it than that, but now's not the time to talk. You say the people who took *Banshee* here to Aslan Station transferred to *Cormorant.* Any idea of their course?"

Vincent cut in. "Lieutenant Liatt just commed me. He's been tracing various out-system vessels. He thinks he has *Cormorant.* It took him a while to sort her transponder out from all the surrounding traffic."

"And?" Michael said.

"She's heading out-system, but since she's not hyper-capable, she's probably heading for a rendezvous of some sort."

Alice nodded sharply. "*Kwahe'e.* I'll bet anything she's going to meet *Kwahe'e.*"

"*Kwahe'e?*" Judith asked.

Alice swivelled her chair so she could look directly at Judith. "Parents never think their kids notice things. I've noticed a lot of things—like *Kwahe'e.* It's a hyper-capable vessel, not large. Technically, she's a small, fast interstellar transport for corporate VIPs, but she's large enough to transport small, valuable cargos, too. In fact, that's what she spends most of her time doing. Those cargos aren't precisely illegal—at least I don't think so—but they aren't exactly the sort you want other people to connect to a prominent politician and business executive."

"So they'll transfer Ruth to *Kwahe'e*," Judith said. "And *Kwahe'e* will be the ship that meets with Ephraim."

"That's how I see it," Alice said. "Now what do you plan to do? You can't chase them down and shoot at them—for one thing, there's too much chance the little girl will get hurt. What was your plan once you located them?"

❊   ❊   ❊

Michael was momentarily stunned, especially when he saw the confident look Judith turned toward him. He'd never expected a chase out-system. He'd thought the kidnappers would go to another planet—probably Sphinx—and once downside he and Vincent would be able to recruit help from the local Palace Security detachments. They would have helped and kept their silence afterwards. Now, this . . .

Alice came to his rescue. "I have an idea. Let me in on this. We'll do a two-ship approach. I'll com *Cormorant*, make some excuse for us meeting up: additional supplies probably. That should slow them. Then I'll take *Banshee* out to intercept."

"What if they contact whoever hired them," Judith asked, "and find out there are no such supplies?"

Alice smiled sadly. "I'm willing to bet that they were never given a contact number. Too dangerous."

"I agree," Michael said. "Why use a cutting edge avatar program and then create such an easy avenue for tracing? Okay. But I'm not sure I like the idea of your taking *Banshee* out."

Alice flared. "Don't you trust me, Mikey? Do you think I'd condone kidnapping a small child? Or do you think I'm not capable of handling my own company's ship?"

Michael held up both hands in a gesture half-surrender, half-self-defense.

"Easy! I wasn't thinking either. I was thinking about you. You're going to be in serious trouble with your parents as it is. If you don't participate any further, you'll be able to cover yourself: say we put pressure on you; say we lied and told you that we were authorized to take *Banshee*."

Unspoken in this was what they all knew. Even if—when— Ruth was recovered, the Ramsbottoms would go unpunished. The kidnappers themselves might stand trial, but they would know nothing about their principals. Even if they did, actually proving the connection to the Ramsbottoms would probably be difficult... not to mention its providing the very scandal they were trying to prevent. Therefore, Alice would have to deal with the wrath of whichever parent was behind this plot.

Alice shook her head, anger gone, a curious sadness taking its place.

"Michael, if either of my parents is involved in this, I don't care how much trouble I get into with them. Let me help. Let me prove to you that not all the Ramsbottoms are so given to ambition as to forget basic human decency."

Judith spoke before Michael could frame an appropriate reply. "I'll trust you. Now, we're wasting time. I'll go with you, since *Banshee* is likely to be the ship to make actual physical contact with *Cormorant*."

Vincent Valless turned to Michael. "I'm sorry, Your Highness, but I cannot permit you to make contact with the kidnappers' vessel. It would be too dangerous. However, if you will agree to go back to *Ogapoge* without protest, then I will join *Banshee*'s crew and provide some protection."

Michael wanted to scream, to protest: "It's *my* job to protect her!" But he knew he didn't have that choice. He tried to keep his voice level as he replied.

"Very well, Vincent. I'd like someone else to go with them, as well."

"I have already arranged for that," Vincent said, a ghost of a smile touching his lips. "Todd Liatt and another member of your security force will be joining us momentarily. That will provide firepower and back-up piloting, should they be needed."

Michael nodded. "Thank you for your foresight and initiative, Vincent."

He tried to make his words gracious, but he knew his tone failed to keep up the illusion. Fine. He would accept his exile, but there was nothing in the rules of etiquette that said he had to be happy about it.

Michael turned to Judith and forced a smile. "At least those of us on *Ogapoge* can trail you and provide pressure to cooperate if that becomes necessary. Even if they spotted us on the way out from Manticore, they've ony got civilian instruments. They won't be able to identify us without our transponder code, and I can disable that once we're out of the press of near-planet traffic."

Vincent Valless coughed softly. "We can even do one better, sir. Ships carrying members of the royal family have some flexibility in regard to supplying precisely accurate identification."

"Brilliant!" Michael said. "We'll do that then. Reset the transponder to show us as an ore freighter or a tourist barge, whichever is more appropriate for the area."

At that moment, Todd and the female security officer came around the corner into *Banshee*'s berth. Michael knew without being told that another of the operatives waited in the corridor to escort him back to *Ogapoge*.

Behind him, Michael could hear Alice making contact with *Cormorant*. She'd refused visual contact, and was telling whoever had answered the call she had added supplies they were to take with them. Something in how she inflected her words implied a reward or bonus. Michael was impressed.

Todd and his companion needed no additional instructions. Further chat would only slow their mission. Since neither *Banshee* nor *Ogapoge* was hyper-capable, it was crucial that they intercept *Cormorant* before she met *Kwahee*.

As Todd passed Michael, he reached out and clasped his friend firmly on one shoulder. "Don't worry, roomie. I'll look out for her."

His words were almost inaudible. Michael was grateful. He knew Todd meant what he said, and he knew, too, that Todd was admitting what Michael himself had hardly dared acknowledge.

He loved Judith Newland. If anything happened to her, the universe would go dark and all the suns at the interstellar core could not shed enough light to brighten it once more.

✳   ✳   ✳

Judith watched Michael leave *Cormorant*, eagerness to find Ruth warring with a sinking sensation in her breast. Resolutely she turned away and strapped herself into one of the front row of passenger seats.

At Alice's suggestion, Todd was taking over as pilot.

"I want to keep an eye on *Cormorant*'s movements. I also want to scan for *Kwahee*. Hopefully, she's well out-system, but we can't count on that."

"Good," Todd said. "You're captain. Sing out if you need me to alter course."

Judith had lived on Manticore for over two years now, but the easy manner in which Manticoran men worked not only with, but also *for* women still could astonish her. Grayson men treated their women far better than Masadans did, but even so women were considered very much the "weaker sex."

Men should try childbirth, Judith thought with a momentary return of the hatred that had driven her to flee Masada. *They should try menstrual periods. They should try chasing around day and night after squalling little children, coping with a thousand crises in a single day, solving everything from medical emergencies to diplomatic breakdowns. Let them try that for a solid week, then see if they still call women weak!*

But Judith couldn't maintain her wrath. Todd wasn't condescending to Alice, not even with the excuse that he was a Navy officer and she a civilian. He recognized that here Alice had the expertise, and so she should be in command. Vincent Valless had introduced Galina Caruso, his female counterpart, without the least hint that she was anything but another security officer.

Get out of your own head, Judith thought, *and face what's going on.* She leaned forward to better attend to the minor drama playing out between Alice and *Cormorant.*

Cormorant had acknowledged Alice's com message—not without a certain degree of suspicion. The kidnappers had seemed particularly suspicious because she was aboard the very ship *they* had just abandoned, but she had managed to put exactly the right note of exasperation into her own voice as she agreed that their joint employers were idiots. She had been remarkably convincing, and they had finally accepted that the "additional cargo" represented some afterthought—one that would benefit the kidnappers as much or more than anyone else.

Although the kidnappers were obviously unhappy, greed had tilted the balance. They had reduced acceleration almost to zero to allow her to catch up, so *Banshee* and the disguised *Ogapoge* overtook *Cormorant* rapidly.

Judith was trying to relax in her seat when Galina moved forward and took the seat next to her.

"You're determined to board *Cormorant* with Ms. Ramsbottom?"

"Yes."

The single word held heat and fire, and Galina nodded. If she'd ever been inclined to argue the wisdom of Judith's decision, she gave it up now as clearly useless.

"Is it likely the kidnappers have seen you before?"

Judith blinked, a cascade of unwelcome thoughts flooding through her mind.

"Yes. One of them diverted me while the other took Ruth." Judith's voice broke, and she steadied herself. "But I'm still going in. It's likely Ruth is still unconscious, but if she isn't, she's going to be afraid. She's going to need me."

"I understand."

Galina's tone of voice said that what she understood was that Judith needed to see Ruth—alive and well—as soon as possible.

"Sometimes," Galina said, "a security officer can serve best by not looking like a security officer."

"Sometimes," Vincent Valless cut in with a wicked grin that made Judith think this tactical point had been a point of contention between them before, "it's best if the guard dog shows his fangs. However, this time you're right, Galina. We should take off our tunics. Without the rank and department badges, we can pass for shiphands."

Galina Caruso nodded. "Good."

She returned her attention to Judith. "I've had some training in disguise. If you'd permit me, I may be able to buy you a few necessary minutes."

"My luggage is in the carry bay in the back," Alice said from her post at the control console. "Help yourself. Judith and I are not exactly the same size, but there's make-up and stuff you might find useful."

Judith's initial response was to protest, to remind them that the whole point of her boarding was to be able to reassure Ruth. How could she do so if she didn't look like herself?

But her protest died unspoken. Galina was right. All it would take was one of the kidnappers recognizing her, and everything would go to hell.

While Todd brought *Banshee* closer and closer to *Cormorant*, Judith let Galina work on her. Her hair was restyled into a tight braid coiled at the back of her neck. From Alice's personal luggage a change of clothes was selected, including a tinted hairnet that did much to dampen the distinctive auburn highlights of Judith's hair into a muddy brown.

"I could make your face up so your own mother wouldn't know you," Galina said, fussing with the collar of the understatedly stylish jacket Judith now wore in place of the work shirt she'd been wearing, "but that's hardly worthwhile since I can't do anything about your eyes. The color is so unusual. If we were in a port, contact lenses would be an easy fix, but we can't get them out here. You're just going to have to keep your gaze lowered."

That will be easy enough, Judith thought. *Neither Grayson nor Masadan men like their women to be saucy. Meeting a strange man's gaze was distinctly saucy—and so something she still found hard to do.*

"Why don't we both wear masks?" Alice suggested. "We don't have any of the fancy nano disguise gear aboard, but a cloth over the face should be enough. Given the care that has gone into protecting the identity of the principal in this case, I think bare faces would be more suspicious than covered. I have some scarves in my luggage that should do."

"I've seen them," Galina said, pulling one out and experimenting with how to best twist it into a concealing mask.

Alice continued, "I've been trying to think how to justify two of us coming aboard. A bodyguard would be a direct challenge. I think we're both going to need to carry something aboard. There are some crates in the back, but they're not very large. If they ask about the contents, we'll have to come up with something believable that's also small enough to fit into a crate that size."

"We could be bringing personal weapons," Judith cut in. "Or high tech trinkets. For all they claim to hate technology, there is a faction on Masada that craves higher tech weaponry and ships. Ephraim Templeton—with whom *Kwahe'e* will be rendezvousing—is among those. If you can imply that they are to bring a present of such in addition to the child..."

Judith's voice broke, and she couldn't say anything further, but Alice was nodding. "That should work. I'll carry one box. You carry another, larger one. The size will give you an excuse to focus on the box, rather than any people aboard. I won't say exactly what the boxes contain, just hint at valuable presents. Greed should do the rest."

"Sounds good," Valless said. "Or at least workable."

"We've been granted permission to dock *Banshee* to *Cormorant*," Todd said. "Everybody take their places."

They did. The two ships mated air locks and Alice Ramsbottom, her attractive face and thick honey-colored hair now concealed beneath a mask made from an artfully twisted dark blue scarf, handed Judith a large box.

"Act as if it's heavier than it is," she reminded, taking up her own burden. "And stay behind me."

Judith nodded. Her heart was pounding, but she couldn't tell whether from anticipation or fear. The box Alice had handed her was heavy enough to remind Judith to act as if it was a real burden, but not overly inconvenient—especially for a young mother who regularly slung her growing child up over her hip and carried her about.

Just on the other side of that hatch, Judith thought. *Just on the other side of that hatch. Ruth is there. Ruth . . .*

Judith stepped forward almost treading on Alice's heels in her eagerness. *Pryderi*-class ships, to which the *Cormorant* and *Banshee* belonged, were not overly large. Unless the kidnappers still had her in a crate, in just a few steps, Judith was going to see her little girl, see her alive, hold her.

Voices from ahead of her forced Judith to concentrate on something other than her thudding heartbeat.

"Just hand the boxes here," commanded a man's voice. "We'll take over."

"Oh, no," Alice said, a breezy laugh underlying her words. Judith admired her poise. "Not so easy, buster. I've orders to have these signed for—and I was told to direct your attention to the seals. They're sequential. The code for opening this box," she hefted the one in her arms, "will be released to you when the other one is delivered along with your other parcel. Until you agree, well, I can walk backwards as easily as not."

Alice took a step back, and Judith had to scuttle to get out of her way.

There was a long pause, then the male voice spoke, "Right. Fine. This has been a bizarre job all along. Why shouldn't it keep being weird?"

Alice strode forward. Judith followed closely, keeping her eyes downcast as if concerned about her footing. Behind her, she could sense another presence, Valless, she guessed, making sure his charges didn't go beyond where he could help.

Alice entered *Cormorant*. Judith followed close behind her and couldn't resist a glance to see if Ruth was on any of the passenger seats.

Her timing couldn't have been worse. The woman she knew as Dulcis McKinley was standing mid-way down the aisle between the rows of seats watching as Alice set her box down on one of the seats in the front row. McKinley had glanced casually over at Judith and their eyes met.

For a moment, Judith thought that it wouldn't matter, but McKinley was good at her chosen profession for a reason. She'd stood in an apartment hallway, holding Judith's attention while her partner snatched Ruth. She wasn't likely to forget those distinctive green eyes with their contrasting ring of brown—especially as the mask that hid the rest of Judith's face accented those incredible eyes.

"You!" Dulcis McKinley said, half-gasp, half-scream. "Ward! It's a trap!"

Her hand dropped to her waist, possibly reaching for a holstered weapon.

Judith didn't pause. Gone was her anxious anticipation. Gone was any fear or indecision. Returned was the fierce decisiveness that had let a child of ten believe that she could steal a spaceship and escape to the stars.

Raising the box she carried in her arms, Judith threw it across the intervening rows of seats, catching McKinley firmly in the chest.

McKinley stumbled, catching herself against the nearest seat. Judith sprang onto the seat nearest to her and flung herself over, leaping with the agile accuracy of desperation.

Behind her, she was aware of the man Alice had been speaking to giving a sharp cry of pain.

Vincent Valless's voice was saying something, but Judith didn't hear any of the details. She had her hands on Dulcis McKinley's throat and, despite the difference in their sizes, was shaking the other woman so hard the woman's elegant head snapped back and forth on her long neck.

"Where is she! Where is Ruth?"

✳   ✳   ✳

Michael Winton supposed that he should be glad that maneuvering a little ship like *Ogapoge*, a vessel of a sub-class he hadn't flown for quite a while, demanded a fair amount of his attention.

One of the two remaining security officers had moved up into the co-pilot's seat and was now scanning the surrounding area.

"Sir, we have a bogie." The man recited coordinates. "Matches the description Alice Ramsbottom gave us of *Kwahe'e*. It's closing on where *Banshee* and *Cormorant* are docked."

Michael had had *Ogapoge*'s weapons systems at ready, but he had dearly hoped to avoid using them.

"Have they spotted us?"

"We were scanned, but I believe our transpoder code was sufficient." The corner of the security officer's mouth twitched in an almost grin. "I believe they were distracted to see the ship with which they expected to make a clandestine rendezvous docked with another."

"We'll keep an eye on *Kwahe'e,*" Michael said, changing his heading slightly in case interception became necessary, "but we're not going to do anything. *Kwahe'e*'s playing it safe. Let's not force her to change her mind."

"Aye-aye, sir."

Michael's hands flowed over the controls, his brain composing various messages. He couldn't query *Banshee* lest the call be overheard. Little passenger ships like this didn't always have the tightest communications systems, and this wasn't the time to take a risk.

He'd just have to wait and watch. Wait and hope. Wait and dread.

❋   ❋   ❋

"Ruth is in the back!" Dulcis McKinley almost screamed the words. "She's in one of the crates. She's fine. The crate is set up like a little bed. I was checking on her just a moment ago. She's still sleeping."

Vincent Valless came toward them, his bulk crowding the aisle. "I'll take custody of this lady," he said to Judith, "if you want to check out her story."

Judith nodded. Galina Caruso had joined Alice in the front of the cabin, and the male kidnapper was sitting down. Judging from his artificially stiff posture, Galina must have had immobilizing restraints.

Interesting, Judith thought, *what she carries around as part of her routine gear.*

But the thought was just cover, empty speculation to keep her from thinking about that crate in the cargo bay at the back of the ship. There was only one large enough to carry Ruth, and it wasn't overly large, but then a sleeping child didn't take up that much room.

She was at the crate, checking the latches, forcing them up, feeling the lid slide up and back.

And there was Ruth, still disguised as a dark-haired little boy. She lay asleep, curled on her side, her thumb tucked in her mouth, an unfamiliar toy—a little woolly lamb—cuddled into the middle of her body.

She was breathing, and as Judith touched her, she stirred. Her sleepy sigh was the sweetest sound Judith had ever heard.

"She's here. She's all right. She may be coming around."

McKinley no longer fighting, philosophically resigned to the changed situation, nodded confirmation.

"She should be. We gave her a mild sedative, just enough to be able to move her without her fussing. Even that should be wearing off within an hour. We had no desire to harm her—or even to make her uncomfortable."

"Lucky for you," Judith said, gathering the sleeping child to her and standing as easily as if Ruth weighed nothing at all. "So very, very lucky for you."

*   *   *

Kwahe'e had peeled back into the dark anonymity of the outer system when *Cormorant* and *Banshee* had undocked and both had turned their courses to the inner system. Perhaps by then they had noticed *Ogapoge* hanging watchful in the fringes; certainly her captain, skilled in skulduggery as he apparently was, had known when absence was the better part of valor.

The three ships had flown in company back to Aslan Station. There *Cormorant* and *Banshee* had been tucked into their reserved berths. *Ogapoge* alone made the trip back to Manticore, carrying with them what Michael Winton was inclined to view as a very precious cargo.

Many of those aboard had at least some medical training, and Dulcis McKinley's statement that Ruth had been only lightly drugged was confirmed. They had decided to let the child sleep off the drug naturally. At this point, a stimulant might be more shock than aid.

Todd piloted the ship. Alice Ramsbottom, looking very serious, acted as co-pilot. Her parents—Michael was willing to bet George Ramsbottom, rather than Babette, was behind the plot—might never come to trial. However, for Alice herself there seemed to be no doubts as to their involvement. Her world was due for some major changes.

The four security officers settled in the rear of the passenger compartment, and for the first time since his return home Michael found himself more or less alone with Judith.

She looked relaxed but tranquil. Ruth slept sprawled over both their laps, creating a curious but not in the least unpleasant intimacy.

"She's safe," Judith said, stroking the child's dyed brown hair. "And you're safe. It's odd. I never thought of myself as a danger to you."

Michael cleared his throat, awkward yet curiously at peace. "I guess what I thought I'd kept to myself must have been more obvious than I realized."

"You love me," Judith said simply. "I can see that now, and I . . ."

She turned and took his hand in hers, then stretched up so she could kiss him softly on one cheek, "And I love you. I never let myself realize how deeply I cared for you until that moment came when you were willing to sacrifice your honor and that of your family to save Ruth—and even though Ruth is the moon and the stars to me, I couldn't let you do that. I couldn't let you hurt yourself, not even to save her."

All too aware of the array of security officers in back of them, Michael settled for sliding his arm around her shoulders.

"Thank you," he said softly. "Thank you so very much for loving me."

"You are very welcome."

"I don't suppose you'd consider marriage? My sister won't mind. In fact, now that I think about various things she's said to me, I think she may have suspected for a long while who held my heart."

"Ask me."

"Will you marry me, Judith?"

"I will."

This time Michael did kiss her. It was a very chaste kiss by the standards of a newly engaged couple, but held a considerable amount of promise.

"There are a lot of people who aren't going to like this," Judith said. Then, to Michael's delight, she laughed. "But after everything we've faced together, I don't think mere disapproval is going to change a thing."

"No," Michael said, holding her close against his side. "It's not going to matter at all."

❊   ❊   ❊

George and Babette Ramsbottom read the handwritten note together.

"Dear Mom and Dad,

"I know what you've been doing—about the kidnapping and how you were willing to send a small child into exile and possibly death if that would further your political aims. I know you thought you were doing the best thing for the Star Kingdom, but I'm afraid I don't agree.

"I also know you've cleverly arranged matters so that the people you've hurt so terribly—powerful and highly placed as they are—can't touch you without the information that would come out in a trial damaging both them and the causes they value without hurting you nearly as much.

"After all, you two only have your jobs, livelihood, and personal freedom at stake. They'd be risking the welfare of the Star Kingdom and that of her new Grayson allies. They won't put the kingdom at risk, so you're safe.

"Or at least you're safe as long as I keep my mouth shut. You may have thought I never noticed just how contrived your supposed enmity is, but I've been aware of the deception for years. I know about your clandestine meetings. I know how you've manipulated your political and professional allies precisely because they believe you two are estranged, and that therefore information shared with one would never, ever be learned by the other.

"Can you imagine what would happen to you if word of your cozy arrangement was released by such an unimpeachable source as your own daughter? I think you do. You'd be ruined socially, politically, and probably financially. I suppose you'd still have each other, but not much else.

"This letter is to inform you that your freedom to act is going to be restricted from this point on. Although Prince Michael will not move against you on the matter of the kidnapping of his soon-to-be stepdaughter, Ruth, I want you to know he knows—not just suspects—that one of you was behind the kidnapping. So even though you're getting away with this crime, you're going to be under observation from this point on. Take care.

"Therefore, think twice or even three times before attempting anything even remotely like this again. Play your political games as you will, but leave the innocent out of it. If I even suspect you're involved in anything in the least criminal, I'll shout the truth about you to every newsie on the beat. And I'll be very, very convincing. You'll be ruined.

"Since it's never a good idea to be the only one with a dangerous secret, I've confided in someone I trust completely. His name is Todd Liatt. He's one of Prince Michael's closest friends. Todd will be given a copy of this letter, and copies of certain other documents and holos in my possession—see attached file—and will pass them on to Prince Michael if anything happens either to me or to... well, to anyone at all. And I understand from Todd that he's made... insurance arrangements of his own, in case you should suddenly feel particularly adventurous.

"I'm writing you this, rather than confronting you in person, because I know you for resourceful and ruthless souls. Given that you're not likely to be overly pleased with me, I don't think I'll be living at home for a while.

"Don't worry about me, though. I won't be on the streets. Judith of Masada has invited me to come and live with her. Her new—well, new to them, anyhow—relationship with Prince Michael means Judith needs a crash course in all the social graces and political complications she's going to face as fiancée and eventually wife to a member of the royal family. Judith has asked me to be her coach. I'll be drawing a good salary, so don't think threatening to cut off my allowance will have any effect.

"Why haven't I exposed you right off? Well, you are my parents, and I do love you, strange and manipulative creatures that you are. Don't disappoint me by suddenly getting dumb.

"Love, your daughter,

"Alice Ramsbottom."

An Act of War

Timothy Zahn

The People's Republic of Haven, it was said by those who knew it well, had never been anything but a depressing study in contrasts.

On the one hand were the upper elite, the movers and shakers of the People's Republic, the ones who put up the brave and arrogant front for the rest of the galaxy. They were the ones who spoke of freedom and equality in the glowing tones that had swayed so many of their fellow elitists onto their side, in the Solarian League and elsewhere.

On the other hand were the vast majority of the people themselves, the poor and disenfranchised and demoralized. They were the ones who took their dole and tried to survive on it, all the while keeping their mouths shut lest a discordant note amid all that glowing equality get them vanished where their mouths would be kept shut for them.

Haven in time of war was just more of the same. A lot more.

Still, there were compensations, Charles reminded himself as he picked up the exquisitely cut crystal tumbler from the polished wood table and took a sip of the excellent brandy his hosts had pressed on him. As the deprivations of a wartime economy squeezed all but the *very* top levels of the elite, it also squeezed out the sweat of desperation among the movers and shakers.

Especially when those same movers and shakers looked to be losing that war.

The two men across from Charles lifted their eyes from the

papers he'd set on the table before them, locked eyes briefly and wordlessly with each other, then turned again to Charles. "So you're saying this will work on *any* sensor array?" the taller one, Armond, asked cautiously. "Even military ones?"

"Even military ones," Charles confirmed. "Provided, of course, that you can get the sheath wrapped around the transmission line leading from the actual sensor to the computer or viewscreen."

"If you'll forgive me, this seems just a little too easy," the shorter one, Miklos, said, a hint of suspicion in his voice.

But only a hint. Armond was the head of one of the Peeps' most distinguished electronics firms, and Miklos was his chief tech, and Citizen Secretaries Rob Pierre and Oscar Saint-Just were breathing down their necks in the most ominous possible way. The Manticoran technological edge was slowly but steadily grinding away the Peeps' numerical advantage, and Haven desperately needed something to turn that around. A fresh infusion of Solly technology would be just what the doctor ordered.

And if Armond and Miklos could buy it under the table and pass it off to Pierre and Saint-Just as their own creation, so much the better.

"Of course it's easy," Charles explained, adjusting the level of patience in his voice to match the level of suspicion in Miklos's. "The hard part is never the tech, but the execution. But as I say, if you can get the Redactor in place, you can put basically anything you want on the other person's screen."

"Including nothing?" Armond asked.

"Including nothing," Charles assured him. "Your attacking ship can come right into energy range, and they'll never even see it."

Armond nodded, running his finger gently across the smooth plastic of the sample Redactor that Charles had brought to this particular session of show-and-tell. "A cloak of invisibility," the Peep murmured.

"Or a hundred cloaks," Charles said. "You can actually program the Redactor to erase *everything* within sensor range that's running a PRN transponder."

"Yes, but a *hundred* of them?" Miklos asked, frowning.

Charles shrugged. A hundred ships really *was* more than the Redactor could handle. But if he'd learned anything over the years, it was to never backtrack. "Or even more," he said. "It all depends on how much money you're willing to spend." He gestured toward the device on the table. "Now, this model only has enough processing power to erase one or maybe two ships. But I know where I can get my hands on advanced models that can handle up to probably even two hundred."

"Those are much larger, I assume," Miklos said. Beside him, Armond pulled out his phone and quietly answered it.

"Not as much as you might think," Charles said. "Our processors and storage are far more compact than anything you're likely to find around here." He gave the other a faintly mocking smile. "Even on Manticore," he added.

Miklos's expression changed subtly, and Charles knew that he had them. The Manties were the bugaboo in this part of the galaxy, respected or feared by pretty much everyone around them. And rightfully so. Their tech, particularly their military tech, was head and shoulders above anything else that could be had out here. Not as good as Solly stuff, of course, but the League was highly resistant to letting their tech leak out into these backwater areas.

Which was where people like Charles came in.

"Yeah, well, the Manties aren't miracle workers," Miklos said sourly as he picked up the general spec sheet again and began skimming down it. "Where exactly is the memory listing—?"

"Hell and fury," Armond cut him off as he slammed down his phone and swiveled in his chair. Grabbing the remote, he tagged the big presentation video screen that took up most of the room's east wall.

"What's the matter?" Miklos demanded.

"Watch," Armond growled.

The screen came to life, showing a scene from somewhere on Manticore. In the center, amid an array of flags and other Manty governmental and military embellishments, was a podium.

And standing at the podium was Honor Harrington.

The Honor Harrington.

Charles felt his mouth drop open. Harrington was *dead*—he and everyone else in the civilized universe had watched her execution. Yet here she was, thin, drained, and missing an eye and arm, but with the fire and spirit in her voice and face that had made her a legend among even some of the Sollies.

He grimaced as the obvious explanation belatedly came to him. Yes, he'd seen her execution. But it had been an HD, which had furthermore been provided courtesy of Saint-Just and his State Security thugs.

Apparently, reports of her death had been greatly exaggerated.

Surreptitiously, he looked at Armond and Miklos. Both men's expressions showed the same surprise and disbelief that Charles himself had been feeling a moment ago. But they, too, were rapidly sidling up on the truth.

And growing rapidly beneath their bewilderment was the hard edge of anger.

Because they too had undoubtedly watched the hated Harrington's execution over a year ago. They'd probably had a few drinks to celebrate the event afterwards, and savored that moment during the bitterness of defeat and pullback and more defeat. Now, however the Manties had pulled it off, that small victory had been snatched away from them.

Even Peeps, Charles mused, must eventually get tired of being lied to by their leaders.

Armond took a deep breath, coming back from somewhere in an unpleasant distance. He thumbed the remote, and Harrington's image and speech vanished in midword. "Well," he said. "Isn't *that* interesting?"

"Events out here never fail to amaze me," Charles murmured. "At any rate—"

"Yes," Armond cut him off. "My apologies, Mr. Dozewah, but I think we're going to have to end things for today. Can we pick it up again tomorrow morning? Say, around ten o'clock?"

"Certainly," Charles said, taking a last sip of his brandy and standing up. "Feel free to look over the documentation. I'd ask that you don't take the papers out of this building, though."

"Of course," Armond said, reaching across the table for a quick handshake. "We'll see you tomorrow."

"I'll look forward to it." Charles started to step away from the table. Then, pretending he'd almost forgotten, he reached over and picked up the Redactor. "I have to take this with me, of course."

"Of course," Armond said, his mind clearly elsewhere. "Have a pleasant evening."

A minute later Charles was walking down the sidewalk toward his hotel two blocks away, trying to figure out what Harrington's unanticipated return was going to do to the Manty/Peep war and, more importantly, to Charles's own sales pitch.

The most immediate effect would be to put Pierre and Saint-Just into the grandmother of all snits, which was probably why Armond had cut the meeting short. The government would be sending out messages to all their top weapons designers, demanding results *now,* and Armond was probably trying to figure out what he was going to say when the empty-faced State Security emissaries came calling.

The real question was whether Armond's CYA speech would include a mention of Charles and his magic Redactor.

Maybe he should just cut his losses and get out. He could get a berth on the next liner heading for League space—hell, for *anyone's* space—and leave this dirty, grimy, depressing world and its evil people behind him—

"Charles Dozewah?"

Charles jerked. The two men had come up behind him, silently and smoothly and professionally. "Yes," he confirmed cautiously.

One of the men held out a gold-embossed identity card. "State Security," he said. "Come with us."

Charles looked at the other man. There was something in his stance that said he was hoping for an excuse to get violent. "I'm a citizen of the Solarian League," Charles protested.

"Yes, we know," the first man said. "Come with us."

❋　　❋　　❋

They took the Redactor, of course, along with his clothing and jewelry. A full search followed, clearly designed to be as intrusive and humiliating as possible. After that, they gave him a jumpsuit and soft shoes and put him in a private cell about the size of four coffins.

And for six days they just left him there.

It was an old technique, of course. The captive was given time to brood and worry about all the possible things his captors might be preparing to do to him.

Still, there were other, equally ancient techniques that were even worse. These they did not use. They fed him regularly, though the gruel was thin and tasteless. The cell's sanitary facility at least afforded a modicum of dignity, though accessing it was somewhat challenging in a room where the ceiling was too short for him to stand upright.

More interestingly, they allowed him a full period of sleep each night, uninterrupted by lights, noises, or rough hands. If

Charles didn't know better, he would think he was being treated like a VIP prisoner.

He *did* know better, of course. Whatever forbearance the Peeps might be showing right now on account of his Solly citizenship would take a sharp turn downward the minute they figured out exactly who he was.

Even that level of courtesy would vanish completely once they figured out what he knew.

Because Charles knew things. Things that no non-Peep should ever know. Including some things that no one outside of Saint-Just's own top people should know. If his interrogators found out he knew those things, he would learn just how barbaric the People's Republic of Haven could be. He had to make sure no one discovered the extent of his hidden knowledge.

Or else he needed to find a way to use that knowledge to his own advantage.

It was just after breakfast on the seventh day when his cell was unlocked for the first time and a pair of large dour men hauled him out of his cracker-box kennel and took him down a plain gray corridor to an interrogation room.

The interrogator was already seated on the far side of a heavy-looking table, his dark gray suit a match for the gray of the walls, ceiling, and floor. "Charles Dozewah?" he asked briskly, his eyes on the papers in front of him as the guards cuffed Charles to an equally heavy wooden chair across from him.

"Yes," Charles said. The interrogator was much older than he'd expected, somewhere in his mid-fifties. Possibly even older than that, depending on which generation prolong he was. That by itself was ominous, since in Charles's experience younger trainees were usually given first crack at new prisoners in order to hone their skills.

"Or is that Charles Navarre?" the interrogator corrected himself, finally looking up and peering unblinkingly into Charles's face.

Charles suppressed a grimace. So they'd figured it out. He'd hoped they wouldn't, but down deep he'd known it was inevitable. "Who?" he asked anyway, just in case.

"Charles Navarre," the interrogator said. "The man responsible for the destruction of the People's Naval Ships *Vanguard* and *Forerunner*. Not to mention the theft of a sizeable sum of the People's money."

"Ah—*that* Charles Navarre," Charles said. "Though technically speaking, the *Forerunner* was an Andermani ship."

The interrogator's expression didn't even crack. "Thank you," he said as he started to gather his papers together. "That's all we wanted to know."

"Actually, it isn't," Charles said, forcing his voice to remain calm even as his heartbeat suddenly picked up. Was that all they wanted to know before they turned him over to the torturers? "I'd like you to get a message to Citizen Secretary Saint-Just for me. Tell him that I know about Ellipsis, and that in three days everyone else will, too."

A slight flicker of something might have touched the interrogator's eyes as he finished collecting his papers and stood up. He gave Charles one final probing look, then circled the desk and left the room. Charles's two guards stepped to his sides and started uncuffing him from the chair.

They took their time, with the result that the interrogator was nowhere to be seen by the time Charles and the guards returned to the corridor. Mentally, he crossed his fingers; but instead of heading back toward his cell, they led him off in a different direction entirely.

So the gamble had failed. They were indeed taking him to a torture room. Not for the gathering of information—the interrogator should have asked at least a few questions if information was what they wanted—but for the simple animalistic pleasure of revenge for the little con he'll pulled all those years ago.

Considering how much that scam had cost the People's Republic, they were likely to make his death as slow and lingering as possible.

He had been stripped naked and strapped to a table when the interrogator arrived and held a brief and inaudible conversation with the black-gloved man who seemed to be in charge of Haven's version of the Inquisition. A minute later, a clearly unhappy torturer bit out an order, and Charles was unstrapped and hauled off the table. The interrogator led him down the hall to the guardroom and pointed him to one of the showers.

The cubicle contained badly missed soap and an even more badly missed razor. Charles made full use of both, and when he emerged a few minutes later, he felt like a new man. The interrogator was waiting with a set of Peep clothing; silently, he handed it to his prisoner. Charles dressed, and then waited as the interrogator added a set of wrist and ankle chains to the ensemble.

He was double-checking the locks on the wrists when his eyes suddenly met Charles's. "If you're lying," he said, his voice dark and deadly, "not even God will have mercy on you."

This time it was Charles's turn not to speak. The interrogator held his gaze another few seconds, then jerked his head toward the door.

Five minutes later, they were in a sealed van, driving down the streets of the capital.

✻　　✻　　✻

Citizen Secretary Oscar Saint-Just was looking a little pale today, Charles thought as a set of palace guards marched him across the expanse of the State Security dictator's office. Or maybe this was his normal skin tone, and the publicity photos and HDs of him were routinely touched up. Certainly a man who could create an entire fraudulent HD of a Manty naval officer being hanged wouldn't balk at having a little cosmetic work done on his own image.

Just as the interrogator had on their first meeting, Saint-Just pretended he didn't see Charles as the prisoner was marched to his massive desk and secured to a chair in front of it. Unlike the chair in the prison, this chair was at least comfortably padded.

The guards strode out, and Saint-Just continued to work in silence. Charles sat motionlessly, cultivating his patience, knowing the other would make the first move when he deemed the time was right.

Two minutes later, it finally was.

"So," Saint-Just said, setting his papers aside and eyeing his visitor. The interrogator had been quite good with the cold, deadly stare, but Saint-Just had the man's efforts beat hands down. "You're here to plead for your life."

Clear and direct, with no word or mind games. Rather as Charles had expected. "Actually, Citizen Secretary, I'm here to offer a deal that will benefit us both."

"Really," Saint-Just said. "And why should I believe anything you say? Because of this?" He reached into a drawer and pulled out the Redactor Charles had been dangling so enticingly in front of Armond and Miklos.

"Neat little gadget, isn't it?" Charles asked, slipping automatically into sales-pitch mode. "It feeds whatever image you want into a ship's sensor line—"

"It's useless," Saint-Just cut him off, tossing the Redactor contemptuously toward an unoccupied section of his desk. "A typical warship has hundreds or thousands of sensor lines. Your shipyard agent would have to have a dozen accomplices working overtime to deal with all of them."

"It does exactly what I claimed," Charles pointed out. "I never vouched for its practicality."

"As you also never vouched for the practicality of the Crippler?" Saint-Just countered.

Charles winced. The Crippler had been at the heart of his last scheme against the People's Republic, a beautiful little gadget that could collapse a ship's wedge from a million kilometers away. And like the Redactor, it had worked exactly as advertised... up to its inherent limits. "The Crippler worked perfectly against the proper targets," he reminded Saint-Just evenly. "And the Redactor would work equally well against, say, a freighter with its considerably fewer number of sensor systems."

"That might be useful if the People's Republic was engaged in large-scale piracy," Saint-Just said acidly. "We're not. We're in the middle of a war. How do you know about Ellipsis?"

The old, traditional out-of-the-blue change of subject. Even men as subtle as Saint-Just occasionally fell back on the obvious ones. "I have information sources everywhere," Charles said. "Most of them nameless, unfortunately, so I can't tell you where this particular tidbit came from."

Saint-Just's lip twitched. "The Navy, no doubt."

"Could be," Charles agreed. "I imagine they weren't pleased when you took everything away from them."

"No, they weren't." Saint-Just cocked his head. "And how exactly is it that you think the universe will know about it in three days?"

"Messages have already been sent out," Charles said, as coolly and calmly as if it were actually true. "If I should disappear for more than ten days—and trust me, there are people, even on Haven, who are always kept informed about my movements and whereabouts—those messages will lead their recipients to everything I know about the ship."

Saint-Just's expression twitched, just noticeably, on the word *ship.* "And you don't think we can beat those names out of you before that time limit is up?"

Charles shrugged, forcing down a shiver. "It's possible," he conceded. "But if you try and fail, you'll be throwing away the best resource to come across your path for many a day."

"The *Ellipsis*?"

Charles gestured toward his chest. "Me."

For a long moment Saint-Just sat motionless, eyeing Charles like a tiger sizing up a prospective bit of lunch. Then, his gaze softened, just a bit, and he settled back into his chair. "Tell me everything."

Charles took a careful breath. Right here, right now, was his only chance to prove to Saint-Just that he was worth more alive than stretched out on a torture rack.

And the first part of that proof, as Saint-Just had demanded, was indeed to tell him everything. "The *Ellipsis* is a Manty heavy cruiser, *Star Knight*-class, which you got hold of early in the war," he said. "My source was a little vague on where it came from, but I've always assumed it was attacked by pirates while escorting some VIP."

"Actually, it was escorting a freighter taking missile technology to Alizon," Saint-Just said. "And its attackers weren't *exactly* pirates."

"Ah," Charles murmured. There were long-standing rumors that the Peeps had hired a number of pirate gangs as privateers. "At any rate, it squared off to fight, and the last thing the freighter saw as it made its getaway was the cruiser being pounded to rubble. It was assumed destroyed, the rest of the Manties went on with their lives, and the People's Navy towed what was left of the cruiser back to a hidden dock somewhere and started taking the thing apart."

"Yes," Saint-Just said, his eyes hardening with the memory. "For all the good it did them."

"Indeed," Charles said, nodding. "The Manty captain may not have gotten around to giving the destruct order before the command deck was hit, but he would certainly have put out the slag order to destroy anything of real tech value aboard."

Saint-Just's lip quirked in another smile. "Your source is very well informed."

Charles shrugged microscopically. "Some of it's just simple logic," he said. "The fact that the PRN isn't using any of the Manty tech, even the less advanced secret stuff from that early in the war, means nothing was found."

"Oh, a great deal was found," Saint-Just corrected, his face darkening. "There were personal service manuals in various lockers and a few hard copies of routine diagnostics that were still intact. There were also quite a few slagged blocks that used to be secret Manty technology. The Navy's R and D people promised they would be able to get something out of them."

"Which will happen any day now, of course," Charles said, nodding. "Yes, I know the routine. The military never quite gives up, yet never quite delivers on their promises. Meanwhile, as they've poked around uselessly, you've formulated a far better plan for the ship, one that would bring dramatic results in weeks rather than years."

Saint-Just's eyes came back from his contemplation of the People's Navy and their stubborn uselessness. "You're indeed well informed, Mr. Navarre," he said, very quietly. "Would you care to tell me what exactly these plans consist of?"

"On that, I can only speculate," Charles said, again suppressing a shiver. If Saint-Just ever even suspected there was a leak in his own upper echelon, he would have Charles taken apart, molecule by molecule if necessary, until he had a name. "Since I assume you've got the Navy restoring the ship for you—grudgingly, no doubt, since they'd rather use the refitting facilities for their own damaged ships—I further assume it's for some kind of covert op that you're hoping will embarrass the Manties. Raiding League freighters, possibly, in the hope of turning more Solly sympathy—and weapons—toward the People's Republic."

"Really," Saint-Just said, again favoring Charles with that tiger smile. "You think I would fight this hard—that I would throw every bit of my own prestige against Naval small-mindedness—just so I could blame Manticore for some shipping harassment? You insult me, Mr. Navarre."

"My apologies, Citizen Secretary," Charles said hastily. "As I said, I'm just thinking aloud. The other possibility is that you plan some kind of infiltration into enemy space, either into the Manticore system itself or that of one of their allies." Had there been a twitch of Saint-Just's lip when the Manticore system was mentioned? "The former would certainly be the more audacious," he continued.

"Only with great risk comes great reward," Saint-Just said. "Now tell me which specific target I have in mind."

Charles braced himself. His life literally hung on his next

words. "To be honest," he said, "I don't believe there *are* any genuinely viable targets."

Saint-Just's eyes remained steady on him. "Explain."

"Let's look at the possibilities," Charles said, forcing himself not to rush. He had to get the whole analysis out before Saint-Just summarily ordered his head taken off. But at the same time, he had to remain calm and professional about it. "The two obvious choices are the Manties' big space stations: *Hephaestus* at Manticore, and *Vulcan* at Sphinx. Taking out either of those would effectively cripple the Manties' spaceborne industry, which would have huge ramifications for both their civilian and military arenas."

"Yet you just said they weren't worthwhile targets."

"Oh, they're worthwhile enough," Charles said. "They're just not viable. No matter what kind of false transponder and ID codes you're able to put aboard the *Ellipsis,* the chance that the Manties will let the ship get within range are slim to none. Even if you can get it close enough to launch missiles, the fixed defenses around either station would almost certainly take them out before they could do any damage."

"Sphinx's orbital radius is slightly over twenty-one light-minutes from the primary, with a system hyper limit of only twenty-two light-minutes," Saint-Just said, watching Charles closely. "That means the *Ellipsis* could come out less than a light-minute from Sphinx and *Vulcan.* That would put it well within missile range."

"I believe that the actual number is even better, only twenty-seven light-seconds," Charles said. "But what most people don't know—though I'm sure you do—is that any ship that comes out of hyper less than three light-minutes from Sphinx is automatically attacked. If the *Ellipsis* tried coming in that close to the station, it wouldn't even get a chance to use whatever ID you'd set it up with."

"So my admirals have informed me," Saint-Just said. His face was still unreadable, but Charles thought he could detect a slight softening of the Peep's expression. Maybe he'd already heard these numbers and arguments from his own people, which would only help Charles's own credibility. "But I never expected it to be anything but a suicide mission."

"I understand," Charles said. "But even a suicide mission has to have *some* reasonable chance of success. Coming out three light-minutes from *Vulcan* would put *Ellipsis* just barely into missile range, but there isn't a reasonable chance that it could hit the station from that distance before the Manties' defenses came into play."

"Then we simply ram the station," Saint-Just said. "Accelerate as much as possible, for as long as possible, and as the Manties start shooting back, rotate to present its wedge to the defenders."

"At which point it would become a ballistic projectile, not accelerating and with a completely predictable trajectory," Charles said. "It would be child's play for the Manties to program a missile to come in sideways and either down *Ellipsis's* throat or up its kilt."

"And worse...?"

Charles frowned. "Excuse me?"

"You've done an excellent job of mimicking my military advisors," Saint-Just said calmly. "Now tell me: what is the even more disastrous risk I would be taking by sending the *Ellipsis* to ram *Vulcan*?"

Charles felt a surge of panic, ruthlessly forced it down. This was obviously some sort of test, with Saint-Just trying to see just how bright or how informed he was.

Only Charles didn't have a clue as to where the Citizen Secretary was nudging him. What could be worse than a failed mission and wasted lives?

"You disappoint me," Saint-Just said into the lengthening silence. "And you a Solly, yet."

And finally, Charles got it. "You're talking about the Eridani Edict," he said, wincing with the thought. "If the *Ellipsis* should miss the station and hit Sphinx..."

"The entire Solarian League Navy would arrive on Haven's doorstep," Saint-Just said, his tone icy. "Never mind the fact that the offender would demonstrably have been a rogue Manty ship, and that the subsequent destruction would have been merely a terrible accident."

Charles stared at the impassive face across the desk. Was that, in fact, Saint-Just's actual plan? To pretend the *Ellipsis* was attacking *Vulcan*, hoping it would "accidentally" destroy Sphinx instead? "It wouldn't matter," he said between suddenly frozen lips. "The League wouldn't believe either. They'd come to Haven, all right, and they'd dismantle your military and government right down to bedrock."

"I suppose." Saint-Just shrugged. "Pity."

"Indeed," Charles said, struck by the grotesque irony of the word. Pity was an emotion Saint-Just himself probably hadn't felt in decades. "But that is unfortunately the reality we face."

Saint-Just smiled faintly. "So it's *we*, now, is it?"

Charles winced. "Forgive the impertinence, Citizen Secretary," he said, ducking his head humbly. "Part of a salesman's job is to identify with his client, all the better to find a mutually satisfactory solution to the client's needs."

"And what are my needs, Citizen?" Saint-Just asked. "Or perhaps we should simply skip to the mutually satisfactory solution you mentioned."

"What you need is to get the Manties off your back," Charles said, his heartbeat starting to pick up again. "An attack on their manufacturing infrastructure would be one way to do that, except that it's obviously something they expect and are therefore prepared for. But there's a better way, one that doesn't rely on Manty carelessness or gullibility."

He cocked his head. "We precipitate a war between the Star Kingdom and the Andermani Empire."

"Interesting," Saint-Just said, his eyes going a little flatter. "Also ironic, given that was exactly what we were trying to do when you came to the PRN with your magic Crippler weapon."

"Not precisely," Charles said, wishing the other would stop bringing that up. His role in that debacle had almost certainly earned him a death-by-torture sentence, which was why he'd waited all this time before venturing back into Peep space in the first place.

On the other hand, the existence of that death sentence was probably precisely why Saint-Just kept bringing it up. Bargaining, after all, was a game for two. "What you were trying back then was to irritate the Manties by using a captured Andermani ship to harass their shipping," he continued. "What I'm proposing would leave the Manties completely out of the loop by persuading the Andermani to declare war on *them*."

"Really," Saint-Just said. His voice was still flat, but Charles could see the first glimmerings of real interest behind those hardened eyes. "The Emperor seems very much disposed toward Manticore."

"I think I can change his mind," Charles said. "Are you interested?"

Saint-Just studied him a moment. Then, giving Charles a slight smile, he settled back into his chair. "Tell me more," he invited.

Charles had gone over the plan twice, and was trying to figure out a third way to come at it, when Saint-Just abruptly lifted his hand. "Enough," he said briskly. "Colonel?"

Charles frowned; but before he could say anything he felt the tingle of a hypospray in the back of his neck. He twisted his head around, his vision suddenly going blurry.

He got just a glimpse of the stern-faced interrogator before the darkness took him.

✻ ✻ ✻

He came to in a hospital bed. The interrogator was sitting at his side, contemplating him as someone might gaze at a particularly repulsive insect just before bringing a large rock down on top of it.

Only instead of the gray civilian suit he'd been wearing in the interrogation cell, he was now resplendent in a full State Security colonel's uniform. Above the pocket a small name plate read *Mercier.*

"Congratulations on your promotion," Charles managed through a desert-dry throat.

"Let me make two things clear," Mercier said, ignoring Charles's attempt at pleasantries. "You're alive for one reason and one reason only: Citizen Secretary Saint-Just thinks you can be of use to us. The assessment as to whether or not you're living up to that potential is mine alone." His eyes flashed. "And just for the record, I was a friend of Captain Vaccares. You *do* remember Captain Vaccares, I trust?"

Charles's dry throat went a little drier. Vaccares had been the captain of one of the ill-fated Peep ships from the whole Crippler scam. "I remember him very well," he said. "For what it's worth, I never intended for any of the men and women involved to die."

"You would certainly recognize the paving material of the road you're traveling," Mercier said acidly. He waved a hand around him. "Would you like to take a guess as to why you're here?"

Charles looked at the IV stands and gleaming medical monitors. "I'm sure you're dying to tell me."

"Interesting choice of words," the other said. "You've just been implanted with a slow poison drip. Very nasty stuff. So nasty that if you don't get a milliliter of a special antidote every twelve hours, you'll die." He reached into his tunic pocket and pulled out a flat metal flask. "This antidote, to be specific."

"Which you'll no doubt be in charge of doling out?"

"Exactly," Mercier said. "If you try to tug on your leash—in fact, if I even *suspect* you're tugging on your leash—I'll dump the whole batch down the sink and sit back to watch you die."

"Understood," Charles said. Strangely enough, his throat was feeling less dry than it had a minute ago, despite Mercier's threat. "But you won't have to worry about that. I have a hundred million reasons to make sure this goes exactly as planned."

Mercier's lip twist twisted. "Yes; the hundred million Solarian credits you cajoled out of Citizen Secretary Saint-Just."

"You disapprove?"

"Citizen Secretary Saint-Just's agreements are his own affair," Mercier said stiffly. "Me, I would have thought letting you leave with your life would be more than enough payment. Especially after all you've already cost the People's Republic."

"This will more than make up for it," Charles promised. "Trust me."

Mercier smiled coldly. "Of course. One last thing."

He stepped to the side of the bed, his smile vanishing, his eyes dark and cruel as he gazed down into Charles's face. "This is the last time you'll see me in this uniform," he said. "From now on, I'll be traveling in civilian clothing, and you'll refer to me as Citizen Mercier. *But.*" He tapped his colonel's insignia. "These will always be here, even if you can't see them. Aboard the *Ellipsis* I will have full authority, over you and over the mission."

"Understood," Charles said calmly. "Incidentally, we'll need to stop by a storage locker on the south side of town before we head out to wherever you have the *Ellipsis* stashed. There's some specialized equipment I'll need to pick up if we're going to make this work."

For a moment Mercier just gazed down at him. "Not a problem," he said at last, stepping back with obvious reluctance. "Your clothes are in the cabinet over there. Get dressed."

❉　　　❉　　　❉

Charles had never been inside a Mantie *Star Knight*-class heavy cruiser before. Nor had he ever gotten up close beside one. But he'd seen plenty of pictures and HDs, both interior and exterior shots.

So, apparently, had Saint-Just's people. The *Ellipsis,* as near as Charles could tell, was perfect.

"I'm impressed," he commented to Mercier as the ship's commander led the way onto the command deck. "My congratulations,

Citizen Captain Tyler. If I didn't know better, I would swear I was on a Manty ship."

"You've been on many Manty ships, have you?" Tyler asked, looking suspiciously at Charles from beneath painfully thin eyebrows.

"None at all, actually," Charles assured him, making a mental note not to make any more comments like that. Captain Tyler was a True Believer, a zealot of the most fanatical kind.

But then, every crew member he'd met so far aboard the *Ellipsis* had had that same hard gleam in his or her eye.

In retrospect, it was hardly surprising. Saint-Just would hardly have chosen anyone but True Believers for what was essentially a suicide mission.

"Citizen Navarre's past activities are none of your concern," Mercier spoke up, his own tone managing to echo Tyler's own fervor while at the same time warning the captain to drop the subject. "You've prepared our quarters as specified?"

"You've been given adjoining officers' berths near the command deck," Tyler said. He gave Charles one last lingering look, a look that said he would obey orders, but that he was senior enough to obey them in his own way and on his own schedule.

So much of Peep communication these days, Charles mused, seemed to be on the nonverbal level. Harder for someone to prove insubordination or treason that way, he suspected.

"Good," Mercier said. "Once we've confirmed that all our equipment has been properly brought aboard and stowed, you'll take us out of dock and head immediately for the Karavani system."

"Everything you brought aboard the pinnace has been stowed," Tyler said, his tone implying that if his guests ended up missing something they would have no one to blame for the oversight except themselves. "Will there be anything else?" he added, gesturing to a yeoman.

"As soon as we're underway I'll need to begin my work," Charles said. "I'll need full access to the equipment crawlspaces—One-D and Four-A to start with. I'll also need—"

"You'll *what*?" Tyler demanded.

"—full downloads of all recent news transmissions coming from the Star Kingdom," Charles continued, ignoring the interruption. "Your uniforms and interior décor look fine, but we'll want to confirm every detail is up to current Manty—"

"Absolutely *not*," Tyler snapped. "You're going to stay as far away from my equipment as I can keep you. What kind of fool—?"

"Captain." Mercier's voice was quiet, but it cut off Tyler's budding tirade as quickly as if the colonel had slapped a skinsuit patch over his mouth. "What Citizen Navarre is requesting is vital to the success of this mission. You *will* permit it."

Tyler drew himself up to his full height. "This is *my* ship, Citizen Mercier," he said, his voice as quiet and deadly as Mercier's. "My authority aboard it is absolute. If I say the answer is no, then the answer is no."

Mercier cocked his head to the side. "In that case, Citizen Captain, I would have no choice but to bring the matter to the attention of Citizen Secretary Saint-Just."

Some of the blood drained out of Tyler's face. "Citizen Secretary Saint-Just?" he asked carefully.

"It was he who personally authorized this mission," Mercier said. His tone was flat, without a single hint of the gloating Charles might have heard from a lesser man. Like Tyler himself, Mercier was a True Believer, with no room in his soul for anything as petty as personal power issues. "I assumed you knew that."

Tyler's eyes flicked to Charles as if seeing this foreign civilian for the first time. "No, I...no," he finished lamely.

He was probably telling the truth, Charles knew. No one aboard the *Ellipsis* would have been told of Saint-Just's personal involvement with the plan, not even the captain's personal watchdog, People's Commissioner Ragli. No matter how suicidal the mission might be, there was always the chance that someone might survive long enough to be questioned, and Saint-Just would have made sure that no such avenue could ever lead back to him.

It was the way of all tyrannies, Charles knew from his reading of history. What always astonished him was not the secrecy and paranoia, but how the True Believers in those tyrannies never seemed bothered by those things.

Mercier let Tyler's discomfort hang in the air for another two seconds. Then, without another word, he turned and gestured to the yeoman still hovering just outside eavesdropping range. "We're ready now," he told her. "Show us to our quarters."

The yeoman looked at Tyler. The captain nodded confirmation, and she stepped forward. "Certainly, Citizen," she said, gesturing back at the door behind them. "This way, please."

✳   ✳   ✳

Later, in the privacy of his own quarters, Charles searched every square centimeter of his body—or at least every square centimeter he could see—for the spot where they'd implanted the poison drip. If he could find it, there was a chance he could get the damn thing out.

But there was nothing. No quick-healed incisions, no scars, no warm spots or subtle bulges where a micro capsule might have been slipped beneath the skin. For all the evidence of his eyes and fingertips, Mercier might have been blowing complete smoke.

But Charles knew better. Men like Mercier never bluffed about things like this. Not when they didn't have to.

Whatever they'd done to him, it was clear Charles wouldn't be reversing it any time soon.

✳   ✳   ✳

Lyang Weiss looked up from the note, his stomach churning, his fingers squeezing the paper hard with annoyance. This was *not* what he needed today. "Thank you," he told the messenger standing in front of his desk. "You may go."

The woman nodded, did a precise about-face, and left the room. Weiss waited until the door had closed behind her before letting free the curse that had been trying to get out ever since he'd spotted the signature on the note.

Even so, he kept the curse short and his voice low. An Andermani embassy had certain behavioral guidelines, after all, and even a lowly assistant military attaché was expected to conform to those standards. Or perhaps *especially* a lowly assistant military attaché.

With a sigh, he turned his attention back to the note. *Important developments to occur within three weeks at Karavani,* the note read. *Vitally important you have an observer present.*

And that was it. Two sentences, plus a signature. About as annoyingly cryptic as a man could get.

What the *hell* was Charles playing at this time?

It wasn't like the man's information wasn't usually good. Indeed, some of the tidbits he'd tossed Weiss's way—for sizeable sums of money, of course—had been extremely interesting, both to the embassy here on Haven as well as to Weiss's patron back in the Empire. Charles was a Solly, after all, and a source with contacts in the League's upper echelons was a good thing for a military attaché to have.

What made the whole relationship so stomach-roiling ambiguous was the fact that, at least on the official paper of those same Solly upper echelons, Charles didn't seem to exist.

So who was he? The choices seemed almost pathologically bipolar: either he was a nobody, a two-bit con man who liked to pretend he was someone and had access to just enough information and gadgetry to back up that pretense, or else he was such a high-level agent that the League itself had done a serious scrub job on his past.

The Peeps seemed to lean toward the former explanation, at least according to the handful of slightly vague references Weiss had been able to dig up. But then, the Peeps had been wrong before. Most recently, and most spectacularly, with Honor Harrington.

Despite his annoyance with Charles, Weiss had to smile at that one. Though the Empire was officially neutral in regards to the Manticore/Haven war, it was hardly a secret that the Emperor's private sentiments were on the side of the Star Kingdom, at least for the moment. Lady Harrington—Duchess Harrington now, he corrected himself—had come onto the Andermani political and military radar very early in her career, and her star had been rising ever since. Weiss's own patron had met the woman once, and Weiss knew her execution on trumped-up charges had turned Andermani sentiment even more against Haven.

Only now, the truth of that "execution" had been blown across the galaxy, along with the Peeps' sordid little secret. Pierre and Saint-Just would be scrambling to cover their butts from the resulting firestorm, and Weiss knew just how dangerous both men were when backed into a corner.

Setting the note aside, Weiss keyed his computer. First step was to find out just what and where this Karavani was.

It was a Peep system, of course, but one so small and unimportant that its description barely filled three pages. It was a border system, completely uninhabited except for a small mining operation in the rings of the fifth planet and a courier transfer station in orbit around that same planet. It was about the last place in the known universe anyone would want to visit.

Unless, that is, the would-be vacationer was carrying a load of contraband Solly weapons and equipment. The third of the three pages on Karavani was an Andermani Intelligence report suggesting that the system was being used by Solly sympathizers to transship the officially banned technology being sent under the table to the People's Republic.

Was that what Charles was suggesting? That the Andermani should see if they could catch the Sollies and Peeps in a violation of League neutrality?

Weiss looked at the note again. No. Even if catching them red-handed would actually accomplish anything, that didn't feel like Charles's style. He was always more flamboyant than that, even while he tried to stay under everyone's radar.

But whatever was about to go down, Weiss would bet heavily it would be worth sending someone to watch.

Or maybe even going himself.

He keyed his com for the ambassador's office. "This is Weiss," he identified himself to the secretary. "I need to speak to Ambassador Rubell as soon as possible."

      ❅   ❅   ❅

The crawlspace was dark, narrow, and stifling, and for a ship that had been so recently renovated it was surprisingly dirty. But with ingenuity and a certain looseness of the joints that he'd been born with, Charles managed to get the Echo hardware in place. One down, he told himself as he worked his way through the oily dust. Twenty-seven to go.

Mercier had been waiting alone when Charles first wriggled his way in through the access panel. But he wasn't alone now. "Citizen Captain," Charles puffed as he pulled himself back out into the fresh air of the corridor. "What brings you here?"

"I wanted to check on your progress," Tyler said, looking Charles up and down with obvious distaste. No crewman of *his*, Charles guessed, would ever get so filthy carrying out his duty. "I also wanted an actual explanation as to what you were doing down here."

"Understandable," Charles said. "Unfortunately, as I told you earlier, this technology is extremely secret and, frankly, isn't supposed to be out here at all. I'm afraid that's all I can tell anyone."

Tyler folded his arms across his chest. "Make an exception," he ordered.

Charles shook his head. "I'm afraid—"

"Make an exception," Tyler repeated, his voice the temperature of liquid hydrogen.

Charles looked at Mercier. But for once, both men were clearly in agreement.

And it wasn't like the theory of this wasn't well-known anyway. "Fine," Charles said with a sigh. "What active sensors do is shoot out focused beams of microwave or visible-spectrum radiation, which then bounce off a target and return to the sender, frequency-shifted with the relative velocities between—"

"We know all that," Mercier interrupted.

Charles nodded. "Right. Well, what the Echo system does is tie in your passive sensors with your own active sensors and communications array so that when a wave packet strikes the hull and starts back, your own active sensors send out a perfectly matched packet that's shifted a hundred eighty degrees out of phase."

Tyler grunted. "Won't work," he said. "Your phase-inverted packet can't catch up with the reflected pulse, which means that the leading edge of the reflection will still make it back intact."

"You would be right," Charles agreed, "*if* the sensors were embedded directly into the hull. But if you'll check your specs, you'll see that your sensor arrays extend anywhere from three to ten meters out from the main hull. That gives the Echo enough lead time—about three nanoseconds per meter—to analyze the packet and create and kick out the phase-shifted duplicate."

"It can do all that so quickly?" Tyler asked, looking down at the bag on the deck with a hint of respect.

"It can," Charles assured him. "It's not as perfect as using a sensor-absorbing hull coating, of course. But this is simpler and much easier to retrofit a ship with. And under normal conditions it will render you adequately invisible to most active sensors."

"Provided our wedge is down, I presume," Mercier said. He was eyeing the bag, too, a thoughtful gleam in his eye.

"Of course," Charles agreed. "There's no way for any add-on like this to conceal the level of gravitic energy that a warship's wedge normally puts out. But as long as you keep the wedge at minimal power while we're moving across the Karavani system, your conventional stealth systems should be good enough to keep that from being any sort of problem. The transfer station's sensors certainly won't be good enough to pick us up at that distance, and we should be in place well before our Andermani friends arrive."

He cocked an eyebrow. "Oh, and by the way, the Echo equipment itself is completely shielded and fail-safed. If anyone aboard should let his curiosity get the better of him and try to see what's inside, it'll instantly slag itself into an inert lump of silicon and metal."

Tyler smiled thinly. "I'm sure there are ways around that," he said. "But for now, I have my orders."

"Assuming the Echo works as well as you claim, will it be for sale after this is over?" Mercier asked.

"Perhaps," Charles said cautiously. If the League ever caught him peddling this kind of stealth technology outside Solly territory... "But let's deal with one thing at a time, shall we?"

"As you wish," Tyler said. "You said you were also tying in the communications system?"

Charles nodded, impressed in spite of himself. He hadn't expected either man to notice that off-handed comment as it went by. "Obviously, an add-on like this has its limitations, and it can be overwhelmed if enough ships are firing their active sensors at you at the same time. I'm not expecting that to happen on this particular mission, but adding the com system and its transmitters into the mix gives us more to work with, and therefore a higher margin of error. There's no point in taking any chances we don't have to."

"Reasonable enough," Tyler said, a bit doubtfully. "And you have twenty-seven more of these things to install?"

"Correct," Charles said. "And since it will take progressively more time to attach each one and calibrate it to the others already in place, I'd appreciate it if I could get back to work."

"Of course," Tyler said. "You're certain there's nothing my techs can do to assist you?"

And perhaps happen to accidentally glance over his shoulder as he keyed in the activation codes for the black boxes' self-destruct mechanisms? "I'm afraid not," Charles said. "It would take more time to teach your techs how to do it than it would take me to do it myself."

"Ah," Tyler said, smiling thinly. He didn't buy Charles's excuse for a minute, of course. Not that Charles had expected him to. "In that case, I'd best let you get back to work. We're only four days out from Karavani, after all."

"On the vector I gave you?" Charles asked.

Tyler's eyes flashed. He might not mind an occasional lie, at least not when he knew he was being lied to. But having his professionalism questioned was another matter entirely. "Of course," he said. "You just get your magic stealthing in place, and let me handle the People's ship."

Charles thought about apologizing, decided he was tired of massaging Peep egos, and just nodded. Tyler eyed him for another moment, then turned and stalked away.

"You're sure you're going to be ready in time?" Mercier asked.

"If I can avoid long, repetitive conversations, yes," Charles said. "Anyway, the stealthing doesn't have to be totally on-line until the Andermani arrive."

"Yes," Mercier said. "I trust you've remembered that, poor sensors or not, the mining station *will* spot our hyper footprint."

"And will be perfectly happy to log our mining ship transponder," Charles said. "Once we've established who we are, we'll load that particular transponder aboard a pinnace, and float it into that collection of floating rock near where we'll be arriving. As long as we keep our wedge at low power after that, the station won't even notice us while we head for our jump-off point. And probably wouldn't care even if they did."

Mercier scowled. "Sloppy," he said, making the word a curse.

Charles shrugged. In actual fact, he doubted the station's casual attitude toward visitors was accidental. This wasn't the first time the Peeps had brought their illicit Solly shipments through Karavani, and Saint-Just and his friends would hardly want stalwart and conscientious officers like Colonel Mercier manning the local sensors. "In this case, sloppy is good," he said. "It'll make our job that much easier."

"I suppose." Mercier gestured to Charles's bag of goodies. "Where do we go next?"

Charles consulted his list. "Eight-C."

Mercier nodded. "Fine. The lift is back this way."

❋   ❋   ❋

"The extractor is the trickiest piece of equipment in the operation," Chief Engineer Fisher said as he led Weiss though the slightly grimy corridors of the Smith-Nobuko Mining Center orbiting Karavani 5. "It breaks down on a regular basis, and it's practically impossible to find new parts for. If the Clauswitz Conglomerate decides they're interested in partnering with us, renovating or replacing it would be the best thing they could bring to the table."

"Understood," Weiss said, feeling his patience straining dangerously close to the breaking point. The three weeks Charles had specified in his note were over, Weiss had been treading water here for over a week, and Chief Engineer Fisher was about to drive him out of his mind.

It was a decent enough cover story, he supposed, especially given that Ambassador Rubell had had to come up with it essentially on the fly. Weiss was supposedly doing a favor to an Andermani space mining firm that was looking to expand its interests into the People's Republic. Clauswitz had settled on Smith-Nobuko, the ambassador had told the Citizen Commerce Secretary, and had deftly maneuvered the other into suggesting Karavani as a place for Weiss to begin his unofficial enquiries.

State Security would undoubtedly have had a fit about letting an Andermani diplomat wander the People's territory untethered this way, especially out to a suspect system like Karavani. But the whole thing had happened so quickly that StateSec had apparently been left out of the loop.

Which wasn't to say Ambassador Rubell wouldn't be delivered a strong protest, and Weiss subsequently delivered an equally strong official reprimand once he returned to Haven. Still, a rap on the knuckles would be worth it if Charles's tip paid off.

Only so far, it hadn't.

Weiss continued down the corridor, listening to Fisher's running commentary with half an ear as he tried to decide what to do. In the nine days he and the diplomatic courier boat *Hase* had been here not a single additional ship had come calling. The only other vessel in the system, in fact, aside from the station's own small collection of pinnaces and carriers, was a mining ship surveying a collection of floating rocks a quarter of the way across the system.

Meanwhile, Fisher and his people were wining and dining Weiss with the surface heartiness and hidden tension of people who desperately need an influx of capital if their business is going to survive.

Everyone knew the price war demanded from the militaries of the nations involved. Fewer people truly appreciated how deeply the devastation extended to every other level of society.

Weiss could almost wish he really *was* scouting for Clauswitz, that he could give these men and women some hope. But he wasn't; and even if he had been, he knew he couldn't in good conscience help the miners out of their economic pit. Anything that helped one segment of Peep society ultimately helped Pierre and Saint-Just, as well. Both officially, and on a personal level, that was something Weiss couldn't do.

So he would eat their food, and smile at their jokes, and make vague statements that sounded hopeful but really weren't.

And unless something interesting happened, in two more days he and his ship would be out of here.

They had passed the extractor, and Weiss had graciously turned down the offer to get close up and personal with the balky machinery, when his com signaled. "Excuse me," he said, and keyed it on. "Weiss."

"Sir, this is Captain Forman," the *Hase*'s commander said. "My apologies, sir, but I was checking over the ship's logs, and I noticed you haven't made an entry in two days. May I remind you that regulations state you're to log every day's activities in a timely fashion?"

Weiss felt his heartbeat pick up. That was the code signal he'd set up with Forman. Something was finally happening. "You're right, of course," he said. "I'll come back and fix it as soon as Citizen Fisher and I have finished our current inspection."

He signed off. "Is there trouble?" Fisher asked anxiously.

"Just some paperwork I've been neglecting," Weiss assured him. "I'm afraid my ambassador is something of a stickler for such things."

"In that case, you'd best get to it at once," Fisher said. "We can inspect the cryonic facility later."

"If you're sure it's all right," Weiss said.

"Absolutely," Fisher said, pathetically eager as always to accommodate his guest. "We can pick this up again when you're free."

Fifteen minutes later, Weiss was back aboard the *Hase*. "What do we have?" he asked Forman as he strode onto the bridge.

"About six hours ago a ship came out of hyper," the captain said, pointing to a spot on the system chart. "Its transponder identified it as the freighter *Figaro*, out of Haven. It signaled to the station that it was here to pick up an ore shipment."

Weiss eyed the position and vector numbers floating beside the freighter's image on the display. "Interesting that he came out way over there instead of closer to the facility," he commented. "Not pulling a lot of gees, either, is he?"

"No, he isn't," Forman agreed. "The captain did say he's having some trouble with his compensators, which could be why he's accelerating so slowly. That wouldn't explain his entry point, though."

"No," Weiss said. "Still, nothing that can't be explained by sloppiness or stupidity."

"Yes, sir." Forman touched another spot on the display. "But then, an hour ago, *this* ship came out of hyper: Solly transponder—the *Winter Vixen*—heading for Haven with humanitarian supplies. The captain signaled that he's having trouble with his nodes—nothing serious, but he preferred to be in an inhabited system while his crew worked on them."

"Again, not unreasonable," Weiss said.

"Not by itself, no." Forman smiled tightly and gestured to the navigator. "But being the suspicious type, I had Ibo run a few numbers." A fresh set of heading and acceleration figures appeared, this group beside the Solly's position. "And then, just out of curiosity, I had him do a position/time comparison." He gestured again, and a pair of intersecting lines appeared across the display.

Weiss stiffened. Five and a half hours from now, the two ships that had casually entered the system from different directions, and ostensibly on different errands, were going to come within a few thousand kilometers of each other.

And if both held their current accelerations, not only would they meet but they would meet at virtually identical velocities. "A nice, private little rendezvous," Weiss murmured.

"*And* taking place far enough from the station that no one here is likely to even notice if any cargo changes hands," Forman said. "Certainly not if they do it properly." He raised his eyebrows. "The question is, should we see if *we* can get a better view?"

Weiss chewed his lip. The fact that the *Winter Vixen* was a Solly ship strongly implied that any transshipments would indeed be of interdicted Solly tech. If he could catch them in the act, the Emperor could either expose the trafficking and stop it, or else keep it secret and use the knowledge as a lever against Haven at some future date.

But while an Andermani diplomatic courier boat might officially enjoy diplomatic immunity, such immunity wouldn't hold up very well against laser-head missiles, should either side of the transaction decide they didn't want to leave witnesses behind. "Do we have anything aboard we could send out in that direction?"

he asked Forman. "Maybe strap a sensor buoy to a remote or load it aboard a cutter and see how close we could get it before the rendezvous?"

"We might," Forman said doubtfully. "Not much difference between sending a remote and going out ourselves, though. They'd know where it came from, and if they didn't want witnesses they could still come here and make sure we didn't live long enough to tell anyone."

Weiss looked over at the nav display. "What if we sent out a sensor and headed immediately for the hyper limit? Could we get out before they could reach us?"

"Certainly," Forman said. "The problem is that by the time the probe reached them we'd be so far away that it would be trivial for them to block any signal the probe tried to send to us."

Which would make the whole exercise pretty futile. "What if we wait until we get some data and then head out?"

Forman shook his head. "By then the Solly, at least, would probably have enough velocity advantage to catch us. Greg?"

"It would definitely be a long shot on their part," Ibo said, his hands skating over the nav board like a skilled surgeon. "Depending on exactly where we aimed we might make it to the hyper limit before they overtook us." He pointed to one of his displays. "But he'd be within missile range for the last twelve and a half minutes before we could get out. The Peep might be, too, assuming he's faking his low acceleration."

"A simple 'no' would have sufficed," Weiss said, scowling at the two incoming ships. So that was that. He and the entire Andermani Empire could suspect all they wanted, but it looked like that was all they were going to get this time around. "Fine," he said, turning away. If Charles thought he was going to get paid for *this* one, he was out of his mind.

"Wedge!" Ibo snapped.

Weiss spun back around. "Where?"

"There," Forman said, pointing at a spot off to the side of the two incoming freighters. "About three light-minutes from the incoming Solly; eleven and a half from us. Just outside the hyper limit."

Weiss felt his forehead crease as he eyed the new marker, then looked over at the sensor display. "That doesn't look like a normal alpha transition," he said.

"No, it doesn't," Ibo agreed sounding as puzzled as Weiss felt.

"Definitely a spike of gravitic energy, though. Maybe he's having some trouble with his nodes." He bent over his instruments. "Let me see what I can coax out of the readings."

"Got a reaction," Forman said tightly. "The *Winter Vixen*'s ... looks like he's veering off."

Weiss chewed at his lip. The gravitic energy from the new-comer's wedge traveled instantaneously, but the radio signal from its beacon awasn't nearly so quick. Even if the *Hase* sent out an inquiry right now, it would be nearly half an hour before the newcomer's transponder gave them an ID on him. "Can we tell from the wedge what kind of ship it is?" he asked.

"It's definitely a warship," Forman said grimly. "The wedge strength alone shows that. A heavy cruiser, I'd say, or possibly a battlecruiser."

"But no way to know whose?"

"Not at this distance and with a courier boat's sensors," Forman said. "But from the Solly's response, I'm guessing it's *not* a Peep."

"Speaking of Peeps, there goes the freighter," Ibo said, pointing. "Veering off. And in roughly the same direction as the Solly, interestingly."

"Trying to rearrange their rendezvous before the bogie can reach them?" Weiss hazarded.

"If they are, it's a fool's hope," Forman said. "They'd both have to redo their entire acceleration profiles, which isn't exactly practical with a warship bearing down on you."

"And of course there's nowhere for them to go with the war-ship between them and the hyper limit," Weiss murmured.

The words were barely out of his mouth when the numbers floating beside the Solly's position abruptly changed as he angled even farther away from the warship and doubled his acceleration. "Uh-oh," Forman said grimly. "Looks like the Solly's gotten a positive ID. And he does *not* like it."

"Like that's going to help him any," Ibo muttered. "He's already inside the bogie's missile range."

"Unless the bogie's plan is to run him down and get whatever he's carrying for himself," Weiss said. "Or is that even possible at this point?"

"The bogie can certainly catch him," Forman said doubtfully. "Whether he can disable him without destroying the cargo is a different question."

"He's not even going to try," Ibo said, his voice grim as he hunched over his displays. "More wedges—fast ones. The bogie's launched a full missile salvo." He looked up at Weiss. "He's targeting the Solly, sir."

Weiss curled his hands into helpless fists. The League was officially neutral in this war, which among other things meant that its ships were to be left strictly alone. As a representative of another neutral power, it was Weiss's duty to do whatever he could to make sure that neutrality was respected.

But if the *Winter Vixen* was carrying interdicted cargo, it couldn't hide behind either Solly neutrality or Solly protection. Regardless, with the *Hase* sitting here at the station with cold nodes, there was nothing Weiss could do even if he wanted to. Even a challenge and warning-off would take over eleven minutes to get to the combatants.

"Make the best recording you can of the incident," he told Ibo. "At this point, that's all we can do."

The seconds ticked by in silence. Weiss watched in horror-edged fascination as the markers indicating the missiles steadily closed on the Solly freighter. The Peep, meanwhile, was gunning away for all he was worth on his own chosen vector. So far, at least, the bogie was ignoring him.

Or maybe he was just waiting until after he'd dealt with the *Winter Vixen*.

There was a chime from the com. Stepping to Ibo's side, Weiss touched the key. "Weiss," he said.

"It's Citizen Fisher," the chief engineer's taut voice boomed from the speaker. "I've just been informed there's an unidentified ship in the system that appears to be firing on a pair of incoming freighters."

"That's correct, Citizen Fisher," Weiss said. "Though for whatever comfort it might be, the bogie so far hasn't attacked your own ore freighter."

"Never mind our freighter," Fisher said, a terrified bewilderment in his voice. "Who *is* it?"

Weiss looked at Ibo. The navigator had a grim set to his jaw. "I don't know," Weiss told Fisher. "I'll look into that and get back to you."

"Yes, but—"

"I have to go now," Weiss said. "I'll get back to you."

He cut off the signal before Fisher could reply. "How are we doing?" he asked.

"Ninety seconds to impact," Ibo said. "And you were right— that was *not* a normal translation footprint." He looked up at Weiss, his expression dark. "Because I don't think it was a normal translation."

Weiss grimaced. There it was, out in the open. The thought all three of them were undoubtedly thinking, and undoubtedly trying to avoid. "Are you suggesting there's a wormhole terminus in this system?" he demanded.

He hadn't intended the words to come out nearly so harshly. But Ibo didn't flinch. "I know it seems unbelievable that something like that could exist in an inhabited system without anyone having spotted it," he said evenly. "But that was definitely not a normal translation footprint, and it definitely *was* consistent with a wormhole transit spike."

"Was *consistent* with a transit spike?" Weiss asked. "You can't tell for sure?"

Ibo shrugged helplessly. "Our sensor suite isn't exactly warship-class," he said. "But there *are* only two options. If it wasn't an alpha transition, a wormhole is the only other possibility."

"We'll try doing an analysis of the recording later," Forman said, his voice suddenly quiet. "There it goes."

And as Weiss looked at the main display, the missiles reached the *Winter Vixen*.

There was no flash, of course. As the bogie's transponder signal and emission pattern were still crawling toward them, so the light and gamma radiation from the freighter's burst fusion bottles would be another ten minutes in arriving.

For the moment, at least, all there was to see was the Solly's wedge disappear.

"One down," Forman murmured. "Shall we try for two?"

Weiss held his breath. But the attacker seemed uninterested in the Peep freighter still running frantically away from him. Angling course back toward the edge of the system, he instead kicked his acceleration up to four hundred gees and headed for the hyper limit. "It would appear he's gotten what he came for," he said.

"Apparently so." Forman cocked an eyebrow. "The question is, did *we*?" he asked.

Weiss gazed at the fleeing bandit. "Oh, yes," he said softly. Charles was going to be paid for this one, after all.

In fact, the man might just be in for a bonus.

✳   ✳   ✳

The *Ellipsis* was nearly to the hyper limit, and Charles was having a post-action discussion with Mercier in his quarters, when Captain Tyler strode furiously in.

"Look at this!" the captain snarled, jabbing the report practically in Charles's face. "Look at the damage the alpha nodes took from that damn fool fake transit energy burst you insisted on."

"What of it?" Charles asked, trying briefly to focus on the waving report. "I warned you that there might be some problems."

"You didn't say anything about this much damage," Tyler bit out. "That one burst probably cost them half their working life."

"Which is why we have a fully-equipped tender waiting at the rendezvous point," Charles reminded him.

Tyler snorted. "And did you bother to mention *that* part to Citizen Secretary Saint-Just?" he demanded "Do you have any idea how much this will cost to fix? Or how much it's going to cost us in acceleration and hyper speed until it is?"

"Yes, I do," Charles said coolly. "Do *you* have any idea how ridiculous a captain of State Security sounds crying over a little damage to his ship?"

It was, in retrospect, probably not the best thing he could have said. Tyler's eyes widened in anger or disbelief or both, and an instant later the report that had been waving beneath Charles's nose had been replaced by the muzzle of the captain's pulser, pressed against his throat.

"Captain!" Mercier snapped, taking a step forward.

"Keep out of this, Citizen," Tyler ordered, his voice as crazy as his eyes. "This man is a traitor and an enemy. Why not just kill him here and now?"

"Because if you do, this whole thing will have been for nothing," Mercier warned him. "Including the destruction of that tech shipment."

And *that*, Charles knew, was what was really gnawing at Tyler's gut. He'd given the orders as Charles had instructed, had sent the missiles flying in a calm, controlled voice. But it had been abundantly clear to everyone on the *Ellipsis*'s bridge that he was doing it under protest, and against a simmering lava bed of fury and frustration.

Not that Charles could blame him. The illicit traffic in Solly tech was the only thing that gave Haven even a chance of countering the Manties' superior equipment. To have blown up one of those shipments—worse yet, to have blown up one of the shipment providers—had probably left Tyler feeling like he'd just cut off one of his own hands.

He was hardly alone in that, either, though Charles wasn't about to tell him that. The freighter attack had also been Saint-Just's biggest sticking point when the scheme had first been pitched. Charles had had to talk long, hard, and fast to get him on board with it, and even then the Citizen Secretary hadn't been very happy about it.

And Saint-Just had just had to sign off on the orders. He hadn't had to be the one to carry them out.

Which didn't change the fact that the man who *had* carried out the orders was currently holding a gun to Charles's throat. "I understand your frustration, Citizen Captain," Charles said, his voice sounding odd with the pressure of the gun at his throat. At least, that was what he assumed was affecting his voice. "But this entire scheme depends on the Andermani believing there's a wormhole terminus in the Karavani system that the People's Republic hasn't discovered but that the Manties have. We—the *Ellipsis*—have to *be* those Manties, which means we have to do everything a Manty would do under similar circumstances. As to the damage to the Alpha nodes, I do regret that. But the Andermani were watching, and our appearance had to look as much like a wormhole arrival as possible."

"Fine," Tyler said bitterly, his finger still pressed on the pulser's trigger. "We've done all that. So tell me why we still need you alive."

"Because he has to be the one to follow up with the Andermani," Mercier said. "No one else can point them the right direction and spring the trap on them."

"And what exactly is this trap?" Tyler demanded.

"The details are in your sealed orders," Charles told him. "You'll be able to open them at the rendezvous, after you drop us at our courier boat and the tender gets to work on your nodes."

For another long moment the pulser muzzle remained pressed against Charles's throat. Then, slowly, the pressure eased. "Any surprises in those orders?" the captain growled.

"No," Charles assured him. "At least, nothing that should be a problem for you."

For another moment Tyler continued to grip his pulser, as if still trying to decide whether to use it. Then, reluctantly, he returned the weapon to its holster. "We'll reach the rendezvous in six hours." He looked at Mercier, then back at Charles. "Until then, both of you will stay out of my way."

"As you wish," Mercier said, inclining his head. "The People's Republic will look forward to your fulfillment of your orders."

"The People's Republic will not be disappointed," Tyler said shortly. "Good day, Citizens." Turning, he strode from the room.

Mercier looked at Charles. "You play with fire, Citizen," he warned. "He might easily have lost control and shot you."

"Should I have babied him instead?" Charles countered. "He's a StateSec officer. He knows the sort of duty he might be assigned to."

"As do we all," Mercier said. "*Your* duty right now is to not get yourself killed until your part in this is over."

At which point, the Peeps would step in and take care of that? Probably. "Thank you, Citizen Mercier," Charles said, managing a wan smile. "I'll keep that in mind."

"See that you do," Mercier said. "Go get a glass of water. It's time for your antidote."

✦   ✦   ✦

Weiss had been back at his post in the embassy for nearly a week before Charles finally responded to his calls. "Sorry for the delay," the Solly apologized on Weiss's secure line. "I've been busy with something across town and couldn't get free long enough to return your calls."

"That's all right," Weiss said. "We need to meet."

"We will," Charles promised. "But not right now. I've just taken a new house in the Grandee District, and it needs some renovation before it'll be ready to receive visitors."

Weiss frowned. With the momentous events that had just happened at Karavani, Charles was squandering his time with *real estate*? "You're not serious."

"Of course I am," Charles assured him. "It's an investment, not only in my future but in my present. Nothing says enthusiastic supporter of the People's cause like a foreigner buying a piece of the People's land."

He had a point, Weiss had to admit. Buying property on Haven automatically put the buyer under extra governmental scrutiny, and no one would do that if they weren't as pure as a

New Berlin snowfall. Assuming Charles passed all the hurdles, he would come out of the experience considerably lower on the Peeps' list of suspicious characters.

"The downside is that StateSec will be watching the new place for awhile until they're convinced I'm not up to anything," Charles continued. "Two weeks, three at the most, and it'll be safe for you to drop by."

Weiss hissed a quiet German curse. This was incredibly bad timing on Charles's part, in his opinion. But with the process already underway, the only thing they could do was see it through and wait for StateSec to get bored and move on.

Besides, there were other things Weiss could do in the meantime to keep this particular ball rolling. "Understood," he said. "Let me know when it's safe to meet."

"I will," Charles promised. "*Auf wiedersehen.*"

It was actually closer to four weeks before Weiss finally got the message he'd been expecting. It was short and unsigned and waiting in his inbox when he arrived at his desk: *1522 Rue de Leon, today, 10:20 am.* Charles, it appeared, was finally ready.

So was Weiss.

The address turned out to be a modest home in a neighborhood that had once been on the upper edge of Havenite elite but which had since fallen on somewhat harder times. Resisting the urge to look furtively around him, Weiss walked up to the front door and rang the bell.

Charles had the door open almost before the chime's echo had faded away. "Come in," he murmured, doing a quick visual sweep over Weiss's shoulder as the Andermani slipped in past him. He closed the door behind his visitor and then led the way down a hallway into a small study reeking of fresh paint. "Sorry about the smell," he apologized as he gestured Weiss to one of a pair of chairs in the center of the room. "A wise old ex-spy once told me that redoing a room with a metal-based paint would play havoc with any bugs in the vicinity."

"I hope you used two coats," Weiss said as he sat down in one of the chairs.

"Three, actually," Charles said as he took the other. "Plus all the rest of the bug-sweeping routine, of course."

He took a deep breath. "Well. The fact that you're here implies you took my advice and sent an observer to the Karavani system."

"I did you one better: I went myself," Weiss said. "So tell me. Did I really see what I thought I saw?"

Charles's gaze locked on Weiss's face like a weapons targeting system. "I don't know," he said, his voice cautious. "What do you think you saw?"

Weiss braced himself. "I believe I saw a Manty ship come through a heretofore unknown wormhole terminus."

Some of the rigidity vanished from Charles's face and body. "I was right," he murmured. "It really *is* there."

"You weren't sure?"

Charles waved a hand. "I'd heard rumors," he said. "I spent— oh, hell; *years*—putting pieces together, analyzing thousands of reports, following the movements and activities of hundreds of Manty ships. It was only in the past three months that I began to suspect what was really going on."

"What *is* going on?" Weiss asked. "I mean, here's the problem. According to our Intelligence people, the Peeps have been bringing Solly tech into the Karavani system for at least the past few months. Why haven't the Manties hit them before now? Or are you suggesting the Manties have hit other shipments and the Peeps somehow didn't notice?"

"Even StateSec isn't *that* stupid," Charles said dryly. "No, from everything I've been able to pull together, the Manties have known all about these Karavani handoffs, but have been biding their time and saving their thunder for the big score. Actually, there are some indications that they've been subtly nudging at the Peeps' other transshipment points, herding their operations to Karavani. This shipment was supposed to be the big one, the one with actual Solly missiles and stealth technology and who knows what else."

Weiss winced. The People's Navy with Solly missiles and stealth tech. God help the Manties, and everyone else in the region, if that ever happened. "Well, they won't be getting anything from *that* shipment, anyway," he said. "The *Charger* took care of that."

"The *Charger* was the ship the Manties used?"

Weiss nodded. "It was keeping its ID quiet, but that's what our analysis of its emissions gave us. Any thoughts as to why they didn't just go back out through the wormhole instead of running for the hyper limit like they did?"

"They may have been a little rattled by the unexpected presence of an Andermani courier boat in the system they were hitting," Charles said. "I'm guessing they hoped you hadn't picked up the terminus's precise location and didn't want to give you another chance to locate it by exiting the same way. Besides that, the hyper limit's obviously the closer escape route. The less time they gave you to study them, the better. What kind of energy spike did you pick up?"

"It was fairly small," Weiss told him. "And frankly, I have to say that this whole thing is starting to drift into the interesting-but-not-very-useful category. Unless you want to run ore freighters to Manticore, there's not a lot in Karavani that anyone would want. And while I'm sure the hyper-physicists would have a field day trying to figure out how a wormhole terminus can be twice as close to the hyper limit as any previously mapped terminus, that's not exactly of galaxy shaking importance in the middle of a war, either."

Charles gave him an odd look. "Who said the other end of the wormhole is in the Manticore system?"

Weiss frowned. "It's not?"

"Why do you think I came to you with this in the first place?" Charles asked, frowning in turn. "The other end of the wormhole doesn't come out in Manty space.

"It comes out inside the Andermani Empire."

❈   ❈   ❈

For a long minute Weiss just stared at his host, his eyes wide, his mouth hanging slightly open. Charles sat perfectly still, letting the other have his moment. If he could convince Weiss, then the ball would continue rolling.

If he couldn't, he would probably be back in the Peeps' torture chamber by dinner time.

He was pondering that unappetizing possibility when Weiss seemed to shake himself. "Where?" he asked.

Charles started breathing again. "I'm not absolutely sure," he said. "But I believe it's somewhere along your border with Silesia, possibly in or near Irrlicht. It's a small system with four uninhabitable planets and a couple of asteroid belts—"

"Yes, I've heard of it," Weiss said. "Why do you think the terminus is there?"

"I've noted a significant number of reports describing attacks on Silesian pirates by unidentified ships in that area," Charles said. "Even asteroid miners don't stay in Irrlicht full-time, which means Manty ships coming and going wouldn't even be noticed.

My guess is that they've quietly set up a base somewhere, probably in the outer belt, to run their operations from."

Weiss pursed his lips, then abruptly shook his head. "No," he said firmly.

Charles felt his heart skip a beat. "I can show you the data," he offered.

"No, I mean you're wrong about the only two termini being in Karavani and the Empire," Weiss said. "Karavani to Irrlicht has to be somewhere close to four hundred light-years. The terminus we saw at Karavani is far too close to the hyper limit for the wormhole to stretch that far in a single gulp. There has to be a junction somewhere considerably closer—sixty to eighty light-years away at the most."

"Eighty light-years won't get you to Manticore," Charles said, frowning in feigned thought.

"No, but it could get you within forty or fifty light-years of Yeltsin's Star," Weiss said.

"You mean like somewhere in the middle of nowhere, where no one's ever thought to look," Charles said, nodding. Not only was Weiss falling right into step on this, but he was even filling in details Charles now wouldn't have to bring up himself. Perfect.

"Exactly," Weiss said. "And if the other arm—or *another* arm; at this point we have no idea how many there are—goes all the way to Irrlicht, it would come out a good three or four light-hours out from the system. Plenty of distance to ensure even those transient miners never notice the energy spike when the Manties come out."

"Yeltsin's Star," Charles said with just the right touch of sudden understanding. "Of course."

"Of course what?" Weiss asked.

"I've always wondered why the Manties bothered to open contact with Grayson in the first place," Charles said. "And why they then went to such lengths to make allies out of them."

"Possibly because they're damn good fighters," Weiss said wryly. But his eyes were distant and thoughtful. "Interesting idea, though."

"Regardless, I daresay this is something you need to get back to the Empire with immediately," Charles said. "Enjoy your voyage. I presume you've brought my fee for the information? Possibly with a bit of a bonus included?"

"I have it, yes," Weiss said, his eyes narrowing slightly. "Are we in some kind of hurry?"

"What do you mean?" Charles asked guardedly.

"I mean you seem anxious to get your money and send me on my way," Weiss said.

"I'm not anxious about anything," Charles protested, putting a bit of subtle discomfort into his voice. "I've given you everything I have. I want my money; you want to lay this out in front of the Emperor and collect your commendation. Nothing mysterious about it."

"But you *haven't* given me everything," Weiss countered. "You just said you could show me the data on the Manties' anti-pirate operations running out of the Irrlicht system."

"Oh, well, I can't show you *all* the data," Charles hedged. "Technically, that belongs to a colleague of mine."

Weiss sat up a bit straighter. "You never mentioned any colleagues," he said, his voice suddenly ominous.

"It's all right—I've known him for years," Charles hastened to assure him. "In fact, I've recently made him my partner."

"Really," Weiss said, his tone not mollified in the slightest. "This is *not* something you should be springing on me, Charles. Not here, and certainly not now."

"I'm sorry if I've upset you," Charles said apologetically, suppressing both a shiver and, paradoxically, a sly smile. If Weiss was upset at this revelation, he could imagine how Mercier was reacting to it as he eavesdropped on the conversation from upstairs. "But there's nothing to worry about. He's hardly going to betray us. Not a Manty in the middle of Peep territory."

"He's a *Manty*?"

"A disaffected one, of course," Charles said. "Come now, *Herr* Weiss—where else did you think I'd gotten all my data on Manty ship movements?"

"Yes, of course." Weiss paused, his narrowed eyes those of a cutthroat spades player trying to read his opponent. "This complicates things a bit."

Charles felt a stirring in his gut. "What do you mean?" he asked carefully.

"But it should still work," Weiss said, as if thinking aloud. "After all, two passengers can be transported nearly as cheaply as one."

"Hold on," Charles said, pressing back into his chair. "Two *passengers*?"

"Of course," Weiss said. "As you said, this news has to be taken to the Empire at once."

"So take it," Charles said. "Give me my money and go."

"I'm afraid that's impossible," Weiss said coolly. "We need to make sure nothing leaks out to the Manties before we've found the Andermani terminus. Unfortunately, that means you and your colleague will have to be our guests for awhile."

"And if we refuse?" Charles asked.

Weiss's expression went diplomat-impassive. "I hope you won't make me insist."

Charles looked down at the Andermani's waist, as if only just now noticing the subtle bulge of a hidden weapon.

Mercier was also armed. Would he be willing to use his pulser against a foreign diplomat? Charles didn't know, but he had no intention of finding out the hard way. "Let me get this straight," he said slowly. "All you want us for is to help you find the Andermani terminus?"

"That's all," Weiss assured him. "Once we've found it, we can start sending cruisers of our own through and start our own quiet survey of the thing."

"And you're not going to be convinced of all this until you do that?"

"Let me put it this way," Weiss said. "Until we *are* convinced, you don't get paid."

For a moment Charles gazed at him. Then, he exhaled a long sigh. "Fine," he said. "But bear in mind that *Herr* Mercier and I are now on the Andermani clock, and we charge by the hour."

"Then we'd best be going, hadn't we?" Weiss said, standing up. "Go collect your friend, grab your data chips and any personal items you want to bring along, and let's get to it. My car and driver are waiting down the block."

Mercier, to Charles's relief, played his part perfectly. He came downstairs at Charles's summons, accepted his new position as Charles's colleague without flinch or glare, and even added in a bit of verisimilitude by telling Weiss that his task upstairs had been to watch for possible StateSec lurkers. He accepted the offer of a trip to the Andermani Empire with just the right degree of surprise, followed by the right level of reluctant agreement.

But Charles wasn't fooled. Mercier was furious, and Charles had no doubt that he would be hearing about it the minute he and the Peep were alone.

Fortunately, that minute was likely to be a long time in coming.

Weiss made a number of quiet calls in German from the car, and instead of going back to the Andermani embassy the driver took them directly to the spaceport. A diplomatic pinnace was waiting, the pilot giving them barely enough time to get settled in their seats before lifting and heading out to the orbit where the embassy's three ships were parked. Charles made a private bet with himself that they were headed for the larger and more luxurious consular ship, and promptly lost as they instead swung in close beside a courier boat. Apparently, Weiss and Ambassador Rubell had decided speed was more important than comfort.

The courier's captain had already begun his own preparations, and in less than an hour they were underway, heading for Haven's hyper limit at nearly six hundred gravities. They had barely left orbit when Weiss called for lunch, and he, Charles, and Mercier settled down to a surprisingly but gratifyingly well-laid table.

Charles ate mechanically, his full attention on Weiss's smoothly casual interrogation of Mercier and the Peep's equally casual and surprisingly good answers. Either the colonel was a far more competent StateSec agent than Charles had realized, with the training to make up—and remember—answers on the fly, or else he'd spent the entire trip since leaving the rendezvous house working out a detailed cover story for himself.

Regardless, his performance seemed to satisfy Weiss's curiosity, both the personal and the professional aspects. When lunch was over, he offered his guests a game of cards. Charles accepted; Mercier pleaded fatigue and headed aft to their quarters.

With Mercier gone, Weiss's casual probing now shifted targets. But Charles was an old hand at this, and even with his mind split between Mercier and the card game he was able to answer or deflect everything Weiss threw at him.

Finally, as the afternoon lengthened toward dinnertime, Charles realized he couldn't put off the confrontation any longer. His twice-daily milliliter of antidote was due soon, and he needed to leave himself at least a little time beforehand to talk Mercier out of whatever quiet rage or suspicion the other was nursing.

As on the *Ellipsis,* the courier boat's captain had assigned the two passengers adjoining berths. Charles keyed his door open, and with only a little trepidation walked inside.

Mercier was waiting for him, lying on the narrow bunk with his arms folded behind his head. He seemed perfectly relaxed, but as Charles looked into his eyes he had the sudden image of a snake lurking in the dust by the side of the road waiting for an unsuspecting traveler. "I came for my drink," Charles said, deciding to try pretending nothing had happened.

"Did you, now," Mercier said, his voice a perfect match for his coiled-snake eyes. "What makes you think I'm going to give it to you?"

"What did you want me to do?" Charles countered, glancing reflexively around the room. But Mercier had had more than enough time to sweep the place for bugs. "He wanted proof, and I could hardly show him data I didn't have."

"And so you throw that little grenade into *my* lap?"

"You don't know the man, remember?" Charles explained patiently. "You're a stranger and a renegade, and you could hardly be expected to turn sensitive material over to him just because he asks nicely. That buys us time, and with enough time we can reach Irrlicht and not have to show them any data at all."

"Is that what you think will happen?" Mercier asked. "That was your plan?"

"That was my improvisation," Charles corrected. "Improvisation is what happens when plans actually hit atmosphere."

"Let me tell you what I think." Leisurely, Mercier pulled himself upright off the bunk. "*I* think you deliberately engineered this little trip, including the part about getting us off Haven without giving me any chance to contact my people. *I* think this was your plan from the very beginning: a way to get you out of reach of the retribution you knew will come crashing down on your head if the plan fails."

"So I escape from Haven and then die twelve hours later?" Charles demanded. "How does that gain me anything?"

"I don't know," Mercier conceded. "I still don't believe for a minute that this was Weiss's idea."

"Then you need to credit him with more intelligence," Charles said. "And while you're doing that, I suggest you look past your emotional haze and realize that this is the best possible thing that could have happened. Now, instead of Citizen Captain Tyler having to bear the whole brunt of the scheme's execution on his own, we'll be on hand to cover any holes and tweak any glitches at the Andermani end. It couldn't have turned out better if I *had* engineered it."

"You talk well, I'll give you that," Mercier growled. But the rattlesnake look in his eye was starting to fade. "Fine—we'll play it your way. Not that I've got much choice at the moment. But let me just throw one more item into the mix."

He reached in his pocket and pulled out his flask. "I have only enough of this stuff to last another month. That's a trip to Andermani space at courier boat speeds, a trip back to Haven, plus a couple of weeks in the Irrlicht system for the scheme and its aftermath." He raised his eyebrows. "If the job takes any longer than that, you're going to die."

"I understand," Charles said. "But as Citizen Secretary Saint-Just himself said, only with great risk comes great reward."

Mercier gazed at him in silence another minute. Then, his lip quirked in a sardonic smile. "You're a cool one, Citizen," he said. "I could almost wish you were on our side."

"I *am* on your side."

"Only for the moment," Mercier said. "And only for that hundred million Solly credits."

Charles shrugged. "Read your history, Citizen Colonel. For the moment, and for profit, is how most wartime alliances are made."

"But ideology is why a warrior is willing to die," Mercier countered. "People like you never understand that." He gestured contemptuously and started unscrewing the flask's cap. "Go get your water. I'll measure out your dose."

✳   ✳   ✳

The trip from Karavani to Irrlicht took four weeks at the *Ellipsis*'s top speed. Citizen Captain Tyler spent most of the trip rereading his orders, drilling his crew for the task ahead, and brooding.

A suicide mission, Citizen Secretary Saint-Just had called it when he'd first offered Tyler the post as *Ellipsis*'s commander. Certain death, but a death that would bring the war with the Manticore Royalists to a sudden and victorious end. Tyler had accepted without hesitation; for, after all, death in the service of People's Republic was the highest goal any of her men or women could aspire to.

But he'd had these past four weeks to study the strategy, and to think about the possibilities. Citizen Navarre's plan was both cunning and brilliant, and it was indeed likely to end in Tyler's own death. And Tyler was still willing to give his life for his nation.

But if the *Ellipsis* could achieve its goal and yet survive, would that not be even better?

The more he'd considered the question, the more he'd decided that it was neither a violation of command nor ethics to try to achieve that end.

Which was why the *Ellipsis* was no longer in the Irrlicht system, as ordered, waiting for the Andermani to come in response to Citizen Navarre's tale of an unknown wormhole terminus in their territory. Instead, he was moving with the deliberate slow clumsiness of a light freighter through the Mischa's Star system, heading on an intercept course toward a small convoy of Andermani freighters.

And as they flew toward destiny, he wondered at the strange name of this ship he'd been given.

Why *Ellipsis*? It was a question that had occupied many of the ship's officers and crew in their idle moments, first during the trip to Karavani, then during the hasty refitting from their tender after all that damage to their alpha nodes, and finally during the longer voyage to Irrlicht. Was it the fact that its namesake grammatical mark, three periods in a row, was an indication of something unseen or otherwise not there? But the ship had had that name long before Citizen Navarre had been brought aboard.

Unless Citizen Secretary Saint-Just had had Navarre and his contraband Solly stealth system waiting in the wings the entire time. A man as brilliant as Saint-Just should never be underestimated.

Perhaps it was the word itself, derived from the ancient Greek for falling short. Not that the *Ellipsis* would fall short in its duty, but that it was named with the confidence that the Manty defenses that were the mission's original target would fall short in their efforts to stop it. Or perhaps it was the dots of the grammatical mark themselves, that in the aftermath of the *Ellipsis*'s success the galaxy would connect the dots in a way that led away from Haven.

But that was vain speculation, a waste of the People's time and energy. What mattered was not the ship's name, but that its captain and crew would go down in history as the saviors of the People's Republic.

The convoy was well within missile range now. Not only that, but its escorting heavy cruiser, having been completely taken in by the fake transponder and People's Commissioner Ragli's fluent German and expertise in all matters Andermani, was already starting to reposition itself to accept this "lost" newcomer into the convoy's flight pattern.

"Prepare to launch missiles," Tyler ordered, feeling his lips pulling back into a tight smile. The first salvo would target the escort, hopefully disabling it before it could respond in any significant way. The second attack would target the largest of the convoy's freighters.

"Citizen Captain, we're nearly to identification range," the sensor officer warned. "Estimate three minutes to tag point."

"Thank you, Citizen Lieutenant," Tyler said, feeling the glacial calm whispering through him, the single-minded focus that made for both a good naval officer and a good patriot. The multiple layers of the *Ellipsis*'s false identity would fool the Andermani only so long, after which the People's ship would be close enough for the cruiser's sensors to penetrate the sheep's clothing and detect the wolf lurking beneath it.

But the Andermani would hardly be expecting an enemy ship to come this deep into its territory. In fact, the cruiser's captain was so arrogantly confident that he was even flying with his sidewalls down. By the time he realized the truth, it would be too late.

"One minute to tag point," the sensor officer announced.

The tag point was only an estimate, of course, and it wouldn't be smart to push the numbers too far. Tyler counted down the seconds, watching the screen for any hint that the escort might have realized something was wrong.

The theoretical timer was down to fifteen seconds when Tyler decided it was time. "Fire one," he ordered.

It was beautiful, in the way that space combat was always beautiful, particularly when taking down a warship from an anti-democratic regime like the Andermani Empire. The missiles shot from *Ellipsis*'s tubes, their wedges flashing into existence as they bore down at a thousand KPS^2 acceleration on the cruiser. There was a balance-point moment as the cruiser's captain belatedly saw his death approaching and tried desperately to get his sidewalls up in time.

The missiles won the race. Their warheads overwhelmed the point defenses and burst into brilliant swathes of X-ray fire that slashed across the cruiser's hull, burning through electronics, bulkheads, and human flesh alike. The cruiser's wedge flickered and dropped in strength as its alpha nodes went, then dropped again as one of its fusion bottles went into emergency shut-down.

For a moment Tyler considered seeing if a second salvo would finish it off completely. But he had a limited number of missiles, and there would be much bigger fish to fry soon enough. "Fire two," he called.

It wasn't nearly as soul-satisfying to attack an unarmed freighter as it was a warship. But it was still spectacular. The lone missile shot smoothly into the gap between the freighter's stress bands and sent its energy burst directly into the rear alpha nodes. And since a typical freighter didn't *have* any beta nodes, that meant the wedge went down completely, leaving the ship dead in space and its crew and cargo helpless against another attack.

Again, Tyler was tempted. *Bigger fish,* he reminded himself. *Bigger fish.* "Helm, veer off," he ordered. "Full acceleration, minimum-time course to the hyper limit. Com, give me transmission." He considered. "Make it a tight focus," he added. "Keep my uniform out of sight."

He got acknowledgments from both stations. Adjusting his expression into a cool, stern mask, he touched the transmit button. "That was your first and only warning," he intoned. "The next time we discover an illegal arms shipment on its way to our enemies, we will blow the culprit, its escort, *and* the rest of the convoy out of the sky."

The commander of the crippled cruiser was starting to sputter a reply when Tyler cut off the transmission. "Time to hyper limit?" he asked.

"Three hours twenty minutes," the helm replied.

"Good." Tyler took a minute to study the long-range displays, searching for anything that might be able to catch the *Ellipsis* before he could escape from the system. But he'd planned his attack carefully, and there wasn't a single thing the Andermani could throw at him.

And with that, all he had to do was take the *Ellipsis* back to Irrlicht and wait.

He smiled as he once again swept his gaze over the long-range displays. Citizen Navarre's plan had indeed been brilliant.

Now, with a single violent stroke, Tyler had made it even better.

❊   ❊   ❊

The *Hase* made one stop, at one of the outlying systems of the Andermani Empire, after which the plan had been to head directly to New Berlin. To Charles's surprise, though, they had barely reentered hyper-space when Captain Forman announced they were making instead for Mischa's Star.

He wouldn't give any reason for the sudden change in course. Neither would Weiss.

It was another two days to Mischa's Star. Weiss was on the bridge with Forman when they exited hyper-space, and Charles contrived to have a question to ask the attaché that coincidentally required him and Mercier to be there at the same time.

The first thing he noted as they emerged back into n-space was that the *Hase's* course wasn't taking them toward the inner system. The second was that the course they *were* taking seemed to lead to a small group of freighters a couple of hours' travel inside the hyper limit.

The third was that, whatever had happened here, the Andermani were taking it seriously. Seriously enough that they'd sent both a military repair ship and a seven-million-ton *Seydlitz*-class superdreadnought to the scene.

And not just *any Seydlitz*-class superdreadnought.

"*Derfflinger* to courier boat *Hase*," the clipped voice of the huge warship's traffic coordinator came over the *Hase's* com. "You are cleared for approach. Follow the prescribed vector; a pinnace will meet you at your parking slot to pick up Attaché Weiss and your passengers."

"Acknowledged," Forman said.

Charles looked at Mercier, noting the grim edge to the other's standard poker face. Whatever had happened, the Peep was just as much in the dark as Charles was.

Casually, Charles walked over to Weiss's side. "The *Derfflinger* is Herzog von Rabenstrange's ship, isn't it?" he asked.

"That's correct," Weiss said. His voice and manner were as grim as they'd been for the past two days, but Charles could hear a touch of pride beneath the concern. "You won't have known this, but he's been my patron for most of my governmental career."

"Really," Charles said with feigned surprise. Of course he'd known of Weiss's relationship with the Andermani duke. It was the reason he'd picked Weiss as the point man for this operation in the first place. "He's, what, fourth in line for the throne?"

"Third," Weiss said. "More than that, he's a cousin and close confidant of the Emperor. That's why I sent word directly to him as soon as I returned from Karavani."

"And he asked us to meet him *here*?"

"Actually, he asked us to meet him at New Berlin," Weiss said. "But events have dictated otherwise." He gestured at the screen.

"A merchant convoy was attacked here a few days ago, its escort badly damaged and one of the freighters disabled."

"They were attacked *here*?" Charles asked, his stomach tightening. Was this some bizarre coincidence? "What was it, pirates?"

"Apparently not," Weiss said. "The attacker was running a false ID code, but the escort's captain believes it to have been a Manty heavy cruiser."

Charles shot a look at Mercier. There was nothing in the *Ellipsis*'s orders about attacking Andy merchantmen. Or of leaving Irrlicht at all, for that matter. "That seems... strange," he said.

"At the very least," Weiss agreed. "I understand that the admiral will be briefing us personally once we're aboard."

"I'll look forward to that," Charles murmured, and wandered away from Weiss again.

What in *hell*'s name was Tyler playing at?

✳   ✳   ✳

The pinnace was waiting precisely where the traffic coordinator had said it would be, and arrived alongside the *Hase* within minutes after the courier boat dropped its wedge. Half an hour after that, their black-uniformed *Totenkopf* Marine escort ushered the three visitors past two similarly uniformed Marines into one of the *Derfflinger*'s conference rooms.

Three men were waiting at the table, all of them resplendent in Andermani naval uniforms. At the head of the table was Rabenstrange himself, flanked by his intelligence officer, Commander Chiro Schmidt, and a man in a captain's uniform whom Charles didn't recognize. All three Andermani were looking grim, but the captain's expression carried an additional edge of shame and smoldering anger. Spread out strategically around the walls were another half dozen armed *Totenkopfs*.

"*Herr* Weiss," Rabenstrange said gravely as Weiss led the party into the room. "It's good to see you again, Lyang."

"And you, My Lord," Weiss said, just as gravely, "though I would have preferred happier circumstances. May I present my guests: Charles Navarre of the Solarian League, and Thomas Mercier of the Star Kingdom of Manticore."

"Welcome aboard the IAN *Derfflinger*," Rabenstrange said. His gaze flicked across Charles, evaluating him in that single glance, then settled onto Mercier. "Your countrymen, *Herr* Mercier. What exactly are they up to?"

"I don't know, My Lord," Mercier said, his voice pitched even darker than Rabenstrange's and Weiss's. "And with your permission, may I state that they're no longer *my* countrymen. I fear the Manticore I grew up on no longer exists."

"Perhaps," Rabenstrange said. Clearly, he was a man who didn't jump lightly to conclusions. "We shall see." He gestured to his right. "This is Commander Schmidt, my intelligence officer—" he gestured left "—and Captain Vien of the IAN *Eule,* the ship whose convoy was attacked here twelve days ago. Captain, perhaps you could give our guests a brief summary of those events."

Charles listened in fascination and ever increasing horror as Vien detailed the disguised cruiser's approach, its sudden attacks on him and the freighter under his care, and the mysterious warning the attacker had given before fleeing the system. By the time a copy of the transmission was played, with the visual proof that the attacker was indeed Captain Tyler and the *Ellipsis,* it was such a complete lack of surprise that Charles didn't need to worry about his face giving anything away. Mercier, he was certain, was in equal control.

"Comments?" Rabenstrange invited when Vien was finished.

Protocol, Charles knew, required him to allow Weiss the opportunity to speak first. But the other remained silent, and after a moment Charles cleared his throat. "I suppose the first and most obvious question is whether we're certain the freighter was not, in fact, carrying any armaments."

"What difference does that make?" Vien snapped. "For Manticore to attack an Andermani vessel carrying *any* Andermani cargo within Andermani borders is a blatant act of war."

"Captain," Rabenstrange said quietly.

With a visible effort, Vien regained control of himself. "My apologies, Admiral," he said. He paused. "And to you, as well, *Herr* Navarre."

"The fault was mine," Charles said, ducking his head and trying furiously to come up a more politic way to get to the point he'd been trying to make. Tyler's irresponsible action had been way over the line, but there was nothing Charles could do about that now. What he *could* do was use the occasion to help solidify the tentative conclusion that the mysterious attacker was, indeed, a Manty. "I'm simply trying to find some reason for the attack, rational or otherwise. May I ask the freighter's name?"

"The *Krause Rosig*," Rabenstrange said. "And since you ask, it was carrying machine parts, farming equipment, electronics, and foodstuffs."

"The *Krause Rosig*," Charles repeated, frowning in thought. "Thomas, wasn't there a Peep arms freighter in that last intelligence report that was supposed to be flying with an Andermani ID and the name *Crossroads*?"

"I was just wondering about that," Mercier agreed without even a fraction of a second's hesitation. "Its real name was the *Overland*, as I recall."

"Right," Charles said, turning back to Rabenstrange. "*Krause Rosig—Crossroads*. I wonder if this could have been an honest mistake, My Lord, with the Manties either garbling the report of the arms freighter's name or the convoy list."

"An *honest mistake*, you say, *Herr* Navarre?" Vien demanded. "A military intrusion of Andermani space, an *honest mistake*?"

Charles winced. "Another poor choice of words on my part," he said. "My apologies. I'm simply trying to make some sense out of this."

"There is one other possibility, My Lord," Weiss spoke up hesitantly. "Perhaps the Manties were concerned about security in the matter which I recently reported to you."

"Yes." For a moment Rabenstrange eyed his protégé. Then, turning to Vien, he nodded. "Thank you for your time, Captain," he said. "You may return to your ship now. As soon as Commander O'Hara and her investigators have finished examining the damage, I'll give orders for your repairs to be expedited."

"Thank you, Admiral," Vien said. Standing, he saluted both Rabenstrange and Schmidt, nodded to Weiss, then strode past the Marines and left the room.

Rabenstrange turned to Schmidt. "Commander, perhaps you'd be good enough to take *Herr* Weiss and *Herr* Mercier to the duty mess down the hallway and offer them some refreshment. While you're there, have someone assign them quarters. We'll be leaving within the hour."

"Yes, *Herr* Herzog." Schmidt rose briskly to his feet and gestured toward the door. "Gentlemen?"

"As for you, *Herr* Navarre," Rabenstrange added, "I'd like a word with you in private, if I may."

Mercier flashed an unreadable look at Charles as he stood up, but made no comment as he followed Weiss and Schmidt from the room.

The door closed behind them, leaving Charles and Rabenstrange alone with the six Marine guards. Apparently, Charles mused, this was what passed for privacy with a member of the Andermani royal family. "How may I help you, My Lord?" he asked.

Rabenstrange pursed his lips. "You can begin by telling me what exactly you're up to."

Charles frowned. "I'm not sure I understand."

"You're a Solly, or so you claim," Rabenstrange said. "Yet here you are, involving yourself in matters the Solarian League has unequivocally stated are none of its citizens' business."

"Yet many of my fellow citizens *are* so involved," Charles pointed out. "The shipment of contraband Solly weaponry which *Herr* Weiss observed in the Karavani system is merely one proof of that."

"Granted," Rabenstrange said. "Which brings up interesting questions of its own." He leaned back in his chair. "For example. You alert *Herr* Weiss to this shipment, and in adequate time for him to witness its arrival. Oddly enough, it happens that the Manties also learn about it, also in sufficient time to send a ship to destroy it."

"As *Herr* Weiss has no doubt informed you, I have certain sources of information," Charles reminded him. "As to the Manties' timely arrival, I expect *Herr* Weiss's report has given an explanation for that."

"Yes, it did," Rabenstrange said. "Information which I note also came from you. The question thus becomes whether all this valuable information came *to* you or *from* you."

Charles shook his head. "You give me far too much credit, My Lord," he said. "I merely glean interesting bits of information out of the vast collections gathered by others."

"Perhaps," Rabenstrange said. "I also can't help noticing that you seem to be playing both sides of this situation."

"I don't understand," Charles said carefully.

"Allow me to lay it out for you," Rabenstrange said, the temperature of his voice dropping a few degrees. "You send *Herr* Weiss to Karavani with the express intent of betraying to him a supposed deep Manty secret. Yet only moments ago you actively defended those same Manties in this attack upon Andermani sovereignty." His eyes narrowed. "So are you with the Manties, or against them?"

Charles shook his head, a bit of relief seeping into him. Rabenstrange had the right idea, but was a comfortably safe distance from the actual truth. "I'm on no side but my own, My Lord," he assured the admiral. "I'm simply a businessman, trying to wrest a small profit from a vast and uncaring universe."

"And how is this profit to be made?" Rabenstrange asked.

"I was hoping to rely on Andermani gratitude," Charles said. "If I'm right about—" he glanced at the nearest Marine "—the matter of which you've already heard, I have no doubt the Empire stands to reap substantial economic benefits." He waved a hand. "All I wish for my services is a small finder's fee."

Rabenstrange smiled faintly. "And this small fee would amount to . . . ?"

"As I said, I would rely on Andermani gratitude."

For a long moment Rabenstrange gazed thoughtfully at him. Charles held the other's eyes evenly, putting every bit of honest capitalistic sincerity into his face and body language that he could. "The courage of your convictions does you credit," the admiral said at last, his tone carrying a faintly mocking edge. "Does your colleague share that same purity?"

"Hardly," Charles conceded. "*Herr* Mercier's motivations are so complex that even I sometimes have trouble following them. But I can handle him."

"I hope so," Rabenstrange said. His eyes flicked to the Marine directly behind Charles. "If we do have to take over that duty, *Herr* Mercier will regret it. So, very likely, will you."

"Understood, My Lord," Charles said, and the shiver that ran up his back was completely genuine. The *Totenkopf* Marines had a reputation that extended even to the League's normally oblivious public. "Will that be all?"

"For now, yes," Rabenstrange said. "If you wish, you may join the others."

"Thank you, My Lord," Charles said, standing up. Now came the equally tricky task of convincing Mercier that he hadn't used his time with Rabenstrange to betray their mission. The *Totenkopfs* might be able to take down the StateSec man if he got out of line, but probably not before Mercier did the same to Charles. Nodding to Rabenstrange, he turned toward the door.

"One more thing," Rabenstrange said from behind him.

Charles turned back. "Yes?"

And froze at the deadly look on the admiral's face. "Who are you?" Rabenstrange asked softly.

Charles felt a fresh surge of adrenaline flood into him. "*Herr* Weiss has already told you that," he managed, fighting to keep his voice steady. "I'm Charles Navarre of the Solarian League."

"I don't think so," Rabenstrange said. "In his dispatch *Herr* Weiss expressed a certain lack of clarity concerning your identity. I therefore took the liberty of doing a more extensive search than he was capable of with the limited resources at his disposal. Including variant spellings, there are approximately one hundred and thirty thousand Charles Navarres on the League's citizen lists." He paused. "None of them appears to be you."

And suddenly Mercier was the least of Charles's worries. "There must be some mistake."

"No," Rabenstrange said flatly. "There isn't."

Charles grimaced. When the big lie doesn't work, as the old saying went, try mixing in just enough truth to wash it down. "All right, you've caught me," he said with a sigh. "My real name is Charles Blake. I'm an investigative journalist, writing for the *Star Universal* and affiliated sites under the name Rufus Perry. You may have read some of my reports?"

"No," Rabenstrange said again, just as flatly. "Can you prove this?"

"If you mean do I carry ID in that name, no," Charles said. "Working undercover this way, I can't take the chance someone will stumble across something that compromises my identity while I'm on a story. I can of course give you references, but they're all on Earth or other League worlds, which means they aren't going to do either of us much good at the moment."

"Mm," Rabenstrange said. He was clearly still a long way from being convinced, but at least he no longer sounded ready to offer his *Totenkopfs* a little exercise. Maybe he *had* heard of Rufus Perry, even if he hadn't read any of the columns. "And this story you fed *Herr* Weiss?"

"One hundred percent true, My Lord," Charles assured him. "I've been sensing something funny about the regions in question for a long time. When I finally figured out what was going on—" He let his lip twitch. "Let's just say journalism is a tough game, and the scars are starting to show. It occurred to me that quietly presenting this to the Empire instead of laying it out in front of a bunch of jaded readers who couldn't see the longer picture if you silk-screened it on their corneas might allow me to retire with grace and a certain degree of comfort."

"Somewhere out of reach of Manty reprisals?" Rabenstrange suggested.

Charles winced. "If at all possible, yes."

"And you think this time I should believe you?"

Charles spread his hands. "Whether you do or not, I didn't make up the Manty ship that attacked the *Eule* and *Krause Rosig*," he said. "Nor can I make up a—you know what—in the Irrlicht system. Put me under guard if you wish, but I urge you to get to Irrlicht with all due speed. That's where all the answers lie."

For another few seconds Rabenstrange continued to gaze at him in silence. Charles waited; and after what seemed like forever the admiral gave a microscopic nod. "I'll want a list of those references," he said.

"Of course, My Lord," Charles said. "I have them in an overlaid code on one of my data chips. I can have a decoded copy for you within the hour."

"No need," Rabenstrange said. "The *Derfflinger*'s cryptologists haven't much to do right now. They'll enjoy the challenge."

Charles suppressed a grimace, but there was nothing for it but to comply. Opening his data chip holder, he selected one at random and set it down on the table in front of him. "Will there be anything else, My Lord?"

"Not at present," Rabenstrange said. "One of the Marines outside will take you to the others."

Charles nodded, and once again turned to the door. This time, Rabenstrange let him escape.

✳   ✳   ✳

To Charles's relief, Rabenstrange didn't take him up on the suggestion that he be clapped in irons, or whatever the IAN used in its brigs. On the contrary, as they headed toward Irrlicht it almost seemed that the crew members assigned to watch over the passengers went out of their way to treat him better than they did Mercier or even their own countryman Weiss. No doubt it was all part of some arcane plan on Rabenstrange's part, pressuring the passengers with lopsided kindness in the hope of forcing open a few interesting and illuminating cracks.

If that was his goal, it was a waste of everyone's time. Mercier, no doubt reading the situation the same way Charles was, made a point of not reacting to any of it, but simply maintained his brooding expatriate persona.

Two days of hyper-space travel later, they reached the Irrlicht system.

"We're here," Rabenstrange announced, swiveling in his command chair to look at the three passengers he'd had brought onto his bridge. "*Herr* Navarre? Any thoughts?"

"Unfortunately, no," Charles admitted. "I'm ninety-nine percent sure this is the place, but I have no idea where exactly the terminus might be located. *Herr* Weiss's analysis suggested it would be two to four light-hours outside the system, but there's no way to know where. On the other hand, if the Manties have a base in the outer asteroid belt somewhere, we should be able to find it, shielded or otherwise. Once we have the base, we should be able to pull records of the terminus itself."

"It's a reasonable place to begin," Rabenstrange agreed, swiveling back around again. "Captain Preis?"

The flag captain nodded and turned to the helm. "Take us in slow—two hundred gees," he ordered. "Bow and sidewall sensors, set up a crisscross search pattern, starting at *null-null*. Stern sensors, search outward for anything that might indicate a gravitic or spatial anomaly. Deploy the LACs with similar instructions."

Turning toward the faint point of light in the distance that marked the system's sun, the big ship headed forward.

There was a breath of displaced air as Weiss stepped to Charles's side. "This is it," he murmured.

"Yes," Charles murmured back. "Did I hear Captain Preis mention LACs?"

"Yes, two of them," Weiss confirmed. "They came with us from Mischa's Star, tractored to the hull. They'll ride escort for us, as well as help with the search."

"Ah," Charles said, nodding. "What was the *null-null* reference?"

"That's *zero-zero*, the part of the outer belt directly ahead of us," Weiss explained. "The miners who occasionally come here to try their luck call the belt the Double Diamond because it has two relatively small, relatively dense areas, with the rest of the ring much more open and empty. Since those are the two likeliest places for the Manties to hide a base, we might as well start with one of them."

"Yes, that makes sense," Charles murmured.

Weiss peered oddly at him. "You all right?"

"I'm fine," Charles said. "Just nervous, I suppose."

"About what?"

Charles shook his head. "Just nervous."

"Ah." Weiss studied him another moment. Then, without another word, he drifted away.

Charles bit back a curse. That bit of unfocused weirdness had probably cost him ten points' worth of class in Weiss's estimation. But right now, he couldn't care less what Weiss thought about him.

The *Ellipsis*'s orders, coming from Saint-Just himself, had been to wait at Irrlicht for Charles and Mercier to bring in the *Derfflinger* or a ship of equal size and status. But Tyler had taken his ship to Mischa's Star instead, and had furthermore risked the entire mission just to shoot a few missiles at a cruiser and a harmless freighter.

The question—the crucial, damnable question—was *why?* What had Tyler thought he could accomplish?

Had he wanted to stir up the Andies to come charging into Irrlicht? But Charles had already promised he would do that, and Saint-Just had accepted that promise, and that should have been good enough for Tyler. Had he hoped an attack would irritate the Andies into sending a big, important ship to investigate the suspect system? But Charles had promised to do that, too.

So why had Tyler deviated from the plan? More importantly, were there other such deviations waiting down the line?

Charles didn't know. But sometime in the next few hours, he had damn well better figure it out.

✳   ✳   ✳

"ID confirmed," the *Ellipsis*'s sensor officer announced. "It's the IAN superdreadnought *Derfflinger*, Admiral Herzog von Rabenstrange's flagship."

"Excellent," Captain Tyler said, leaning back in his seat and smiling one of his wolfish smiles. It was all going exquisitely according to plan, Navarre's overall scheme and Tyler's improvements to it. The Imperials had taken the bait, and now the cousin and close friend of the Andermani Emperor himself was aboard the ship bearing down on him.

Navarre's plan had been a bold one: point the Andermani to the Irrlicht system and talk them into sending a ship to investigate; have the *Ellipsis* "appear" from its supposed wormhole, spot the "unexpected" intruder, and attack under the guise of a Manty ship jealously defending "its" wormhole; damage the Andy as much as possible before his own destruction; and then let nature and Andermani militarist pride take its course. Tyler had never doubted for a minute that it would work.

But Tyler had now seen the inherent risks of straining his alpha nodes in order to create the fake wormhole footprint. He could do permanent damage to them, and here in the Irrlicht system there was no PRN tender standing by ready to repair that damage. Or worse, the energy surge might blow the impeller rooms and destroy the entire ship. That would end Citizen Navarre's plan right there and then.

Besides, wouldn't it be better if, instead of merely damaging the Andermani ship, the *Ellipsis* was able to completely destroy it?

Of course it would. Not only would it enable the People's Republic to retain the *Ellipsis* for future service, but the Emperor's outrage at the Royalists would be orders of magnitude greater.

So Tyler had taken it upon himself to modify Navarre's plan. And now, thanks to that initiative, this new, better result was all but guaranteed.

Because under the original plan, there was no way of knowing which direction the investigating ship might come from. The two large clusters of this so-called Double Diamond asteroid belt were more or less equidistant from New Berlin, and a captain coming from the Andermani capital could basically flip a coin as to which cluster he chose to investigate first.

But one of those two clusters was on an almost direct line from Mischa's Star. By creating an additional "Manty" incident there, an incident that would most likely be investigated by the same ship already tasked with the Irrlicht probe, Tyler had given the *Derfflinger* an obvious choice of which cluster to examine first.

The cluster that the *Ellipsis* itself was even now skulking inside, its wedge at low power, its ID beacon silent, its wonderful new Solly stealthing rendering it all but invisible.

"He's stabilized his approach vector, Captain," the navigator reported.

"Acknowledged," Tyler said, studying the nav display. It would have been even more perfect if he could have known precisely where the *Derfflinger* would be coming in. Then he could have lain quietly along the Andermani's approach vector until the Imperial lumbered unsuspectingly into point-blank energy range, where a single salvo of laser and graser fire poured down its unprotected throat would gut even a superdreadnought like a fish. Not only would that have finished him off in a single blow, but it would have had the extra irony of being exactly the same technique the accursed Royalist Honor Harrington had used in her cowardly attack on the People's task force during her escape from Cerberus.

But alas, it wasn't going to be so neat and clean. Even coming from a known position, the *Derfflinger* had any number of approach vectors to choose from, with no way for Tyler to know where to lie in wait for him.

Which was why, as far back as the repair work on his alpha nodes, he'd conceived this new scheme instead.

"Prepare to get underway," he ordered. "Minimal wedge, full stealthing, course as previously laid in."

"Yes, Citizen Captain," the helmsman acknowledged.

Tyler settled back in his seat. No, this new plan wouldn't be as neat and clean as a graser ambush. But it would be just as spectacular.

And in the end, the *Derfflinger* and Admiral Rabenstrange would be just as dead.

✽   ✽   ✽

The *Derfflinger* was six hours into the Irrlicht system when she spotted the wedge.

"Given its current vector, and assuming constant acceleration and heading, it has to have come from right about here," the superdreadnought's tactical officer said. She tapped a command into her console, and a blinking icon appeared on the flight deck's master plot.

"Even if they'd been under complete emissions control, the recon drones' active sensors should have picked it up when they swept that area," Captain Preis pointed out.

"Yes, sir," the officer agreed. "Best explanation is that it was shielded somehow."

Preis grunted and turned to the communications display which linked his position on *Derfflinger*'s command deck to Rabenstrange's flag bridge.

"I think, Admiral, we may have found our camouflaged Manty base. If they got some kind of super stealth that can hide a starship, I don't see any reason it couldn't hide a basing facility just as well. Especially if the facility's built into an asteroid, as well."

"Perhaps," Rabenstrange agreed. "Any ID on the ship?"

"Configuration, emissions, and impeller signature are consistent with a Manty *Star Knight*-class heavy cruiser," the tactical officer reported. "So far, nothing else."

For a moment Rabenstrange sat quietly. Then he gave a short nod, as if he'd come to a decision. "The base can wait," he said. "Plot an intercept course with that ship. If they're the ones who hit Mischa's Star, we're going to want to have a serious conversation with them."

There was a flurry of acknowledgments, and the maneuvering plot shifted as the big superdreadnought began altering its course. In the midst of all the activity, Charles caught Mercier's eye and gave a small nod toward a relatively unoccupied part of the bridge. Mercier frowned, but nodded back, and began drifting that direction. Charles did likewise, feeling the eyes of the silent *Totenkopfs* on him the whole way, and a moment later he and Mercier were as alone as they were going to get.

"What exactly is he doing?" Mercier murmured.

"That was *my* question," Charles murmured back as he pulled out his reader. "Give me a chip—any chip. We need to look like we're consulting on something. This isn't the plan, Mercier. What the hell is Tyler playing at?"

"Why ask me?" Mercier countered, digging a chip out of his pocket and handing it over.

"Because he's your countryman, and you've got a better handle on his psychology than I do," Charles said, plugging in the chip. It turned out to be a collection of classic novels. "Could he have lost his nerve and be making a run for it?"

"Don't be absurd," Mercier scoffed. "Besides, if he was, why turn off the stealthing? Unless you think it might have failed."

"No," Charles said firmly, looking over at the tactical display. Mercier was right: if the *Ellipsis*'s stealthing hadn't been on earlier, the *Derfflinger*'s sensors would have spotted it long ago. So why turn it off now?

Unless Tyler *wanted* Rabenstrange to see him.

A hard knot settled into Charles's stomach as he looked at

the display with new eyes. There was no way Tyler could have known exactly which approach vector Rabenstrange would come in on. But what he *could* do was quietly move the *Ellipsis* to a particular point, and then time his appearance from stealth in order to nudge the *Derfflinger* onto a pursuit vector.

A carefully prepared pursuit vector . . .

"Tell me something," he murmured to Mercier, looking back at his reader. "That tender we brought to Karavani to fix any damage the *Ellipsis* might sustain in that raid. It was a general supply/repair/ammunition ship, right?"

"Correct," Mercier said.

"Loaded with a typical grab-bag of weaponry?"

"Again, yes," Mercier said. "What are you—?"

"Including a selection of laser-head mines?"

For a moment Mercier just stared dumfounded at Charles. Then, the corners of his lip twitched. "Excellent," he said. "Well done, Captain."

"You think so?" Charles bit out, fighting to hold onto his temper. "Let me set you straight. It may not matter to you whether or not you die today. But if Tyler succeeds in luring us into a minefield, the whole plan will die right here and now."

"What are you talking about?" Mercier asked, frowning. "Destroying the *Derfflinger* would be perfect."

"No, it would be disastrous," Charles retorted, gazing intently down at the reader, knowing that every *Totenkopf* eye was on them. He had to make this look good. "Think it through. The *Ellipsis* has to be seen coming out of a wormhole—well, Tyler's screwed that part up already. But never mind. More importantly, he has to be seen in Manty uniform, he has to challenge Rabenstrange with Manty claims to the system, *and* he has to inflict some serious damage before supposedly popping back down the rabbit hole. All of that requires *that he leave some actual survivors.*"

Mercier's expression abruptly changed. "Oh, hell," he murmured. "But there would still be escape pods, right?"

"After a bunch of mines have delivered a down-the-throat X-ray laser barrage?" Charles asked. "You tell me. Besides, a few random engine room or medic staff survivors would be useless— they won't have seen any of the show we've worked so hard to set up. Whatever else happens, the command deck has *got* to survive intact, or this whole thing will have been for nothing."

Mercier swore viciously. "Damn him to hell," he muttered. "What do we do?"

"We get off this vector as fast as we can," Charles said grimly, pointing to a random part of the reader's display. "Here—we've just discovered indications that the wormhole terminus is on a vector about ten degrees starboard of us. *That's* what we really want to go look at, not some random marauding Manty ship. Think you can convince Rabenstrange of that?"

"Why me?" Mercier countered. "You're the one he likes."

"No, I'm the one he doesn't trust," Charles countered, thrusting the reader into his hands. "It has to be you."

"He's not going to believe me," Mercier insisted, his voice starting to sound a little ragged as he took the reader. "What do I show him for proof? A random page from—what is that?—*A Study in Scarlet*?"

"It's overlay-encrypted," Charles explained patiently. "That's all you have to say—I gave him that same spiel a couple of days ago. Now *go*."

For a moment Mercier gazed at the reader in silence. "Fine," he said. "Wait here. I'll take care of it."

He headed toward the command chair. The two *Totenkopfs* standing guard there moved to cut off his approach, stopped at a word from Rabenstrange and allowed him to pass. Mercier stepped to the admiral's side, and for a minute they spoke together in voices too low for Charles to hear. Rabenstrange nodded, and as Mercier walked away he turned to Captain Preis and murmured new orders.

"Well?" Charles asked as Mercier returned.

"He agrees that three vessels will be able to herd the Manty ship more efficiently than one," Mercier said calmly. "So he's going to take my suggestion and move the two LACs into flanking positions outside our wedge."

Charles felt his mouth drop open. "*What?*"

"You were concerned that the *Derfflinger* might die with all aboard," Mercier reminded him. "A group of mines facing a superdreadnought and two LACs will certainly ignore the smaller ships, which means there will now be at least two LACs' worth of survivors. And since Tyler will be delivering his message on broadcast instead of tight beam, they'll see and thus be able to report everything." Giving Charles a tight smile, he walked away.

Charles stared after him, his pulse thudding in his throat. So the *Derfflinger* would be destroyed, Rabenstrange would be killed, and the Emperor would declare war within hours of hearing the news. All nice and neat and made to order.

Never mind that Mercier himself would die along with everyone else. From his point of view, this was indeed the ideal solution. *True Believer*...

"You all right?"

Charles started. With his brain and gut tied in knots, he hadn't even noticed Weiss's arrival. "No, I'm not," he said, trying desperately to get his brain on line again. Rabenstrange might not listen to him, but he would certainly listen to Weiss. "I can't shake the feeling that we're in danger."

"We're a warship," Weiss said dryly. "We're allowed to be in danger."

"Not like this," Charles insisted. "There's something wrong here. I can feel it."

"Relax, *Herr* Navarre," Weiss said, an edge of amusement to his grimness. "We're a superdreadnought. They're a heavy cruiser. There's very little they can do to trouble us unless we get careless."

"I know," Charles said. "It's just...listen, did you read the report of Honor Harrington's escape from the Peep prison planet?"

"I read what the Manties released," Weiss said, frowning. "Plus the extra material Imperial Intelligence was able to get. Why?"

"I keep thinking about the way she hit that incoming Peep task force, the attack that got her the rest of the transport capability she needed to get the prisoners out," Charles said. "As I understand it, she basically slid up between the two halves of the force on her thrusters, and since she didn't have her wedge up and blazing she was able to sneak into energy range before they even spotted her."

"Mainly because the Peeps were being sloppy and not doing proper scans," Weiss said slowly. "But I see your point. You think there's an ambush waiting out there that the cruiser is trying to draw us into?"

"I don't know," Charles said, feeling sweat gathering beneath his collar as he carefully walked his delicate line. He couldn't have the *Derfflinger* destroyed, but he also couldn't have Rabenstrange break off the pursuit completely. "All I know is that something about this is popping red flags like crazy."

"Let me talk to the *Herr* Herzog," Weiss said. He smiled faintly. "The fact that Charles Navarre is actually concerned—about anything—is all by itself worth bringing to his attention."

He left Charles's side and moved over to the command chair. This time, the *Totenkopfs* didn't need to be told to let him through. For a moment he and Rabenstrange conversed, again too quietly for Charles to listen in. Then, with a nod, Weiss stepped away.

Again, Rabenstrange spoke to the flag captain, who nodded and stepped over to the communications station. As he finished, Rabenstrange swiveled around, caught Charles's eye, and gestured him forward. Suppressing a grimace, Charles obeyed.

"My cryptologists have been looking over the data chip you gave them," Rabenstrange commented as Charles arrived beside him. "So far, they haven't been able to find the overlay code you spoke of."

"I'm not really surprised, My Lord," Charles said. "As I mentioned, my life out here depends on no one figuring out they have an investigative journalist looking over their shoulders. If you'd like, I'd be happy to decode a copy of the references for you."

"Perhaps later." Rabenstrange nodded toward the screen and the starscape in front of them. "I understand you're concerned that we're flying into an ambush. Any particular reason why?"

"Not really, My Lord," Charles said, painfully aware of the two watchful Marines standing bare centimeters away from him. "But in my line of work, you learn not to ignore your gut feelings."

"And yet that same gut tells you that Manticore might actually be foolish enough to precipitate a war with the Empire while still fighting for her life against Haven?"

Charles shrugged. "I know it sounds insane, My Lord," he conceded. "But politicians sometimes do insane things. Who knows what the Manties might do in response to a perceived threat against their legitimate security concerns?"

Rabenstrange snorted, a gentle, thoughtful sound. "Interesting that you should put it that way," he murmured, his voice that of someone drifting into memory. "Several years ago I sat in my quarters aboard this very ship with a rising young Manty officer. I remember saying those exact words to her: 'No one can predict where competing ambition and completely legitimate security concerns will lead interstellar powers.'"

"Perhaps one of those tipping points has been reached," Charles offered. "Perhaps *Herr* Mercier is right that the Star Kingdom of that long-past conversation no longer exists."

"Perhaps," Rabenstrange said. "We shall soon see."

❄   ❄   ❄

"The *Derfflinger* is approaching the mine field," the *Ellipsis*'s sensor officer reported. "Still bearing true."

"Acknowledged," Tyler said, smiling in satisfaction and anticipation. At the *Derfflinger*'s current speed and acceleration, Rabenstrange would have perhaps twenty seconds between the time the mines activated, lighting off their drives and heading directly toward the superdreadnought, and the point where their laser heads burst into a searing torrent of X-rays and flooded the ship with death.

A death that would be as complete as it was awesome. The *Derfflinger* was coming straight into the field, which meant the mines' energy bursts wouldn't even have to expend any of their energy cutting through the ship's sidewalls. They would have a clear shot straight down the Andermani's throat.

Tyler gave a little snort of contempt. And those twenty seconds would be just enough time for Rabenstrange to see that death coming, and to realize it was his blundering that had killed his ship and his crew. "Still bearing true?" he asked, just to make sure.

"Yes, sir," the sensor officer said, peering closely at one of his displays. "But the LACs have altered position. They've moved from flanking points to a lead-and-tail configuration: one ahead and slightly above the *Derfflinger*, the other astern and beneath."

Tyler snorted again, but this time it was a snort of contempt. So Rabenstrange had finally started to wonder if this was too easy, and had sent his LACs ahead and behind to take the brunt of any sneak attack that might be lurking along his path. So much for any propaganda that the Empire's leaders actually cared about the lives of their subjects. Rabenstrange had sent the LACs' crews out to die in his place, probably without even a second thought.

But it would do him no good. The mines weren't especially smart, but they weren't stupid, either. Their computers would have no trouble picking out the better target and locking onto it. All Rabenstrange would accomplish by putting the LACs out there would be to leave a few witnesses behind.

Which was all to the good, of course. *Someone* had to survive to take back word of the attack, along with a recording of the speech Citizen Charles had written for Tyler to deliver. After all, New Berlin had to know who exactly to declare war on.

He took a final look around his bridge, taking in the Manty equipment and Manty uniforms all around him, preparing to deliver his message with full Manty arrogance. The Emperor would know, all right.

And by the time the *Ellipsis* arrived back at Haven for its heroes' welcome, the Star Kingdom would be in a two-front war even they couldn't possibly win.

"Ninety seconds to minefield," the sensor officer announced.

"Acknowledged," Tyler said. Smiling again, he settled back to watch the show.

✳   ✳   ✳

Charles was standing silently beside Weiss, gazing across the bridge and wondering what death would feel like, when the tactical display abruptly exploded into activity. "Mines!" the tactical officer snapped. "*Many* mines, one point three million klicks, bearing zero-zero-two, zero-one-zero!"

Charles caught his breath, staring at the swarm of wedges arrowing straight toward the *Derfflinger*'s bow. So that was it. He'd been right, all the way. Tyler had sprung his trap, and there was no way Rabenstrange or anyone else would be able to react before the terrible energies of those mines slashed through its open throat, killing and destroying everything in their path.

"Acceleration zero," Captain Preis called, his voice calm and even.

"No!" Charles barked reflexively. Killing the *Derfflinger*'s forward acceleration was exactly the *wrong* thing to do. Preis had to use that acceleration to twist the ship sideways, to try to put as much of sidewalls as possible between them and the approaching laser heads. "Captain—"

He broke off as Weiss grabbed his arm. "Wait," the other said, his voice as calm as Preis's.

Charles wanted to snap out a curse, to remind Weiss about the horrible death screaming toward them. But it was too late for that. It was too late for anything. Clenching his hands into impotent fists, he waited for death. Abruptly, incomprehensibly, the stars in the main display vanished, and the insane thought flashed through Charles's mind that without even a flash of vaporized bulkheads he had somehow been killed.

And then, with a surreal silence, utterly divorced from the

noise and the fury he had expected, the mines simply . . . disappeared from the tactical display.

An eerie stillness descended on the bridge. Charles stared at the tactical, fighting against his frozen mind, trying desperately to figure out what had happened. Out of the corner of his eye he could see Weiss watching him in grimly amused expectation.

And then, finally, he got it.

He turned to Weiss. "Very nice," he said quietly. "The LAC, right?"

Weiss nodded. "Standard Andermani military minefield doctrine," he said. "You wait for the mines to activate and lock on, kill your forward acceleration and go ballistic, then turn your escorts over to put their wedges between your throat and kilt and the mines." He smiled tightly. "A doctrine partially developed by Admiral Herzog von Rabenstrange himself."

"With a bit of inspiration from Hancock Station," Rabenstrange added. He had swiveled around, Charles noted, and his eyes were squarely on him. "Do we have an ID on that cruiser yet?"

"Yes, sir, he's finally started broadcasting," someone called. "It's the RMN *Charger*, Captain William Grantley commanding. Intelligence data shows no current location or assignment for either ship or commander."

"We've reached extreme missile range," another voice put in. "Firing solution plotted and laid in."

"Acknowledged," Rabenstrange said. "Well, *Herr* Navarre. It appears your gut was right."

"So it would seem," Charles said, forcing as much calmness as he could manage into his voice. It wasn't a lot. Distantly, he wondered how Mercier was reacting to the situation, but didn't dare look at the Peep to find out. "Well executed, My Lord. What now?"

Rabenstrange swiveled back around again. "They've had their shot," he said quietly. "Now it's our turn."

✳   ✳   ✳

"No!" Tyler screamed at the bridge crew, at the *Derfflinger*'s intact image on the screen in front of him, at the universe at large. "No, no, *no!*"

The attack couldn't have failed. It *couldn't*. The setup had been perfect, the *Derfflinger*'s insertion vector had been perfect, the mines' operation had been perfect. It simply wasn't possible for

Rabenstrange to have come up with that blocking maneuver so fast, let alone have executed it.

He felt his lips pull back in a snarl. Of course. Navarre. Tyler had no idea how the slimy little Solly had pulled this off, but he knew beyond a stealthed doubt that Navarre was behind it somehow.

He drew himself up in his command chair. "Stand by to transmit," he bit out. So Navarre had ruined his chance to destroy the *Derfflinger* and strike a solid blow for the oppressed Andermani people. Fine. He would just have to let the Manties do it for him.

"Transmission ready," the com officer called.

"Make sure it's a wide focus," Tyler reminded him. Navarre had insisted on that, to the point of underlining the order. The Imperials needed to see a Manty bridge, hear Manty-style orders, and see a whole group of up-to-date Manty uniforms. Only then would they truly be convinced that the Manties were the ones responsible for the attack.

"Wide focus, aye," the response came.

Tyler smiled again. Royalists against Imperials... and when it was over, the People's Republic would be there to gather together the pieces and bring freedom to the oppressed of both nations. Tyler's only regret was that he wouldn't be there to see it.

He let his smile fade, and set his face in a dark, Royalist glare, and touched the switch. "This is Captain William Grantley of the RMN *Charger*," he announced. "IAN *Derfflinger*, you are trespassing on territory claimed by the Star Kingdom of Manticore. Leave at once, or face the consequences."

❊   ❊   ❊

"...or face the consequences."

Weiss stared at the com display, his stomach a single hard knot of horror and disbelief, his brain battling to make sense of what his ears and mind were telling him.

But he couldn't do it. Even after the evidence of Mischa's Star, even after the casual violation of Imperial territory and property that that attack had demonstrated, this sudden ultimatum was more than his mind could wrap itself around.

Because he *knew* the Manties. He'd met many of them, soldiers and politicians both, in the days before the war. He'd spoken with them, dined with them, interacted socially with them. Some were geniuses, some were merely competent, and others were fools who clearly owed their positions to family name and political influence.

But never had he sensed from any of them the sort of arrogant galactic-level supremacy or false-smile, hidden-dagger scheming that he'd felt from so many of Haven's politicians. The Star Kingdom was proud, certainly, and all too often that pride swerved across the line into annoying cockiness.

But cockiness was one thing. A deliberate invasion, a deliberate act of war, was something else entirely.

But he couldn't ignore the evidence of his own eyes. It was all right there, staring him in the face. He'd been aboard a number of Manty warships, though the Manties themselves probably weren't aware of that, and the bridge stretching around and behind Captain Grantley was without a doubt that of a *Star Knight*-class heavy cruiser.

"RMN *Charger,* you have violated Imperial Andermani territory," Rabenstrange was saying, the admiral's voice faint through the hissing of blood in Weiss's ears. "It is *you* who will strike your wedge and surrender your ship and crew."

"I think not, Admiral," Grantley said. "You can destroy me if you choose, but that won't change the facts of this situation."

"And those facts are...?" Rabenstrange asked.

Weiss frowned, tearing his eyes from Grantley's image and looking at Rabenstrange. There had been something odd in the admiral's voice just then.

He frowned harder. Because it wasn't just Rabenstrange's voice. The admiral's face was still grim, but to Weiss's amazement he could the hint of a smile twitching at the corners of the other's lips.

Weiss had known men like that, men who went into battles with smiles of anticipation, especially battles that promised to be unmitigated slaughters. But Rabenstrange wasn't like that. He was a servant of the Crown, going into battle when he had to, or was ordered to, and never simply because he enjoyed it.

Or did he? What did Weiss really know about his patron, anyway?

"The fact that the Star Kingdom hereby lays claim to this system and everything within it," Grantley said evenly. "We now have vested interests here, interests that we *will* defend."

"With your fleet fully engaged against the People's Republic of Haven?" Rabenstrange countered. "Surely your leaders aren't foolish enough to take actions that would open up a second front."

Grantley smiled, a thin, evil thing. "Your intelligence services are slipping, Admiral," he said. "We have new weapons and delivery systems which will end the war with the Peeps within three months at the latest." The smile vanished. "And when we've finished with them, you'd better pray that the Star Kingdom hasn't found someone else who needs to be taught a lesson about the galaxy's new realities."

"Is that a threat?" Rabenstrange asked softly.

"Take it as a threat, a warning, or a simple statement of fact," Grantley said. "But take it seriously."

"Oh, I will," Rabenstrange promised. "As seriously as the new reality demands."

He turned to Weiss. "Well, *Herr* Weiss?" he asked quietly, his voice as calm and cool as if he was asking which wine the attaché wanted with dinner. "Do you see it?"

Weiss stared at him. *Do you see it?* What kind of insane question was that? "I'm sorry, My Lord?" he managed.

"The larger picture, Lyang," Rabenstrange said, lowering his voice even more. "Ignore Captain Grantley. Take in the larger picture."

Weiss looked back at the screen, as bewildered as he'd ever been in his life. Grantley hadn't moved, his defiant glare still blazing from the screen like the laser head of one of his own mines. Behind him, the bridge was still a *Star Knight*-class bridge, and the people sitting or standing at their consoles were still clothed in the proper Manty uniforms...

And then, Weiss saw it.

Or rather, he saw *her*.

She was standing at one of the fire-coordination consoles at the rear of the bridge, just over Grantley's left shoulder, her expression as grim and defiant as the captain's own. Her lips were moving as if she was speaking, though her voice from that distance would of course be inaudible on Grantley's pickup.

Only she shouldn't be here. She *couldn't* be here.

He looked back at Rabenstrange. The admiral was smiling openly now, a smile like the approach of death itself. "I see it, My Lord," Weiss said.

"Excellent." Rabenstrange nodded his head fractionally to the side, then swiveled his chair to look behind him.

Weiss turned. Over the past couple of minutes Charles had drifted back to the rear of the bridge and was now standing beside Mercier, the two of them flanked by a pair of *Totenkopfs*.

"Tell me, *Herr* Navarre; *Herr* Mercier," Rabenstrange called, loudly enough for the entire bridge to hear as he gestured toward the screen. "Which one of you knew I'd personally met the Duchess Honor Harrington?"

A violent twitch jerked at Mercier's body, his head twisting sharply as he looked at the screen.

His eyes widening as he belatedly caught sight of Harrington's impossible presence behind Captain Grantley's defiant scowl.

Rabenstrange lifted a finger. "Take him," he ordered.

Mercier must have known in that instant that he was a dead man. But he was clearly not the sort to simply roll over and accept his fate. Spinning half around, he threw himself like a striking rattlesnake at the nearest of the Marines, one hand jabbing toward the other's eyes, the other making a grab for the guard's holstered pulser.

But these weren't ordinary Marines, or even ordinary Andermani Marines. The *Totenkopf* dropped smoothly into a crouch, letting Mercier's jabbing fingers shoot harmlessly over his head, simultaneously dropping his hand to his holster in an attempt to catch his attacker's hand and pin it there. Mercier snatched his hand back just in time, leaning away and shifting the direction of his lunge toward a row of engineering monitor consoles and a pair of crewwomen goggling at him from behind them.

He was four steps from his potential hostages when a precisely-aimed burst of pulser darts shattered his body into a spray of blood and raw meat.

Someone swore feelingly. "Enough of that," Rabenstrange said coolly. "Lieutenant Ling, call the medic bay and have them remove the body for examination." He cocked his head. "Now, as to you, *Herr* Navarre."

Weiss dragged his eyes away from what was left of Mercier and looked back at Charles. The Solly was standing exactly where he had been, except that now he was bowed slightly over at the waist with two *Totenkopfs* pinning his arms behind his back. "Nicely done, My Lord," Charles said, his voice as calm and cool as Rabenstrange's. "May I ask a favor before I'm taken to the brig?"

Weiss looked at Rabenstrange, wincing at the implied arrogance of that request from an enemy prisoner to his captor. But the admiral merely raised an eyebrow. "Ask it quickly."

"After you deal with Citizen Captain Tyler and his captured

Manty cruiser, I'd ask that you have your medics give me a complete examination," Charles said. "The late Citizen Colonel Mercier implanted me with some kind of poison drip, the antidote to which is probably now well mixed with his own bodily fluids. You have approximately six hours in which to either find and remove the drip, or else synthesize more of the antidote."

"And if we don't?" Rabenstrange asked.

Charles gave the admiral a lopsided smile. "If you don't, you'll never know exactly what happened here today."

"*Herr* Herzog, the enemy ship has launched missiles," the sensor officer announced.

"Point defense on alert; stand by for a response," Rabenstrange said. "Take the prisoner to sickbay." He swiveled back around. "And," he added over his shoulder, "get that mess off my bridge."

✻   ✻   ✻

The first thing Charles noticed when he awoke was a glass jar sitting on the tray beside his sickbay bed. Inside the jar was a small, spiny insectoid creature about the size of a tick.

The second thing he noticed was that his wrists and ankles were anchored securely to his bed's rails. Clearly, the Andermani weren't taking any chances with him.

Under the circumstances, Charles could hardly blame them.

He had seen a corpsman twice, and the doctor once, and had been fed a small, disappointingly bland meal when Rabenstrange finally made the appearance Charles had been expecting. "You're looking well," the admiral commented, giving Charles's restraints a quick but careful look before pulling a chair to the foot of the bed and sitting down.

Not that Charles would have tried anything, even if he'd been so inclined. Not with a pair of silent *Totenkopfs* taking up positions at Rabenstrange's shoulders. "I'm feeling well, too, My Lord, thank you," he said. "Given the time that's passed since our last conversation, and the obvious fact that I'm still alive, I gather your medics were successful."

"The evidence is right there," Rabenstrange said, nodding toward the jar. "The poison drip was actually nothing more than a parasite, probably genetically altered, that your friends introduced into your alimentary canal. It had lodged in a fold in your small intestine, where it could feed happily away as it secreted its poison into your system."

"Clever," Charles said with a shiver. "I'd wondered why I couldn't find any incision scar."

"Well, you have one now," Rabenstrange said. "And be assured that it's already been added to the *descriptive features* section of the dossier we're preparing on you." He smiled faintly. "I thought you might want to save us some trouble by filling in the rest of the details."

"I'll do what I can," Charles said, gazing into the admiral's face and trying to figure out what exactly he should say. "But first, I assume you want to know what this whole *Ellipsis* mess was about."

"I think we've already deduced most of it," Rabenstrange said calmly. "The Peeps scrounged up a *Star Knight*-class cruiser from somewhere, restored it, and were hoping to start a war between New Berlin and Manticore." He raised his eyebrows. "I would say, in fact, that the biggest question still remaining is what *your* part was in the whole thing."

Charles pursed his lips. "To be perfectly honest, the whole thing was my idea. Well, most of it was," he hastened to add. "The attacks on the *Eule* and *Krause Rosig* were entirely Citizen Captain Tyler's doing. My plan would have left no casualties other than among the Peeps who were perpetrating the deception in the first place."

"And the Sollies aboard the freighter in the Karavani system."

"They were bringing in weapons," Charles said bluntly. "As far as we were concerned, their lives were already forfeit."

Rabenstrange cocked his head. " 'We'?"

Charles grimaced. "I suppose there's no putting the genie back into the bottle now, is there?" he said. "Very well. My name is— well, my real name is irrelevant. Just call me Charles. I'm part of an organization of League citizens who strongly disagree with our government's gutless neutrality in the Haven/Manticore war. We see Haven as not only a threat to every other star nation around it, but also an oppressive regime that deals out chaos and death to its own citizens. Since the League as a whole hasn't seen fit to get involved on the side of justice, we've decided to do so on our own."

"Interesting," Rabenstrange said. "*Herr* Weiss had mentioned that you have access to unusually extensive information sources."

"They're actually more extensive than even *Herr* Weiss realizes,"

Charles told him. "At any rate, we'd heard of this *Ellipsis* project that Citizen Secretary Saint-Just had going under the table. We didn't know what exactly his plan was, so I went to Haven, ostensibly to hawk some Solly tech, hoping to pick up some fresh intel."

"What kind of tech were you offering?" Rabenstrange asked.

"A pretty useless kind, actually," Charles assured him. "It was a system for feeding false images into a warship's sensors, thereby creating confusion during battle. The catch is that the equipment has to be hard-wired into the enemy warship itself, and you'd need an incredible number of the things in place in order to blind *all* the ship's sensors. Still, it looked good on paper, and I was well on the way to adding some much-needed credits to our coffers when State Security picked me up.

"But they made a mistake. Instead of interrogating me immediately, they put me in solitary for six days. I assume that was supposed to soften me up. Instead, it gave me time to think."

"And so you came up with this plan?"

"I settled first on three long-term goals," Charles said. "First, to eliminate the *Ellipsis*, because whatever use Saint-Just was planning for it I knew it would be devastating to Manticore and could conceivably shift the momentum of the war in Haven's favor." He cocked an eyebrow. "The ship *has* been eliminated, hasn't it?"

Rabenstrange grimaced. "By its captain's hand, yes," he said sourly. "He blew his fusion bottles once it was clear he couldn't escape and couldn't inflict any serious damage on us. I'd hoped to capture the ship at least partially intact for examination."

"Which was undoubtedly why Tyler chose to scuttle it," Charles agreed. "So: goal one accomplished. Goal two was to destroy as much incoming Solly tech as possible. That was actually much easier. Once I'd presented my plan and gotten Saint-Just on board, the Peeps themselves were kind enough to point me to Karavani and the biggest clandestine shipment to date. In order to spark Andermani interest, I argued, as well as add verisimilitude to the tale, a Manty ship had to be seen destroying it. Goal two, accomplished."

"But why the wormhole story?" Rabenstrange asked, frowning. "Did Saint-Just really believe I would fall for it?"

"Why not?" Charles asked. "It's not like wormholes come equipped with ID beacons announcing their presence." He started to spread his hands, stopped as the restraints brought his arms up short. "The point is that I needed something that was potentially valuable enough for Manticore to risk war with New Berlin over *and* offer the kind of power or maneuverability that would make Manticore think it could *win* a war with New Berlin *and* convince Saint-Just that New Berlin would recognize both those factors and conclude it had to immediately come down hard on the Star Kingdom before it finished off Haven and turned its full attention against them. A heretofore unknown wormhole system was perfect for the part."

"The image of Duchess Harrington," Rabenstrange said slowly. "That was your false-image device, wasn't it?"

"Very good, My Lord," Charles said, inclining his head. "Yes, fortunately for me it works just as well on com feeds as it does on sensors. The Peeps were kind enough to give me access to all news broadcasts, ostensibly so that I could make sure the *Ellipsis*'s crew's uniforms were perfect. I simply took the Manties' own report of Harrington's return from Cerberus, matted the image into Tyler's broad-focus feed, and left her to be a big red flag when he came on with his dramatic challenge."

"Clever," Rabenstrange grunted. "But what if I hadn't noticed her?"

"If you hadn't, someone else on New Berlin surely would have when they were analyzing the records of the incident," Charles said. "Unlike the imaginary RMN *Charger* and the equally imaginary Captain Grantley, the Manties would have no problem proving Harrington's whereabouts at the time of the incident." He shrugged. "But I really wasn't worried. I knew your reputation, and I was pretty sure you'd spot her and realize the whole thing was a scam."

"Is that why you brought in *Herr* Weiss?" Rabenstrange asked. "To lure me into the picture, knowing I'd met Duchess Harrington during one of her Q-ship operations in Silesia?"

"I actually knew nothing about that," Charles said, completely honestly for once. "I mostly wanted *Herr* Weiss—and by extension, you—to sweeten the pot for Saint-Just. He had to be convinced that this scheme was the best possible use of his captured Manty ship, and promising that the Emperor's cousin himself would be involved was a big help in that regard."

"Indeed." Rabenstrange's expression darkened. "Now explain why you didn't tell me all this when you first came aboard and I had you away from your watchdog. Why didn't you tell me then?"

"Would you have believed me, especially in the aftermath of the *Eule* attack?" Charles countered. "Besides, if we hadn't played it exactly according to the script, Tyler might have sensed something had gone wrong and simply taken the *Ellipsis* back to Haven. Not only would Saint-Just still have the ship available for some other insane purpose, but he would also have the Solly stealth tech I put aboard as window dressing for the wormhole illusion. It was supposedly fail-safed, but I couldn't take the risk that the Peep techs might be able to be coax some of its secrets out of it."

For a long moment Rabenstrange gazed at him in silence. "You speak well," he said at last. "Perhaps some of it is actually true. You mentioned *three* goals?"

Charles grimaced. "The third was to stay alive," he said. "Or at the very least to die quickly and not in one of StateSec's torture chambers. No matter how well I did with the other two goals, I figured I was going to get that one."

"Are you sure?" Rabenstrange countered. "What makes you think the Andermani don't have torture chambers of our own?"

Charles felt his stomach tighten. "Actually, I was hoping that, in light of my confession—and along with the contact information I'm going to give you to establish my identity and credentials— that you might see your way clear to letting me, shall we say, walk away quietly?"

"I'll certainly take those names," Rabenstrange said. "But as to what happens to you, that decision is in the Emperor's hands."

"Yes, I thought it might be," Charles said with a sigh. "Still, it was worth a try."

"Meanwhile, I'm told you need your rest," Rabenstrange said, standing up. "If it makes you feel any better, I'll make every attempt to be present during your hearing."

"Thank you, My Lord," Charles said. "Tell me: will your testimony help or hurt my case?"

"I have no idea," Rabenstrange said. "Until we meet again, *Herr* Navarre."

"Until then, My Lord," Charles said, bowing his head. "And when you next see Duchess Harrington, do say hello for me."

✳   ✳   ✳

Duchess Honor Harrington reached up to rub at her missing left arm, suddenly seemed to remember it wasn't there, and lowered her hand back to the treecat draped across her lap. "That," she said, "has got to be the most bizarre story yet of this war. And considering some of the things the Peeps have pulled, that's saying a lot."

"Which is why *Herr* von Rabenstrange asked me to come here

personally to tell you about it, Your Grace," Weiss said, wishing he didn't feel so damned intimidated in her presence.

But he couldn't help it. And actually, considering who she was and what she'd accomplished over the relatively few years of her career, a certain amount of awe was hardly out of place. "And as long as I was coming here anyway, he also wanted me to bring his personal congratulations on your escape from Peep custody, and to wish you a speedy recovery."

"That was very kind of him," the duchess said. "Please thank him for me." She inclined her head thoughtfully. "Though it seems to me that you have those two backward."

Weiss glanced at the three armsmen standing their loose but wary semicircle behind her, then at the treecat, who looked much more relaxed than the armsmen but was undoubtedly watching him just as carefully as they were. "I'm not sure I understand, Your Grace," he said.

"I simply meant that the fact that you came here instead of going to Cromarty or White Haven or anyone else in government suggests you don't intend to tell them about this latest outrage on Saint-Just's long list of such atrocities," Harrington said. "In which case, instead of that revelation being the primary reason for your visit, with Herzog von Rabenstrange's congratulations being an afterthought, it's actually the other way around."

Mentally, Weiss shook his head. Tough, competent, resourceful, and the damn Manty could read minds, too. "That's correct, Your Grace," he conceded. "The Emperor is convinced that Manticore was in no way responsible for what happened at Mischa's Star and Irrlicht. But he also knows there are those in the Empire who would have their doubts. He feels there's nothing to be gained by allowing the story any more general exposure than it's already been given." He raised his eyebrows. "I hope we can count on your discretion in this?"

"Absolutely," Harrington said, and Weiss could hear no equivocation or uncertainty in her voice. "If releasing the story would raise tensions between Manticore and New Berlin, by all means let's keep it quiet. The last thing any of us wants is to allow Saint-Just to pull even a modest victory out of his failure."

She shifted her hand to stroking position along the treecat's jaw. "Which of course leads immediately to the question of why tell even me about it?"

"Two reasons, Your Grace," Weiss said. "One, Admiral von Rabenstrange thought you would appreciate hearing how you helped expose the Peep treachery in this matter, even if you weren't actually there at the time."

"Never let it be said that I didn't do all I could to strike out for truth and justice," Harrington said dryly. "Especially when all it requires me to do is stay home and read a book. Anything else?"

"Yes," Weiss said. "Before he was taken off the *Derfflinger,* our mysterious friend Charles asked the admiral to give you his greetings the next time he saw you. On the off-chance that he wasn't just blowing smoke, we hoped that you might actually know him, or know of him, and could shed a little light on who he really is."

"I'm afraid not," she said, shaking her head. "I can run your holos through the facial-recognition files if you'd like, but I doubt ours are any more extensive than yours. The references he gave you didn't pan out?"

"Not a single one of them," Weiss said ruefully. "Most of the names were fictitious; those that weren't belonged to people who flatly and categorically denied even knowing of his existence."

"I suppose that's not really surprising," Harrington said. "Still, maybe a little vigorous interrogation will shake loose something solid."

Weiss sighed. "I doubt that, Your Grace," he said. "Between his transfer from the *Derfflinger* and his expected arrival on New Berlin, he somehow managed to disappear."

One of the guardsmen shifted position slightly but remained silent. "Interesting," Harrington said. "Any idea how?"

Weiss shrugged. "Such feats usually involve friends, violence, or money. Since we found no bodies lying around, we assume it was one of the other two. But so far we haven't been able to figure out which."

"Maybe he'll be smart and go to ground," Harrington suggested.

"He doesn't strike me as that type." Weiss cocked an eyebrow. "But it occurs to me, Your Grace, that if he really *does* know you—whether or not you know *him*—it's possible he might come calling on his way back to the League."

"An intriguing possibility," Harrington said softly. "Let's hope he does. I'd like to meet the man."

She looked over her shoulder at her armsmen. "I'd like it very much."

"Let's Dance!"

David Weber

She hated pirates.

She'd *always* hated pirates. Even when she'd been a little girl, first discovering historical fiction, she'd never confused them with the jolly buccaneers of certain particularly bad novels (thanks in no small part to her father's experiences during his military career). Even if she'd ever been inclined to think romantic thoughts about them, her own middy cruise here in the welcoming Silesian Confederacy would have cured her of the temptation forever.

So far, this afternoon's experience hadn't done much to change her mind. Judging from the reports she'd already received, it wasn't going to, either.

"How bad is it, Everett?"

Years as a Queen's officer kept Commander Honor Harrington's Sphinxian accent crisp and clear, unshadowed by emotion, as she asked the question. But her brown eyes were hard with the anger of bitter experience as she gazed at the tactical display and the icon of the "freighter" flashing the transponder of the Confederacy Merchant Ship *Evita*.

She rather doubted that was the ship's real name, but it would do.

"Not good, Ma'am," Lieutenant Everett Janacek, RMMC, the youthful—extraordinarily youthful, actually—commanding officer of HMS *Hawkwing*'s embarked Marine platoon, replied from *Evita* over the com link from his battle armor.

Janacek, like Honor herself, was a third-generation prolong

recipient, and he'd come aboard less than three T-months earlier, as Lieutenant Shafiqa ibnat Musaykah's replacement when ibnat Musaykah went home for promotion and command of her own company. Honor was still getting to know him, and she'd found it necessary more than once to remind herself that whatever he might sometimes seem like, he was a commissioned Marine officer, not a friendly puppy still growing into its outsized feet. At twenty-three, he looked like a well grown pre-prolong sixteen-year-old, and she often felt he seemed as young as he looked. Without the third-generation therapies developed to accelerate the maturation of the physical brain and neural processes—*and*, she reminded herself, *gestation periods*—which prolong would otherwise have retarded (which had been the real obstacle to administering prolong in mid- or even early adolescence), he *would* have been, but not today. If he'd been more ancient than *Methuselah*, he would have sounded old and bitter beyond his years today.

"There hasn't been any resistance since we came on board, Ma'am," he continued. "These . . . people aren't stupid enough to try something like that against battle armor. But we've found prisoners. A *lot* of prisoners, I'm afraid."

He paused, and Honor felt her treecat companion, Nimitz, press comfortingly against the side of her neck as she closed her eyes.

"Let me guess," she said, and her soprano was calm, almost dispassionate. "These are the people they kept alive for technical support." Despite herself, her firm mouth grimaced. "Among other things."

"That's what it looks like, Ma'am." Janacek's voice was much grimmer and harsher than Honor's had been. Of course, he was standing there actually looking at the pirates' captives. "A couple of them are pretty far gone," he continued. "They don't even seem to realize who we are. I think they think we're just members of the ship's crew they haven't met yet. That's . . . pretty bad, Ma'am." He swallowed, and she heard him draw a deep breath before he continued. "Some of the others are a lot more together than that, though. According to them, they're the 'lucky' ones."

"And they probably are, Everett."

This time Honor allowed herself to sigh. She also shook her head, although Janacek had no visual of her on his helmet com.

Actually, she knew, *Hawkwing* had been more fortunate than usual to find any captives—however badly abused they might have been—to rescue. Quite a few pirates tended to take a page from genetic slavers when they realized they might be boarded by a warship. Inconvenient witnesses tossed out an airlock might very well never be noticed at all, especially by the sort of sensor techs one all too frequently encountered in the Silesian Confederacy Navy. Of course, in Honor Harrington's opinion, there wasn't much difference between a pirate and a slaver; scratch the surface of one of them, and you'd find the other close under the skin. That was one reason she'd identified herself as a Manticoran as soon as she summoned *Evita* to surrender. The Royal Manticoran Navy had adopted a simple policy: if slavers or pirates put slaves or captives out an airlock, the slavers or pirates in question followed as soon after as possible.

You just have to find an argument they can understand, *I suppose,* she thought coldly.

"I assume that, with Her Majesty's Marines' normal efficiency, you've thoroughly searched the ship?" she went on out loud after a moment in a deliberately lighter tone.

"Yes, Ma'am. KK—I mean Platoon Sergeant Keegan—took personal charge of that."

Honor nodded. Kayleigh Keegan (also known as "Gunny Keegan" or, more informally, simply as "KK") was Janacek's platoon sergeant, the senior noncom of *Hawkwing*'s Marine detachment. She'd been in the Royal Manticoran Marine Corps since Everett Janacek's tenth birthday, and her expertise in bringing along young and very junior Marine lieutenants was one reason she'd been assigned to a ship as small (and elderly) as *Hawkwing*. If Gunny Keegan said a ship had been "thoroughly searched," then that ship had, indeed, been thoroughly searched. A few stray microbes might have escaped her attention, but Honor wouldn't have cared to place any wagers on it.

"We turned up a couple of hideouts, but we've got them all in cuffs and under guard now, Ma'am," Janacek said.

"Good. How many warm bodies are we talking about, Everett?"

"I'm afraid we don't have a definitive count on their prisoners yet, Ma'am," the lieutenant said a bit apologetically. "We're working on that, but the best I can tell you so far is that we've got at least thirty-five or forty of them. I do have a hard count on the pirates, though. We make it a hundred and eighty-one—and from the looks of their crew quarters, Platoon Sergeant Keegan estimates that they sailed with at least half again that many more originally."

Honor's right eyebrow rose at the number. It was scarcely a total surprise, but the sheer size of the other ship's crew would have been abundant proof of what she was even without the captives Janacek had found on board, and even without the minor fact that *Hawkwing* had surprised *Evita* in the act of firing on an Andermani merchantman.

Honor's own command had a total complement of less than three hundred. Of course, *Hawkwing* (known affectionately to her crew as the "*Hawk*") was no spring chicken—in fact, she was a unit of the old *Falcon* class and just under forty-eight T-years old, which made her thirteen T-years older than her present commanding officer. But she was still a warship, packed full of weapons, sensor systems, communications gear, and small craft, with the large crew all of that implied.

The vessel she'd just captured, on the other hand, had clearly started life as a standard J Class hull from one of the Timmerman Yards in the Solarian League. At four million tons, *Evita* dwarfed *Hawkwing*'s seventy thousand tons into insignificance, but freighters were basically just big empty places in which to store things, and a standard J Class ship's company would have been no more than forty—fifty, at the absolute outside—despite the Solarian tendency towards manpower-intensive designs. Pirates, on the other hand, always needed redundant personnel to crew any prizes they might happen across, not to mention needing the manpower for minor chores like boarding captured ships, slaughtering their crews, raping and torturing their prisoners, or all the other little diversions they found to keep themselves entertained.

The most immediate implication of the numbers Janacek had just given her, however, was that there was no way in the world all of those pirates and their captives could possibly be crammed aboard *Hawkwing*. The destroyer simply didn't have enough life support, even if there'd been any place to physically put that many people. Which meant any prize crew she put aboard the other ship would have to be big enough to ride herd on the captured pirates, as well as operating *Evita*'s essential systems, and she simply didn't have a lot of people she could spare.

Not without overloading everyone else even more badly, anyway, she thought with a mental grimace, then shrugged.

It's not as if it's all *bad,* she told herself. *One thing those "technical support" people are going to want is to get as far away from that ship as possible. So if I've got to put thirty or forty of my people over there to wind it up and make it go anyway, maybe we can clear the space to fit all of them in aboard the* Hawk, *at least.*

"All right, Everett," she said. "I'll be sending some more of our people over there to help you out and take control of the ship's systems. I'm not sure exactly how many yet—I'll talk that over with the exec and the master—but that shouldn't take too long. In the meantime, get their prisoners ready to come aboard. Tell them we need our doctor to check them out."

"That's going to be true enough, Ma'am," Janacek said even more grimly. She heard him inhale again, even more deeply. "Ma'am, it looks like at least three-quarters of the people they kept alive are women."

"I assumed that would be the case, Everett," Honor said gently. "Trust me, I understand—and so will Lieutenant Neukirch."

"Yes, Ma'am." Janacek's tone might have been just a bit less grim, but any improvement was slight. Not that Honor blamed him. For whatever reason, pirate crews tended to be heavily male in composition. As if to compensate for that, the minority of women who joined them tended to be the worst of the lot, in Honor's opinion, but that gender inequality helped explain why pirate crews also tended to prefer keeping *female* technicians alive to help deal with their shipboard needs.

After all, Honor thought harshly, *they might as well keep them alive for more than one purpose.* Her nostrils flared, and she gave herself a mental shake. *There are times I wish we had a female surgeon aboard, but at least Mauricio's been around the block enough times. He's seen more than enough rape trauma out here in Silesia.*

"In the meantime," she went on to Janacek, allowing her voice to show no trace of her thoughts, "I'm assuming your new ship's previous owners had set up some sort of security arrangements to keep their...technicians under control?"

"Yes, Ma'am. You might say that."

It was obvious from Janacek's tone that the captives' living conditions had been decidedly suboptimal. That was nice to know.

"How many of your prisoners do you think you could cram into the same space if you pushed hard?"

"At least two thirds...if we pushed hard, Ma'am. If we *really* pushed hard, we might even get them all in."

"I see." It was obvious the lieutenant was thinking exactly what she was, Honor reflected. "I assume that by 'really pushed hard' you mean it would be effectively standing room only, Lieutenant?"

"Yes, Ma'am."

"That's what I thought." Honor paused for a moment, then shrugged. "Well, that's a pity, but I'm afraid the security arguments for keeping them under confinement are pretty overwhelming, Lieutenant. So they're just going to have to put up with it, aren't they?"

"I'm afraid so, Ma'am," Janacek agreed without any particular sign of regret.

"Then see to that, if you would. I'll have the first small craft over there to lift the evacuees off as quickly as possible. Go ahead and start moving them out of the confinement area now."

"Aye, aye, Ma'am."

"Otherwise, for now, sit tight, Everett. We'll be sending in the first reinforcements along with the evac craft." Honor paused for a moment then smiled slightly. "You did a good job today, Lieutenant."

"Thank you, Ma'am." The pleasure in Janacek's voice was obvious.

"Harrington, clear," she said, then turned to the two officers who'd been standing behind her listening to her conversation with Janacek.

Lieutenant Commander Taylor Nairobi, her executive officer, was about four T-years older than she was. He was also seven centimeters shorter, with brown hair, dark eyes, and eminently forgettable features. In fact, in many ways, he had the bland, inoffensive look of a mousy little file clerk who didn't get out much—the kind of person who was still described with the ancient word "geek." On the other hand, those dark eyes met other people's eyes very levelly, and they were capable of becoming extraordinarily icy when the occasion required it. No one who'd ever seen Commander Nairobi when *Hawkwing* went to action stations—or who'd been unfortunate enough to appear before the exec on report—was ever likely to confuse him with anything remotely mouselike. Unless, of course, the mouse in question came equipped with long, sharp fangs.

Lieutenant Aloysius O'Neal, on the other hand, was the oldest member of *Hawkwing*'s complement, almost thirty T-years older than Honor. In fact, he was a first-generation prolong recipient, and his hair and bushy mustache were liberally streaked with silver. When she'd first taken command of the destroyer the better part of three T-years ago, she'd been a little afraid the absurd difference between their ages might make her uncomfortable about giving him orders—or, worse, make him resent *taking* her orders. But her concerns had disappeared quickly; O'Neal's was a very reassuring, low key presence, and he'd taken the difference in their ages in stride. In fact, she wondered occasionally if the air of composed, comfortable self-sufficiency he carried around with him was the result of his having long ago accepted that he'd simply never caught the "interest" for promotion to a higher rank...or if it was the *reason* he'd never caught that interest.

One thing she was positive of: if he'd only been younger, begun his career when she'd begun her own, he would never have ended up stalled as a mere lieutenant. The Royal Manticoran Navy's worst flaw, in her opinion, had always been its susceptibility to cronyism thanks to the tradition of patronage. Junior officers with powerful patrons advanced rapidly, and when there were only so many slots to go around, that meant junior officers *without* powerful patrons got passed over for promotion in order to make room for the ones who did have them. The fact that the Star Kingdom of Manticore's navy had always been decidedly on the small side, especially for a star nation with such a huge merchant marine, compounded the problem. And the introduction of first-generation prolong to the Star Kingdom seventy T-years ago had only made that situation still worse, given how long naval careers were now likely to last.

But things were changing these days. The naval buildup King Roger had begun in response to the threat of the People's Republic of Haven's imperialism continued to accelerate under Queen Elizabeth, which made far more slots available than ever before. And another welcome side effect of the Navy's rapid growth was that the officers who opposed the patronage system—and, to be fair, there'd always been more than a few of those—were beginning to pry its fingers loose from the Service's windpipe.

Not that they've managed to pull it off completely, she reminded herself grimly, remembering certain influential enemies of her own. *But people like Admiral Courvoisier have made enough progress that if Al were just starting out today, there's no way someone as good as he is would've gotten stuck as a lieutenant.*

There were times when she wondered (and worried about) what

was going to become of O'Neal. His many years of experience, combined with his relatively low rank, made him an ideal fit as *Hawkwing's* sailing master, but that position was being phased out by the Navy. It was taking longer aboard smaller starships— largely, Honor had concluded, because someone in the Admiralty recognized what a valuable learning resource veteran officers like O'Neal provided the inexperienced commanders of ships like destroyers. Yet it was happening even there, and it wouldn't be so very much longer before there were no more sailing masters at all, so what was going to become of him once the transition was complete?

Of course, she was probably worrying too much—her mother had certainly twitted her for that often enough! Sixty-one wasn't even middle age for a prolong recipient, even a first-generation one like O'Neal. A lot of people were still coming to grips with the way prolong permitted multiple careers, but with O'Neal's skill set, he'd be invaluable to any merchant shipping line. And if he didn't want to move over to merchant service, he'd have plenty of time to go back to school and learn an entirely new profession, if he chose to.

In the meantime, she reminded herself once again, *why don't you just go on concentrating on how lucky you and Taylor are to have Al around. I don't know about Taylor, but I know I've learned an awful lot from him!*

"You heard?" she said, and both of them nodded in confirmation.

"Al," she continued to the sailing master, "I think this is going to be your job. I want you to pick yourself a set of watch-standers and an engineering crew ASAP."

"Mahalia's going to raise hell if I pick the ones I really want, Ma'am," O'Neal pointed out with a moustache-shadowed smile.

"I'll deal with Mahalia," Honor told him with a lurking smile of her own, then jabbed an index finger under his nose. "But that's not a hunting license for you to go down into Engineering and deliberately pick people you know are going to piss her off, understood?"

"Aye, aye, Ma'am!" O'Neal's smile turned into the sort of grin any urchin might have envied, and Nimitz bleeked the equivalent of a chuckle from his place on Honor's shoulder as the sailing master's gray eyes laughed at her.

"I mean it, Al!" she said warningly, despite the telempathic treecat's obvious amusement at whatever he was sensing from O'Neal. In fact, given Nimitz's sense of humor, that amusement only made her even warier.

"I know you do, Ma'am. And I'll be good—promise."

Honor regarded him with a trace of lingering suspicion. Lieutenant Mahalia Rosenberg, *Hawkwing*'s engineering officer, was dark-haired, dark-eyed, and strong-nosed, with a thin, studious face. She was about Honor's own age, and also, like Honor, from the planet Sphinx. In point of fact, she was from the city of Yawata Crossing, not that far from Honor's birthplace in the Copper Wall Mountains, although she was one of the minority of the city's citizens who weren't even remotely related to the Harrington clan.

For the most part, Honor approved of Lieutenant Rosenberg. She was good at her job, industrious, intelligent, an excellent chess player, and usually good company. But there was something about Aloysius O'Neal that simply rubbed her the wrong way. Despite the sailing master's easy-going personality, he and Rosenberg seemed constantly on the brink of some sort of spat. They were like oil and water—or possibly more like flint and steel, given the effortless way they struck sparks off one another.

She gave him one more moderately suspicious look, then transferred her attention to Nairobi.

"In addition to whoever Al thinks he's going to need to run the ship, we'll have to leave at least a couple of squads of Everett's Marines aboard as a security element, Taylor. That's going to make some holes in your watch lists."

This time, the executive officer's nod seemed a tad less cheerful. The Royal Manticoran Marine Corps was larger than similar services in a lot of star nations, but that was partly because its personnel were tasked not simply as the Navy's ground combat component and boarding force but also as integral members of their ships' crews. No one was going to mistake a Marine for a trained naval rating, but they served on weapons crews, in damage control parties, and in search and rescue duties aboard ship. Coupled with the naval personnel O'Neal was going to need, sending half of them to another ship was going to cost Nairobi over fifteen percent of his total warm bodies.

"Be thinking about which squads we can give up with the least repercussions for our shipboard organization," she told him.

"And I'm thinking we're going to want either Everett or KK over there to help Al keep an eye on things. In fact," her eyes twinkled suddenly, "if we can find a tactful way to do it, it might not be a bad idea to leave *both* of them over there. That way KK could keep an eye on Everett, too."

"Yes, Ma'am," Nairobi replied, and despite any problems he might foresee, there was a hint of the twinkle in his own eyes... and less unhappiness in his voice than she'd expected.

"While the two of you work on that, I'll get Aniella"—Honor twitched her head in the direction of Lieutenant Aniella Matsakis, *Hawkwing's* astrogator—"started laying out our course to Saginaw."

Both Nairobi and O'Neal looked at her. The exec did a better job of hiding his reaction (probably because O'Neal didn't seem to be trying especially hard to conceal *his*), but it was obvious neither had experienced any sudden thrill of delight when they heard her announcement. Which was fair enough; she wasn't enthralled by it herself. Unfortunately, her orders left her little choice.

As far as Honor was concerned, the Silesian Confederacy was more of a continual, ongoing meltdown into anarchy than anything she would have dignified with the title of "star nation." The local elites had an absolute stranglehold on political and economic power and they were even more corrupt than most of the closed oligarchies one found all too often in the Verge—that vast, sprawling hodge-podge of independent star systems and tiny star nations spreading out beyond the Solarian League. Technically, the Star Kingdom was part of the Verge itself, although the Manticoran Wormhole Junction gave it a direct connection to the very heart of the League, despite its physical location. But Manticore was also a prosperous, well-educated, and politically stable society where upward mobility was the rule, not the exception, which made it a very different proposition from a typical Verge star nation.

The Confederacy differed from most of those other star nations, too, if not in precisely the same ways. Or in anything *like* the same ways, when it came down to it. Silesia was far larger than Manticore, for example, with many times the systems and inhabited planets. It also had a large population, decent education (for the children of the oligarchs, at least), a fairly modern (if decidedly second-tier) tech base, and semi-decent healthcare. Given all of those factors, the Confederacy should have been a going concern, but it wasn't.

Like the even larger People's Republic of Haven, although for very different reasons, Silesia's self-inflicted wounds had turned what ought to have been a thriving, well-off star nation into a shambles. Many of its individual planets or star systems were at least reasonably stable (if not particularly prosperous, by Manticoran standards), and the Confederacy as a whole offered an enormously lucrative market to the Star Kingdom, given the fact that local industry was so hugely underdeveloped. But one of the main reasons for that lack of local development was the way the oligarchs siphoned every possible dollar out of the Silesian economy through graft, bribery, peculation, and outright theft. They were deeply embedded predators, concentrating a stupendous percentage of the Confederacy's total wealth in a relative handful of pockets, and that suited them just fine. *They* weren't suffering, after all.

Even that would probably have been bearable, if they'd been willing to limit their depredations to the economy. Unfortunately, politics, personal power, and money were even more thoroughly intermixed—and far more bare-knuckled—in the Silesian Confederacy than they were most places. Political power was concentrated just as completely (and in the same hands) as economic power, and the kleptocracy which controlled both saw them only as tools its privileged members could use to improve their own positions vis-à-vis one another. Graft, corruption, and kickbacks would have been bad enough, but piracy was a thriving, long-standing tradition in Silesia...mainly because the First Families of Silesia had always been in bed with the aforesaid pirates. They were willing enough to prey on domestic shippers, but they were even happier to pillage the merchant ships of other star nations when they ventured into Silesian space.

And, just to make the mess complete, someone in Silesia was always prepared to do what abused, pauperized, exploited people were always sooner or later driven to do: rebel. Honor doubted there'd been a single year in the last T-century or so in which at least one "independence" movement hadn't been waging armed rebellion against the Confederacy's central government. They seldom accomplished much, but that didn't keep a lot of people from getting killed in the process. And, as Honor had discovered on her own middy cruise, one reason so many people got killed was because the very oligarchs they were rebelling against actually found ways to exploit the situation and make money off of it until the situation finally got bad enough the Confederacy Navy was called in to put down the rebels.

Which always seemed to be accomplished with the maximum possible firmness (and bloodshed). Officially, that was to deter future rebellions. If it just happened to wipe out most of the people who could have fingered certain extremely wealthy oligarchs as their primary weapons providers, that was pure serendipity, no doubt.

In Honor's opinion, the best thing the Star Kingdom could have done for the people of Silesia would be to ship in several million free pulsers—or, better yet, several *billion*—and the ammunition for them.

Unfortunately, the Foreign Office hadn't been interested in Commander Harrington's deep insights into the nature of Silesia's internal dynamic before *Hawkwing* had departed on her current deployment. Which meant her orders were to support the Star Kingdom's official foreign policy towards the Confederacy. And it had been made crystal clear to Commander Harrington that, as part of the Navy's cheerful and willing support of the foreign policy of Her Majesty's Government, she was to cooperate with the local authorities. In particular, she was to cooperate with the Honorable Leokadjá Charnowska, Governor of the Saginaw Sector, who was (according to the Foreign Office) a leading spokesperson for Silesian-Manticoran cooperation and happened to be closely related to the Confederacy's current head of state. Charnowska, Commander Harrington had been informed in no uncertain terms, was a very important—and very large—fish who was making a significant difference in her sector. She was firmly committed to maintaining public order and supporting and protecting interstellar commerce and trade. As such, Commander Harrington was to do all in her power to support the sector governor's reforms and to encourage and strengthen Charnowska's pro-Manticore leanings.

Honor intended to do her best to comply with her orders, but she'd been to Silesia before. Because of that, she'd made a point of finding and interviewing as many merchant factors and skippers who'd had firsthand familiarity with Saginaw as she could, and their accounts had painted rather a different picture from the Foreign Office's rosy assessment.

After two and a half T-months on station, everything she'd seen suggested they'd been right. However pro-Manticore Sector

Governor Charnowska might be, the Saginaw Sector still seemed to have just as many pirates—and just as much local corruption—as any of the Confederacy's *other* sectors. None of which filled her with optimism where Charnowska herself was concerned. In the Navy, a ship's captain was both morally and legally responsible for the performance of her command. Honor was well aware that civilian—and especially political—hierarchies were seldom run on quite such a black-and-white basis. Even granting that, however, she suspected that any disinterested observer would conclude that at least some responsibility for the sector's condition had to be laid at the feet of Manticore's good friend, the Sector governor.

"You know, Ma'am," Nairobi said in a carefully neutral tone, "we did catch them in the act." He twitched his head at where the master plot showed the icon of the Andermani freighter *Sywan Oberkirch*, still close aboard. "We've got *Oberkirch*'s people's testimony, as well as our own tac recordings. And then there are the prisoners Lieutenant Janacek found aboard the pirate. That's pretty conclusive evidence *Oberkirch* isn't the first ship they've attacked."

"I'm aware of that, Taylor," Honor said just a bit more coolly than was her wont.

"I think what Taylor's trying to say, Ma'am," O'Neal put in, "is that under interstellar law, there's—"

"Thank you, Al," Honor interrupted. "I'm also aware of the relevant provisions of interstellar law. And we're still going to Saginaw. So let's be about it."

"Yes, Ma'am."

O'Neal's response could not have been more respectful, yet it was obvious he saw no good reason to make the four-day voyage from their present location in the Hyatt System all the way to the Saginaw System and the sector's capital. He'd *probably* have been willing to at least shoot them first, but Honor didn't doubt for a minute that he would also have been perfectly willing to see how well pirates did trying to breathe vacuum.

Which was, after all, the traditional penalty for pirates who'd been—as Nairobi had pointed out—caught in the act.

But it's not what's going to happen this time, she told herself. *Not when the Admiralty was so clear about the need to stay on Charnowska's good side.*

She tried very hard to tell herself that was the only reason she'd rejected O'Neal's solution to the problem. That it had nothing

at all to do with squeamishness, or any desire to pass the buck
for the execution of almost two hundred human beings. She was
almost sure she believed herself... but only almost.

❋   ❋   ❋

"So over all, Ma'am," Surgeon Lieutenant Mauricio Neukirch
said, "I'm as satisfied with my patients' condition as I probably
have any right to be."

Which isn't any too damned pleased, his tone and body language added.

"Pretty bad, was it?" Honor asked gently, and the powerfully
built doctor drew a deep breath, then nodded.

"Yes, Ma'am. It was." He grimaced, and his dark brown eyes
glittered with unaccustomed anger. "There's a couple of them—"

He broke off and shook his head.

"A couple of them are going to need lots of counseling, Ma'am,"
he went on after a moment, his expression bleak. "One of them,
especially. I haven't had time to really sit down with her yet, but
one of the others told me she was serving on a family-owned
ship. One of her sisters and at least two of her brothers were
crew members. She was the youngest—she's only about twenty-
three—but she was holding down the assistant engineer's slot
when these... people took their ship."

He closed his eyes, his broad shoulders sagging as he sat in
the comfortable chair in Honor's day cabin.

"The brothers never made it off the ship. From what the woman
who was telling me about it had to say, it would've been God's
own mercy if her sister hadn't, either. And she got to watch it
all, of course."

His jaw clamped, and Honor made herself sit back and inhale
a deep draft of cleansing oxygen.

Mauricio Neukirch, despite his last name, had been born and
raised on the planet of San Martin. His mother was a physician,
and his father had been a senior undersecretary in the Trevor's
Star system government before the Havenite conquest of San Martin, seventeen T-years ago. Dr. Neukirch had managed to refugee
out to the Star Kingdom with four of her five children, of whom
Mauricio—then in his second year of college—had been the eldest.

The eldest to *survive,* that was. His older sister had been an engineering officer in San Martino's navy; her ship had been destroyed
with all hands during the San Martinos' desperate fighting retreat

to cover the Trevor's Star terminus of the Manticoran Wormhole Junction long enough for the refugee ships to break free. Mauricio's father had been shot by the Peeps' occupation force a few T-months later, after they broke his cell of the San Martin resistance.

Yet despite all that had happened to him and to his family, Mauricio was one of the gentlest, most compassionate people Honor had ever met. Which was why he hated pirates even more than she did, if that were possible.

"At any rate, Ma'am," the surgeon lieutenant continued in a determinedly more normal voice, "I don't think we're in any danger of losing any of them because of their injuries. That's better than it could be. Thomas and I are going to be keeping a pretty close eye on them until we're positive of that, though."

"Good, Mauricio. Good."

What he really meant, Honor reflected, was that he and his senior sickbay attendant, Chief SBA Thomas Dwyer, were going to be keeping an especially close eye on one particular patient. One Neukirch didn't want to officially designate as a "suicide watch" situation.

"In that case," she went on after a moment, "I'll let you be about whatever it is you need to be doing. Keep me informed, please. Especially if the young woman you mentioned needs to talk. Nimitz can help a lot, sometimes, in situations like that."

"Yes, Ma'am, he can," Neukirch agreed, climbing out of his chair and producing his first smile since entering her cabin. He looked affectionately at the treecat napping on his bulkhead perch. "If that little bugger could only talk, Skipper, he'd make one hell of a counselor or therapist!"

"Speaking from personal experience," Honor told him with a somewhat lopsided smile of her own, "he manages pretty darned well *without* being able to talk."

✳   ✳   ✳

"Captain, we have a communications request for you from the Confed cruiser *Feliksá*. It's from a Commodore Teschendorff," Lieutenant Florence Boyd said.

Honor looked across the bridge at her attractive, platinum-haired, sapphire-eyed com officer. Boyd was three or four T-years younger than Honor, but she was also a second-generation prolong recipient, which meant she actually looked older than her commanding officer.

And on her, *it looks pretty darned good, too,* Honor thought with more than a touch of envy, remembering the way her own *third*-generation prolong had stretched out her gawky, overgrown horse adolescence. Was *still* stretching it out, really, as far as she was concerned, she thought, running a hand over her close-cropped hair. Boyd, she'd noticed, never seemed particularly lacking in male companionship.

Nimitz made a small sound of amusement from the back of her command chair as he followed the familiar thought through his person's emotions. She smiled and reached up to rub his ears, but her almond eyes simultaneously narrowed thoughtfully. *Hawkwing* had crossed the Saginaw System's hyper limit just under forty-one minutes earlier with a normal-space velocity of eight hundred kilometers per second. She'd been accelerating steadily towards Jasper, the system's single inhabited planet at just under four hundred and nineteen KPS^2 for that entire time, and her velocity relative to the planet had increased to 10,905 KPS. She was still almost an hour from her scheduled turnover point, and over an hour and a half from Jasper.

More to the point, she'd announced her presence to the system traffic control authorities immediately after crossing the limit. It had taken almost nine minutes for her transmission to reach planetary orbit, and another nine minutes for Saginaw Traffic Control's acknowledgment to get back to her, but she'd been cleared for a standard approach without any unusual questions.

And no one at STC had mentioned anyone named "Teschendorff" to her. Which was particularly interesting because the senior officer here in Saginaw was supposed to be one Rear Admiral Gianfranco Zadawski.

She glanced at the master plot and found the caret which indicated the transmission's source, blinking steadily under the tactical icon of a heavy cruiser at a range of two light-minutes. The icon's appended vector information indicated that the *Feliksá* was headed out-system at a leisurely two KPS^2 on an almost reciprocal course, and she and *Hawkwing* were closing at a combined rate of just over sixteen thousand kilometers per second.

"And would it happen that we know who Commodore Teschendorff is, Florence?" she asked.

"I have him in our ONI database as the commander of a Confed cruiser squadron, Skipper," Lieutenant Commander Nairobi offered before the com officer could reply. Something about the exec's tone raised one of Honor's eyebrows, and he shrugged. "According to our latest information on him, he's supposed to be over in the Hillman Sector, not here in Saginaw."

"Really?" Honor rubbed the tip of her nose thoughtfully.

It was always possible their information was simply out of date and the Confederacy had changed this Teschendorff's assigned station since the Office of Naval Intelligence had last heard about him. For that matter, there could be any number of reasons for him to be hanging around Saginaw even while he was officially assigned to a neighboring sector, especially given that Saginaw boasted one of the Confederacy's larger naval shipyards. But the Confederacy Navy had a tendency to leave its squadrons permanently assigned to specific sectors and naval bases. Personally, Honor thought that was a not insignificant part of the many problems Silesia faced; leaving the same ships (and ships' companies) assigned to the same stations for literally years on end encouraged them to establish all sorts of long term relationships with the local population and authorities. Most places that might have been a good thing, but here it was only one more opportunity for the people who were supposed to be suppressing piracy and smuggling to be co-opted by the people who were *doing* the pirating and smuggling.

"Do we have any more information on him?" she asked after a moment.

"Not a lot, Ma'am." Nairobi shrugged slightly. "We've got some boilerplate bio, but not any real details."

"I see."

Nairobi's reply was scarcely surprising. ONI did its best to keep tabs on the Confederacy Navy's senior officers, but trying to keep up with all of them was a daunting task. Besides, more and more of the RMN's intelligence capacity was being consumed by its far more important concentration on the People's Republic. Much as Honor would have liked to, she couldn't really fault that prioritization, but it was making things even more difficult for starship commanders assigned to commerce protection duties here in the Confederacy.

"Very well, Florence. Go ahead and put him through to my display."

"Yes, Ma'am."

An instant later, a gray-eyed man in the uniform of the Silesian Confederacy Navy appeared on Honor's com display. His dark blond hair was going noticeably lighter at the temples, which suggested he was probably first-generation prolong. In which case, he was probably about Honor's father's age.

"Good afternoon, Sir," she said politely. "How may I be of service?"

"Good afternoon, Commander," the blond-haired man replied after the inevitable light-speed lag. "I'm Commodore Mieczyslaw Teschendorff, and my flagship's tactical section has informed me you appear to have a prize in company. Which led me to wonder if there might be some way the Confederacy Navy and I might be of service to *you*?"

Honor kept her eyes from widening, despite Teschendorff's unusually direct manner. Relations between the Royal Manticoran Navy and the Confederacy Navy were often strained, in large part because many of the Confederacy's naval personnel deeply resented Manticore's long-standing tradition of "interfering" here in Silesia. Unlike some Manticorans, Honor had always found that perfectly understandable. No doubt a great many of those who resented Manticore's presence were indeed—as the majority of her own fellows were automatically wont to opine—in the pockets of the very pirates, smugglers, and slavers they were supposed to be hunting. But even (or especially) those officers who were doing their level best to discharge their own and their service's responsibilities were bound to resent the way Manticore's intrusiveness underscored their inability to deal with their star nation's internal problems. The fact that quite a few Manticoran officers, over the years, had made that same point to them in thoroughly undiplomatic terms didn't help, she was certain, yet even if every Queen's officer had been a paragon of diplomacy (which they weren't, by a long shot), they would still have been—by their very presence—a crushing indictment of the Confederacy's internal corruption and the CN's ineffectuality.

That inevitable tension between the Confederacy Navy and the RMN had produced quite a few testy exchanges over the years. What it had *not* produced was a tendency for CN officers to go out of their way to be any more helpful to the Manticoran interlopers and they absolutely had to be.

Nor, for that matter, she thought, would very many Confed

Navy tactical sections have realized so quickly that *Hawkwing* was accompanied by a prize ship. *Hawkwing* hadn't informed system control of *Evita*'s status when she checked in with the STC, and she hadn't said a single word to this *Feliksá*. Even granting that the cruiser's tac people had been sufficiently on their toes to notice *Hawkwing*'s arrival in the first place (which had scarcely been a given), deducing that the merchant vessel with her was a prize wouldn't necessarily have followed. The logical conclusion upon detecting a Manticoran destroyer in company with a freighter would have been that the destroyer was *escorting* the freighter, not that she'd captured it.

Unless, of course, she thought rather more grimly, *they recognized the freighter's emissions signature and already knew she was a pirate. Which raises the interesting question of exactly* how *they'd know that, doesn't it, Honor?*

"I appreciate your courtesy, Commodore," she said out loud, "but I believe we have the situation under control. We've already notified system control of our arrival, and we've been cleared for planetary approach."

She sat in her command chair, waiting while her transmission crossed the light-seconds to *Feliksá,* and then while Teschendorff's response crawled back to *Hawkwing.*

"I assumed you would have, Commander," the Silesian said then. "On the other hand, we both know how warships can find themselves...tied up while planet-side authorities deal with all the legal formalities. If, as I suspect is the case, you intend to lay charges against your prize's crew for piracy, you could find yourself anchored here in Saginaw for quite some time. I, on the other hand, as a senior officer of the Confederacy Navy, could take them off your hands immediately. In which case, you wouldn't have to spend any additional time here in-system waiting for the wheels of justice to turn."

Honor had her expression well in hand, but she found herself wishing fervently that she and Teschendorff were face-to-face, where Nimitz could sample his emotions. The treecat was an all but infallible lie detector, although his inability to manage human speech meant there were often times she had to guess about exactly what his reaction to someone meant. Fortunately, they'd been together for the better part of a quarter T-century, so she'd had lots of practice. *Un*fortunately, not even Nimitz could parse someone's emotions from the other end of a com link two light-minutes long.

On the face of it, Teschendorff's offer could be no more than the sort of courtesy a senior officer could be expected to extend to a visiting naval officer who'd happened across criminals operating on the senior's astrographic turf. And he certainly had a point about how many days—or weeks—a warship could find herself rusting away in orbit while she waited for planetary legal personnel to get around to collecting all her evidence and taking all the relevant statements. But this was Silesia. Altogether too many of the Confederacy Navy's senior officers were prepared to go much further than simply turning a blind eye to the operation of pirates in their bailiwicks. From her own experience, Honor figured the odds were at least even that what Teschendorff really wanted was to collect "her" pirates so he could...release them back into the wild as soon as he'd seen *Hawkwing*'s back.

It was always possible she was doing him a disservice, but she wasn't inclined to bet anything valuable on the possibility. Besides, there were those orders about cooperating with Governor Charnowska.

"I deeply appreciate the offer, Sir," she lied pleasantly through her teeth, "but I'm afraid my instructions from my own Admiralty are fairly specific." That much, at least, was actually the truth. "In particular, the Confederacy government has informed Her Majesty's Government that it wishes to pursue a closer integration of our operations here with your *civilian* legal authorities."

She decided to let him speculate on just how those instructions of hers might envision bringing that about, and waited for his response. Four minutes later, the image on her display frowned very slightly, then smoothed its expression and shrugged.

"In that case, Commander Harrington, I wish you the best of luck. Governor Charnowska and Admiral Zadawski do have a reputation for moving expeditiously in cases like this, so perhaps you won't be tied up here in Saginaw as long as you might be elsewhere, after all."

Teschendorff paused for a moment, as if on the edge of terminating the conversation, then smiled slightly, although it didn't seem to Honor that the expression managed to reach as high as his eyes.

"*Feliksá*'s just completed some overdue repairs to her forward impeller ring, Commander," he said. "We're conducting trials and letting the builder's reps be sure everything is where it's supposed to be before heading back to our own station. It's probably going to take us at least a few more days. Perhaps we'll run into one another on Jasper."

"Perhaps so, Sir," Honor replied courteously.

"Well, on that note, Teschendorff, clear," the commodore said four minutes later, and her display blanked.

✣ ✣ ✣

"Thank you for seeing me so promptly, Your Excellency," Honor said as Sector Governor Charnowska's aide ushered her obsequiously into the governor's office. Her guide, Honor reflected, should have had "Flunky" embroidered across the back of his tunic in fluorescing letters.

"Thank *you* for coming planet-side to see me so promptly, Commander Harrington," Leokadjá Charnowska said graciously, holding out her hand as she stood and walked around the end of her enormous desk to greet her visitor.

The aide disappeared as if by magic, and the governor didn't appear any more displeased by that than *she* was, Honor reflected, studying the other woman unobtrusively. Charnowska made quite a striking first impression. She was a good twelve or thirteen centimeters shorter than Honor, with dark red hair, large, intense brown eyes, and a graceful carriage, and her smile was as gracious as her tone.

"Under the circumstances, Ma'am, I thought I should make my manners as soon as was convenient for you." Honor hoped Charnowska didn't realize her own smile was more than a little forced. She didn't like politics even in the Star Kingdom; in no small part, she admitted to herself, because she didn't *understand* politics. And she liked them even less when she found herself forced to interact with foreign politicians, particularly at such a high level.

On the other hand, it comes with the white beret, doesn't it? she reminded herself sardonically.

"'Under the circumstances,' Commander?" Charnowska repeated, quirking one eyebrow and tilting her head slightly.

"Yes, Ma'am. When my ship first arrived on station, Admiral Zadawski informed me you were out of the system, which, obviously, made it impossible to pay a courtesy call on you before I had to leave again to begin checking in on Manticoran business and shipping interests in the area. I regret that, especially since my instructions from the Admiralty lay particular emphasis on the desirability of fully cooperating and coordinating my own operations here in protection of Manticoran commerce with the sector's civilian government." She gave a deprecating smile. "I think one of the things my superiors had in mind when those instructions were issued was for me to make certain I wasn't stepping on anyone's toes." She allowed her smile to disappear and shrugged ever so slightly. "I'm sure no one here in the Confederacy needs to be reminded that there have been too many instances in which Manticoran naval officers have—unintentionally, of course—irritated or offended your authorities by taking... unilateral action to resolve problems they've encountered. My orders make it quite clear that my superiors desire me to avoid following those unfortunate examples."

Honor felt vaguely ill at her own mealymouthed platitudes. In a general sense, there was nothing wrong with what she'd just said. In fact, it was what a naval officer of a foreign power ought to be saying—and doing—when she found herself operating in the sovereign territory of another star nation. Unfortunately, that assumed the star nation in question was able (or willing) to exercise an effective police power in its own star systems.

"I see."

Charnowska gazed at Honor for a moment, then nodded towards the huge, panoramic windows of her office, inviting the Manticoran officer to accompany her as she strolled across to them. She folded her hands behind her, gazing out across the capital city of Onyx, while Honor stood a respectful pace behind her and to the right.

"I'm pleased to hear what you've just said, Commander," the governor said. "I happen to be one of the Silesians who believe we ought to be cultivating closer—or perhaps I mean more cordial— relations with the Star Kingdom. As you say, there have been entirely too many past instances of irritation and offense—going both directions, I'm sure," she added just tardily enough to make it clear she meant exactly the opposite. She turned her head and smiled at Honor. "I think it's time the Confederacy and the Star Kingdom turned over a new leaf, and I'd be delighted for that process to begin right here in Saginaw."

"Thank you, Your Excellency," Honor murmured.

"And, in connection with that, are there any service needs your ship might have?" the governor inquired.

"We would like to take on some fresh foodstuffs, Your Excellency. And while we're in Saginaw, I'd like to give my people an opportunity for liberty here on Jasper."

"Of course, Commander!" Charnowska's smile was both broader and more genuine than it had been. "I'm certain the port's entertainment facilities would be delighted to separate your spacers from any loose currency they might have weighting down their pockets."

"That *is* the way it seems to work, Ma'am," Honor agreed with a smile of her own.

"Very well, I think we can consider that agreed to. Is there anything else I can do for you today, Commander?"

"No, Your Excellency." Honor bowed slightly. "There are some additional matters which will have to be dealt with, of course, but I'm sure Admiral Zadawski and I can handle them without involving your office. And, of course, I'll hold my officers and personnel in readiness for any additional testimony or statements which may be required."

"Testimony or statements about what, Commander?" Charnowska asked, turning to face her fully with what certainly looked like an expression of genuine puzzlement.

"About the crew of the *Evita*, Ma'am."

"Of the *Evita*?" Charnowska's look of puzzlement deepened. "What are you talking about, Commander?"

"I'm sorry, Your Excellency," Honor said. "I assumed Admiral Zadawski had already informed your office. The *Evita* is a Silesian-registered freighter—although I'm quite confident her papers are false—which *Hawkwing* took in the act of piracy in the Hyatt System. We brought her in with a prize crew on board late yesterday, your time. And, in accordance with my instructions, I handed her and the prisoners over to Admiral Zadawski. Well, actually," she corrected herself scrupulously, "I informed him of the circumstances and that I would hand her and her crew over to the local authorities with considerable relief as soon as it was convenient for him to put his own people on board."

"Well," Charnowska said rather tartly, "I'm pleased you've

brought this up, Commander, because no one *else* has informed me of the situation. I suppose it's possible the message simply hasn't reached me yet, but from what you've just said, should I assume it has not yet been 'convenient' for Admiral Zadawski to relieve you of your responsibility for this vessel?"

"Ma'am, I didn't mean to sound as if I were criticizing the Admiral." Honor hoped she sounded at least a little more sincere than she actually felt. "It's not as if it were any sort of emergency, after all. My people have the situation aboard *Evita* under control. I would like to get them back aboard ship, and, obviously, to hand this responsibility over to your people, but it's not going to hurt us any if it takes another day or two."

"Perhaps not, but it's a poor way to reward your cooperation with us," the governor said. "I assure you, Commander—your people will be relieved of their responsibility for this ship as soon as possible."

✳   ✳   ✳

"Oh, stop being so grumpy, Stinker!" Honor said.

The cream-and-gray treecat stretched out along the back of the chair across the table from her only regarded her through grass-green eyes and flirted the very tip of his tail. Nimitz had not been overjoyed by her decision to leave him aboard ship during her courtesy call on Sector Governor Charnowska.

"Not everyone is delighted to see a treecat coming along on official port visits," Honor continued, leaning back in her own chair and folding her arms. "I explained that to you. Again."

Nimitz made the soft sound that served him in place of a sniff of disdain, and Honor felt her lips twitch.

"You're not going to make me feel guilty about it, you know," she told him firmly. "I'll take you with me if I get back down there for something less official, but without the governor's specific invitation—or permission, at least—I'm not taking you to any meetings with her. It's just one of those rules you and I have to put up with sometimes."

The slight flattening of Nimitz's ears made his opinion of "those rules" clear. And, although Honor had no intention of admitting it, she tended to agree with him. Not only that, but she very much wished she'd had him in range to sample Charnowska's emotions during their conversation. After all the years they'd been together, he *understood* Standard English better than many humans she'd met. They'd also evolved their own set of signals, and she'd learned to read his reactions and body language with remarkable acuity, as well. The insight that gave her into the emotions of others had served her well upon occasion, and she wished she'd had it with her earlier today.

She started to say something else to the 'cat when a soft, musical chime sounded and she pressed the admittance stud, instead. Her briefing room door slid open, and Rose-Lucie Bonrepaux, *Hawkwing*'s senior steward, stepped through it. Chief Steward Bonrepaux was a few years older than Honor, with sandy hair, brown eyes, an oval face, and a pronounced Havenite accent. Her parents (both engineers) had managed to refugee out of the People's Republic when Bonrepaux was less than five years old, and they'd settled in the Star Kingdom. The entire Bonrepaux family had the fierce immigrant loyalty and patriotism that often put nativeborn Manticorans to shame, and although the steward was a tiny woman—a full dozen centimeters shorter than Honor—she was also an elemental force of nature when it came to running the destroyer's food services organization.

"I've got that tray you wanted, Skipper," she said now, offering a large plastic tray under an opaque cover.

"Thank you, Rose-Lucie," Honor replied as the steward set her burden down on one end of the table.

"And Commander Nairobi asked me to tell you Lieutenant Janacek and his party will be returning aboard in the next fifteen minutes or so."

"Thank you," Honor repeated, and Bonrepaux nodded and headed back out. The door closed behind her, and Honor returned her attention to Nimitz.

"As I said," she told him firmly, "you're not going to make me feel guilty. However..."

She reached out a long arm to lift the lid off the tray, and Nimitz's flattened ears perked upright. Bonrepaux had delivered a stack of the chicken salad sandwiches of which Honor was particularly fond (and which helped provide the calories her genetically enhanced metabolism required) and a moisture-beaded bottle of Old Tilman. But in addition to the sandwiches and beer, there was a neat pile of freshly cut celery sticks, as well.

Nimitz flowed down from the chair back and began to sidle across the table towards her, and Honor chuckled. All treecats had an absolute passion for celery, for reasons neither Honor nor any other human had ever been able to figure out, and Nimitz's passion was even stronger than most. He paused, nose a quarter-meter from the tray, whiskers quivering, tail swishing, clearly torn between greed and the need to maintain his proper air of long-suffering martyrdom at having been left behind when she went dirt-side.

It was, alas, a hopelessly unequal struggle, and one long-fingered true-hand darted out and claimed one of the crisp, green stalks.

"*Gotcha*," Commander Honor Stephanie Harrington murmured softly.

❊   ❊   ❊

"Welcome back aboard, Everett," Honor said as Lieutenant Janacek stepped into her briefing room twenty-five minutes later. He started to come to attention, but she only pointed at the chair whose back Nimitz had been decorating when Bonrepaux dropped off the bribe-loaded tray.

"Sit," she said.

"Thank you, Ma'am."

The youthful Marine settled into the indicated seat, and Honor leaned toward him slightly, resting her forearms on the table and clasping her hands lightly.

"I've been looking over your reports," she continued, coming straight to the point. "Now that the Silesians have taken possession of your prisoners, I'm sure they're going to want all the paperwork and evidentiary material as quickly as possible. So I thought I'd ask if there's anything you think should be added to your existing remarks."

Janacek didn't reply immediately, and Honor's right eyebrow rose millimetrically. Nimitz looked up from the stylus he'd been playing with, cocking his head, ears pricking, and Janacek glanced at the 'cat before he turned back to Honor.

"Ma'am, I don't know that it's something that ought to be added to the reports for the Sillies—I mean, the Silesians," he corrected himself quickly.

He might have colored just a bit, although it was difficult to tell, given the olive complexion which went so strangely with his arctic blue eyes. Honor's mouth twitched ever so slightly, but she had herself well in hand. She refused to laugh at his self-correction and embarrass him even further.

"What I meant to say, Ma'am," he went on, his tone edged with gratitude for her restraint, "is that I noticed something that seemed...odd to me. Out of kilter."

"'Out of kilter' exactly how?" Honor asked.

"It's just... Well, Ma'am, right after we took the *Evita*, those were some pretty unhappy pirates. I mean, alleged pirates." He managed to not—quite—roll his eyes as he added the qualifier the Silesian legal system insisted upon. "I think a lot of them expected us to just shove them out the lock," he continued. "When they figured out we weren't going to do that, they calmed down some, but they still seemed pretty damned nervous, if you understand me."

He looked at her, and she nodded. If she'd been someone captured in the act of committing piracy, she'd have been fairly nervous herself, she supposed.

"But then they found out we were taking them to Saginaw, Ma'am," Janacek said. "And when that happened, they got a lot less nervous, somehow."

"They did?" Honor murmured.

"Yes, Ma'am." Janacek was clearly relieved to have gotten out his observation without having her tell him he was imagining things. At the same time, he looked as if he might have felt better if she *had* told him that.

Honor would have felt better if she'd been able to tell him that, too. But young Lieutenant Janacek, despite his occasionally brash youthfulness, wasn't the sort to imagine things like that. And given the normal state of affairs in Silesia, there were entirely too many reasons why his observation might have been right on the money. She found herself wondering about Rear Admiral Zadawski's apparent delay in informing Sector Governor Charnowska's office about *Evita*. It was entirely possible that it was one more example of why Janacek's observation might not be mistaken.

Which was not a possibility Commander Honor Harrington especially cared to contemplate.

"Well, Everett," she said finally, "it may have been as simple as relief at the prospect of getting out of quarters as packed as the ones we crammed them into." It was evident from Janacek's expression that he didn't buy that particular explanation any more than she did. "At any rate," she continued more briskly, "I think you're probably right that it's not something we need to add to our reports or depositions for the local authorities."

"No, Ma'am."

"In that case, welcome back aboard. Go get yourself settled back into your quarters. And I'll expect you to join me, the exec, the master, and Lieutenant Hutchinson for dinner tonight."

"Yes, Ma'am."

Janacek stood, and this time he did come to attention.

"Dismissed, Lieutenant," Honor told him.

❋　　　❋　　　❋

Honor settled herself more comfortably into the pinnace's seat as the small, sleek craft separated from *Hawkwing* and sliced into the upper reaches of the planet Jasper's atmosphere.

It was, she acknowledged, a beautiful planet. Fractionally larger than Old Earth, its gravity ran about one percent higher than humanity's birth world, which made it only about seventy-five percent that of Honor's own home world. Of course, the majority of planets humanity had chosen to settle had gravities lower than Sphinx's, and she was accustomed to feeling light on her toes when she visited other worlds.

The two planets had very similar hydrospheres, however, and almost exactly the same axial inclinations, which was pleasantly homey. On the other hand, Jasper's orbital radius was less than half that of Sphinx, which gave it a far shorter (and far warmer) year. One, in fact, which was almost identical with that of the planet Manticore.

She watched the display on the passenger compartment's forward bulkhead as the pinnace arrowed towards Onyx and wondered once again how the city had avoided ending up known as "Landing" or "First Landing" or "Footfall" like most other capitals. It made a change, at least, she reflected as Onyx's buildings grew rapidly larger on the display.

For that matter, she'd noticed on her previous visits that the system and sector capital looked far more welcoming than many a Silesian city she'd visited. Its broad avenues, green belts, parks, and water features were clearly evident on the display driven by the pinnace's forward optical head, and she saw remarkably little evidence of the slums which were so much a part of the typical Silesian urban landscape. They were there—she knew they were, and if she looked closely, she could find them—but they seemed less extensive than usual, and she told herself that was a good sign.

Frankly, at the moment, she could use any good omens she could find. *Hawkwing* had orbited Jasper for over five days now, and after taking custody of her prisoners, the evidence, and the various detailed reports and depositions (from her own personnel, the pirates' freed captives, and *Sywan Oberkirch*'s complement), the planetary authorities seemed to have had very little to say to Commander Harrington or her ship's company. There was no way of knowing how much of that was due to simple bureaucratic inefficiency and how much to deliberate delay on the part of Rear Admiral Zadawski and/or his staff, or even—for that matter, and despite her apparent attitude—on Sector Governor Charnowska's part. For that matter, Honor supposed it was entirely possible she was simply over-refining on a perfectly unexceptionable and easily explained series of delays. It wasn't as if the Silesian Ministry of Justice was any more efficient than any other part of the Confederacy's government. Or as if that government as a whole felt any burning urgency to appear to kowtow to Manticoran concerns with piracy, for that matter. At least some of that was perfectly understandable, however, given the two star nations' past history, and lack of urgency didn't necessarily equal a refusal to act. Nonetheless, there were times she'd found herself rather wistfully wishing she'd gone ahead and taken Commodore Teschendorff up on his offer. He'd certainly been right about how long this looked like taking, at any rate!

Not that it was all bad. She had, indeed, been able to grant liberty to most of her people, and Lieutenant (JG) Ottomar Mason, her logistics officer, had managed not only to revictual the ship, but also to scrounge up several other items which had been in short supply. She was pleased he'd been able to do that, but even more by the opportunity to get the members of her crew some time planet-side. It was good for people who lived so much of their lives in the sealed environments of their starships to actually smell open air and maybe even find the opportunity to walk on a beach somewhere, or soak up a little sun—a point Taylor Nairobi had made to *her* just this morning.

"Unless I'm mistaken, Skipper," he'd said after completing his daily report, "everybody aboard the *Hawk*'s managed to get dirtside . . . except you."

"Nonsense," she'd retorted. "I've been planet-side three or four times."

"And every time it's been to call on the governor or for some other official appointment," Nairobi pointed out. "Not exactly what I'd call a 'liberty,' Skip."

"But—"

"Don't start making excuses." Nairobi's stern tone had been rather undermined by the twinkle in his eyes. "Just say, 'Yes, Mr. Exec, I believe you have a point. And while I'm down there sampling the local cuisine, I believe I'll keep an eye out for a new cookbook for my father's collection.'"

Honor had opened her mouth once more to protest that she had entirely too much paperwork to go gallivanting off, but she closed it again. First, because Nairobi had a point. She needed to spend some time on a real, living planet just as badly as any of her crewpeople did. Secondly, because the fact that all of her visits had, in fact, been official, meant Nimitz hadn't been planet-side, either. Despite what she might have said to him after her courtesy call to Sector Governor Charnowska, he didn't have to look mournful to make her feel guilty for denying him that treat. If human beings needed time in a nonartificial environment, that was even truer for someone with the keen senses of a treecat. And the exec's last shot had been a shrewd one, as well, since most of her officers had discovered that she did indeed make it a habit to collect cookbooks for her father.

Which was how she found herself headed for the Melchior Rajmund and Emiliá Reginá Stankiewicz Interstellar Spaceport (universally referred to as simply "Capital Spaceport" for fairly obvious reasons) this rainy spring day.

✳   ✳   ✳

"Well, if it isn't Commander Harrington!"

Honor turned in surprise, and her almond eyes widened as she found herself face to face with none other than Commodore Mieczyslaw Teschendorff.

Who, she discovered, was one of the tallest human beings she'd ever met.

Honor Harrington was accustomed to towering over virtually every woman she met, and of being as tall as—or taller than—most men, as well. Teschendorff, however, stood well over two meters in height. She wasn't used to looking across at someone else's third or fourth tunic button, and from his solid, broad-shouldered physique, it seemed evident that his height wasn't the product of a low-gravity homeworld environment, either.

"Commodore Teschendorff," she responded after a moment, coming to attention and saluting. He returned her Manticoran-style salute with a somewhat less crisp rendition of the Silesian version, then gazed interestedly at the silky-coated treecat on her shoulder.

Nimitz looked back at him, green eyes bright and alert, one true-hand resting lightly on top of the white beret that marked Honor as the commander of a hyper-capable starship of the Royal Manticoran Navy. The 'cat's ears were up, his head tilted slightly to one side, and Honor felt the soft, heavy plume of his tail switching ever so gently from side to side against her back.

"So, Commander," Teschendorff said, "am I correct in assuming that your companion there"—he nodded in Nimitz's direction—"is a Sphinxian treecat?"

"Yes, Sir. He is." Honor didn't quite manage to conceal her surprise at Teschendorff's question. Very few of the people she'd met outside the Star Kingdom of Manticore had any clue what a treecat was.

"I thought it might be." Teschendorff looked pleased, then chuckled at her expression. "Xenobiology and botany are hobbies of mine, Commander Harrington," he explained. "I'm particularly interested in nonhuman sapients, and I understand your Star Kingdom's Constitution formally recognizes treecats as the planet Sphinx's native sentient species. They're tool-users, I believe?"

"Yes, Sir, they are," Honor replied, and realized she was torn between pleasure that Teschendorff obviously really did know something about the 'cats and a native Sphinxian's almost instinctive protectiveness towards the furry arboreals.

"Fascinating. That makes *two* nonhuman sapients in your Star Kingdom, now that you've established that protectorate over the Basilisk System. That has to be a record for a star nation with so few star systems."

"I believe it is," Honor agreed.

Teschendorff nodded, still contemplating Nimitz with obvious fascination and pleasure, and she wondered if the Silesian had also heard about the 'cats' telepathic abilities. That particular treecat capability was one which the humans who knew them best went to some length to downplay except with people they knew well and trusted. There'd been a few nasty incidents early on in human-treecat relations, especially when unscrupulous bio researchers—the planet Mesa came to mind—had tried to acquire specimens of treecats in order to probe their reputed telepathy.

"Well!" Teschendorff said after a few more seconds, almost visibly shaking himself. "May I ask what brings you to the fair city of Onyx, Commander? Official business, or personal?"

"Personal, this time, Sir."

"Indeed?" Teschendorff regarded her thoughtfully for a moment, then seemed to come to a decision.

"As it happens, Commander Harrington, I'm here on personal business this morning, as well. *Feliksá* has finished her trials, and Captain Holt and I will be returning to our station in Hillman in the next day or so. So I thought I should spend today visiting one of my favorite restaurants here on Jasper. I was stationed here for some time, you know."

"No, Sir," Honor replied (not entirely truthfully), "I didn't know that."

"Well, I was. And I have to say that it was my experience when I was here that Jasper's cuisine is superior to most. Have you had the opportunity to sample it yet?"

"I'm afraid not." Honor smiled. "As a matter of fact, Nimitz and I"—she indicated the treecat on her shoulder as she named him—"are just on our way to repair that omission."

"Really? Did you have a particular restaurant in mind?"

"Not yet, Sir."

"Well, if you'll forgive me for pointing this out, you might find it just a bit difficult to gain admittance to most of our restaurants—including, I'm afraid, almost all the better ones—with what most of the local citizenry is going to persist in regarding as a 'pet' on your shoulder."

Honor grimaced at the reminder. It wasn't as if she hadn't had that experience more than once. Even some *Manticoran* restaurants reacted that way.

"What I was thinking," Teschendorff went on before she could respond, "is that I've never actually had the opportunity to make a treecat's acquaintance. If you and—Nimitz, was it?—wouldn't object to my making the most of that opportunity, it would be my pleasure to invite you as my guest to one of my own favorite restaurants. One where I feel reasonably confident my own modest endorsement might convince the management to regard him as yet one more diner and not someone's pet."

Honor gazed at him, feeling Nimitz on her shoulder, and wondered exactly what lay behind that invitation. It was possible that it was as simple as Teschendorff was suggesting. On the other hand, it had been Honor's experience that the universe normally wasn't quite that straightforward. And the intensity with which Nimitz continued to regard the Silesian officer suggested that he found something about Teschendorff just as fascinating as Teschendorff appeared to find him, which raised all sorts of interesting questions.

But if, in fact, Teschendorff had any sort of ulterior—or at least so far unstated—motives for his invitation, the only way to find out what they might be was to accept it. Besides, the opportunity for an officer of her own seniority to make the acquaintance of a senior commodore in someone else's navy didn't come along every day.

"In that case, Sir," she heard herself say, "Nimitz and I would be honored to accept."

＊　　＊　　＊

Commodore Teschendorff's restaurant of choice turned out to rejoice in the name of Chez Fiammetta's del Shenyang. Honor was no linguistic expert, but that name seemed even more gloriously mangled than usual to her, and she experienced a distinct twinge of doubt as she and Nimitz followed Teschendorff across an antique walkway of rain-glistening bricks and through its relatively modest front door.

She wasn't a bit surprised when the maître d' raised both eyebrows and began an automatic protest at the sight of Nimitz, but if she'd had any doubt about Teschendorff's status as a regular, the speed with which the maître d' surrendered to the commodore's "explanation" would have banished them. As far as she could tell, no money even changed hands, yet within minutes, the two of them—and Nimitz—were seated at a linen-draped table looking out through multi-paned doors at a garden. The restaurant was built in a hollow square around the garden, and there were dining tables scattered among local flowering shrubs with brilliant blue leaves and crimson blossoms around the small fountain which formed the garden's centerpiece. Under less damp conditions, they must have been the best seats in the house, she thought a bit wistfully.

A waiter materialized at Teschendorff's elbow.

"Have you had the opportunity to sample any of the local wines, Commander?" the commodore asked.

"Actually, Sir, I'm not particularly fond of wine. Or, rather, I'm afraid my father is a much pickier wine snob than I am, and I've tried to avoid falling into that particular snare."

Teschendorff chuckled and shook his head, and she smiled at him.

"What I would like to sample, if I may," she continued, turning to the waiter, "is the local beer. I'm particularly partial to the dark beers or a good lager."

"I see."

The waiter's accent didn't sound like any of the local accents Honor had yet heard, and his complexion was considerably darker than a typical Jasperite's, as well. His eyes went a bit distant for a moment as he appeared to think deeply, then they sharpened again.

"If I may, Ma'am," he said then, "perhaps I might suggest the Lanzhou Dark. In my personal opinion, it's the best of our house beers."

"I'll second that, Commander," Teschendorff put in.

"In that case, let's go ahead and give it a try," Honor said with a smile.

"And I'll have my own usual, John," Teschendorff told him.

"Of course, Sir. And for your companion, Commander?" the waiter asked, looking courteously at Nimitz in the highchair she'd requested.

"For now, Nimitz will just have ice water, thank you." Honor was pleased—and more than a bit surprised—that he'd asked.

"Um, should I bring it in a *glass*, Ma'am?"

"That would be fine," Honor told him with another, broader smile. "I think a straw might be in order, though."

"Of course," he murmured again, and departed.

❖   ❖   ❖

What followed was among Honor's more . . . unusual gastronomical experiences. The restaurant's apparently absurd name, it turned out, was an accurate reflection of its culinary offerings. Honor had no idea whether or not Chez Fiammetta's was remotely typical of

Jasperite restaurants, but its cuisine was a unique—and surprisingly delicious—fusion of Old Earth's French, Italian, and Chinese cookery. At Teschendorff's suggestion, she began with a soup course—a lemongrass gnocchi with shrimp—accompanied by a crisp green salad with seared tuna (although the fish in question didn't look a thing like the Old Earth—or Sphinxian—species of the same name) and ginger dressing. The entrée was a house specialty which she could only think of as chow mein with prawns and Italian sausage in Alfredo sauce, garnished with ripe olives, which sounded bizarre, at best, but turned out to be extraordinarily tasty. And at Teschendorff's suggestion, she added the House *Profiteroles au Chocolat* for dessert, which turned out to be equally delicious . . . despite the touch of licorice in the hot chocolate sauce and even though it had never occurred to her to try coconut ice cream instead of vanilla.

Nimitz had been equally well cared for, with a *Carpaccio de Boeuf* with a side order of celery sticks stuffed with a pesto and cream cheese blend. Teschendorff had watched with evident interest (and amusement) as the treecat devoured his meal with impeccable table manners, and their waiter seemed equally fascinated by his unusual diner.

It turned out to be one of the most pleasant meals Honor had ever enjoyed in Silesia, and Teschendorff turned out to be an equally pleasant dinner companion. He did, indeed, ask a great many questions—all of them intelligent and thoughtful—about both Nimitz and the Medusans who inhabited the sole oxygen-nitrogen planet of the Basilisk System, and unlike many Silesians she'd met, he appeared to be equally willing to answer questions about his star nation, in return. She was careful not to ask the sort of questions which might give offense, yet on more than one occasion, he ended up discussing aspects of the Confederacy's endemic instability with what she privately considered to be devastating frankness for any serving Silesian officer.

All of which led her to reappraise his initial offer to take *Evita* off her hands.

"Well, Commander," Teschendorff said finally, "I've enjoyed the conversation and the company, but I'm afraid I have an appointment."

He laid his folded napkin on the table and stood. Honor rose as well, but he waved her back into her chair.

"There's no need for you to run off, Commander Harrington,"

he told her with a smile. "I know you said you weren't a 'wine snob,' but there's an orange blossom Muscat I wish you'd try."

"Commodore, you've been entirely too generous—" Honor began, but Teschendorff only shook his head with another, broader smile.

"You and Nimitz have put up with more than enough questions to leave me in your debt," he told her. "Besides, I fully intend to turn in the receipts for our repasts as part of my professional training and networking budget."

She looked at him for a moment, then shrugged and smiled back at him.

"All right, Sir. I still think you're being too generous, but I'm greedy enough to go ahead and take you up on it, anyway."

"Good! It's been a pleasure, Commander. I hope we encounter one another again."

He half-bowed, then turned and walked away, pausing on his way out of the restaurant to say something to their waiter.

A moment later, the waiter appeared at Honor's elbow with a wine bottle for her examination. He extracted the cork, and she went through the entire sniffing, tasting, and approving ritual just as if she actually knew what she was doing.

As with the rest of Teschendorff's suggestions, this one turned out to be excellent, and she sat back, looking out the windows at the garden while she enjoyed it. The rain had stopped, and shafts of sunlight reached down through the breaking banks of charcoal cloud to wake winking reflections from the wet brick walkways and splash the flowerbeds and shrubbery with bursts of brilliant, rain-drenched color.

She was just preparing to leave Chez Fiammetta's, not without a certain regret, when her waiter reappeared.

"Do you require anything else, Commander Harrington?" he asked her.

"No," she told him with a smile. "No, thank you. You've taken wonderful care of Nimitz and me."

"You're entirely welcome, Ma'am," he replied, then cocked his head to one side. "Excuse me," he continued, "but I couldn't help overhearing some of your conversation with the Commodore, especially about your companion here." He nodded slightly in Nimitz's direction. "I gathered that you were Manticoran. Given what you had to say about treecats and where they come from, I was wondering if you'd happen to be from Sphinx, yourself?"

"Yes," Honor said a bit slowly after a moment, her eyes narrowing. "As it happens, Nimitz and I are both from Sphinx."

"Well, I couldn't help wondering—especially given . . . Nimitz's presence—if you might happen to be related to Dr. *Allison* Harrington?" Honor's narrowed eyes widened suddenly. "She's from Beowulf, originally," the waiter went on a bit quickly.

"As a matter of fact," Honor replied even more slowly, "Dr. Harrington is my mother."

The waiter's eyes widened, yet Nimitz was watching him closely now, and Honor had the impression that the man wasn't really surprised by the fact that she was Allison Benton-Ramirez y Chou Harrington's daughter. He seemed more surprised by the fact that she was a naval officer . . . or that she was here on Jasper, perhaps. She wasn't certain why she thought that, but the impression was quite strong.

He seemed to hesitate for a moment, as if making his mind up about something, then cleared his throat.

"Forgive me, Ma'am. I'm sure I seem to be poking my nose into your affairs, and I apologize for that, but I didn't really expect to encounter Dr. Harrington's daughter here in Silesia. Now that I have, I can't help wondering if you happen to share your mother's views on genetic slavery."

Honor managed not to blink. She knew bizarre coincidences abounded, and she'd experienced more than a few of them herself, yet nothing had prepared her for the possibility of encountering someone who actually seemed to know her *mother* here in Silesia. Nor could she imagine where this conversation was headed. Still, there was only one honest answer to the question he'd just asked.

"Yes," she said, looking him levelly in the eye. "Yes, I do."

"Somehow," he murmured, "that doesn't really surprise me."

"May I ask why not?" she inquired, grasping the dilemma firmly by the horns.

"Why I'm not surprised, Ma'am?" He smiled crookedly. "I haven't seen your mother in a great many years, Commander, but I know several members of her family—your family, I suppose, for that matter—on Beowulf quite well, actually. And I'm familiar with its history."

"And is there a specific reason that you've drawn this to my attention? Besides a simple desire to reminisce about my Beowulfan relatives, I mean?"

"Actually, there is," he said in a much quieter voice. "I don't think this is the time or place to explain it all, though. Is there some way I could reach you aboard your ship...without anyone knowing?"

Honor's eyes were no longer merely puzzled. They'd narrowed and hardened, yet despite the intensity of the gaze she bent upon the waiter, she was watching Nimitz out of the corner of her vision, as well. The 'cat's ears were upright but pointed in the waiter's direction, his slit-pupilled eyes were intent, and the very tip of his tail curled up in a sort of frozen question mark. Whatever else might be happening here, Nimitz obviously sensed no immediate threat.

Which, coupled with the waiter's last question, gave Honor furiously to think.

"I can't answer that," she said finally. "I can tell you that any conversation with my ship would be completely secure from *our* end, but I'm not in any position to vouch for its security from *this* end."

She didn't bother to add that any breach of her ship's communications security from the Jasper end would be a serious violation of all sorts of solemn interstellar agreements. Nor, from the look in his eyes, was he surprised by her response. Or happy about it, for that matter.

"It happens," she heard her own voice continuing, without any conscious decision on her part, "that no one expects me back aboard in the next two or three hours, though."

The waiter brightened visibly.

"In that case, Commander," he said, "I mean, given that you've got some time to kill before returning to your ship and that it's stopped raining, I wonder if you've seen Wozniak Park?"

"I beg your pardon?"

"Wozniak Park, Ma'am. I mean, Mikolaj Wozniak Memorial Park. It's named for the first Saginaw Sector governor, Mikolaj Wozniak. It's quite close, actually—only about three and a half kilometers from here—and it's famous throughout the system for its landscaping and water features."

"No," she said, watching his expression closely. "No, I haven't had the opportunity to visit it yet."

"Well, I'd really hate for you to miss it," he said. "Especially if you don't have to be back aboard your ship for another couple of hours. I think"—he looked straight into her eyes—"that you'd find it well worth your time."

Honor glanced at Nimitz one last time. The treecat still seemed fascinated by the waiter, but she saw no sign of threat response in his body language, and she looked back at the man.

"I appreciate the advice," she told him. "And, given the strength of the recommendation, I may just try to take a look at it before I head back to the port."

❋   ❋   ❋

"Tell me, Stinker—do *you* think I've lost my mind? Because I've got to tell you," Honor Harrington shook her head, gazing out across the sparkling blue waters of Mikolaj Wozniak Memorial Park's central lake, "*I'm* pretty sure I have!"

She and Nimitz sat on a bench which was still slightly damp under a sky which had turned into crystal blue banded with chunks of still dark-bottomed clouds. Sunlight highlighted the upper portions of those clouds dramatically in dazzling white, and Honor found herself wondering if today were some sort of local holiday, given the number of obviously school-aged children who seemed to be materializing out of thin air. Dozens of remote-controlled boats dotted the lake's surface, including some of the best working sail-powered vessels Honor had ever seen. At least one of them had three fully rigged masts, and as she watched, the model—probably the next best thing to two meters in length—came about, head sails and yards resetting themselves smoothly. Others churned busily about under power, and despite the relatively cool weather (for Jasper; for Sphinx, it was actually quite warm), a couple of dozen kids were wading in the lake's shallows. More were tearing about madly in some local variant of tag, and shouts, laughter, and squeals of delight wafted from playground equipment and a magnificently muddy soccer field in a backdrop of such utter normalcy that it was hard to remember she was really here to do anything but enjoy the park.

Nimitz didn't seem to have any trouble remembering that, though. As she finished her question, he stood straight up right in her lap, turning to face her, and laid the palm of one long-fingered true-hand against her cheek, then shook his head in an unmistakable "no." She looked down at him, and her lips quirked in a smile.

"I'd feel better about your diagnosis if you hadn't so happily gone along with some of the other incredibly stupid things I've done in my life," she told him severely. "Like, oh, buzzing the commodore during the Regatta, for example. You and Mike both thought that one was a wonderful idea, if memory serves."

The 'cat bleeked, wrinkling his muzzle and twitching his long whiskers at her. She grinned back at him, although there was a certain degree of truth to her accusation. Nimitz had the soul of a practical joker with a particularly low sense of humor, and he'd gleefully aided and abetted her in more than one outrageous Academy prank. The incident with the Regatta was simply the most spectacular one for which they'd been *caught*.

She chuckled and wrapped both arms around him, lowering her head until the bottom of her chin rested gently on top of his skull. They sat quietly, admiring the park—which truly was as beautiful as the bizarre waiter had told her it was—and the radio-controlled sailboats slicing across it on the brisk afternoon breeze, and her smile slowly faded.

It was never a good idea for the captain of a Queen's ship to go traipsing off on her own, and Honor was well aware of that minor fact. If she hadn't been able to figure it out on her own, she'd sat through literally dozens of security briefings which would have made the point for her quite nicely. There were any number of ill-intentioned souls who would just love to get their hands on the sort of information a starship commander could provide. Or, for that matter, on the ransom money the Royal Navy might decide to pay to get her back before all that information got compromised.

Up until the point she'd headed for this park, any threat to her personal security had been minimal. The spaceport and its immediate environs were probably the best policed areas of the entire planet, since it would never have done for tourists and important business travelers to find themselves robbed, assaulted, or abducted. Chez Fiammetta's had been no more than a couple of kilometers outside the port itself, and she and Teschendorff had made the trip to it in an air taxi, so security hadn't been much of an issue then, either.

It was now...and she knew it.

She hadn't taken any taxis to get to the park. Instead, she'd walked, and more than one set of curious eyes had followed the space-black-and-gold Manticoran uniform along the damp, shaded sidewalk. Now she was simply sitting here, holding Nimitz in her lap on the lakeside bench, and she had no doubt that if Nimitz had been wrong about the waiter's emotions the two of them had to present an incredibly tempting target to anyone who wished her—or Manticore—ill.

Of course, there were targets... and then there were *targets*. Anyone who'd never seen a Sphinxian treecat in action could probably be excused for thinking of Nimitz as primarily an adorable, fluffy pet. For that matter, the 'cat went to considerable pains to project exactly that image. The truth was rather different, given his ability to sense the emotions of any potential enemy at ranges of up to a couple of hundred meters, especially if those emotions focused upon him or his person. Then there was the fact that a treecat's natural weapons were astonishingly lethal, especially for a creature of its diminutive size. And in addition to Nimitz's abilities and weaponry, there was the three-millimeter pulser in the shoulder holster under Honor's tunic. It wasn't as heavy as the weapon she'd habitually carried in a belt holster from the time she was twelve whenever she ventured into the Sphinx bush with Nimitz, but it ought to be sufficient to deal with just about anything smaller than a hexapuma. It was her constant companion whenever she went dirt-side on her own, and she routinely shot "High Expert" on the Navy and Marine pistol courses.

None of which changed the fact that she was sitting here, enjoying the breeze as it caressed her short-cropped hair, on a bench in a public park on a Silesian planet at the invitation of a man she'd never met before who seemed to know an awful lot about her and her family. If she hadn't actually lost her mind, she'd certainly managed to display enough questionable judgment to get on with.

Nimitz twitched in her arms, and she straightened. The treecat turned his head, looking along one of the paths, and she followed his gaze, then stiffened ever so slightly as she recognized the waiter. He saw her at about the same time she saw him, and something about his body language suggested a combination of both surprise and relief.

He looked both ways, up and down the path and across the lake, then quickened his pace very slightly, strolled up to her, and waved one hand at the bench on which she sat.

"May I join you, Commander?"

"It's a public bench," she pointed out, and he smiled slightly.

"So it is," he agreed, and settled gingerly into place.

She studied him frankly, and he sat patiently, giving her time. His eyes were a peculiar shade of amber, almost yellow, and his dark complexion had an odd cast which wasn't quite like anything she'd ever seen before. Not surprisingly, probably, given the variations the two thousand years of mankind's Diaspora had worked into the basic warp and woof of humanity. But there was something about him . . . something—

Her thoughts chopped off abruptly as he opened his mouth and stuck out his tongue.

It was an absurdly childish gesture . . . except that it wasn't. Given her family history, she knew exactly what she was looking at as he showed her the barcode of a genetic slave on his tongue.

He let her look at it for an instant, then closed his mouth, and this time his crooked smile was bitter.

"I told you I knew your family on Beowulf, Commander," he said. "In fact, I once met your mother personally, although I doubt she remembers it. She was barely out of high school at the time."

"Mother's memory might surprise you," Honor replied. She knew she sounded as if she were playing for time—since she was—but she also chuckled. "Mind you, that memory of hers can be pretty selective when it suits her purposes."

"And yours, Commander? Can your memory be selective when it suits *your* purposes?"

Honor regarded him thoughtfully for several seconds, then shrugged.

"I'm not going to answer that just yet," she told him. He looked a question at her, and she flicked her right hand in a throwing-away gesture. "I'm not going to give you any sort of carte blanche, not until I've got some idea what this is really all about, and I'm not going to pretend I will, either. I don't imagine you'd have gone to all the trouble of inviting me to meet with you out here if you didn't have something fairly significant on your mind. If you want to go ahead and tell me about it, I'm willing to listen. I'm not willing to give you any guarantees about what I'll do if I don't like what I hear."

She held his gaze very levelly.

"Bearing that in mind, do you want to continue this conversation? Or should we both just sit here and admire the lake?"

"You're rather more direct than your relatives back on Beowulf, Commander. Did you know that?"

"I take after Daddy's side of the family in that respect, I think," she said, and he snorted.

"That's certainly *one* way to describe him," he said feelingly, and Honor allowed one eyebrow to arch at the fresh evidence that he knew a very great deal, indeed, about her and her family.

He sat looking at her for several more thoughtful seconds, then gave his head an odd little toss. It was a decisive gesture, and he turned sideways on the bench to face her fully.

"In case you're wondering, Commander, I didn't have any idea you'd be anywhere near the Saginaw System before Commodore Teschendorff walked you into the restaurant. I mean, I don't want you thinking my presence here on Jasper has anything to do with *your* presence here on Jasper. It's just one of those things that happens every once in a while, however unlikely they may seem."

Honor watched him levelly, but Nimitz's right hand-foot pressed very gently against her thigh in the signal that told her the waiter was telling her the truth.

"I suppose I can accept that coincidences happen," she said.

"When I began to realize who you might be—to be honest, it was Nimitz that started me thinking about it, then I saw your eyes." The waiter shook his head. "Did you know you have your mother's eyes?"

"It's about the only part of her I *did* get," Honor said wryly. Her own overgrown gawkiness had been an even more painful cross to bear during her prolong-extended adolescence because of her own mother's exquisite, almost feline beauty. Honor loved Allison Harrington dearly, but there was still a part of her which couldn't quite forgive her mother for being so much more beautiful than she herself would ever be.

The waiter started to say something, then shook his head and changed whatever it had been into something else.

"Working here in Onyx, I hear things," he said. "In fact, I hear lots of things. For example, I hear that the *Evita*'s case has already been resolved. In a manner of speaking."

"Resolved?" Honor repeated sharply, straightening on the bench. "What do you mean, '*resolved*'?"

"I mean the good ship *Evita*—and her entire sadly misunderstood and maligned crew—has mysteriously vanished," the waiter told her. He watched the shock and fury welling up in her eyes, then shook his head. "Surely that's not a *complete* surprise, Commander!"

Honor managed not to glare at him. Nimitz quivered against her with the barely audible sound of a snarl which wasn't directed at the waiter but fully mirrored her own rage. Then her nostrils flared, and she grimaced.

"No," she admitted. "Not a *complete* surprise. I wish it was."

"I'm sure you do."

The waiter's amber eyes were oddly sympathetic, almost gentle, yet she saw something else under the sympathy that was anything but gentle.

"I'm well aware of Governor Charnowska's vocal support for a closer, more cordial relationship with the Star Kingdom, as well, Commander," he continued. "I'm afraid, though, that the situation in this sector is . . . less than ideal, shall we say?"

"I'm sure it is." Honor leaned back. "On the other hand, I hope you won't be offended if I say it's obvious to me that you have some sort of information you want to share with me. Besides the disappearance of the *Evita,* I mean. You know as well as I do that I'd have found out about that soon enough on my own. So let's take it as a given that you dropped it on me to get my attention and demonstrate that you really do 'hear things' here in Onyx. Now suppose you tell me exactly who you are and exactly what it is I'm sitting here on this bench to hear about?"

He blinked at her directness, then chuckled, yet she sensed a new and deeper tension. It wasn't anything overt, nothing she could have pointed at, but she didn't need Nimitz to recognize the tautness of someone approaching a threshold or Rubicon. Then he drew in a lungful of air, let half of it out, and shrugged.

"My name is John Brown Matheson, Commander. My mother adopted the last name—Matheson—for the first officer of the Havenite heavy cruiser that captured the slaver she was on. I chose 'John Brown' when I joined the Audubon Ballroom."

Despite herself, Honor's eyes widened. The Ballroom was officially listed as a terrorist organization even by the Star Kingdom, which wasn't too surprising in light of the atrocities it was prone to inflict upon the employees and customers of Manpower, Incorporated. Simple executions were seldom enough for the vengeful ex-slaves and children of slaves who filled the Ballroom's ranks. Quite a few of them were fond of a ditty from an old pre-space operetta about "making the punishment fit the crime," and they had centuries of crimes to punish . . . and imaginations which were both inventive and grisly. Which was why even the Star Kingdom, which had hated and opposed the interstellar genetic slave trade for centuries, and which thoroughly sympathized with the victims of that trade, wasn't prepared to endorse the sort of carnage the Ballroom all too often wreaked.

Which, in turn, explained exactly why no serving officer of the Royal Manticoran Navy had any business at all sitting on a park bench talking with an acknowledged member of what was arguably the bloodiest—and certainly one of the most successful— organization of "terrorists" in the explored galaxy.

She ought to stand up immediately, nod pleasantly to him, and be on her way. She knew that perfectly well.

"And just why would a member of the Ballroom want to talk to *me*?" she asked instead.

The waiter—Matheson—didn't actually move a muscle, yet somehow he seemed to sag in relief, anyway. None of which showed in his voice as he continued in the same matter-of-fact tone.

"When I said this situation in Saginaw was 'less than ideal,' I was guilty of just a bit of understatement. As a matter of fact, the situation here in Saginaw is a hell of a lot worse than that, Commander Harrington. And at least a quarter of the rot is coming out of the Casimir System."

"Casimir?"

Honor couldn't keep a flicker of surprise out of her own voice. She knew relatively little about Casimir, but from what she remembered off the top of her head, Casimir was a K0 star with seven planets and a fairly extensive but not especially spectacular or valuable asteroid belt. Unlike most star systems, it did have two habitable planets, although Anná, the innermost of the two, was no great prize. Beatá—twenty percent larger and two light-minutes farther out than Anná—was supposed to be a much nicer proposition, although both of them combined had little more than five hundred million inhabitants.

"Casimir," Matheson said flatly, then snorted harshly. "I don't blame you for being surprised. The reason there's so much grief coming out of Casimir right now is that the people responsible for it deliberately picked what you might call an out-of-the-way spot to set up shop."

"And who might those 'people' be?" Honor asked, watching his expression closely.

"Manpower." Madison's flat, uninflected tone made the single word the filthiest obscenity in his vocabulary.

"Manpower's established a major slave depot in Casimir," he continued in a marginally less passion-flattened voice. "It's rapidly becoming the primary transshipment point for the slave trade here in the Confederacy, as well as for several other independent star systems out this way."

Honor knew from Nimitz's reaction that Matheson wasn't lying to her, but that didn't mean what he thought was the truth actually was, and for the life of her she didn't see any logical reason for Manpower to put one of its clandestine slave-trading depots in Silesia. That thought must have showed in her eyes, because Matheson shook his head.

"Before you decide I don't know what I'm talking about," he said, "think about this. The wealthy and corrupt families here in the Confederacy are even wealthier—and a lot more corrupt—than their counterparts most places. Let's face it, the entire Confederacy doesn't have a pot to piss in compared to the Star Kingdom or the Solarian League, but people with the right connections can still squeeze an obscene amount of money out of their less fortunate neighbors. People with the right connections to become, oh, a system governor—or even a *sector* governor—let's say. And whenever there's that much money and that much economic corruption floating around, personal corruption and degeneracy are never far behind. That's why the Ballroom has so many people scattered around the Confederacy. The kind of sick SOBs who dabble in 'pleasure slaves' or who simply prefer the sorts of 'resorts' someone with connections to Manpower can offer them, are thicker on the ground out here than in a lot of places."

He held Honor's eyes for a moment, and she nodded slowly.

"On the other hand, I never said the Casimir depot is just for the slave trade. Manpower's got connections with any black market or illegal trade you'd care to name, and the Jessyk Combine is using Casimir as a transfer point for all kinds of cargoes no one wants to bring openly through customs, even here in the Confederacy." He grimaced, lips working as if he wanted to spit on the ground. "There're billions of Solarian credits worth of illegal goods and services—slaves, drugs, black-market weapons, stolen technology, you name it—being handled through Casimir, Commander. We didn't find out about it immediately, of course, but it's been going on for over two T-years now, and 'business' is growing steadily."

She believed him, Honor realized. She would have believed him even without Nimitz's endorsement of his truthfulness. And she also found herself wondering if it was remotely possible Commodore Teschendorff had deliberately steered her to Chez Fiammetta...and to this particular waiter.

On the face of it, that was even more ridiculous than anything Matheson had told her. Teschendorff was a *commodore*, with an entire squadron of heavy cruisers under his command. What possible reason could an officer that senior have for deliberately putting the captain of a mere destroyer—and one which belonged to a foreign star nation, at that—into contact with a terrorist organization just so it could pass her this kind of information?

Yet even as she asked herself that question, she realized it might not be ridiculous at all. If Matheson was right about what was going on in Casimir, and if it had been going on as long as he said it had, then even the Confederacy Navy would have heard the odd hint about it by now. Which meant that if the Confeds weren't doing anything about it, it was because they'd been *told* not to. Some of them—a lot of them—were probably being paid off directly by Manpower, Jessyk, and the other outlaws and criminals using Casimir's services, but there had to be more to it than that. And given what Matheson had just said about corrupt sector governors, Honor had a sinking sensation about who was most likely to be protecting Casimir.

Which could just explain exactly why Commodore Teschendorff might have embarked on something as Byzantine as deliberately throwing Honor together with Matheson—assuming, of course, that the commodore knew or suspected enough about Matheson's Ballroom connections to steer her that way. If she'd been a senior officer who thought something like Casimir was going on in a sector adjacent to her own assigned duty station—somewhere where she herself had no authority—and she had reason to know it was being protected at the highest level, she might just want to draw it to the Star Kingdom's attention, as well.

Especially given the Manticoran position on the Cherwell Convention and the genetic slave trade in general.

Great, she thought sardonically. *He and Matheson between them are telling the skipper of a single destroyer that's almost fifty T-years old about it. If Matheson's right about everything that's going on there, it'd take at least a couple of cruisers—not to mention a battalion or so of Marines—to do anything about it! And that doesn't even consider the fact that I'm under orders to cooperate with Charnowska. I can just imagine how the Admiralty's going to react if I go charging off and poke my nose into an illegal operation on this scale being carried out with the full knowledge and approval of the pro-Manticore sector governor we're supposed to be supporting!*

"I really appreciate your willingness to tell me all this," she said after a moment in a rather snappish tone. "But has anyone bothered to tell the *Silesians* about it? I mean, it *is* their star system."

Matheson didn't even bother to reply. He simply gave her a look that was so pitying she felt herself blush. But she also shook her head stubbornly.

"All right, forget I asked that. But I can hardly justify taking some sort of unilateral action—which is what you're really asking me to do, as we both realize perfectly well, even though at this particular moment I don't see a whole lot that I *could* do—without at least mentioning 'my' suspicions to the local authorities."

Matheson looked a lot more than just skeptical, and she shook her head again.

"If you're right about what's going on—and I don't know anything that would prove you're not—you're handing me a live hand grenade and inviting me to look for the pin. You know it, and I know it. And I'm sure you also know I've got my own orders from the Admiralty. To be perfectly honest, I'm of the opinion that those orders and the supplementary instructions I was given to go with them will pretty much preclude my doing anything at all about this beyond informing my own superiors about it as quickly as possible."

Disappointment flickered in Matheson's amber eyes, but she continued doggedly.

"I didn't say that was what I *wanted* to do; what I said is that it's what my orders will *limit* me to doing. And before I can do even that much and figure that anyone's going to listen to me, I have to be able to tell them I at least discussed the situation with Sector Governor Charnowska. Believe me, no flag officer is going to authorize an operation against an installation in sovereign

Silesian territory on the say-so of a mere commander—and one who's been hobnobbing with Ballroom terrorists, at that!—without having all of the formal i's dotted and t's crossed. It's just not going to happen.

"On the other hand, if Charnowska *doesn't* know about it, then it's my duty to tell her. And if she *does* know about it—if she's actually involved in it herself—she may decide it's time to cut her losses and shut things down before the Admiralty does do something about it unilaterally."

Matheson's expression made it abundantly clear that if she truly believed Charnowska would do anything of the sort she had no business wandering around without a keeper to wipe the drool off her chin. She half expected him to say so, but instead, he only shrugged.

"I don't think it will do a bit of good," he told her frankly, instead. "On the other hand, if you think that's what your duty requires you to do, I'm sure it's what you're going to do. I hope you'll keep the source of your information confidential, though?"

He raised both eyebrows, and she gave him an irritated, choppy nod. Of course she wouldn't tell Charnowska where she'd gotten it!

"Sorry," he apologized as he correctly interpreted her nod. Then he shrugged again.

"As I say, I'm sure you'll do what you think you have to do. At the same time, I'm about equally sure it won't do any good at all." He reached into his pocket and extracted a slip of paper with a handwritten com combination on it. "If I'm right about that, and if you decide you'd like to talk some more about this with me, call this number—from a ground station, please." He twitched his head in the direction of the miniature sailboats scudding across the lake. "Ask for Betsy and mention the sailboats on the lake here. Maybe you'll even decide to buy one from her."

He met her eyes as he held out the piece of paper, then stood as she took it.

"Good luck, Commander," he said, and walked away down the path, whistling.

＊　　＊　　＊

"Good morning, Commander Harrington."

Sector Governor Charnowska's smile was just as gracious as it had been the first time Honor met her, but somehow it seemed less welcoming to her this time. Perhaps it was because *this* time she'd gone ahead and brought Nimitz to the meeting. Charnowska might simply be one of those people who didn't like pets, although, if Honor had had to venture a guess, she would have bet on the governor's irritation stemmed less from any ingrained distaste for pets than from the fact that her visitor hadn't even asked if she could bring the pet in question along.

Or maybe it doesn't have a single thing to do with Nimitz one way or the other. Maybe *it's because she's been keeping an eye on me and doesn't approve of the people I've been talking to. And wouldn't* that *suggest all sorts of "interesting" things?*

"Good morning, Governor Charnowska," she said warmly, shaking the proffered hand. Then she waved her left hand in Nimitz's general direction. "I don't believe you've met Nimitz, Ma'am?"

"No, I haven't," the governor agreed, and behind her own careful expression, Honor gave a mental nod. Charnowska's tone answered at least one question. The governor clearly thought Honor was "introducing" her to a mere pet. Charnowska was willing to be pleasant and reasonably courteous about it, but it was clear that—unlike Teschendorff—she had no idea Sphinxian treecats were their home world's native sentient race.

Or of their rumored telempathic abilities.

"I promise he'll behave himself," Honor said out loud, playing to Charnowska's preconceptions. "He doesn't get off the ship very often, and he needs fresh air even more than most of us two-footed people do."

"I quite understand, Commander." Charnowska beckoned for Honor to follow her to what was obviously the governor's favorite position, in front of the windows once more. "Your request for this meeting mentioned something about . . . 'disturbing information' which has come to your attention, I believe?"

"I'm afraid that's true, Your Excellency," Honor replied in a considerably more formal, sober tone.

"That sounds ominous." Charnowska smiled briefly. "What sort of 'information,' Commander?"

"One of my people from *Hawkwing* picked up on a conversation in one of your local restaurants," Honor told her—truthfully enough, as far as it went—then paused.

"What sort of conversation?" Charnowska asked a bit impatiently.

"It was about the Casimir System, Your Excellency." Honor wasn't looking at the governor or trying to read the Silesian's expression; she was looking out the window and letting Nimitz read something considerably deeper than mere facial muscles. "According to what she heard, Manpower is operating a full-fledged depot in Casimir. Apparently, it's been going on for some time without its coming to the local authorities' attention."

"Nonsense!" Charnowska said sharply. Then she drew a deep breath and shook her head. "Pardon me, Commander. I don't wish to appear to be discounting your information out of hand, and I certainly wouldn't want to suggest that I feel anything but grateful for your having brought it to my attention. Officially informing the Confederacy of such a possibility, even when it turns out your information is an error, is exactly the sort of mutual cooperation I've been urging my colleagues here in Silesia to pursue—and welcome—for so long. At the same time, however, I feel quite confident your information *is* in error." She smiled again, even more briefly. "To be honest, it sounds to me as if someone realized your crewman was listening and decided to feed the 'foreigner' a false rumor as some sort of joke."

"Really?" Honor turned to face her as Nimitz's left true-foot pressed firmly against her spine, just below her shoulder blade, in the 'cat's signal that Charnowska was lying.

"I think that's the most probable explanation, at any rate," the governor said. "There could be any number of other explanations, of course—including the possibility that your man simply misheard something."

Honor wondered if the governor's use of the male pronoun meant Charnowska hadn't heard her own *female* pronoun, or if it was deliberate. If the other woman did know it was Honor herself who'd had the conversation in question, she might be using the wrong gender intentionally as a way to disguise the fact that her people had placed Honor under surveillance.

"Well, obviously Casimir is a Silesian system, not a Manticoran one," Honor observed. "And it's in the Saginaw Sector, of course, which means it's your jurisdiction. Not to mention the fact that it also means you undoubtedly have better contacts and sources of information than I do." *Which doesn't say one word about what you* do *with any information that comes your way.* "Still, my information is that the conversation was quite intense. If it was some sort of prank, the people behind it seem to have been playing it for all it was worth."

"People sometimes find peculiar things humorous, Commander," Charnowska said a bit more frostily. "And, while I may wish this weren't the case, it's also true that Manticorans aren't exactly what one might call universally beloved in the Confederacy." There was very little of a smile in the flash of bared teeth she showed Honor this time. "I'm afraid any number of Silesians would find it enormously entertaining to play something 'for all it was worth' if they could convince a Manticoran to believe nonsense or act foolishly on the basis of false information."

"I hadn't actually considered that possibility, Your Excellency." Which was also true; and she *still* wasn't considering it, either. "Do you really think it was as simple as that?"

"Yes, Commander, I do." The look Charnowska gave her clearly implied that she thought Honor was being particularly slow.

"Then you probably have a point." Honor tried to sound a bit penitent, like a relatively junior officer who'd just realized she was irritating a powerful foreign political figure. "In fact, I feel sure you do. Still, *Hawkwing* will be hypering out in a couple of days. Would you like us to stop in at Casimir on our way to Hyperion?"

"Hyperion?" Charnowska arched one eyebrow.

"Yes, Your Excellency. I've been instructed to touch base with the Hauptman Cartel's resource extraction operation there. Casimir would only take us day or so out of our way."

"Commander Harrington, I'm sure your time would be better spent in Hyperion than in Casimir. The Hauptman operation there is large enough to represent a significant economic resource for the entire sector, and, to be frank, I'm delighted your own government has made it a point to support and nurture it."

"I entirely agree," Honor said, doing her very best to play the part of the aforesaid relatively junior officer who was now scurrying to find some way (as unobtrusively as possible) of offering the aforesaid powerful foreign political figure an olive branch. "At the same time, as I said, visiting Casimir wouldn't delay us very much, and—"

"I appreciate your willingness to be of assistance," Charnowska said, "but I see absolutely no need for you to visit Casimir. And, to be frank, Commander, I'm not sure it would be either . . . tactful or wise."

"I beg your pardon, Ma'am?" Honor widened her eyes.

"I don't wish to belabor this point, particularly since I'm

fully aware that you're simply trying to be helpful and to pursue your instructions to cooperate and coordinate with the sector government."

Charnowska's tone was firm, even a bit cold, but not really unpleasant... yet.

"Having said that, however, I feel I should point out to you that Casimir, like Saginaw itself, is a Silesian star system and the sovereign territory of the Silesian Confederacy. I am, as I said, firmly of the opinion that there's nothing to this rumor your crewman overheard. Assuming he interpreted what was being said correctly, it was almost certainly exactly what I've already called it—a prank. It would be most unfortunate if in the pursuit of such an ill-founded assertion a Manticoran warship were to be perceived as interfering in Silesia's internal, purely domestic affairs. I'm sure"—Nimitz's left true-foot pressed even harder than before—"that you would have absolutely no intention of interfering in that manner. It might not *appear* that way to the local population and authorities, however, which would be... unfortunate."

The steadiness with which her eyes met Honor's made it quite clear who she intended to experience any "unfortunate" consequences.

The governor held her gaze for a couple of heartbeats, then inhaled and smiled brightly.

"Nonetheless, Commander," she said, "just to be on the safe side, I'll pass your comments on to Admiral Zadawski and also to our civilian investigative agencies. I'm sure they'll look into it carefully. In fact, since you were courteous enough to bring this information to me in the first place, I'll *insist* they do so and personally share their findings with you on your next visit to Saginaw. Will that be satisfactory?"

"Oh, completely!" Honor lied with deliberate haste. "It was never my intention to provoke some sort of an inci—um, I mean, *misunderstanding*, Your Excellency! I simply thought that since I'd brought the matter up, it might be helpful if I—That is, if I were able to come back to you and *confirm* that nothing untoward is going on there," she finished a bit lamely.

"I understand. We here in the Confederacy are quite capable of looking into this sort of rumor for ourselves, though, you know." The governor smiled, but it was obvious she was getting in another lick on a clearly rattled foreign naval officer whose misplaced zeal and credulity had gotten her into deep water.

"Of course you are, Your Excellency," Honor agreed fervently.

"Well, then!" Charnowska's smile broadened. "Was there anything else I could do for you today, Commander Harrington?"

"No, Ma'am. I'm—That is, I've taken up enough of your valuable time. I'm sorry to have disturbed you with something like this."

"Not at all," Charnowska said affably. "If you don't mention such rumors, there's no way anyone can dispel them for you, is there? And, to be fair, what seems painfully obvious to those of us who live here is likely to seem far less obvious to visitors from other star nations. I appreciate the fact that you did attempt to alert us to something we might not have been aware of."

"Thank you, Your Excellency." Honor managed to inject just a hint of obsequiousness into her answering smile. "With your permission, I'll withdraw now."

"Of course, Commander Harrington. Please feel free to contact me again if the need should arise."

"Oh, I will, Ma'am," Honor assured her.

But, she added mentally, *not as quickly as I'm going to contact Betsy to discuss sailboats.*

✳   ✳   ✳

"Hello?"

There was no visual on the display in the spaceport restaurant's com cubicle. Honor detested the small, cramped, mini-closets most public places offered for people who wanted to use their coms. She suspected the small size was partly due to the fact that so few people needed to use public com facilities, even on relatively backward planets like those here in Silesia, but she suspected even more strongly that the proprietors of places like this restaurant figured anyone who was using their com was doing it for reasons of privacy. They certainly made a point of posting theoretically "discreet" notices in highly visible places proclaiming that privacy (and security), and they charged an arm and a leg for their services and equipment.

Unlike the majority of the Silesians who might find themselves using this cubicle, however, Honor had brought along some interesting equipment of her own, as well. Using it for this particular purpose (or, at least, when she intended to contact these particular *people*) stretched several regulations right to the snapping point, and even with it, no guarantee could be perfect. But Manticoran tech was considerably better than anything one was likely to encounter in Silesia, and according to the palm-sized display on the small device on the shelf beside the com, no one happened to be tapping this line.

Probably, she reminded herself.

"I'm sorry," she said. "There's no image at my end, so I hope I have the right number. I'm trying to reach Betsy. I wanted to discuss the sailboats I saw on the park lake yesterday."

"It's the right number," the faceless voice said. It sounded like an older woman's, Honor thought. Or, at least, like a voice which was *supposed* to sound like an older woman's. "I'm afraid she isn't here just now, though," it continued. "You just missed her, actually. In fact, I believe she's on her way to the park right now. Did you want to buy one of the boats from her?"

"I wanted to discuss it, at least," Honor replied. "I sail quite a bit at home myself, and I've got a couple of younger cousins who'd probably really enjoy playing with them. From what I could see yesterday, I think it would actually be pretty fair early training for the real thing."

"Several people who've bought them said the same thing," the voice agreed. "If you want to talk to her, she'll probably be down at the lake for the next—oh, at least for a couple of hours. Maybe longer, if she's teaching one of her classes."

❉   ❉   ❉

Someone who'd been adopted by a treecat, Honor discovered, had certain advantages when it came to making covert contact with an unknown individual for the first time. There were actually three kiosks selling the remote-controlled sailboats by the park lake, but Nimitz steered her directly to the one she wanted with the unerring accuracy of a good radar tech.

The young woman behind the counter—"Betsy," Honor presumed—had the same olive complexion and oddly amber-colored eyes as John Brown Matheson. She also had Matheson's nose, although in a thankfully much more feminine version. In fact, she was quite attractive in a dark-haired, slender-yet-already-opulent way, and Honor suppressed a grimace. If "Betsy's" tongue carried a barcode, Honor was willing to bet that it was for one of the "courtesan" models—otherwise known as sex slaves.

"Yes?" the young woman (she couldn't have been much over eighteen or nineteen T-years old, prolong or no) said pleasantly as Honor walked up to her kiosk. "Can I help you...Captain?"

The slight pause and rising eyebrow which accompanied her greeting made it clear she was guessing at Honor's rank.

"It's Commander, actually," Honor replied. "And I think you may be able to. Someone told me that if I wanted to buy a couple of the sailboats I saw wandering around the lake yesterday, I should look for Betsy. Would it happen I've found her?"

"As a matter of fact, you have." The young woman gave her a bright, dimpled smile.

"Good!" Honor smiled back. "I was impressed enough by them that I definitely want one of my own. And—worse, from my perspective, if not from yours—I think I probably need at least a half dozen more of them, too." Her smile broadened slightly. "I've got a whole passel of cousins back on Sphinx, and each of them is going to want one of her very own when they see mine."

"Oh, my!" Betsy chuckled. "That's probably going to cost you a pretty credit, Commander!"

"Better I take a hit to the bank account than bring home too few to make everyone happy," Honor said with a fervency which was actually more than half genuine.

"Well, in that case, could I suggest you look at our custom line?"

"Custom line?" Honor let just a hint of buyer's wariness creep into her voice and cocked her head.

"Yes. My dad and older brother build the hulls for me, and for a slight up-charge they can give you just about any hull form you want. For that matter, I could show you our deluxe models. Most of them are single-masted or twin-masted, like the ones here in the kiosk, but we can build them with significantly upgraded control systems."

"You can?" Honor discovered that her interest was genuine, and Betsy smiled again.

"Oh, yes. Dad built one just last month that was a perfect scale model of one of the Old Earth clipper ships. You know about clipper ships?"

"Yes. Yes, I do, as a matter of fact," Honor said, remembering the three-masted ship she'd seen sailing grandly across the lake on her previous visit.

"Well, Dad got copies of the original plans from *Smithsonian-Britannica* and modeled a ship called the *Lightning*, with each sail on each mast individually controlled. And last year, my brother built a five-masted barque that was almost two and a half meters long."

"You did mention a *slight* up-charge, didn't you?" Honor asked even more warily, and Betsy laughed.

"You have the look of a true aficionado, Commander. People like you are likely to have a bit more elastic definition of 'slight' when it comes to something you're really interested in."

Betsy, Honor decided, didn't need a treecat to recognize a sucker when one of them walked up to her kiosk. Whatever else happened, she felt sure her bank account was going to take that hit before this was all over.

"Given the fact that I strongly suspect I'm about to give you the equivalent of a full week's worth of business," she said, "would it be possible for me to sit down and discuss their handiwork with your father and your brother?"

"Oh," Betsy's tone was light, but her eyes were suddenly dark and very steady, "I think that would be a *very* good idea."

✳   ✳   ✳

It didn't take Betsy long to turn the kiosk over to one of her friends. Obviously, most of the park's hucksters were accustomed to looking out for one another, and the young man she'd waved over simply nodded and stepped behind the counter.

As soon as he did, Betsy beckoned to Honor, and the two of them set off down one of Onyx's innumerable brick sidewalks.

Betsy kept up a steady flow of conversation about her sailboats as they walked, and Honor's genuine interest was sufficiently piqued to let her keep up her end without *too* much strain, despite the mingled anticipation, wariness, and anger (at Sector Governor Charnowska, not Betsy) bubbling away inside her.

The walk was longer than Honor had really expected, and as the brick sidewalks turned into ceramacrete—and then into badly *maintained* ceramacrete—she realized they were straying into one of those slums most Silesian cities boasted. The people around her were more poorly dressed, and the majority of them looked like they were probably stuck in minimum-paying jobs or eked out a living as causal labor. Yet few of the faces around her had that sullen, closed-in look she'd seen too often in other Silesian cities, and while it was obvious no one was falling over herself to perform street or building maintenance, the neighborhood was significantly cleaner than many of the rundown, hopeless, dead-end stews Honor had seen on more than one world. Nimitz's head was up, his ears pricked, as he savored the emotions flowing around them, and Honor found his obvious relaxation reassuring.

Several people looked at her and Betsy curiously. They couldn't be in the habit of seeing foreign naval officers with exotic pets on their shoulders in these parts, but no one commented, no one stopped them, and as they made their way deeper into the neighborhood, Honor realized that that was precisely what it was—a *neighborhood*. A community, where—like the kiosk operators by the lake—people looked after (and out for) each other. However rundown and hardscrabble it might be, this was a community of *neighbors*, not simply a gathering of more-or-less strangers who happened to have addresses near one another.

She found that comforting, although she was also aware that looking out for each other could have unpleasant consequences for any outsider who turned out to spell trouble for one of their friends.

After another couple of blocks, she and her guide found themselves outside a rather dingy building with a worn out-looking glowsign that proclaimed that it was "The Onyx Fitness, Exercise, and Health Club." From the looks of things, the Onyx Health Department hadn't carried out any recent inspections, but she followed Betsy up the walk and through the old-fashioned, manual doors.

The interior was a surprise, although Honor scolded herself for the preconceptions which made it surprising. The walls were freshly painted, the floor was worn but spotlessly clean, and the equipment she glimpsed as they walked past several exercise rooms looked well maintained and, in a few cases, virtually new.

Betsy led her down a long corridor, down a flight of stairs, and then out onto the ceramacrete surround of a large indoor swimming pool. There was no one in the water, but a half dozen or so people sat on well-worn benches and chaise longues, watching as she and Betsy approached them.

One of them was John Brown Matheson, who stood and held out his hand.

"Should I assume from your presence, Commander Harrington, that Governor Charnowska didn't seem . . . especially impressed by your information?" he asked.

"Something like that," she agreed. "Actually, what bothered me more was that she didn't seem very *surprised* by my information."

"Ah." Matheson nodded, then cocked his head to one side. "Tell me, Commander—did she also suggest that what might be happening in Casimir wasn't any of your business?"

"Oh, I think you can take that as a given, Mr. Matheson."

"And should we assume you've come to visit us because you don't agree with that particular assessment?"

"Before we go any farther," Honor said quietly, "I think we both need to understand something here. Yes, I'm not so very happy about what you say is going on in Casimir. And I happen to think this is the sort of . . . activity the Queen's Navy is supposed to be discouraging. But that doesn't mean I'm prepared to go charging in there half-cocked with a single destroyer on the simple say-so of someone who—I hope you'll forgive me for pointing this out—has admitted to me that he represents a terrorist organization which everyone knows has its own agenda and hasn't shown . . . a whole bunch of scruples in the past, let's say. What I'm here for is to pursue your information a little further, see where it leads. Frankly, if this operation is on the scale you suggested to me earlier, I don't believe *Hawkwing* has the resources to do anything meaningful about it. In that case, the best I can do would probably be to pass your information along to higher authority—higher *Manticoran* authority—and hope priorities, moral responsibilities, and hardware availability will let older, wiser heads in command of significantly more powerful forces do something about it. Whenever they finally get around to it, that is."

She faced him unflinchingly. She scarcely expected him to be pleased by all the qualifiers she'd just hung on him, but she was darned if she'd lie to him, even by implication.

To her surprise, instead of becoming angry or irritated, he *smiled* at her, instead.

"You may not expect this, but I'm actually pleased to hear you say that," he said.

"You are?" She realized she hadn't managed to completely conceal her surprise, and he chuckled.

"The last thing any of us wants would be to discover that you were some sort of glory hound or, even worse, so stupid you wouldn't recognize potential problems when you met them. Yes, we'd like you to do something about Casimir. And, yes, we're prepared to help in any way we can. But we'd rather have you do nothing than find ourselves with a botched operation. Especially the sort of 'botched operation' which could lead those Manpower bastards to space a couple of thousand inconvenient witnesses."

His amusement vanished with the final sentence, and Honor nodded slowly and soberly.

"I'm relieved to hear you feel that way," she said. "And I'll admit I'm also a little puzzled. I have the distinct impression you people have a reasonable estimate of *Hawkwing*'s capabilities. So why mention this to me at all? From what you've already said, this sounds like something that's going to need a couple of companies of Marines, at the very least, and I've got one *platoon*."

Matheson glanced over his shoulder at the four other men and two women still lounging at poolside behind him. Then he turned back to Honor and invited her with a gesture to accompany him back over to the others. He settled down on one of the benches, beside a woman who looked to be about his own age (and who had the same cheekbones and opulent figure as Betsy) and waved Honor into a battered, tattered, yet surprisingly comfortable chair facing the bench.

"Before we go any farther, to use your own phrase," he said, "recognizing—as we both do—the limits of your ship's capabilities, why are you here? Yes," he waved one hand, "I believe you when you say that if you can't do anything about this situation you'll pass the information on up the line. But you and I both know that when you pass along your information's source, at least some of the people in your Admiralty are going to consider it tainted. So I suppose what I'm saying is that the limit of your capabilities—of what you *could* do, shall we say—would really only matter if you and your destroyer were interested in *trying* to do something about Casimir. Are you?"

Honor leaned back in the chair, rubbing the tip of her nose thoughtfully for several moments, then inhaled a deep breath of chlorine-scented air and shrugged.

"I'm under direct orders to cooperate with Governor Charnowska, Mr. Matheson. That means quite a few of my superiors would be inclined to regard anything I might try to do about Casimir as a clear and serious violation of my instructions. They would argue—correctly, from the perspective of the Star Kingdom's foreign policy—that stepping on the toes of one of the very few Silesian sector governors who's publicly advocating closer relations with Manticore would be...unwise."

They looked into one another's eyes, and Honor felt Nimitz's buzzing purr vibrating against the side of her neck.

"As I say, they'd probably even have a point about that. But the thing is," she said softly, "that sometimes the wise thing and the *right* thing aren't the *same* thing."

Matheson looked back at her for several seconds, then smiled slowly.

"No, they aren't, are they? On the other hand, you're half Beowulfan, Commander. That means you have dual citizenship, as far as Beowulf is concerned, at least. So, given your maternal connections, I imagine you could probably wrangle a commission in the Beowulf System-Defense Force, if worse comes to worst."

That cold, damp sensation around your toes is the water of the good River Rubicon, and he knows it, Honor, she told herself, and leaned towards him.

"In that case, suppose you offer up a few details about this slave depot, Mr. Matheson."

✳ ✳ ✳

Over the next ninety-odd minutes, Honor discovered that Matheson and his friends—all of them obviously had their own ties to the Ballroom—actually had quite a lot of details about Casimir.

Unfortunately, none of them were good.

"So, let me summarize," she said finally, sitting back in her armchair. "According to your information, what we have here is a mixed residential and industrial habitat in orbit around a gas giant that's actually being used as a transfer point for slaves, drugs, and just about any other illegal commodity you'd care to name. Oh, and it's also being used as a support base by at least half a dozen pirates who're fencing their plunder through the smugglers using the habitat. It's got some light defensive armament it's not supposed to have, and there's usually at least one armed vessel hanging around to keep an eye on things. You figure there are probably between five hundred and fifteen hundred slaves being held there at any given moment, plus 'liberty facilities' for the crews of the smugglers, pirates, and slavers wandering through the system. Then there's the service population for those facilities, and probably at least some of these people actually have families, and those families are probably living aboard the habitat. And, finally, as far as you're aware when the bad guys first moved in on the platform, they refused to let the original tech crews—and *their* families—leave. They're still there, doing most of the basic maintenance and even continuing to operate the 'legitimate' side of things. Is that about the size of it?"

"About," Matheson agreed. He didn't seem especially dismayed by Honor's recapitulation, which led her to wonder if she had perhaps been a little over-optimistic about how well he understood the problem.

"Actually, the station's defensive armament is legal, Commander," the dark-haired, dark-eyed man who'd introduced himself as Wolfe Tone said. He appeared to be the local Ballroom's intelligence chief, and Honor had already concluded that he was one of the smartest people she'd ever met. "Before Manpower, Jessyk, and the others moved in on Casimir, when it really was just an industrial platform operating scoop ships in the jovian's atmosphere, Charnowska's predecessor signed off on arming it. It looks to us like the real reason the...call it the current management, is still running the scoop ships is less out of any profit motive than to provide a degree of cover if any Confed naval type who's not in on the deal happens by. Or, of course, if any Manties should pass through.

"Not even the last governor was willing to let it have any really heavy stuff, though. We've got a detailed profile on what it's got, and most of it's pretty mediocre—the kind of outfit designed to stand off the kind of chicken thieves who'd usually be interested in hitting a low-profit target like that."

"That's all well and good," Honor replied. "Unfortunately, a destroyer isn't a lot tougher than a merchant ship when it comes to surviving damage. We can hand it out, but we can't take it. So even relatively light weaponry would pose a significant threat if we got into its range...which, unless I'm mistaken, we're going to have to do if we want to put a boarding party onto the platform."

"Agreed," Tone said.

"And next on the list of problems," Honor went on, "is the fact that according to your information, these yahoos actually keep a guard ship on station."

"That's probably putting it a bit strongly," Boadicea Matheson (who was indeed John Brown Matheson's wife and Betsy Ross Matheson's mother) put in. At the moment, Nimitz lay in her lap, not Honor's, and her hands moved slowly, caressingly, over the 'cat's fluffy pelt. It was obvious to Honor that the green-eyed, auburn-haired woman had been genetically designed as a "courtesan." Honor knew at least a little (which was far more than she wished she knew) about the "training" Manpower inflicted on its pleasure slave lines, and from the way Nimitz had reacted to Boadicea, the abuse she'd survived before managing to escape had left plenty of internal scars. If so, however, they hadn't affected her native wit . . . or courage.

"It's not actually a *guard ship,* Commander," Boadicea went on, her hands stroking, stroking down Nimitz's back while the treecat purred. "That would imply they're actually expecting trouble."

"I see the distinction you're trying to make, Ms. Matheson, and it's probably a valid one," Honor conceded. "At the same time, the fact that this . . . passel of outlaws have managed to agree that at least one of their armed vessels should have hot impeller nodes at all times—and be far enough from the platform to maneuver—shows a lot more forethought than most pirates or slavers ever display. And that, in turn, suggests this outfit is likely to be at least a bit more security conscious—and probably more alert—than we normally see out of them."

"Agreed," Tone said again. Honor looked back at him, and he shrugged slightly. "At the same time, Boadicea's right about how prepared they're really likely to be. They're going through the motions, but it looks to us as if that doesn't actually help a lot. It's as if the fact that they *are* going through the motions makes them feel overconfident, like they've got all the bases covered. And we're scarcely talking about any sort of regular warship. For all intents and purposes they've simply stuck a few missile launchers and some point defense onto merchant hulls, so everything you said about your ship's vulnerability to damage would be true for them, too—in spades."

"Maybe so," Honor said. "It's still going to present a significant problem, though. If nothing else, any ship being used as a pirate is probably going to have better long-range sensors than whatever was originally authorized for this habitat. It'd be close enough to impossible to sneak *Hawkwing* into weapons range of the platform under any circumstances, but giving them extra sensor reach is going to make it even harder."

"We recognize that, Commander Harrington," Matheson said.

"I'm glad, because that's going to be our first serious problem.

When they see us coming, their 'guard ship' is probably going to have the option of running for it instead of standing to fight. If they've got any other ships docked, they'll almost certainly have cold nodes, which means *they* won't be able to run. But if the platform has time to bring its weapons on line, I think we're screwed. Not so much because of the damage they might do to *Hawkwing*, but because all of us know there are innocent bystanders aboard. I'm confident *Hawkwing* could *destroy* the entire platform if it refuses to surrender, but I'm not prepared to murder a thousand or so slaves and innocent technicians who were just unlucky enough to get their platform hijacked right out from under them. For that matter, I'd really rather not include the family dependents of the outlaws as 'collateral damage,' since I've got a hunch most of *them* didn't exactly volunteer, either.

"But even assuming we could somehow deal with the guard ship, then take out or somehow neutralize the platform's own weapons, there's the little matter of how many *people* there are aboard the thing. Even leaving the question of innocent bystanders completely out of consideration, from what Mr. Tone's been able to tell us, there's going to be somewhere between eight hundred and two thousand actual pirates and smugglers aboard, given the permanent crew and whatever ships' companies may be taking advantage of the platform-side facilities. Even at the minimum figure, that's close to three times my ship's total complement. *If* we can get *Hawkwing* into range, and *if* we can neutralize their weaponry, and *if* they're willing to surrender without a fight once we've done those two things, there's no problem. But if they've got the local civilian and naval authorities as deep into their pockets as you people are suggesting, all they really have to do is hold us off until some suitably outraged Confed cruiser comes along to kick my interfering ship out of sovereign Silesian territory. Which probably wouldn't be all that difficult for them, given that sort of disparity in non-naval combat power. Even with my Marines in battle armor, they'd find it awful hard to hack that kind of odds, unless we wanted to use the kind of heavy weapons that would go right ahead and kill all of those innocent bystanders we're trying to keep alive."

Honor looked around at the silent, watching faces, and shrugged unhappily.

"Which is why I said I think we're screwed," she said quietly.

"I don't like saying that, either. At the same time, though, I'm not going to commit to attacking something like this when all indications are that we won't be able to get in clean enough, or have remotely close to the boarding strength we'd need, to pull it off. I won't risk getting that many noncombatants killed if there's so little chance of success."

All of them looked back at her for several moments. Then they looked at each other, and Matheson raised an eyebrow at one of the others—a tall, massively built and extremely ugly man, with a face which looked as if it had been hacked out of a boulder with a blunt object and a complexion darker than Honor's friend Michelle Henke's. He sat straddling one of the chairs, sitting backwards in it with his folded forearms across the top of the chair back and his chin resting on their cushion. He also hadn't been formally introduced yet, however, and Honor wondered what that raised eyebrow was asking him about.

He didn't say anything, only looked back at Matheson for a second or two. Then he shrugged and raised his head far enough to nod, and Matheson turned back to Honor.

"I'm not sure we have any fast and easy answers about how to get close enough, Commander," he said, speaking very, very carefully. "We might, however, be able to find a few more people to fill out your boarding parties."

"More people?" Honor sat for a moment, eyes narrowed in speculation. "What sort of 'more people' did you have in mind?" she asked then, in a tone which was even more careful than his had been.

"Well, that's really more Opener's bailiwick than mine," Matheson said, twitching his head in the direction of the man who'd just nodded. He looked over his shoulder at his companion again. "You want to handle this bit, Opener?"

Honor looked thoughtfully at the man he'd called "Opener." So far, Opener hadn't said a single word, and if she'd known a bit less about genetic slaves, Honor might have been inclined to write him off as someone who was all brawn and very little brain. She recognized the basic genotype—one of Manpower's heavy labor models—and she knew some of those lines really had been designed to be as slow-witted as they might look, just as almost all of them had been designed for limited "service lives." Nobody was going to waste prolong on a slave under any circumstances, but a lot of the heavy labor slaves were deliberately genegineered for maximum strength and toughness at the expense of over-loaded metabolisms which burned themselves out in as little as twenty-five or thirty T-years. Yet some heavy labor required well developed technical skills and the intelligence to support them, and Manpower produced slaves for that sort of requirement, as well. Her mother and her Uncle Jacques had always said that only the pleasure slaves were more dangerous—to their owners, at least—than the heavy labor/technician crosses, and unless Honor was sadly mistaken, this "Opener" was a case in point. She'd recognized both the intelligence and the bitter experience—and steely purpose—in the dark-brown, almost black eyes under those craggy brows, and Matheson's obvious deference to him at this point only reinforced her original impression.

"All right," he replied to Matheson now, sitting up straighter and looking across at Honor.

"I'm François-Dominique Toussaint," he told her in a deep, rumbling voice perfectly suited to his powerful physique and deep chest. He watched her for a moment, waiting to see if she'd make the connection between his nickname and the name he'd chosen as a free person, and what looked like satisfaction flickered in his eyes when she pursed her lips and nodded slowly.

"The reason John said this was my bailiwick, Commander," Toussaint continued, "is that I'm the local Ballroom's dance instructor."

He was still watching her expression, even more carefully now, and she understood exactly why. He'd just informed her that she was sitting beside a swimming pool with the man who was the commander of the Audubon Ballroom's local "direct action" organization. The Ballroom's battle cry—"Let's dance!"—might have struck some people as humorous, but Honor knew too much about the way those dances normally worked out. And "Opener" had just identified himself as the man directly responsible for every bombing, act of arson, murder, and other atrocity committed by the Ballroom in the vicinity of Saginaw. If there was a single human being in the entire Confederacy who a Queen's officer had less business talking to, Honor couldn't imagine who it might be. She could no longer pretend, even to herself, that she didn't know exactly who she was meeting with, and she knew with total certainty that what she really ought to do was call this insanity off, get up, and leave—quickly.

"That's an interesting admission, Mr. Toussaint," she heard herself say instead. "Does it have some direct bearing on this discussion, though?"

"It might," he replied, his tone as calm as hers. "You see, the Ballroom happens to have come into possession of a transport vessel. A slaver." His voice was still calm, yet lava seemed to churn with slow, deadly patience in its depths. "It masses a bit over two megatons, and up until about five T-months ago, it belonged to the Jessyk Combine. Now it belongs to us."

Honor wasn't even tempted to ask what had happened to the previous crew.

"We've managed to come up with the people we need to man its critical systems," Toussaint continued. "I won't pretend we have anything a naval officer would even remotely consider an *adequate* crew, or the bridge officers we really need, but we're capable of basic astrogation and we've managed to keep propulsion and life support on line. In that regard, it's probably just as well it's got so few bells and whistles; there are less things for us to break."

Honor gave a small nod of understanding, and he shrugged.

"For obvious reasons, we're not keeping it here in Saginaw. In fact, we've got it in . . . another star system, let's say. One with no real estate worth developing, where we've managed to cobble together a habitat of our own. Now, this ship is totally unarmed, so even if we had something like a trained crew, there's no way we could use it against Casimir like some sort of Q-ship. But"—he looked very levelly into her eyes—"in that same unnamed star system, aboard that habitat, we've managed to assemble almost twelve hundred experienced fighters. Fighters who all have skin-suits . . . and weapons. We're not Marines, Commander, but one thing we *damned* well are is as motivated as it gets when it comes time to dance."

Honor inhaled deeply and settled back in her chair. She was so far into deep, dark water now that it wasn't even remotely funny. It was one thing to gather information from someone like the Ballroom. It was another to propose to act upon that information in the Star Kingdom's name. Yet bad as both those actions undoubtedly would have been from her superiors' view-point, they could be at least arguably justified. It would be quite another thing for an officer of the Royal Manticoran Navy to actually cooperate operationally in what would undoubtedly be denounced as "an unprovoked terrorist attack" by the very sector governor with whom she'd been ordered to coordinate her activities here in Silesia. In fact, it would be the sort of "quite another thing" which led to interstellar incidents, heated diplomacy, demands for reparations, and the catastrophic end of the officer in question's career.

But without Toussaint's "dancers," she didn't begin to have the manpower to do anything about that depot.

It was that simple. If she staged a raid on Casimir with the Ballroom's support, her career would almost certainly be over. She might be permitted to resign her commission, but it was far more likely to lead to an extraordinarily messy court-martial. Probably even to prison time, given the Ballroom's official—and, frankly, well deserved—"terrorist" label. She never doubted that the majority of the Navy would understand, even approve, but that approval would be cold comfort after the ax fell.

She knew that. And for two or three heartbeats, she quailed from the vista of the future she saw opening before her. Yet she was who she was, and as she'd told Matheson in Chez Fiammetta's, she was her mother's daughter. She knew precisely what Allison Harrington would do in her place, if she had the training, the capability, and the resources. And she knew even more clearly than that what her father would do in her position, because once upon a time, he'd been there.

But in the end, what it came down to was less about what her parents would have thought or felt—less what *they* might have done—than it was about what *she* might do. About the maelstrom where her love for the Navy, the deep, satisfying joy she'd found in her career, met her sense of duty to her Queen and the bedrock of her own principles. She looked cold-eyed at the agonizing loss of that career, at the certainty that men and women she respected would condemn her for deliberately setting out on a course she knew would be devastating to the foreign policy she'd been ordered to support, and remembered something Raoul Courvoisier had told her so many years ago at the Academy.

"In the end," he'd said, "there comes a time when a Queen's officer has to decide. Not follow orders, not seek counsel and advice, not pass the responsibility on to someone else—*decide*. Make a choice. Recognize the costs and the consequences in the full knowledge that people *who weren't there* are going to pass judgment upon him for it without any particular interest in being fair about it. That's the true measure of an officer—of a human being. Right or wrong, popular or unpopular, he has to know where duty, moral responsibility, and legal accountability meet the honor of his uniform and the oath he swore to his monarch and his kingdom. When that time comes, an officer worthy of that uniform and that oath and that monarch makes the *hard* decision, in full awareness of its consequences, because if he doesn't make it, he fails all of them . . . and himself."

She doubted Admiral Courvoisier had ever imagined in his wildest dreams that one of his protégés might someday find herself in the basement of a Silesian health club hobnobbing with admitted murderers and terrorists. Yet when all was said and done, however *hard* the decision might be, it was also a simple one, wasn't it?

"So," she heard her voice say calmly, "tell me more about this ship of yours, Opener. Two megatons, you said? With something that size to work with, sneaking *Hawkwing* into range of the platform just got a lot simpler."

✳   ✳   ✳

Honor watched from behind eyes which were calmer than she actually felt as Chief Bonrepaux poured coffee into her senior officers' cups. She herself nursed a mug of her favored cocoa, but the rest of her officers—with the exception of Surgeon Lieutenant Neukirch, who wasn't present—were all firmly in the official coffee camp with the rest of the Navy. At the moment, however, most of them seemed a bit too preoccupied to properly appreciate their beverage of choice.

Bonrepaux finished pouring while two of her minions placed trays of small sandwiches and other finger food on the table. The chief steward surveyed their work, nodded to them when she found it good, and then twitched her head at the door. They disappeared, Bonrepaux took one last look around, then followed them.

The day cabin door slid shut behind the chief steward, and Honor took a slow sip of her cocoa while she considered the other men and women at the table. It wasn't a particularly large day cabin—*Hawkwing* was only a destroyer, and on the small side compared to her younger sisters, at that, and cubic space for living quarters was limited, even for her commanding officer. The

wardroom was considerably larger, but the wardroom aboard a
Royal Manticoran Navy ship belonged to all of its officers *except*
the captain. The CO was a guest there. It was her subordinates'
refuge and social center, and she didn't intrude upon it unless
she was invited.

Especially not, she thought now, *for something like this.*

"I imagine you've all got a few questions about exactly what
it is we're up to," she said finally, setting her cup neatly on the
saucer in front of her. From their expressions, her last sentence
would appear to be one of the grosser understatements she'd
uttered lately, she reflected, and felt the faint vibration of Nimitz's
almost silent purring chuckle against the back of her neck as he
followed her thoughts, or at least her mood.

"Well, I imagine we *are* all at least a little . . . curious, Skipper,"
Taylor Nairobi said after a moment. His tone was light, almost
whimsical, but his expression wasn't. In fact, there was an almost
hurt look in his eyes, Honor thought. She regretted that, but there
was a reason why, for the first time in the two T-years they'd
served together, she hadn't taken him fully into her confidence.

"I'm sure you are," she said, "and I apologize for leaving all
of you in the dark until now. But I had my reasons—which had
nothing at all to do with my trust or personal and professional
regard for all of you."

"Well, *that* sounds ominous," Aloysius O'Neal observed cheerfully, although his gray eyes were serious and thoughtful across
the table from her.

"That isn't *exactly* the word I'd choose, Al," Honor told him,
"but it's headed in the right direction. In about eighteen hours,
we're going to be arriving at our current destination, and I'm
sure Aniella"—she flashed a smile at the astrogator—"wasn't the
only one who felt a certain degree of curiosity when I told her
where we were going."

The "where" in question was, in fact, a thoroughly useless,
completely planetless red dwarf. The only value it possessed was
as a convenient beacon. Not even the best astrogator could guarantee a pinpoint arrival at her intended destination, and even a
useless star was a lot more visible than any starship. Especially
if the starship in question was doing its best to avoid attracting
unwanted attention. Bad novels frequently had single ships making contact at deep-space rendezvous in the "trackless depths of

interstellar space," but professional spacers knew exactly how much time the ships in question could spend looking for each other, given how much distance even the smallest astrogational error amounted to over the course of a voyage light-years in length.

Unless, of course, there was some convenient, clearly visible target destination they could both make for.

"The reason we're headed there," she continued, "is to meet someone. And after we've done that, we'll be moving on to another destination in company."

"Another destination, Ma'am?" Lieutenant Hutchinson asked when she paused for a moment, and she smiled at the tactical officer.

"It seems there's something rotten in Casimir, Fred," she said, "and we're going to do something about it. You see—"

✳   ✳   ✳

The others had departed, leaving Honor alone with Nairobi and O'Neal. She waited until the door closed behind their juniors, then tipped her chair back, folded her hands over her stomach, and smiled crookedly at them.

"Somehow," she said almost whimsically, "I seem to sense that the two of you are less than totally delighted with this operation."

O'Neal snorted, but Nairobi's expression was anything but amused, and he shook his head almost grimly.

"Skipper," he said, "I hope I'm not out of line to say this, but you're damned right I'm not 'totally delighted' about this little brainstorm of yours." He shook his head again. "No wonder you didn't tell any of the rest of us about it until just now! I suppose I'm grateful you didn't, but what I really wish is that you'd opened your mouth about it in the very beginning so I could've done my damnedest to talk you out of it!"

"To be honest," Honor said calmly, "that's one of the reasons I didn't tell you. I knew you'd try to convince me not to do it, and I also knew you wouldn't succeed." She shrugged ever so slightly. "You'd only have wasted a lot of time, energy, and concern over my sanity. Don't think I don't appreciate the fact that you would've tried to save me from myself, because I do. But since you weren't going to manage to anyway, it just seemed kindest to everyone concerned to avoid the conversation."

"Bull...excrement," O'Neal said, shifting what he'd been about to say in mid-word.

Honor cocked an eyebrow at him, and he snorted again.

"Oh, I don't doubt for a minute that you knew exactly what Taylor would've been saying to you, Skip," the sailing master told her. "And I don't doubt you were just as happy not to have that conversation. But all three of us—and all those people who just left your cabin, for that matter—know the real reason you kept your mouth shut." His eyes held hers unwaveringly. "You're protecting us, and we damned well know it."

"You're right," Honor admitted. "I know the main reason Taylor would've been trying to talk me out of this is that he knows exactly what our orders are, and he'd be trying to protect me from myself. That's one of an exec's jobs, and Taylor's a darned good exec. But it's my job to protect the *rest* of you from myself, when it's necessary, and this is one of those times."

"Let me guess," Nairobi said bitingly. "Before we ever left Saginaw, you recorded a dispatch and sent it off home, informing the Admiralty of your intentions, and also informing them that you had not discussed this with any of us, that you were acting entirely on your own responsibility and authority, and that none of us shared any part in your decision to embark upon this lunacy. Is that about right?"

"About." Honor nodded. "Although I might quibble just a bit over the word 'lunacy,' now that I think about it."

"*I* wouldn't," O'Neal said in a considerably less amused tone.

She looked at him, and he scowled.

"Don't get me wrong, Skipper. Assuming your information's correct, there's probably nothing in the entire Confederacy that needs squashing as much as these bastards do. For that matter, I'm all in favor of somebody doing it. Hell, I'm even in favor of the *Navy's* doing it! But Taylor's exactly right about our orders, and you wouldn't even be considering this—especially not with your . . . allies—if you didn't know Governor Charnowska flat out isn't going to do it. That means you're setting out to deliberately antagonize the person you were ordered to cooperate with, and that you're doing it in company with a flipping batch of *terrorists*! Christ, Skipper, couldn't you find a *bigger* club for her to beat you with? The Foreign Office's going to want you *crucified* for this, and with these Ballroom fanatics cranked in—!"

He pushed himself forcefully back in his chair, both hands shoulder-high in front of him, as if he were throwing something away, and Nairobi nodded.

"It's going to be bad enough, as far as some of the people at Admiralty House are concerned, if we simply don't try to retake this 'liberated slaver' of theirs," he said. "When they find out you've actually cooperated with them, conducted a *joint operation,* they're going to pop gaskets left and right."

"I've considered all of that," Honor told both of them serenely. "And Al's right, that's exactly why I sent off that dispatch making it perfectly clear no one else in *Hawkwing* even knew what I was thinking, far less had any part in planning this. I can testify to that under oath with a clear conscience, and so can all of you. That's important to me. But understand this, both of you—however wise or unwise this may be, we're *going* to do it. The reason I asked the two of you to stay behind when the others left wasn't to give you the chance to change my mind. It was because I want you to have the opportunity to formally state your opposition to my plans before we embark on the operation."

She paused, looking at each of them in turn, hard, before she continued.

"Don't misunderstand me, either of you. I've done everything I can to protect you, but the truth is that if this goes as badly as it has the potential to go—and I'm not talking just about the op, as you both realize perfectly well—that may not matter. You're my two ranking officers. If you don't make your reservations about this operation part of the official record before we carry it out, it's entirely possible that when the smoke clears you'll find yourselves beached right alongside me. I don't want that to happen, especially when this was all *my* idea."

"Let me get this straight, Skipper," Nairobi said after a moment. "Are you *ordering* us to object to your orders?"

"No, I'm just saying that—"

"Well, it's a good thing that isn't what you're doing," the XO interrupted her, "because it would be the *silliest* damned order anyone ever gave! I mean, ordering your subordinates to formally protest your lawful commands?" He shook his head. "Most nitwitted thing I ever heard of!"

"Taylor, don't take this lightly. I'm serious when I say—"

"Skipper, do you think he doesn't know—that we *both* don't know—you're serious?" O'Neal chuckled at her expression. "Of course we do. And of course we both think you're nuts. And of course we both agree with you."

Honor had opened her mouth again. Now she closed it, slowly, and gazed at both of them in silence for several seconds.

"I really wish you'd take my advice on this, both of you," she said quietly. "But the truth is, I'm glad you feel that way."

"Please don't confuse our illustrious sailing master's agreement—or mine, for that matter—with delirious joy and unqualified approval, Skipper," Nairobi said. "In fact, delirious joy and unqualified approval are probably the last two terms I'd use to describe my own feelings at this particular moment. Despite which, I have to go along with him. Assuming these people are telling you the truth, then this really is something that needs doing. But I have to ask you this. Are you genuinely confident they *are* telling you the truth? Or, at least, that they're telling you *all* the truth? God knows I can't fault the Ballroom for how much it hates Manpower's guts, but their own hands aren't exactly spotless, and they've never been above...creatively misrepresenting circumstances, shall we say, to game third parties for the result they want. There was that business in Pelzer, for example, if you'll recall."

"Point," Honor agreed.

There wasn't any actual proof, but ONI's analysts had concluded that the Ballroom—or its sympathizers, at least—had fed deliberately false information to an Andermani cruiser squadron several years ago in order to provoke a raid on the territory of one of the small, independent star systems just beyond the Empire's borders. There wasn't much doubt the government of the Pelzer System had, in fact, been deep in bed with various Mesan interests, quite possibly including Manpower, but the slave trading depot the Andermani had expected to find, catching the system authorities red-handed, had been a figment of someone's imagination. The Andermani incursion, however, had destabilized the system government in question...at which point a "spontaneous" coup (launched, oddly enough, by heavily armed people who appeared quite sympathetic to the suppression of the genetic slave trade and seemed to have had some odd notion that some destabilizing event might be about to occur) had removed it from power. Most of the previous government's leading members had found themselves tried and convicted for crimes ranging from outright treason to malfeasance, bribery, embezzlement, and participation in the slave trade. Three of them had been shot, two had been stripped of their citizenship and permanently deported, and most of the rest had gone to prison for lengthy periods.

The fact that every one of them had been guilty of the crimes for which they were accused, as far as anyone could tell, was all very well. And no fair-minded person could honestly argue that the Pelzer System wasn't far better off—not to mention more honestly and efficiently run—than it had ever been before. But none of that changed the fact that the Andermani's information had been . . . less than completely accurate.

"Taylor, I appreciate your concern, and I understand exactly why you're asking that," she said, "but in answer to your question, yes. These people may be mistaken—for that matter, someone *else* may have lied to *them*—but they aren't lying to me." She unfolded her interlaced fingers and raised her right hand to touch Nimitz lightly on the head. "I took along my furry little henchman here. Trust me, if they'd been lying, Nimitz would have told me."

It would have been inaccurate to describe either of her subordinates as completely satisfied by her statement. On the other hand, both of them had known Nimitz for quite some time now. Whatever the general opinion of treecat intelligence might be, they had no doubt at all that he would have been able to tell his person if she'd been lied to.

"Well, I guess that's that, Taylor," O'Neal said, grinning across at the executive officer. "She's going to do it, whatever we think about it, so I don't see any point in pretending we don't think it's a good idea, too. Do you?"

"To be honest, I can see all kinds of reasons to pretend that," Nairobi said in a considerably more sour tone. "Unfortunately, I'm not a very good liar. Hell, you know I can't even bluff at poker! I'd just look like an idiot if I tried to convince Admiralty House she'd dragged me into this kicking and screaming all the way."

Honor smiled at both of them, then shook her head slowly.

"I think you're both idiots," she told them. "But I'm not going to pretend I'm not relieved to hear you say that. I shouldn't be, but I'm selfish enough to be glad, instead. Thank you both."

"I hope you still feel that way in a few years," O'Neal said, "when you realize that if we'd only argued harder, we might actually have saved all of our naval careers."

❋　　❋　　❋

Honor had no idea what the ship whose icon floated in her display had once been named. And, she told herself honestly, she didn't really *want* to know, either. All that mattered at the moment was that she was here, a concrete confirmation that her Ballroom "allies" could deliver on at least part of what they'd promised.

She sat on *Hawkwing*'s bridge and felt the tension behind her bridge crew's disciplined façade as the destroyer decelerated towards rendezvous with the waiting freighter. That ship was a confirmation for them, as well—confirmation that their CO truly was going to proceed with her entirely unauthorized operation.

She'd come to the conclusion that at least some of her subordinates thoroughly disapproved of what she was doing. Lieutenant Boyd, for example, hadn't been able to hide her repugnance at the thought of associating herself in any way with notorious terrorists. Nor was the com officer alone in that. Lieutenant Mason was obviously glad his position as *Hawkwing*'s logistics officer meant he was going to have very little to do with the murderous Ballroom fanatics. And although Mahalia Rosenberg's deep satisfaction at the notion of destroying a depot like the one Honor had described was evident, her discomfort about the Ballroom was equally evident.

It wasn't that any of them felt any great sympathy for the Ballroom's "victims." Honor suspected there were very few Manticoran officers who felt anything but contempt and revulsion when they considered anyone who dealt in human misery on such an interstellar scale. She certainly *hoped* there weren't, at any rate! For most of them, though, it went even deeper than that, into a corrosive hatred for all the genetic slave trade represented. Yet there was no denying that the Audubon Ballroom had alienated an enormous number of people who sympathized with its stated goal of destroying the slave trade once and for all. Even a great many who had no particular problem with armed resistance were sickened by the Ballroom's unrepentant savagery.

Thanks in no small part to her mother's side of her family, Honor knew a great deal more about the anti-slavery movement in general than the majority of Manticorans ever learned. Her Uncle Jacques was a senior director of the Beowulf-based Anti-Slavery League, the political arm of the abolitionist movement, and she knew that even within the ranks of the escaped and liberated slaves there was a lively, often bitter internal debate between those who endorsed the Ballroom's methods and those who believed such "terrorist excesses" actually strengthened Manpower's hand. The atrocities the Ballroom left scattered in its wake were undoubtedly exactly what the Ballroom claimed—*counter*-atrocities, provoked and driven by all the centuries in which slaves had been routinely, casually slaughtered, tortured, and simply thrown away. But even many who fully recognized that all of those terrible things had happened to slaves were unprepared to accept the Ballroom's counter-terror as justice. Indeed, as the more moderate members of the ASL argued passionately, for the public at large, the Ballroom's operations too often blurred the moral distinctions between Manpower and Manpower's victims.

If Honor was going to be completely honest, she would be forced to admit she shared more than a trace of the moderates' opposition. Despite her relative youth, she'd seen too much human misery—especially here in Silesia—to be in favor of inflicting still more of it, however deservedly, if it could be avoided. But she was also enough of a historian to know excesses like those of the Ballroom were inevitable. That when human beings, whatever their genetic makeup, were treated as expendable, disposable *things* long enough, when they were denied not just freedom but even the vestiges of human dignity, when they were no more than toys to be played with and those they allowed themselves to love could be stripped away from them and disposed of like any other commodity at someone else's whim, then those responsible for abusing them stored up the whirlwind, and no power in the universe could prevent that whirlwind from striking when the opportunity came. It wasn't simply impossible to stop the Ballroom's bitter, impassioned, hating avengers from slaughtering their tormentors, it was unreasonable even to think anyone could.

She'd seen the cold hatred burning in "Opener" Toussaint's dark eyes, and she'd seen its reflection in Boadicea Matheson's green gaze, and she knew nothing short of death itself could stop people who'd endured what they had from exacting the last terrible gram of their vengeance. And deep down inside, she didn't blame them in the least.

Which wasn't to say she approved of the Ballroom's extremism, because she didn't. From a purely pragmatic viewpoint, the moderates had a point about the way in which the abolition movement's opponents could use the Ballroom to blur the distinctions between them and their enemies. Even more than that, though, there was the price people paid for their vengeance, however deserved that vengeance might be. Retribution might taste sweet, and she was prepared to admit that sometimes the victims of evil required avengers more than they did simple justice, but that sweet taste was also a deadly poison. A corrosive brew which truly could—and all too often did—eat away the moral distinctions between the avenger and those she punished.

She remembered something her father had told her once, many years ago, when she was only a child. There were times, he'd said, when a man or a woman confronted evil which had to be stopped. When the only way it *could* be stopped was by violence. She'd known even then that he was speaking from personal knowledge, and she'd listened silently, sitting beside him, his strong and loving arm wrapped around her. It was only later that she'd realized he'd already recognized her own hunger for a naval career. That he was deliberately sharing with her something of incalculable value, something he himself had won through terrible and bitter experience.

"When that happens," he said, "when there's no choice but to kill evil, then kill it. It's your responsibility, your duty, and if you flinch, you fail—not just yourself, but everything important in your life. But if it must be done, if there truly is no choice, then do it because you *must,* not because you want to, and never, ever exult in the doing. That's the price of your soul, Honor—the ability to do what has to be done without turning yourself into the very thing it is that you're fighting against."

I'll remember, Daddy, she thought now, watching the light code on the display coming closer and closer. *I'll remember, I promise.*

❊   ❊   ❊

"Well, Commander Harrington?"

Honor turned her head to look at Samson X, the commander of the ship the Ballroom had renamed *Reprisal,* and raised one eyebrow.

"Well, what, Captain?" she asked mildly.

"Well," he waved one hand at the mass of men and women filtering out of the outsized messing compartment, "do they pass your muster?"

Honor regarded him thoughtfully for several seconds. She knew a bit more about him than he might suspect, courtesy of Wolfe

Tone's briefing. She'd insisted on that before she agreed to commit herself to working with Samson, which was why she knew he'd already been a young adult before he was liberated from a Manpower slave ship very like *Reprisal* by one of the unfortunately few Solarian League Navy officers who made it a point to go after slavers aggressively. That officer (not surprisingly) had come from Beowulf, and the freed slave had been relocated to that world. He'd been just young enough to receive the first-generation prolong therapies Manpower never wasted on its property, and he'd taken the surname of the SLN captain who'd liberated him for his own first name—possibly because of its implications as a warrior for his people. But whatever the reason he'd chosen "Samson" for his first name, the choice of the single letter "X" for his own surname had been an unflinching declaration of how he intended to spend his own life. It was probably the most common single "last name" among the Ballroom's hard-core fighters.

That had told Honor quite a bit, all by itself; Nimitz's reaction to him had told her even more. Samson wasn't quite as dark as Toussaint, and his brown hair had auburn highlights, but under the skin, they were very much alike. Samson was one of those people who'd been intended by nature as a basically nice guy . . . and who really was the sort of total psychopath (where Manpower was concerned, at least) which the Ballroom's critics argued that *all* of its members were. Even without Nimitz's empathic abilities, Honor could almost literally taste the electric tension, the hunger, crackling through him, and she hadn't missed the edge of challenge in his question.

"I didn't come here because they had to pass my 'muster,' Captain," she told him after a moment. "I came here to meet them, and you and your officers, and, frankly, to be sure they actually existed." She smiled slightly. "I'm a naturally trusting soul, but before I commit my ship to an operation like this, I really do feel a certain slight responsibility to be positive my allies are as numerous—and as well equipped—as I've been assured they are." She shrugged. "I haven't done an actual headcount yet, mind you, but at first glance, it looks to me as if Mr. Toussaint's strength estimate was accurate."

Samson looked at her as if he was trying to figure out some way to take offense at what she'd just said, and she made herself return his hot gaze coolly, calmly, as if she were totally unaware of the passionate currents deep inside him.

"Sorry," he said finally, and gave himself a shake. "Sorry, Commander," he repeated in a more normal voice, and managed an almost sheepish grin. "Didn't mean to sound like I was trying to pick a fight. It's just—"

He broke off and shrugged, and Honor nodded.

"I didn't think you were," she said, not quite entirely accurately. "Trying to pick a fight, I mean."

"Actually," he said, "I think part of it's how long I *have* been trying to pick this particular fight. To go after Casimir. We've known about it for better than sixteen T-months now, and we haven't been able to do a thing about it." His jaw clenched. "I don't like to think about how many of our people have passed through that...place while we knew what was going on and couldn't stop it."

"I understand, or at least I come as close to understanding as someone who's never been a slave can," Honor told him quietly.

"I think maybe you do." Samson's voice was calmer than it had been, and his nostrils flared as he inhaled deeply. "It eats at a man," he said simply.

"I'm sure it does."

Honor reached out and laid one hand lightly on his shoulder, feeling the tension in the muscles under her fingers, and looked him squarely in the eye.

"I'm sure it does," she repeated. "But now, I think we should probably meet with your officers. I seem to have a dance card that needs filling, so let's see what we can do about letting someone else feel some teeth eating at *them* for a change."

✳   ✳   ✳

Honor, Taylor Nairobi, and Lieutenant Janacek sat across the dining table in *Reprisal's* wardroom from Samson X and the two men he'd introduced as Henri Christophe and Nat Turner Jurgensen. Christophe was the senior action team commander aboard *Reprisal,* which made him the commanding officer of the combined Ballroom strike force, and Jurgensen was his second in command. It was obvious from Nairobi and Janacek's reactions that they hadn't caught the significance of the two men's chosen names, but Honor had, and she stroked Nimitz's ears with gentle fingers as she considered them thoughtfully.

Despite his name, Christophe had blond hair, blue eyes, and a very fair complexion. He was also small and very nimble—probably from one of the entertainer slave lines; he had the look of a juggler or an acrobat—and she had the distinct impression that he was an incorrigible prankster. A prankster of the Old Earth folk tradition variety: the kind whose wit was as deadly as another's sword. Coyote and Brother Rabbit would have been quite at home with him, she suspected.

Jurgensen was darker than Christophe, with an olive-brown complexion, brown hair, and brown eyes. He was bigger, physically more powerful, and seemed considerably more driven, yet there was no question that Christophe's was the dominant personality.

"Do my people pass muster, Commander?" Christophe asked, probably unaware he was echoing Samson X's question of two or three hours earlier. Unlike the ex-slaver's captain, however, his voice and manner weren't particularly challenging. In fact, they were almost amused.

"As a matter of fact, Mr. Christophe," she confessed, "I have to admit I was favorably surprised." She waved one hand gently. "Don't mistake me. Anyone who's familiar with the Ballroom's operational record knows your people have to be capable. I suppose I'd simply expected something a bit more... informally structured, let's say."

"We *are* a pretty 'informally structured' bunch," Christophe said. "We don't have a lot of use for the sort of military traditions or spit-and-polish discipline of more 'respectable' outfits. But a lot of us—more than a lot of people guess, I think—do have military experience before we ever wind up in the action teams." He shrugged slightly. "We know the difference between soldiers and a disorganized mob, and we're not willing to screw up the way a mob screws up. What we do is too important for that."

Honor nodded slowly. It wasn't as if what he'd just said came as a surprise to her, although she suspected Everett Janacek had been more taken aback than he'd cared to indicate by the professionalism of the Ballroom "terrorists" she and her officers had met and inspected. Unlike Janacek, however, Honor had known for years that the government of Beowulf had a long tradition of covertly assisting the Ballroom. And one way Beowulf did that was to enlist liberated slaves, and the children of liberated slaves, into its own system self-defense force. Beowulf undoubtedly had a greater concentration of freed genetic slaves than any other star system in the explored galaxy, and they repaid the star system which had given them refuge—and in many cases, actively helped liberate them in the first place—with an almost rabid loyalty. Their representation in Beowulf's armed forces was far higher than the simple percentage of the total system population they represented might have suggested, and quite a few of them—possibly even as many as half—stayed in Beowulf uniform.

Most of the others, however, served loyally and well for the term of their enlistment, then left the service... and took their training with them when they joined the Ballroom, instead. Which went a great way towards explaining why they were the "extraordinarily capable" force she'd just called them.

And if there'd ever been any doubt in my mind about the accuracy of Mother and Uncle Jacques' occasional comments about Beowulf's attitude towards the Ballroom, the fact that almost every one of these "ragtag terrorists" has what looks an awful lot like a standard Beowulfan Marine skin suit and standard issue pulse rifle would tend to suggest they were right all along.

Not even Marine skinnies were the equal of battle armor, but they offered far better protection against small arms and grenade fragments than civilian or even navy-issue skinsuits. The Beowulfan Marines' gear was every bit as good as anything the Royal Marines could boast. In fact, it might actually have been a little bit better, and young Lieutenant Janacek had hovered on the brink of waxing indignant as he contemplated the quality of the "terrorists'" equipment.

Of course, that had been before he realized that the people who were going to be *employing* that equipment were probably at least as well trained in its use as his own people were, as well.

Her lips twitched on the brink of a smile at the memory. She tried to suppress it for a moment, then changed her mind and let it out.

"Tell me, Mr. Christophe, if you don't mind. How many years were you in the Beowulf Marines?"

For just a moment, the blue eyes went still and thoughtful, but then he shrugged again and smiled back at her. It was a bit thin, that smile, more like Coyote than ever, but it was also real.

"Eight T-years," he admitted, and glanced at Janacek. "I retired as a captain, actually. They offered me major, if I'd stay in."

Janacek had himself well in hand, Honor noticed, but the lieutenant couldn't keep his own eyes from widening in surprise, and Christophe chuckled in obvious amusement.

"I thought it must have been something like that," Honor murmured, then glanced at Nairobi, who looked marginally less surprised than Janacek. "I think we can probably take it as a given that Mr. Christophe's people can hold up their end, don't you think, Taylor?"

"Um—I mean, yes, Ma'am, I think we can."

"Good."

She looked back at the three men sitting across the table from them.

"I'll want to discuss the boarding operation itself with Mr. Christophe and Mr. Jurgensen, Captain," she told Samson X. "Among other things," she allowed her voice to harden very slightly, her eyes sweeping their faces, "I want to be absolutely certain we're on the same page when it comes to little matters like accepting surrenders. And in what happens to anyone who *does* surrender afterward. If the Ballroom ever expects cooperation out of the Star Kingdom of Manticore again—on any level, gentlemen—you and your people are going to have to demonstrate a certain level of ... restraint in the course of this operation. I hope none of you are going to be offended by my saying that, but I think we all need to be certain we understand it."

The three "terrorists" seemed to stiffen slightly, but no one protested. Then, after a moment, Christophe cleared his throat.

"We assumed that would be the case going in, Commander." His voice was flatter, harder than it had been a few moments before, and his normally cheerful face tightened. "I won't pretend we like it, and I won't pretend Nat and I haven't had to knock a few heads together—in a couple of cases, literally—to get that same message across. But as important as this is to us, and as badly as we want these bastards to pay, we're not about to risk turning the Star Kingdom formally against us by splattering you with Mesan blood."

"I'm relieved to hear it," Honor said quietly. "Believe me, I'm enough of a Beowulfer to understand why the Ballroom is as ... ruthless, let's say, as it is. I won't pretend I approve of all of your actions, because I don't. You probably wouldn't believe me if I tried to pretend otherwise. But I *do* understand what drives you, and because I do, I appreciate how difficult it must have been for you to impress that attitude on your people. I only hope they remember it when the moment comes."

Jurgensen's face darkened, but she shook her head before he could speak.

"I mean that sincerely, Mr. Jurgensen. I don't doubt for a moment that your people understand exactly why it has to be that way, and I don't doubt for a moment that you and Mr. Christophe have emphasized that to them again and again." In fact, thanks to Nimitz, she knew they were telling her the truth about that. "But given what some of your people, or their parents, or their loved ones, must have been through, they have all the legitimate motivation in the universe to tear these people apart. It couldn't be any other way, and it would be foolish—and wrong—of me to suggest it could. So I meant neither disrespect nor to suggest that *you* didn't mean exactly what you said. I truly do hope they remember when the time comes, because I recognize how difficult it would be for *me* to remember in their place."

Jurgensen's taut shoulders eased, and he gave her a curtly courteous nod of acknowledgment. She nodded back, then returned her attention to Samson X.

"As I say, Captain, we're obviously going to have to discuss the boarding operation, but unless we can figure out how to get *Reprisal* close enough to the platform to put Lieutenant Janacek's Marines and Mr. Christophe's people aboard it, there's not going to *be* any boarding action. Which suggests to me that before we worry about that, we need to work out our cunning strategy to get *Hawkwing* close enough to neutralize their defenses."

She smiled almost impishly, and despite his own inner demons, Samson X grinned back at her.

"Now, Commander Nairobi and I"—Honor nodded at her XO—"have been giving that matter a little thought, and what's occurred to us is—"

* * *

Reprisal was a small ship by the standards of most interstellar freight carriers. In fact, she was about the smallest size that was regularly used outside purely local, relatively short-haul traffic. Despite that, *Hawkwing* looked like a minnow beside her. The destroyer massed less than four percent as much as she did. In fact, Honor's ship could have been tucked away in one of *Reprisal*'s cargo holds... assuming, of course, that it wasn't one of the holds which had been reconfigured to carry human freight.

But small though *Hawkwing* might be, she was a minnow with

long, sharp teeth, which *Reprisal* completely lacked. That made the destroyer far more deadly to other starships (or orbital habitats), except for the minor fact that she had to get in range of them before she could hurt them.

Which, Honor thought as she watched her tactical display, *is where the fact that we're such a little guy actually starts working in our favor.*

She smiled faintly, recalling Taylor Nairobi's response when she'd first explained how she intended to sneak *Hawkwing* into the Casimir System. It wasn't that he'd been able to come up with any technical objection to her plan, and he'd come around with something approaching enthusiasm in the end, but it was obvious it offended his sense of the way things were supposed to be. And that he thought it was . . . undignified, to say the very least.

Well, that's fine with me, Taylor, as long as it works, she reflected. *And it's off-the-wall enough that I really don't think they're going to see it coming.*

Her smile grew briefly broader, and she wished Nimitz were in his usual place across the back of her command chair to share her amusement. But the 'cat was tucked away in the life-support module in her quarters, instead. He'd been a bit less cheerful than usual about the separation this time, though. Probably that was because he'd understood that—assuming everything went according to plan—there wasn't really very much chance *Hawkwing* was going to take damage or lose pressure. But, she admitted to herself, it might also have had a little something to do with the fact that when she'd donned her skinsuit, this time she'd strapped on her pistol belt, as well.

Well, he'd just have to put up with it, she thought, her smile fading. He didn't have a skinsuit of his own, and she wasn't going to take any chances with him. Besides—

"Captain, we have a communications request from the freighter," Florence Boyd announced, and Honor concealed a grimace.

The communications officer's distaste for the entire operation hadn't abated in the least, and it showed. The lieutenant's normal cheerful extroversion had turned inward over the past week and a half while Janacek's Marines exercised with their Ballroom "allies" before the two ships headed for their objective. It was as if she were deliberately disassociating herself from the members of *Hawkwing*'s complement who'd embraced the idea of cooperating with such a murderous, bloodstained bunch. She did her duty, but in a far more distant sort of way than before, and she'd turned much more formal. And, as if to emphasize her unhappiness with the entire notion, she never—ever—used *Reprisal*'s name, or the name of anyone aboard her, if there was any way to avoid it.

"Very well, Florence. Put Captain X through to my display, please."

Honor's soprano was unshadowed by any overt reprimand, but Boyd's fair complexion darkened noticeably as her captain quietly emphasized both Samson X's rank and name.

"Yes, Ma'am," the com officer said more than a bit stiffly, and Samson's dark face appeared on the small display by Honor's right knee.

Unlike Honor and the rest of *Hawkwing*'s personnel, Samson was in his regular, comfortably worn-looking shipsuit, not a skinsuit. She wondered for a moment if that was a statement of confidence on his part, or if he simply didn't have one available after outfitting the Ballroom boarding party.

"Captain," she greeted him.

"Commander." His response actually sounded calmer than his voice had been during their planning and training sessions, but his eyes were brighter and harder than ever.

"According to Angelina, we'll be making our alpha translation in about fifteen minutes," he continued.

There was an almost but not quite questioning note to the statement, and Honor suppressed another smile as she heard it. Unless she missed her guess, Angelina Grimké McCutcheon, *Reprisal*'s "astrogator"—like Henri Christophe and Nat Jurgensen—had received her basic training courtesy of the Beowulfan military. Honor rather doubted Angelina had ever been commissioned or formally certified in astrogation, though. In fact, she had the feel of an experienced noncom, probably one who had served as a quartermaster *assisting* trained astrogators rather than doing the math herself, and it seemed evident most of *Reprisal*'s company nursed reservations about her abilities. She clearly did just fine in n-space, but from a couple of things Samson had let drop, it sounded as if her hyper-space astrogation was a bit...problematic.

Maybe it is, Honor thought now, *but she's managed to get them where they were going—so far, at least—without running into anything along the way. Considering my math skills, I'm not going to be throwing any stones at someone who's done that. And sooner or later, I'm sure, someone who was thoroughly trained as an astrogator by Mom's dear old home world is going to come along to relieve her. Assuming nothing unpleasant happens to* Reprisal *in the meantime, of course.*

For the moment, however, it was obvious Samson—and Angelina, for that matter—had breathed a huge sigh of relief when Aniella Matsakis turned up to handle the steering chore for this little expedition. And unlike Boyd, Matsakis seemed to have remarkably few problems with the notion of cooperating with the Ballroom.

"Yes, Captain." Honor decided to let just an edge of her smile show. "That matches our calculations, as well."

Samson's lips quivered, but he managed not to smile back at her.

"Have any last-minute details occurred to you, Commander?" he asked instead.

"No." Honor shook her head. "I think it's the best plan we could put together under the circumstances, and the last thing we need to be doing is trying to make last-minute revisions that are just going to confuse our people."

I wonder if it sounds as peculiar to him as it does to me for a Queen's officer to be referring to Ballroom "terrorists" as "our people"? she wondered.

"Agreed." Samson nodded, then rotated his shoulders and exhaled noisily. "I guess I'm a little more anxious over all of this than I'd like to think I am."

"I imagine we all are," Honor replied, feeling rather touched by the veteran freedom fighter/terrorist's admission.

"Well, I'll get off your com and let you get down to business, then," he said. "Samson, clear."

❖　　❖　　❖

The beep of the com interrupted Edytá Sokolowska at a very inconvenient moment. She ignored it, but it beeped again, less than three seconds later, this time with the sequence which indicated a priority message. She snarled a curse, shoved her bed partner roughly aside, grabbed the remote off the bedside table, and stabbed the acceptance key.

"Yes? What is it?" she demanded, raising her voice to carry across the sleeping cabin to the desktop unit as its display blinked to life.

"We've got an unscheduled incoming," Julian Watanabe said from the display. "One headed for us, not Anná or Beatá."

"What?" Sokolowska got out of bed, ignoring the man who was still in it, and crossed the compartment's carpeted floor towards the com. As she did, she realized she wasn't seeing the icon that indicated it was an audio-only call, and she grimaced and hit the remote button to kill the camera at her end.

"What *kind* of incoming?" she demanded.

"Impeller signature's showing a merchant wedge, probably around two megs," Watanabe replied confidently. As Casimir Station's weapons officer, the platform's sensors (such as they were, at any rate) reported to him. "Definitely not military, anyway. And she's squawking a Jessyk Combine transponder code, but we don't have her in our files."

Sokolowska frowned, using both hands to wipe sweat from her face while she considered what he'd just said.

The whole reason Manpower had moved in on Casimir in the first place was that, despite its strategic location within the Silesian Confederacy, it was a podunk little system which attracted little or no legitimate commerce. No one was likely to notice anything that was going on—especially this far out from the system primary— and any genuine merchantman who did turn up was going to be interested in the two inhabited planets—Anná and Beatá, otherwise known as Casimir I and II—and not Elsbietá, the gas giant the platform orbited. Elsbietá was thirty-three light-minutes from the system's K0 primary . . . which was another reason Manpower had been attracted to the depot; the planet was actually better than fifteen light-minutes outside the system hyper limit. Elsbietá was massive enough to generate a hyper limit of its own, but it was only three light-minutes deep, which meant ships could disappear into hyper a lot faster than they could if someone caught them in the inner system, deep inside the main limit. But all of that meant the huge gas-ball was located in an extraordinarily inconvenient position for almost any other purpose. Even the gasses harvested by the platform's scoop ships were collected by a pair of shuttling short-haul tankers and transported back to Beatá for processing and distribution.

As far as Sokolowska knew, neither of the tankers' crews were aware that anything untoward was happening out here, either. She knew their schedules, and whenever they were due to collect a cargo, any "visitors" headed off to the other side of Elsbietá-3, the largest of the planet's moons, and hid there until the tankers had turned back in-system. Of course, the local system governor most certainly *did* know (and was doing very well for herself out of the knowledge; Sokolowska knew she was, because she personally handled the monthly payoff), so she supposed it was possible the tanker crews knew all about it and had simply been ordered to keep their mouths shut.

The operative point, however, was that Elsbietá was in a hell of an out-of-the-way spot. So, logically, any ship which made her translation into normal-space this far out had to be here expressly to visit the depot. Which fitted with the transponder code Watanabe had reported.

So far, so good. But Edytá Sokolowska hadn't been chosen to run Casimir Depot because she was inclined to take anything for granted, and she didn't like the fact that they didn't have this ship in their database, Jessyk transponder or not. On the other hand . . .

"Have they said anything to us yet?"

"Not yet. But they just got here."

"Sure they have. And how far out are they?"

"About three light-minutes."

"And they've been back in normal-space, what? Five minutes, maybe?"

"Oh." Watanabe frowned, and Sokolowska snorted.

"Maybe I'm just being paranoid, but I think we should go ahead and contact them," she said. "I know they're squawking the right kind of transponder, but that doesn't necessarily mean they're who they say they are."

"Yeah. I'll get right on that."

"And while you're doing that, make sure the ready-duty ship knows what's going on. Who is it right now? Lawson or Tsien?"

Watanabe punched a button, looking at something outside the com's field of view, then looked back up.

"Lawson," he said.

"Great."

Sokolowska rolled her eyes. Emmet Lawson was never going to be confused with anyone's concept of a regular navy officer. He'd been successful at what he did for a long time, but he seemed to be slipping a bit, of late, and he'd never been at the apex of his profession to start with. All of which meant Sokolowska didn't have the liveliest confidence in how he was likely to react if a real emergency turned up.

"Go ahead and inform him we've got an unscheduled arrival," she said. "Do me a favor and stress the word 'unscheduled' when you talk to him, too. You might even want to add 'unidentified,' if you can get his attention."

"I'll do that," Watanabe promised with a lopsided grin. He and Sokolowska had their differences, but their opinions of Emmet Lawson were very similar. Sokolowska snorted at the thought, then glanced back over her shoulder at the man still waiting obediently in her bed.

That was another thing she and Watanabe had in common, she thought.

"How long for them to reach us?" she asked.

"They only carried about twelve hundred KPS across the wall with them, and they're only showing about two hundred gravities. Call it . . . two hours and forty-five minutes, give or take a couple of seconds."

"Then we've got some time, don't we?" She smiled hungrily. "Go ahead and talk to them. Find out who the hell they are. If anything sounds out of line, screen me back ASAP. Otherwise, I'll be up to the command deck in . . . oh, thirty minutes or so."

"Got it." Watanabe smirked on the display. "Have fun."

❊   ❊   ❊

"The platform is hailing us, Ma'am."

Lieutenant Boyd's voice sounded much more like its normal, crisp self, Honor noticed. She'd expected the communications officer to settle down once things actually started happening, but she was still glad to hear it.

"Are they accepting our transponder code so far?" she asked.

"Yes, Ma'am. Or at least they're hailing us as *Rapunzel.*"

"Then I suppose we ought to see just how good our friends' intel really is," Honor said calmly. "Throw it to my display, please."

"Aye, aye, Ma'am."

A moment later, Honor's display lit with the face a youngish looking man with brown hair and green eyes. He appeared to be a pleasant enough fellow, but looks could be deceiving, and he matched the description the Ballroom had given her for one Julian Watanabe. As Wolfe Tone had told her, "He looks like a choirboy, but he's one sick, sadistic piece of work. We've been wanting to meet up with *him* for a long time."

I think you *may just have a bit of a problem surrendering to my "allies" intact, assuming you're who I think you are,* she thought. *Pity about that.*

"*Rapunzel,* this is Casimir Station," the face on her display said. "We read your transponder, but we weren't expecting you. To what do we owe the pleasure?"

Honor smiled into her com pickup. Samson X and Christophe had both been emphatic about who had to handle this particular conversation, and she'd found herself in agreement with their reasoning. *Reprisal's* electronics were a lot less sophisticated than *she* would have wanted if she'd been engaged in an illegal trade which was (depending upon who captured one, of course) punishable by death. They didn't include the ability to play games with outgoing com signals, and anyone associated with Manpower would recognize someone like Samson or Christophe—or, at least, recognize what they *were*—on sight.

Hawkwing's electronics, on the other hand, were far more sophisticated than one would normally have expected out of a destroyer growing so long in the tooth. Partly, that reflected standard Manticoran refit policies, but it also reflected the fact that she was intended for service in Silesia, where the ability to pretend to be someone else was often essential when it came to sucking a potential pirate into range.

Or vice versa.

And even if that weren't true, a corner of her brain reflected, *Samson and his people are too psyched up. I don't care how professional they are, it'd be awful hard for any of them to keep that from showing if they actually had to talk to one of these . . . people.*

"Casimir Station," she said levelly while *Hawkwing's* computers replaced her naval skinsuit with the uniform of the Jessyk Combine, "this is *Rapunzel,* Daniela Magill, commanding. We know you weren't expecting us, but we got orders to divert to you from Caldwell. According to the word we got, there's a Manty cruiser sitting on top of our people there." She shrugged. "We've got places we've got to be, so they told us to drop our cargo off with you, so you could hold them until the Manties clear out of Caldwell and someone else can run them in."

So far as anyone aboard *Reprisal* or *Hawkwing* knew, there was no Jessyk Combine captain named Daniela Magill, nor was there a ship named *Rapunzel* in Jessyk's service. They'd debated trying to pass themselves off as one of the ships the Ballroom had identified as one of Casimir's at least semi-regular visitors. There'd been some arguments in favor of that approach, assuming they could guarantee they had an accurate reading on the transponder code—and emissions signature—of the ship in question. There'd been some downsides, as well, however . . . including the high probability that someone on the platform would have a personal acquaintance with somebody aboard the ship and want to talk to her.

Which was why they'd decided against trying it. To be sure, there were risks associated with fabricating an ID out of whole cloth, as well. On the other hand, nobody could possibly know everyone who worked for something the size of Jessyk. Besides, the Caldwell System was far enough away from Casimir to be outside the Casimir depot's operational area, and Manpower's normal procedure was to avoid putting any unnecessary information into its depot databases as a means of limiting damage if those databases should fall into unfriendly hands. It seemed probable the Jessyk Combine, which had worked so closely with Manpower for so long, would follow the same policy, so it was unlikely the station's crew would *expect* to recognize a ship which had been diverted to them at the last minute from so far away. All of which had suggested to Honor that it would be wiser to create an entirely fictitious vessel and a CO to go with it than to try to pretend she was someone they might actually know.

The transponder code *Reprisal* was squawking, on the other hand, was *mostly* genuine. Lieutenant Hutchinson and Lieutenant Boyd had spent several hours carefully altering the ship's number attached to the Jessyk house code, and Honor was confident it would stand up to any scrutiny it was likely to receive—except, of course, in the highly improbable event of that particular number belonging to one of the ships which was *supposed* to be operating in Casimir's vicinity.

Six minutes ticked away while the light-speed signal crossed to the platform and its response returned to *Hawkwing*.

"Aren't we a little bit far out of your way from Caldwell, Captain Magill?" Watanabe asked then.

"Actually, you're a hell of a lot out of the way from Caldwell," Honor agreed in an exasperated tone. "They didn't tell me exactly why I was supposed to dump this cargo on you, either. According to the routing instructions I've seen, though, at least half of it was going to be split off in Caldwell and sent your way." She shrugged. "Maybe they're just figuring they might as well get that part of it closer to delivered. And, to be fair, you were pretty close to our base least-time course to where it is we're supposed to be from where we were when they told us not to go to Caldwell. If you follow me."

Six minutes later, Watanabe grinned at her.

"Actually, I *do* follow you. Scary, isn't it? How big is this cargo of yours, Captain? How much life support are we going to need?"

"It's not huge," Honor told him. "Only a bit over seven hundred. But we've got fifty specials for a pleasure resort. They need to be kept segregated from the others, and they're shipping under pretty high trank levels, so somebody will need to keep an eye on the med levels, too."

"Understood. We can handle all that. I make your turnover in fifty-nine minutes, and arrival here at the station in about another hour and a half."

"That matches our numbers." Honor nodded. "If it's all right with you, though, we'll lighter them across instead of actually docking. We're running behind schedule, and I'd rather not take the time to rig personnel tubes."

"Not a problem from our end," Watanabe assured her. "Do you have enough shuttles, or do we need to send some out to help?"

"We're covered, I think, but thanks. We've already got them pretty well tranked on happy gas; by the time we start packing them into the shuttles, they'll be like sleepy little mice."

Honor allowed herself a nasty smile, and Watanabe smirked back at her.

"Understood," he said. "We'll see you then, Captain."

✳   ✳   ✳

"What a pain in the ass," Emmet Lawson growled as he grimaced at his executive officer.

Lawson, who practically never thought of himself as Ezzo Damasco these days, was built on the small side. He had a wiry, weasel-like quickness, black hair, a dark complexion, and dark brown eyes which looked as if they'd died years ago. He and his XO made an interesting contrast, since Kgell Rønningen was twenty centimeters taller than him, with fair hair, blue eyes, a powerful physique, and an air of gentle good humor.

That seeming good humor was deceptive, however. Like Lawson,

Rønningen couldn't have begun to count how many men and women he'd killed over the last two or three decades. As far as he knew, there weren't any actual interstellar murder warrants out for him... which there certainly were for the man who'd been born Ezzo Damasco back on Old Earth herself sixty T-years before. On the other hand, most of *his* murders had occurred in deep space, far from any officious, watching eyes.

"Well," he said now, shrugging massive shoulders, "it's not really a surprise, is it?"

"I just don't like all this Mickey Mouse bullshit," Lawson grumbled. "Bastards act like they're frigging admirals and I'm some goddammed brand-new ensign!"

Rønningen only grunted. Actually, he was beginning to have his doubts about Lawson. They'd only gotten off with their skins intact last time around by a fluke, as far as Rønningen could see, and that hadn't been the first time Lawson had walked into something. The number of times they could do that and walk *away* again had to be finite. Besides, the whole point in throwing in with the people here in Casimir in the first place had been to ensure a safe place to dispose of their loot and a safe haven for routine maintenance and R&R, and unlike Lawson, Rønningen had no problem pulling his weight in the cooperative effort to *keep* it a safe place.

And, he reflected (not for the first time), it wasn't unusual for a pirate vessel's executive officer to suddenly find himself its *commanding* officer following the mysterious disappearance of the previous CO. Especially when the rest of the ship's officers agreed with the XO in question that the previous captain's... questionable decisions had become a liability.

"All right!" Lawson waved one hand. "Tell them we've received their damned message and we're keeping an eye on things."

"And should I go ahead and bring the weapons up?" Rønningen, who doubled as the ship's tactical officer, inquired.

"Go ahead," Lawson said resignedly.

* * *

"I've got something you should take a look at, Skipper," Lieutenant Hutchinson said, and Honor turned her command chair to face the tactical section.

"What is it, Fred?"

"We're getting good telemetry back from the recon drones," *Hawkwing*'s tac officer said. "Most of it's not too surprising—the

Ballroom guys did a good job digging out the original stats and authorization order for the platform's weapons outfit, and it doesn't look like there've been too many changes from the file copies. But their intel about these people's keeping a ship at readiness looks to have been right on the money, too."

Honor nodded patiently. She'd noticed the icon of the single ship standing fifteen hundred kilometers clear of the platform with her impeller nodes online over a quarter-hour ago.

"Well, Skipper, the interesting thing about it is that we *know* that ship."

"We do?" Honor's eyes narrowed.

"Yes, Ma'am. According to her transponder, that's the Andermani-registry ship *Christiane Kirsch,* but she's got all her active sensors online. We're getting good, solid reads off of them, and according to CIC's records, her *emissions signature* belongs to our old friend *Evita.*"

Honor suppressed the almost automatic reflex of asking Hutchinson if he was sure about that. Frederick Hutchinson was very young—only about four T-years older than Everett Janacek—but he'd been *Hawkwing's* tactical officer for over ten T-months now. He'd demonstrated his competence over those months, and he wouldn't have said what he'd just said if he hadn't double and triple-checked CIC's evaluation first.

That was her first thought. Her second was considerably more bloodthirsty.

"Well," she said aloud, "I suppose we might consider her presence here additional evidence of Governor Charnowska's involvement. If we had naturally suspicious minds, of course." She smiled thinly. "I'm confident the governor could come up with all sorts of perfectly reasonable explanations for how it all could have happened without her knowledge."

"I'm sure she could, Ma'am," Hutchinson replied with a tree-catlike smile.

"On the other hand, it does give us a certain additional...freedom of action," Honor continued. Her tone was almost whimsical, but her almond eyes were as cold as the vacuum outside *Hawkwing's* hull. "Good work, Guns. I think we'll go with Polka One."

"Polka One, aye, Ma'am," Hutchinson acknowledged, and his smile turned even more predatory as he added, "It works for me, Skip."

＊　　＊　　＊

"I thought you said *thirty* minutes," Julian Watanabe observed as Edytá Sokolowska finally arrived on the command deck.

"I did." She gave him the smile of a temporarily—very temporarily—satisfied predator. "But I'm discovering that with the proper...incentive his endurance can be pretty amazing."

Watanabe returned her smile. Both of them had come into Manpower's employ for primarily financial reasons, but there'd been other attractions, as well. Attractions which had a lot to do with why—before their Manpower days, at least—both of them had made it a point to avoid professions which would have required basic psych evaluations.

Watanabe had been reprimanded twice for "excessive wastage of product," which took some doing, given Manpower's usual attitudes. It hadn't come close to disqualifying him from sensitive positions—in fact, Manpower actually preferred people like him in a lot of ways; their appetites gave their employers an extra handle on them—but his pay had been docked for the full price of the slaves—*all* the slaves—on both occasions.

Sokolowska knew all about those reprimands, and she couldn't have cared less, although her own tastes ran to rather more... subtle forms of entertainment. Watanabe was reputed to be inventive, but he used his toys up quickly. Sokolowska, on the other hand, had a lot more of the sharp-clawed cat in her makeup, including the need to savor her play for as long as she could. Physical cruelty was all very well, and no doubt satisfying in its own way, but it palled too quickly for her taste. She found it much more delicious to compel her playthings—male or female—to lavish pleasure upon her. Fear of pain could do that, and inflicting it as she went along added a certain savor of its own to the moment, but she found *psychological* terror an even more satisfying vintage. Which actually made her and Watanabe partners upon occasion. After all, what could drive a man to thoroughly satisfy her libido better than the knowledge that if he failed—if she should happen to be...dissatisfied with his efforts in any slightest way—his preadolescent son or daughter would be sent to entertain Watanabe?

She brushed that pleasurable thought aside and turned her attention to the master display.

The information displayed above *Rapunzel's* icon showed the ship was still about ten minutes from actual rendezvous with the depot. Her velocity was down to 1,176 KPS, and the range was barely 353,000 kilometers.

"Anything more from them about those fifty specials?"

"No." Watanabe shook his head, then cocked it to one side. "It does sound interesting, though, doesn't it?"

"Don't even think about it, Julian." She turned to give him a stern glance. "Management will put up with a lot, but if they say it's so important to keep these separated from the rest, messing with them is a good way to end up with something a lot worse than burned fingers."

"Oh, I know," he acknowledged with a slightly wistful expression. "Still, it does give one to think."

"As long as thinking is all you're doing." She shook her head. "It's not like you don't have plenty to pick and choose from right here on the depot."

He nodded, and Sokolowska turned back to the display, satisfied—or at least mostly so—that he really would keep his hands to himself. Still, she couldn't pretend she was *positive* he would, and the front office would probably tolerate it even if he did...slip a little.

Why he can't just be content with the ones that aren't off-limits is beyond me, she reflected. *Maybe that's part of the attraction for him? The fact that he's flirting with danger himself when he crosses the line?*

Whatever it was, she wasn't even tempted to emulate him. She'd just stick to the low-cost merchandise. Or, even better, do her hunting on the side. Most of the platform's "official" personnel were family men and women, which made them much better suited to her own type of play. And this *was* the perfect opportunity to indulge herself with the sort of toys which were usually harder to "disappear" than mere slaves.

After all, no depot could be left permanently in place, especially not when it was serving so many ends at once. Sooner or later, even as sweet a setup as they had here, with Charnowska and Obermeyer both on the pad, had to come to an end at last. And when the time finally came for Manpower to fold its tent here in Casimir and move on, they wouldn't be leaving any witnesses behind.

✳   ✳   ✳

"Coming up on ninety seconds, Skipper," Fred Hutchinson announced. The fair-haired tactical officer's blue eyes were narrow, focused on his own displays, and Honor nodded.

"Thank you, Guns." Her voice was even calmer than usual, but all of her officers had been with her long enough to know what that meant. "Stand by for separation, Helm."

"Standing by for separation, aye," Aloysius O'Neal responded from where he stood with one hand on the seated helmsman's shoulder and his own eyes on the maneuvering display.

The sailing master's taut voice was noticeably less calm than hers, but its tension was that of concentration, not fear, and Honor glanced at the single icon floating well clear of the platform on the main tactical plot. Under the strict letter of interstellar law, her next preparatory order should be to Florence Boyd, she reflected. Instead, she turned back to the com display by her knee.

"Captain Samson?"

"Standing by for separation," Samson X confirmed over the com. He sounded quite a bit more nervous than O'Neal did, she noticed. Well, considering what even a slight helm error on *Hawkwing*'s part would do to his ship, he had a right to be nervous.

"We will execute separation on my mark," she continued. "Tactical, confirm Polka One."

"Polka One set and locked, Captain," Hutchinson said formally.

"Very well then, people," Honor said, watching the digital display tick down the handful of seconds. "Let's be about it."

There was complete silence on the destroyer's bridge for another seven seconds. Then—

"Execute separation!"

❈   ❈   ❈

One moment, everything was perfectly normal aboard Casimir Depot, proceeding exactly according to plan. *Rapunzel* was less than eight thousand kilometers out, down to barely a hundred seventy-six kilometers per second, ninety seconds from her zero-zero rendezvous with the platform.

The next moment, things changed...drastically.

❈   ❈   ❈

It took a moment for Kgell Rønningen to realize what was happening. It wasn't really his fault—Honor Harrington and her allies had gone to great lengths to ensure that no one would realize what was happening until it was too late. It had never occurred to anyone in Casimir that the "slave ship" plodding so sedately towards the depot might have a royal Manticoran warship tractored limpetlike to its side. That its approach vector might have been carefully chosen to keep that ship in its shadow, hidden from any of its enemies' sensors even after the warship in question broke skin contact. That HMS *Hawkwing* might have carefully positioned herself one hundred kilometers clear of *Reprisal,* still hidden between the roof and floor of the big freighter's impeller wedge, but far enough out to clear the threat perimeter of her own wedge when the time came.

And it had come *now.*

✳   ✳   ✳

"Kill the wedge!" Samson X barked, and his engineer hit the master switch.

Reprisal's wedge disappeared instantly, and a fraction of a second later, *Hawkwing*'s slammed up. The destroyer had cut her tractor connection to the freighter the instant Honor gave the separation order; now she rolled and went to her maximum acceleration—5.14 KPS^2—and raced clear of her enormous companion, even as *Reprisal* rolled much more slowly on gyros and reaction thrusters alone.

Her new heading was the exact reciprocal of *Reprisal*'s. As the two ships continued to roll, they moved the threat perimeters of their wedges away from one another. It took barely nine seconds for *Reprisal* to clear her wedge perimeter, and the big freighter's wedge flicked back up. She turned away, simultaneously continuing her roll, and presented the belly of that wedge to Casimir Depot. All of *Hawkwing*'s highly stealthy recon drones had confirmed that none of the platform's internal weapons were online. Neither of the two ships moored to the platform had any offensive or defensive weapons online, either. Which was fine...but neither Honor nor Samson X intended to take any chances, anyway.

The smaller, far more responsive and maneuverable destroyer went scooting away from her vast consort, and the drones she had deployed on the way in drove CIC's plot even when her own wedge blocked her shipboard sensors. She knew exactly where the depot's "guard ship" was, and she snap-rolled back down to bring her broadside to bear.

While the fact that Honor had positively confirmed that *Evita* was a known pirate vessel might not technically excuse her from the requirement to challenge her before opening fire, she wasn't particularly concerned about that, either. Especially since *Evita* must have come directly here, which meant it was virtually certain she'd had no time to capture fresh "technical support personnel" to replace the ones *Hawkwing* had liberated from her.

There were *only* pirates aboard her . . . and that was what Polka One was all about.

"Target solution!" Fred Hutchinson announced—quite unnecessarily, except that regulations required him to inform Honor—and stabbed the master key on his console.

Hawkwing was no ship-of-the-wall. Nor was she a cruiser. In fact, she wasn't even a particularly modern destroyer. But she still had three missile tubes, four Mark 31 sixty-centimeter lasers, and four Mark 16 point defense clusters in each broadside, and— "ready-duty ship" or not—*Evita* was totally unprepared when the Manticoran demon abruptly materialized, literally out of nowhere, at a range of under six thousand kilometers.

At that range, there was no need for missiles. *Hawkwing's* port broadside lasers knew exactly where she was, and it would have been extraordinarily difficult for her to miss.

*   *   *

"*Shit!*" Kgell Rønningen gasped as his numbed brain raced to catch up with the information suddenly inundating it. "It's a goddammed *des—*"

Hawkwing's number two laser scored a direct hit on *Evita's* command deck. Not that it would have mattered one way or the other. Not a single member of the pirate vessel's crew was in a skinsuit. Not one of them had suspected even for a moment that they might suddenly find themselves under attack. Most of them were in their quarters, many in their bunks, and every single one of them was totally unprepared when Honor Harrington's ship ripped their vessel apart around them.

Evita's hull didn't shatter under *Hawkwing's* fire—it *disintegrated*. The terrible beams of coherent energy punched clear through the vast, vulnerable, unarmored bubble of alloy and life-support. Atmosphere belched from the terrible wounds, and bodies and pieces of bodies were borne out of the ship on the escaping tornado. And then, without warning, her fusion plant blew, and the entire ship vanished in an expanding boil of brilliance.

*   *   *

Edytá Sokolowska and Julian Watanabe were just as stunned as Rønningen had been. Unlike *Evita*'s executive officer, however, they at least lived long enough to realize what was happening.

"God*damn!*" Watanabe blurted.

He wheeled to his own command console and the heel of his hand slammed down on the general quarters button. Alarms began to howl throughout the platform, and men and women looked up in stark disbelief. They were criminals, not military personnel, and they lacked the spinal-reflex training to respond instantly. Shock and sheer, stunned surprise paralyzed all of them, at least briefly.

Not that it mattered.

Hawkwing rolled back down, presenting her broadside to the platform. Honor had never even considered using her ship's main armament against the station. There were far too many innocent noncombatants aboard it for that. But the weapons modules had been boom-mounted in order to get them far enough from the bulbous, asymmetrical hull of the platform to have decent fields of fire. That meant they were far enough from all of those innocent noncombatants for her to target them.

Even so, this was no job for her main energy weapons. Besides, the point defense clusters had a vastly higher rate of fire. Now they opened up, spitting out chained lightning, and Casimir Depot's weapons were blotted away with dreadful, effortless precision.

"Attention, Casimir Depot!" a frozen-helium soprano voice said sharply and crisply over the general emergency frequency. "This is Commander Honor Harrington, Royal Manticoran Navy. Your base's weapons have been destroyed. If either of the ships moored to the station attempts to move in any way, or attempts to activate any weapons system, I will destroy it immediately. There will be no additional warning. If you don't believe me, I invite you to try."

The main com display flickered, and the woman who had introduced herself as Daniela Magill looked out of it at them. Her ship's computers were no longer manipulating the signal, and Edytá Sokolowska's blood ran cold as she recognized the insignia on the skinsuit she wore. It wasn't one any employee of Manpower, Incorporated, was likely to mistake.

"I am fully aware that the original crew of the platform you've seized is still aboard," the almond-eyed woman on the display said coldly. "Be informed that I have sufficient personnel aboard

'*Rapunzel*' to take that habitat away from you, one dead body at a time. Be further informed that if it becomes necessary to do that, I will. And that if anything should happen to the innocent personnel aboard that platform, I personally guarantee there will be quite a *lot* of dead bodies by the time my people are finished."

She paused, letting them see the iron-hard sincerity in those agatelike brown eyes.

"If you surrender, I will guarantee that you will be taken into custody and offered fair trials," she continued after a moment, "but that's the only guarantee I'm prepared to make you. You have five minutes to decide what you're going to do. Personally, I advise you to surrender without further resistance. Otherwise, believe me, you *will* regret it."

＊　　＊　　＊

"What the *fuck* do we do now?" Watanabe demanded, wheeling to stare at Sokolowska. "We're screwed—*screwed!* We don't—"

"Shut up!" Sokolowska snapped. He blinked, and she caught the front of his shipsuit and shook him with a snarl. "That's the goddamned *Manty* navy out there, you idiot!"

Watanabe licked his lips, his face pale. The Star Kingdom of Manticore had made its position on the genetic slave trade abundantly clear: slaving and piracy were legally the same thing as far as the Royal Navy was concerned. Which meant every single Manpower employee aboard the platform was subject to the death penalty...and that "fair trials" or no, this Harrington had all the authorization she needed to convict them on her own authority and execute sentence here and now.

That was true for all of them, but if it should happen that Manticore knew about the specific activities of one Edytá Sokolowska and Julian Watanabe, it would almost certainly be even *more* true for them.

Which completely ignored what the Manties would discover about their actions right here in Casimir if any of the original platform's personnel ever had the opportunity to testify.

"So what?" Watanabe demanded after a moment. "So it's the fucking Manties! What're we going to *do* about it? We don't even have a damned *popgun* left, and if they really send in frigging *Marines*—!"

"Shut up!" she snapped again, then tossed him away from her with a grimace.

"You—Baker!" she barked at a white-faced, paralyzed com tech. "Send a message in clear to Governor Obermeyer. Tell her we're under attack by a Manticoran destroyer, and she'd better whistle this bitch the hell off of us if she doesn't want to go down with us!"

"But—"

The technician stared at her for a moment, then shook himself like a dog flinging off water.

"But Beatá's practically on the other side of the primary from us! I'll have to bounce off one of the relays in the Belt, and if I send in clear, everybody who sees it is gonna know what we're saying! And the transmission lag's going to be better than forty minutes, each way!"

"So code the damned thing!" Sokolowska snarled.

"But the lag—"

"Screw the goddamned 'lag'!" If she'd had a sidearm, she would have shot him where he stood, she thought viciously. "Send... the...damned...message," she ground out, one word at a time. "And make sure that frigging destroyer *knows* you sent it!"

For a moment, she thought the idiot was going to run his mouth some more, but then he closed it with a click, nodded, and wheeled back around to his own console.

"He's got a point," Watanabe said. His voice was calmer and quieter than it had been, although she didn't much like the look in his green eyes. "There's no way in hell Obermeyer's going to be able to 'whistle off' something like this. And even if she could, we're looking at an hour and a half before anything from her could even get back to us!"

"I know that, you idiot." She glared at him. "But you know as well as I do what's going to happen if the damned Manties get their hands on us. On *us*, Julian, whatever happens to anybody else!"

"And this is supposed to stop that from happening exactly how?" he demanded.

"If that bitch out there—that Harrington—knows we've sent the message, she's also going to know we've got all kinds of contacts with the Sillies. Maybe she doesn't realize yet just how badly she could burn her fingers over this one, so it won't hurt a damned thing if we *tell* her, now will it? And in the meantime, I'll be damned if I roll over and play dead for her! She can't crack this platform open without killing those precious 'innocent personnel' of hers, and that's only a frigging destroyer over there."

"What about all those Marines she says she's got aboard '*Rapunzel*'?" he challenged.

"It's probably a bluff! I don't care what she says—I'll bet you that's just a merchie she's picked up somewhere to use for cover to get close enough to us," Sokolowska shot back, and as she did, she realized she actually meant what she was saying. "If they'd had time to put together a *real* assault force, they wouldn't've sent it in with nothing but a *destroyer* to side it, Julian! That entire damned freighter's probably running the next best thing to empty! So all they've probably got over there—*at most*—is a single platoon of Marines, and we've got close to twelve hundred people aboard this orbiting can!"

"None of whom have battle armor," Watanabe pointed out.

"So? Even with battle armor there's still only going to be thirty or forty of them—and that's assuming they've got armor for all of them, which they damned well *won't* have. And even if she really thinks she's got enough Marines over there to take us hand-to-hand, she's going to know some of those people she's so frigging worried about are likely to get caught in the crossfire. So let's see if she's so damned willing to come in here after us if we tell her there's no way in hell we're surrendering and she knows I've already put in a call to the local system government!"

❊   ❊   ❊

"The platform's just transmitted a message, Skipper," Florence Boyd reported. The com officer's reservations seemed to have abated—or receded from the forefront of her thoughts, at least—but her expression was anxious.

"What kind of message?" Honor asked calmly.

"I don't know, Ma'am." Boyd shook her head, blue eyes troubled. "It was encrypted."

"They wouldn't be sending it if they didn't expect someone to hear it, Skip," Taylor Nairobi pointed out from Honor's command chair com display. With the ship closed up for action, he was stationed in Auxiliary Control with the backup command crew, but he was tapped in to everything that was happening on the bridge. At the moment, his expression was less worried than Boyd's . . . but not a lot.

"Or unless it was a bluff," Honor pointed out. The exec looked at her skeptically, and she shrugged. "I didn't say it *was* a bluff; I only pointed out that it could be."

"And if it isn't one?"

"If it isn't one, then it's probably confirmation the Ballroom was right about Governor Obermeyer," Honor said, still in that calm, almost serene tone. "Which wouldn't come as an enormous surprise, now would it?"

"What do you think they're telling her, Ma'am?" Nairobi asked in a quieter voice.

"I imagine they're telling her they're under attack by a Manticoran warship and that she should exercise her authority by ordering us to stand down and leave them alone."

Nairobi looked more worried than before, and Honor gave him a smile.

"It's not as if we didn't see this as a possibility, Taylor," she pointed out.

"Which doesn't make me feel a whole lot better," he replied grimly.

"Maybe not, but—"

"Skipper, the platform's hailing us," Boyd interrupted.

"Put it on the main display, Florence," Honor said, and turned to face it as a chestnut-haired, brown-eyed woman appeared on it. She matched the Ballroom's description of one Edytá Sokolowska.

"Have you made your decision?" Honor asked in a voice of icy calm.

"Damned straight we have!" the other woman—Sokolowska—snarled. "You can take your destroyer and your frigging Marines and shove them right up your ass, lady! The way I figure it, you've got about ninety minutes—max—before you get your marching orders from Governor Obermeyer. What are you going to do to us in an hour and a half with one damned destroyer's worth of Marines?"

She sneered, and Honor wondered if she really believed what she was saying or if she only wanted to convince *Honor* that she did. Either way . . .

"Ms. Sokolowska—it *is* Ms. Sokolowska, isn't it?" Honor smiled very slightly as the other woman failed to completely conceal a flinch of surprise. She let a moment of silence linger, then shrugged.

"Ms. Sokolowska, I trust you don't think I'm stupid enough not to have realized that for you to be operating so brazenly here in Casimir, Governor Obermeyer has to be aware of your activities. Which, I have no doubt, means she's as deeply in bed with you and Manpower as Sector Governor Charnowska."

Sokolowska paled visibly, and this time Honor's smile was a hexapuma's hunting snarl.

"Of course I'm aware of your exalted patrons and protectors, Ms. Sokolowska," she said coldly. "Unfortunately for you, none of them seem to be here at the moment...and *I* am. And it may surprise you to discover this, but neither of them is in *my* chain of command and I don't really *care* very much what they may think of my current actions."

"You're bluffing!" Sokolowska snapped. "I don't care who the hell you think you are, what do you think your own government is going to say if you provoke an incident on this kind of scale?!"

"You really think Charnowska and Obermeyer are going to *admit* after the fact that they were in *Manpower's* pocket?" Honor gave her a half-pitying look. "They'll kick you out the lock like yesterday's garbage, Sokolowska, and you know it. Unless, of course, some of you would care to turn Queen's evidence and testify against them."

"They wouldn't have to admit a thing to demand *your* head!" Sokolowska sounded a bit more desperate, Honor decided.

"Maybe not," she replied, with another of those hexapuma smiles. "On the other hand, maybe I don't really care about *that,* either. And whether I do or not, it's not going to make one bit of difference to what happens out here, in this star system, in the next hour or so."

"You try coming aboard this platform, and a hell of a lot of those 'innocent personnel' you're so damned worried about are likely to get killed," he Sokolowska told her flatly.

"Let's get something straight here, right now," Honor said flatly. "I know all about Manpower's usual operating procedures. I know as well as you do that every one of those people is dead the instant you leave that station and head off to set up shop somewhere else. That was going to happen no matter what. And if I back off now, you're just going to go ahead and kill every single one of them before you blow up your 'depot' and try to disappear into the general system population. So don't think threatening them is going to cause me to change my mind. On the other hand, perhaps you'd care to contemplate the fact that I'm telling you nothing but the truth about the boarders I've got aboard 'Rapunzel.' And I never said they were *Marines.*"

"What?" Sokolowska's eyes narrowed. "What the hell are you talking about now?!"

"I'm talking about the Audubon Ballroom, Ms. Sokolowska." Honor's voice was flatter than ever, and a muscle began to tic at the corner of her mouth. "I've got the next best thing to a thousand of them aboard '*Rapunzel*,' and, trust me, they'd *really* like to dance with *you*."

She stared into Sokolowska's eyes, and silence hovered between them. It stretched out for several seconds before the other woman shook herself and glared at her.

"You're lying. You don't actually expect me to believe that even a *Manty* would actually launch an attack on sovereign Silesian territory with a bunch of goddammed terrorists, do you?" Sokolowska barked a laugh. "Nice try, but that's too much!"

"This Manty is also half-Beowulfan," Honor told her very softly, "and if this is going to cost me my career, so be it. We're coming aboard that platform, Sokolowska, and we're taking every slave, and every innocent worker, off of it with us. And if you're considering going ahead and killing some of them—or even all of them—in an effort to convince us to back off, you'd better think about all the stories you've ever heard about the Ballroom, too. Because the only thing standing between a thousand of them and you is *me*."

"You wouldn't dare." Sokolowska glared at her, but there was a flicker of something very like panic in those brown eyes now. "Even if that freighter of yours *is* stuffed with those lunatics, you wouldn't dare turn them loose on us. They wouldn't just break you for that one—they'd frigging well *crucify* you!"

"I'm willing to take that chance, Ms. Sokolowska ... are you?"

Two pairs of brown eyes locked, and then Sokolowska bared her teeth.

"Damn straight," she said softly. "*Damn* straight. You come aboard this platform, *Commander*. Go ahead. I *invite* you, because, you know what? I don't have a damned thing to lose. So, the instant the first one of your Marines—or one of those Ballroom lunatics—sets foot aboard this platform, I'll—"

Suddenly, with absolutely no warning, Sokolowska's head exploded in a grisly spray of red, gray, and fine, white splinters of bone. Honor heard the high, unmistakable whine of a pulser. Somebody screamed, and then more pulsers were firing.

It seemed to go on forever, although it couldn't actually have been more than a very small handful of seconds. Then, abruptly, another face filled the display. A man's face, with dark eyes and dark hair streaked with silver.

"I'm Kamil Mazur, the senior engineer!" he said hoarsely. "We're not all like that lunatic bitch!"

"Good. Should I assume you intend to surrender, then?" Honor's voice was calm, unshaken by the sudden violence.

"Yes! I mean—" The man shook himself. "I mean, *I'm* ready to surrender, and so are a lot of the others, I'm sure. But not all of them." He grimaced. "Some of the rest are like her—they'll figure they've got nothing to lose. There's no way I could control them, even if I tried."

"Then, Mr. Mazur, I would recommend that you and anyone who agrees with you get down to wherever your prisoners are held and keep them alive," Honor said coldly. "We're coming aboard... and my 'associates' aren't going to be very happy if they find a lot of dead slaves. Do you understand me?"

"I can't—I mean, how am I supposed to—"

"That's *your* problem." Her voice could have frozen a star's heart, and her eyes were pitiless. "Figure it out. And remember this. If you get killed trying to keep them alive, it will probably still be better than what would happen to you if the Ballroom gets its hands on you and they're dead."

She held his eyes for a moment, seeing the warring tides of panic and desperate hope in them, and felt no pity for him at all.

"Harrington, clear," she said.

❋　　❋　　❋

"Down!"

Honor grunted in surprise as someone slammed into her, tackling her and driving her to the deck plates. She hit hard on her shoulder and grunted again—this time in anguish. Whoever had tackled her sprawled across her, and the external mike on her skinsuit brought her the hissing shriek of the heavy tribarrel's darts and the staccato thunder as they struck the bulkhead above her and the hurricane of explosions ripped it apart. The weight across her legs shifted, a pulser whined, someone screamed, and the tribarrel abruptly stopped firing.

The man who'd tackled her—one of the Ballroom fighters assigned to Henri Christophe's command group—rolled aside and came up on his knees, grinning down at her through his helmet visor as she pushed herself up cautiously on one elbow.

"You want to keep an eye out for that kind of thing, Commander," he told her over the com. "Be awful embarrassing to the Ballroom if we go and lose the only regular Navy officer who's ever actually cooperated with us!"

"I'll try to keep that in mind," she told him.

"Good, because—"

He broke off, lunging to one side, as Honor's right hand suddenly snapped up and her pulser fired through the space his helmeted head had occupied a moment before. The Manpower holdout behind him collapsed backward through the door Honor and her companion had just fought their way through, and the grenade he'd been about to throw exploded on the other side of the bulkhead. It was an antipersonnel grenade, and half a dozen of the lethal little flechettes came whining through the open door—none of them, fortunately, on a trajectory that intersected Honor or the Ballroom fighter.

"You want to keep an eye out for that kind of thing," she told him dryly, and heard his half-breathless laugh over the com.

"Sure thing," he said.

He squirmed around to look back through the doorway, then stood and reached a hand down to her.

"Looks like there were—operative word being 'were'—three of 'em," he observed. "Terrible what a grenade like that will do in close quarters."

"The same thought had occurred to me," Honor admitted, letting him boost her back to her feet.

"Yeah, that kind of thing happens."

He shrugged, then his eyes went slightly unfocused as he glanced at the heads-up display projected on the inside of his Beowulfan skinsuit's visor. It wasn't quite as good as the HUD built into a Manticoran Marine's battle armor, but it was a lot better than nothing, and Honor found herself wishing—again—that she had one. Unfortunately, her skinsuit was Navy-issue, and it wasn't supposed to need the sort of tactical display to keep track of this kind of fight. Since, of course, the Navy recognized the self-evident fact that no naval officer, and especially not the commander of a Queen's starship, had any business at all doing something like this.

That was a point which Taylor Nairobi, Aloysius O'Neal, Mahalia Rosenberg, and Fred Hutchinson had all drawn rather emphatically to her attention, and she'd known they were right. She *didn't* have any business in this madhouse. It wasn't the sort of fight she'd trained for, she had zero expertise in this kind of combat environment, and the last thing anyone would have needed was her trying to give orders to people who *did* know what they were doing.

None of which changed the fact that she had to be here, anyway.

"We go *that* way," her companion said, pointing, and she nodded.

"Lead the way. I'll just tag along and try to cover your back."

"So far, you're doing pretty well," he told her with a harsh chuckle. "Come on."

She followed him out of the compartment and down a passageway littered with bodies, its blood-splashed bulkheads scarred by pulser darts, grenade fragments, and the deadly, multi-sided needles of flechette guns. They moved quickly but cautiously, and the thunder of combat roared up again ahead of them as they turned a bend in the passage and caught up with the rest of Christophe's command group.

Another clutch of Manpower holdouts was dug in, covering the approach to one of the main lift banks. However ultimately hopeless their situation might be, for the moment, they had good defensive positions. They'd obviously had time to prepare for this moment, and they'd parked a batch of heavy-duty repair servo mechs across the passage to form a solid breastwork. Now they were pouring out a heavy fire from behind its cover, and Honor saw one of the skinsuited figures in front of her go down in a geyser of blood.

"*Shit!*" her companion snarled, and Honor's jaw clenched.

Somebody on the other side of those servo mechs had a tri-barrel. The good news was that the depot's inhabitants appeared to have had very few heavy weapons. The bad news was that every single one of the ones they did have seemed to have found its way into the hands of one of the "no surrender" fanatics. And while the armored skinsuits most of the Ballroom fighters had brought along offered fairly good protection against standard pulsers, they weren't battle armor, which meant they weren't designed to stop *that* kind of fire.

"Fire in the hole!"

She recognized Henri Christophe's voice and flung herself instantly back onto the deck. A moment later, half a dozen somethings arced up and sailed across the barricade. The boarding grenades were offensive weapons, designed to stun and disorient even skinsuited enemies, but not so powerful that the people who'd thrown them couldn't follow the explosion up quickly. She'd learned that much getting this far, and—

"Let's dance!" Christophe screamed, and as the rest of the command group leapt to its feet and charged the barricade, Honor found herself right in the middle of them.

The next few instants were all mad, bloody confusion—screaming pulser darts, flechettes, even combat knives and vibro blades. Christophe lost three more people on the way in—one dead, two wounded—but fortified position or not, the Manpower thugs were no match in close combat for the Ballroom.

There were no Manpower survivors, and Christophe looked at Honor.

"Sorry about that," he said.

"About what?" She smiled grimly at him. "I didn't hear anybody trying to surrender."

"No, I guess you didn't." He smiled back at her, then checked his own HUD.

"According to the master display, Nat and your Platoon Sergeant Keegan are almost through to the slaves. And your Lieutenant Janacek is punching straight through to Engineering, too," he said, and shook his head in something like admiration. "You don't suppose he'd care to sign up with the Ballroom, do you, Commander?"

"No," Honor said rather repressively.

"I was afraid you'd feel that way."

His com beeped and he looked away from her, focusing on his HUD again, then inhaled in obvious relief.

"Nat and Keegan've gotten through to the slave quarters!" he said, and grinned at Honor. "Sounds like you managed to inject at least a little backbone into that asshole Mazur. Leastways, he and three or four others were down there personally making sure none of their buddies got to the people we're here to rescue."

"Good." Honor managed to keep her vast relief out of her voice, but Christophe obviously heard it anyway, and he flashed her another smile.

"Meanwhile," he went on, extending a handheld display board for her to see, "most of the rest of the holdouts seemed to be concentrated over here, in Delta Sector." He tapped the indicated area of the station with an index finger and grimaced. "Don't suppose they actually think they can get a cargo shuttle or a scoop ship past your ship, do you?"

"Not likely."

Honor studied the display. As he'd said, it showed the heaviest concentration of remaining resistance on the side of the platform's core hull where the scoop ships were berthed.

"I doubt anyone was doing anything as clear as actually 'thinking' about anything," she told Christophe after a moment. "More likely, it was as much instinct as anything else."

"Well, whatever it was, it's convenient as hell for us," Christophe said grimly. "We know where they are, and there's no place for them to go . . . except Hell, of course."

Honor looked at him levelly, and he glared back for a moment. Then he drew a deep breath and shook his head.

"I know—I *know!*" He shook his head again. "We promised, and I'll try. But at this point, given where they are, and given that they know where we have to come from to get to them, I can't make any guarantees about taking any of them alive. Especially since I kind of doubt any of *these* people are especially interested in surrendering in the first place."

"Fair enough," Honor said, after a moment, and she meant it.

The entire reason she'd overruled Nairobi, O'Neal, and the others who'd wanted her to do the sane thing and stay aboard *Hawkwing,* where she belonged, was to glue herself to Christophe. She knew, thanks to Nimitz, that he and Nat Jurgensen had meant it when they promised to avoid atrocities, but there were limits to what could be expected out of flesh and blood. Much as Honor hated Manpower and the genetic slave trade, she knew she couldn't truly appreciate the hatred of someone like the Ballroom's fighters, however hard she tried. And when the stress of combat, and the fresh losses they were going to take among their friends, were mixed into that hatred, Christophe's people would have had to be more than human not to be tempted.

If Everett Janacek had been twice as old, or if he'd had twice as many Marines, or if he'd had to be in half as many places at once with the ones he had, she would have been willing to stay aboard ship. But it had been absolutely imperative for them to smash their way through to Engineering and to the slaves and imprisoned civilians as quickly as possible. Because of that, she'd known going in that her Marines—especially the ones in battle armor—were going to be too spread out across the station to simultaneously take their own objectives and ride herd on their "allies." And despite the deep confidence she'd come to feel in Janacek, she'd also known that to too many of the Ballroom fighters, he was "that snot-nosed kid." She had no doubt he would have done his duty, whatever it required of him, but she'd also known things were far more likely to come apart if she left him to cope with what, after all, was *her* responsibility.

She'd never know whether or not her presence had actually been necessary, but there'd been a time or two when Christophe had glanced her way and she'd felt the hunger quivering around her in the members of his command group. Yet nothing had come of it, and those moments had all been near the beginning of this long, exhausting running fight. Before they'd seen *Hawkwing's* captain's skinsuit splashed with blood—their enemies' and their own—and seen her holding up her own end in a fight they knew as well as she did that she'd never been trained for.

Now she glanced at the display again, then looked back up at Christophe.

"Assuming any of them do want to surrender, we'll give them one last chance," she told him levelly. "After that, if they choose not to, well . . ."

She shrugged, and Christophe nodded slowly.

"No atrocities," he promised.

"That's good enough for me," Honor Stephanie Harrington told him, then looked into his eyes. "So we'll give them their chance, and then . . . we'll dance," she finished softly.

＊　　＊　　＊

"God, what a *mess,* Ma'am."

Surgeon Lieutenant Mauricio Neukirch stood with Honor in what had once been the wardroom of Casimir Depot. At the moment, it had been turned into a dressing station for several dozen casualties, and Neukirch shook his head wearily. He and his sick-bay attendants—ably assisted by a team of Ballroom corpsmen—were haggard with exhaustion, and not just because of the combat casualties.

"I know, Mauricio," Honor said quietly. "I know."

She turned to survey the wounded lying about her. Most of them were Ballroom fighters, but two were her own Marines, and she was conscious once more of the dried blood which had splashed her own skinsuit and of the ache of weariness deep in her bones.

"How bad is the bill?" she asked him finally.

"So far, it looks like three of our people and about thirty of the Ballroom's people, dead," Neukirch said harshly. "We've got two more wounded here, and another half-dozen or so—mostly minor stuff—back aboard ship. The Ballroom's got about twenty seriously wounded—I think most of them are going to make it—and another fifteen or twenty walking wounded. I don't know for sure how many minor injuries their own people patched up."

Honor squeezed the bridge of her nose for a moment, then nodded. It was a steep price, but not as bad as the one she'd feared might have to be paid.

"And the station's legitimate personnel?"

"As far as I know, we didn't lose any of them," Neukirch told her, his expression lightening...slightly, and shook his head in semi-disbelief. "I didn't hear what you said to that Mazur asshole, but it seems to've been effective!"

Honor nodded again. Clearly, the Manpower engineering officer had taken her seriously. She still didn't know exactly how he'd pulled it off—and, to be perfectly honest, she didn't care—but he'd managed to convince at least a dozen others that protecting the Silesian civilians and slaves being held aboard the platform represented their own sole chance for survival. It was fortunate for everyone concerned that the civilians had been confined in the same section of the station as the slaves whenever they weren't actually on duty, and that the "new management" had sealed off all but one of the passages into that section as one of their own security measures. Mazur and his fellows had been able to get into the confinement area virtually unopposed, and they'd only had to hold that single entryway until Nat Turner Jurgenson's fighters and one of Janacek's two squads of armored Marines smashed their way through to them.

"Unfortunately," Neukirch's face tightened again, "I think a lot of them had already been killed before we got here, Ma'am. And most of the ones we're getting out have been through Hell." He shook his head. "I've been too busy patching up people to really examine them yet, but I think a lot of the regular crew—and their families, damn it!—actually had it even worse than the slaves did."

His jaw muscles clenched. "Bad enough for the adults, but the *kids*." His nostrils flared. "These *bastards* used them up like cheap toys!"

"Of course they did, Mauricio," Honor said wearily. He looked at her, and she shrugged. "Slaves are a commodity," her voice was flat, ugly. "They represent cash value. But the people who just got in Manpower's way?" She shrugged again, the motion quick and angry. "They were *freebies*, Mauricio. Nobody in Accounting was going to complain if some of *them* got killed. After all, these people were going to kill them *all* when they left, weren't they? So why not go ahead and *enjoy* themselves first?"

She hadn't even raised her voice, but Mauricio Neukirch had never heard so much soul-deep anger in his CO's voice . . . nor seen so much grief and so much hatred in those calm almond eyes. He started to say something to her, then closed his mouth, looked away, and simply shook his head in silence.

"It's all right, Mauricio."

Honor's voice was suddenly gentle, almost compassionate, and he looked back at her as he felt her hand on his shoulder.

"It's all right," she said again, softly. "At least we got some of them out. On the grand scale of the universe, maybe it doesn't matter at all. But it matters to *these* people. And it matters to *us*, Mauricio. It matters to us."

❖　　❖　　❖

The sound of the bedside com's attention signal pulled Honor up out of uneasy dreams. She woke as she always did, with the instant awareness of her surroundings her years of naval service had drilled into her, yet the ghosts of those dreams—of the things she'd seen aboard the platform, of the shattered faces and the all too often savagely scarred bodies of the captives they'd liberated—floated in her eyes as Nimitz rolled off his customary sleeping position on her chest. He made a disgruntled, sleepy sound, and she quirked a semi-apologetic smile in his direction and caressed his ears with her left hand even as her right reached for the com's acceptance key.

"Yes?" The single word came out crisp and clear.

"Skipper," Taylor Nairobi's voice said from behind the audio-only display's wallpaper, "I think you'd better get dressed and come up here."

"Why?" Honor's tone had sharpened, and her eyes narrowed. It wasn't like Nairobi to play games of the middle of the night, but—

"We've just picked up a hyper footprint at just over fifty-four million klicks. It's a single ship, headed our way at four hundred gravities." Nairobi paused for a moment, then cleared his throat. "It looks a hell of a lot like a Confed heavy cruiser, Ma'am."

"I'll be up directly," she said, and swung her long legs over the side of her bunk.

✳   ✳   ✳

Honor walked onto *Hawkwing*'s bridge less than seven minutes later. Her uniform was immaculate, perfectly arranged, and her short, feathery hair was neatly brushed under her white beret. Nimitz rode high and straight on her shoulder, and her expression was focused but calm.

"Captain is on the bridge!" the quartermaster of the watch snapped. People started to rise, but Honor waved briskly.

"As you were," she said, and crossed to Nairobi as the exec climbed out of the command chair at the center of the bridge.

"I have the ship," she told him, settling into the chair he'd just vacated.

"Aye, Ma'am. You have the ship," he confirmed, and she nodded her head in the direction of the master plot and the icon crawling across it toward them.

"Anything more on our visitor?"

Her voice was considerably calmer than she actually felt. Five days had passed since the savage battle aboard Casimir Depot, and so far, Governor Obermeyer wasn't even willing to talk to them. Well, that wasn't entirely correct. She hadn't even acknowledged receipt of Honor's factual and complete (mostly) reports or the massive stack of supportive evidence *Hawkwing* had turned up aboard the platform (except to reject them out of hand as "unacceptable"), but she'd been more than willing to express her opinion—at some length—of *Hawkwing*'s high-handed, arrogant, and totally unacceptable violation of the solemn sovereignty of the Silesian Confederacy's territory. Whatever might have been transpiring aboard Casimir Depot, it couldn't possibly justify the Star Kingdom's flagrant, unilateral intrusion into the Confederacy's internal affairs and territory. The Confederacy was not some neo-barb single-system little flyspeck on a chart somewhere, she had informed Honor icily, and she intended to demand apologies—and undoubtedly reparations—at the very highest level.

Honor wished Obermeyer's attitude could have come as a surprise. But given the fact that the system governor had been on Manpower's payroll for better than two T-years—a fact which had been amply confirmed by the records they'd captured in Sokolowska's private files—Obermeyer didn't really have any other viable response. She couldn't possibly admit the validity of that evidence, so she was concentrating on so thoroughly attacking and vilifying the evidence's originators that no one would be looking at the facts themselves. While it was always possible her own patrons—starting, no doubt, with Sector Governor Charnowska— were powerful enough to protect her from any investigation which might ensue, she'd clearly decided the best defense was a powerful offense. It was obvious she intended for her own creatively inventive version of events near Elsbietá to be the official one, and she'd been careful to heap scorn on everything Honor had reported to her. She'd treated those reports as no more than the self-serving lies to be expected out of a rogue officer who'd so brazenly violated Silesian sovereignty and, undoubtedly, killed hundreds of Silesian citizens in the course of her lunatic attack on a peaceful industrial platform. She hadn't even taken official cognizance of the liberated slaves and freed Silesian citizens Honor and her allies had found aboard the platform.

All of which makes me wonder if she'd cheerfully "disappear" all of them if we'd just pull out and let her, Honor thought grimly from behind her serene eyes. *It would certainly be more convenient for her if there were no one around to confirm our version of what happened out here, and given that she was willing to climb into bed with Manpower in the first place...*

"Actually, Skipper," Nairobi replied to her question in an odd tone, "we do have a little more. In fact, CIC's identified her."

Honor quirked an eyebrow at him, and he shrugged.

"According to CIC, Ma'am, that's the Confederacy Navy's heavy cruiser *Feliksá.*"

Both of Honor's eyebrows rose this time, and the XO shook his head.

"She hasn't said a word yet, Ma'am, but CIC's confident they're reading her fingerprint accurately."

"I see."

Honor leaned back in her command chair, elbows on its armrests, fingers steepled together in front of her, and her mind raced. *Feliksá* was the last thing she would have expected to see here in Casimir. Given the fact that Commodore Teschendorff was assigned to Hillman, his flagship was at least twenty light-years outside his jurisdiction, and intruding into someone else's private preserve without an invitation simply wasn't done in the Confederacy Navy.

"How long for her to reach us?" she asked.

"She only brought about nine hundred KPS across the wall with her, Ma'am." Lieutenant JG Wallace Markham, Aniella Matsakis's assistant astrogator, had the watch. The brown-haired, hazel-eyed Markham was from Gryphon, with a burr that almost matched Aloysius O'Neal's, and he was only a couple of years older than Everett Janacek. "She's accelerating at roughly two-point-niner KPS squared, so assuming she's headed for a zero-zero with us here, she'll make turnover in about fifty-three minutes, and she should reach us in another hour and ten minutes. Current range is five-three-point-niner million kilometers."

"Thank you, Wallace."

"You're welcome, Ma'am."

Honor thought some more. Should she go ahead and hail *Feliksá*?

If she did, it would take only three minutes for a message from her to reach the cruiser, as opposed to the forty-plus minutes it would take any message from Obermeyer to reach her, even assuming Obermeyer realized who and what she was. It was far from certain that a Silesian system, especially one as poverty-stricken as Casimir, had the sensor ability to identify a target this far out. For that matter, they might not even have detected *Feliksá*'s hyper footprint! And even if they had, Obermeyer almost certainly couldn't know what *Feliksá* was. In fact, her most reasonable assumption would be that it was another slaver or pirate headed in to avail itself of Casimir Depot's hospitality. Which would present her with an interesting quandary of her own. Did she contact the newcomer and warn it to stay away from the platform? Or did she contact the newcomer and encourage it—assuming it was armed—to *attack* the platform and its new tenants? And what happened if she sent a personal message to what she *thought* was an outlaw vessel...and it got received, instead, by a Confederacy Navy cruiser? Now, *there* was an entertaining thought.

Either way, Honor could get a message to the cruiser a lot faster than anything from the inner system could reach her, and opening the conversation on her terms had a lot to recommend it. If nothing else, she could get her version of events in front of Teschendorff before *Obermeyer's* version could possibly reach him.

The flip side to that was that it was evident *Feliksá* was already headed for the platform. She'd shaped her course for it from the moment she made her alpha translation, so she clearly hadn't come to Casimir to conduct any official business in the *inner* system. That suggested several possibilities, especially if one wanted to assume certain devious and underhanded motivations were in play, and given the way Honor had "coincidentally" met John Browne Matheson in the first place...

"Well," she said almost whimsically, "I imagine we'll find out what she's doing here in about two hours, then."

✻ ✻ ✻

In actual fact, it was only a little over ninety minutes later, when *Feliksá* had closed to fifteen light-seconds, that Florence Boyd turned to Honor.

"Ma'am," she said very formally, "we have a com request from *Feliksá*. Commodore Teschendorff asks to speak directly to you."

"Well, it would appear the good commodore knows we're in the neighborhood," Honor murmured, then nodded to the com officer. "Put it on the main display, Florence."

"Yes, Ma'am."

"Commander Harrington," Commodore Mieczyslaw Teschendorff's image said from the main display a few seconds later, "I trust you have at least *some* explanation for this flagrant violation of Silesian sovereignty." He frowned, eyebrows lowered above his gray eyes, and shook his head. "I was shocked—*shocked!*—when I communicated with Governor Obermeyer on my arrival in the system and she informed me of your high-handed actions! Frankly, I would never have *believed* a Manticoran officer of your experience could possibly have been guilty of such an unwarranted intrusion into the Confederacy's internal affairs!"

It seemed to Honor that more than one of the people on *Hawkwing's* bridge cringed. For herself, she only tipped back in her chair, lips slightly pursed.

"I will do you the courtesy," Teschendorff continued in that same grimly outraged tone, "of assuming you at least believed it was essential to move quickly in a case such as this one. That, however, is far too weak a justification to be stretched to cover this sort of high-handed action! Governor Obermeyer has made it clear to me that if, in fact, the incredible things you've claimed about the situation onboard that platform are accurate, no one in Casimir had the least idea any of it was occurring. Surely an officer in Manticoran service, aware of how critical good relations between our star nations are, should have realized that the appropriate course of action, should this information have come into your hands, was to bring it to Governor Obermeyer's attention so *she* could deal with it. She has assured me that had you—as every canon of interstellar law clearly required—informed her of your suspicions, she would have acted promptly and forcefully to investigate your claims. As it is, you have handed all of us the potential for a grievous interstellar incident—one, I fear, which could very well lead to sufficiently severe consequences to more than negate whatever *positive* results your unilateral actions in this system may have achieved."

Honor cocked her head to one side, and it appeared to more than one of her bridge personnel that her lips were twitching.

"I suppose," Teschendorff continued heavily, "that all of us are fortunate happenstance has brought my flagship to Casimir at this particular moment." He shook his head again, his expression hard. "Under the circumstances, my decision to stop off in Casimir in order to allow my personal steward to take sick leave with his family here on his homeworld would appear to have been fortuitous, to say the very least." He allowed himself a harsh snort of amusement. "Frivolous of me, I suppose, in some ways, but he's been with me for the better part of thirty T-years. After that long, he deserves a little extra consideration, I think."

He paused, glowering out of the display, then drew a deep breath.

"I will reach your current position in approximately thirty-four minutes, Commander. I expect to see you here, on my flagship, at your earliest convenience. I trust you'll see fit to honor that... 'request' promptly. Teschendorff, clear."

His transmission ended without allowing her any opportunity to respond, and she tipped her chair back still farther, rocking it from side to side in gentle arcs in the profound silence which followed.

"My," she murmured finally, apparently oblivious to the deeply anxious eyes all about her, "he *does* seem put out, doesn't he?"

＊　　＊　　＊

Hawkwing's pinnace docked neatly in SCNS *Feliksá's* number one boat bay in obedience to instructions from the heavy cruiser's flight operations center. The personnel tube ran out as soon as the small craft had settled into the docking arms, and Honor's flight engineer studied the telltales on his panel beside the hatch.

"Good seal, Ma'am," he announced... in the same tone, Honor reflected, a sympathetic centurion might have used to inform the Christians that the lions were ready now.

"Very well, Chief," she said serenely. "Open the door."

"Yes, Ma'am."

The hatch slid open, and Honor swung herself into the tube's microgravity. She swam gracefully down its center with Nimitz on her shoulder, caught the grab bar at the far end, and swung the two of them back out into *Feliksá's* shipboard gravity. She landed lightly, came to attention, and saluted the bulkhead-mounted Confederacy coat of arms which served the Confederacy Navy as a flag, then saluted the lieutenant wearing the orange brassard of a SCN boat bay officer of the deck.

"Permission to come aboard, Sir?" she inquired politely.

"Permission granted, Commander," the young man replied in a painfully neutral voice. There were no side boys, and no bosun's pipes twittered, but she saw another lieutenant waiting in the background.

"Thank you," she said to the BBOD, and raised one eyebrow at the other Silesian officer.

"Lieutenant Osmulski, Commander Harrington," the chestnut-haired young man said in response to the eyebrow. "I'm the commodore's flag lieutenant. He asked me to extend his compliments and request you to accompany me to his flag bridge briefing room."

"Of course, Lieutenant," Honor said pleasantly. "Please, lead the way."

＊　　＊　　＊

Honor had visited several units of the Confederacy Navy during her various deployments to Silesia. She'd discovered, in the course of those visits, that discipline, training states, and readiness seemed to vary widely from ship to ship. To be honest, she hadn't been very favorably impressed by most of them. She'd tried hard to avoid the sort of institutional arrogance which all too often seemed to typify Manticoran officers' attitudes toward their Silesian equivalents, but she was guiltily aware that she hadn't always succeeded. The truth, she'd concluded, was that the reason so many Manticoran officers looked down their noses at the Silesian navy was that the majority of its ships—and of its ship *commanders*—deserved it.

She hadn't liked reaching that conclusion about anyone's navy, but the sad truth was that in a service riddled with graft, corruption, and the worst sort of patronage, sworn to the service of a government which was even more corrupt and rife with peculation than the navy itself, there was very little incentive for officers to maintain the sort of professionalism the Star Kingdom expected from *its* officer corps. She'd told herself there had to be exceptions to that dreary, depressing state of affairs. Unfortunately, she hadn't met any of them.

Until today.

Despite the occasional hostile glance thrown her way as she followed Lieutenant Osmulski across the boat bay to the lifts, what she was most struck by was the bay's absolute, spic-and-span cleanliness and order. Every single piece of gear was exactly where it was supposed to be, and she suspected Rose-Lucie Bonrepaux would have been willing to serve a meal on its decksole. Every uniform was not simply clean (which was rare enough on most Silesian ships she'd visited) but neat, and the people in them went about their duties with a briskness and a professionalism which would have been right at home aboard *Hawkwing* herself.

Osmulski waved for her to precede him into the lift car, then followed her in and punched in their destination code. He stood facing her, hands folded respectfully behind him, without speaking, until the car slowed, then stopped.

"This way, please, Commander," he murmured, waving gracefully to their right as the doors opened, and Honor nodded.

It was no more than a short walk to the flag bridge briefing room, yet everything she saw along the way only confirmed the impression the boat bay had made upon her. *Feliksá* was a typically over-gunned Silesian design, but as far as Honor could see, every centimeter of her was meticulously maintained, and there was obviously nothing at all wrong with the people responsible for running her.

They reached the briefing room. Its door stood open, and Osmulski nodded to indicate she should enter first. She did, with the flag lieutenant a respectful pace and a half behind her, and found herself facing a seated Commodore Teschendorff and a dark-haired, dark-eyed officer in the uniform of a senior captain. *Feliksá*'s CO, she decided, as Osmulski cleared his throat.

"Commander Harrington, Sir," he announced in a discreet tone.

"So I see," Teschendorff rumbled. He looked at Honor with scant favor, and his flag captain's expression was even grimmer. She looked back levelly, her expression calm . . . and Nimitz's tail hung relaxed down her back as the 'cat cocked his head to one side and regarded the two senior Silesian officers from her shoulder.

"I am required to inform you, Commander," Teschendorff said grimly, "that this conversation is being recorded. That recording will be forwarded to Governor Charnowska's office and, I have no doubt, to the Cabinet. What will happen to it after that, I cannot say, of course. I would not be surprised, however, to find it included in a future formal communication from my government to yours. Is that understood?"

"Yes, Commodore," she replied calmly.

"Then, Commander," Teschendorff said, "allow me to inform you that in all my years of service I have never encountered such a brazen case of an officer's dizzying overstepping of her own, her navy's, or—for that matter—her *star nation's* legitimate authority. You've clearly taken it upon yourself to operate in vigilante style on the sovereign territory of the Silesian Confederacy. You did not communicate your suspicions, or the evidence upon which they rested, to *any* legitimate official or agency of the Confederacy. Instead, you mounted an attack on a Silesian industrial platform, in which—by your own report to Governor Obermeyer—*fatal* casualties exceeded a thousand. Which doesn't even include however many people perished aboard the *Evita* when you blew her out of space without, so far as I am aware, any warning or surrender demand at all! There have been pitched battles between squadrons of *warships,* Commander, in which fewer people were killed!"

He paused, but it was obvious he expected no reply. Finally, he inhaled noisily and shook his head.

"Had you brought your evidence to the attention of the proper authorities, it's highly probable that a properly mounted operation, with the proper support elements in place, could have resolved this entire situation without such a massive level of casualties. I suppose we should count ourselves fortunate that it at least appears your suspicions about conditions aboard the platform were justified. That is *not* to say the actions you took in *respect* to those suspicions were also justified, Commander. That, I feel positive, will not be the view of my government, nor is it my own intention to imply anything of the sort."

He glared at her for a moment.

"However, based on what I've so far seen from the reports and documentation you've submitted to Governor Obermeyer—*after* the fact—I'm inclined to believe that at least the dead—the *many* dead—left in the aftermath of your high-handed actions were, in fact, the pirates and slave traders you've accused them of being. And that fact, Commander, is the *only* reason I'm not going to demand that you and your ship accompany me back to Saginaw so that you might account for your actions to Governor Charnowska in person. Believe me, nothing would give me greater pleasure than to see you attempting to explain yourself to her. Under the circumstances, however, and bearing in mind the need for any *responsible* officer to attempt to minimize the interstellar conse- quences of your actions, I'm not going to insist on that. Instead, I'm instructing you, on my own authority, as the senior officer present of the Confederacy Navy, to immediately depart Silesian space with your vessel. I have no doubt your own superiors will find your efforts to explain this affair away at least as specious as I would myself, and I confidently anticipate that you will soon experience the consequences of their severe displeasure."

He glared at her again, then waved one hand in an abrupt gesture.

"Is there anything you'd care to say in response, Commander?"

"Actually, Sir," she said respectfully, "there are three questions I'd like to ask, with your permission."

"Ask," he said brusquely.

"First, Sir, what would you like me to do with the prisoners my personnel are currently holding aboard the platform? There are approximately six hundred of them, counting the survivors of the platform's crew and the complements of the two pirate vessels—excuse me, of the two *alleged* pirate vessels—which were moored here when we arrived."

"A reasonable question." Teschendorff sounded as if he would have preferred to denounce it as *unreasonable,* assuming he could have found a way to. "And in response," he continued,

"I've informed Governor Obermeyer that, in view of the fact that dealing with so many prisoners would grossly strain her own facilities and system security assets, I will personally take your prisoners into my custody, along with any documentary or physical evidence you may wish to provide, and return them to the Hillman Sector with me. I'm sure we'll be able to get to the bottom of all this there."

"I see. Of course I'll be prepared to hand them over to you at your convenience, Sir."

Teschendorff only sniffed, then waved his hand again.

"You said you had two more questions, Commander."

"Yes, Sir. As you presumably know from my reports to Governor Obermeyer "—*and I'll bet she was just* delighted *to hand* those *over to you when you asked for them,* she thought sardonically— "I was assisted in this operation by several civilian volunteers. In fact, it was only through the assistance of their vessel that I was able to bring *Hawkwing* into effective range of the platform and the pirate vessels—I mean, of course, the *alleged* pirate vessels—in the system. Obviously, they believed I had the authority to request their aid in this operation. Since they acted in good faith within that belief, and since they suffered several fatal casualties of their own in the fighting, I'd like to request your assurance that they will also be permitted to withdraw from Casimir rather than facing any sort of local charges for their actions."

Teschendorff made a noise which sounded remarkably like a growl and drummed the fingers of his right hand on the briefing room table for several seconds. Then, finally, he nodded grudgingly.

"Very well," he said. "Obviously, pirates and slavers are the general enemies of all civilized star nations. I can hardly fault civilian volunteers for being willing to assist a naval officer who—as you yourself just pointed out—they undoubtedly assumed had the authority to enlist their aid in the suppression of such enemies. Under the circumstances, yes, they're free to go."

"Thank you, Sir. I appreciate your generosity."

"I'm not being generous to *you*, Commander," Teschendorff pointed out icily. He let that sentence linger for a moment, then shrugged. "And your third question?"

"In addition to the civilian personnel legitimately assigned to the platform, Sir," Honor said quietly, "we discovered well over nine hundred genetic slaves in holding cells. Obviously, neither

Hawkwing nor *Feliksá* has the life support capability to lift that many people off this platform. For that matter, I'm not certain anyone in the entire Casimir System has that much life support—or, for that matter, that Governor Obermeyer's planet-side facilities would be adequate to absorb that many liberated slaves without subjecting them to crowded, possibly primitive living conditions for some time, at least. The CO of the *Rapunzel*, however, has informed me that he *does* have enviro capacity to take them all aboard his vessel. I believe, under the circumstances, that allowing him to do so, and to transport them either to the Star Kingdom or to some other planet which is prepared to offer them safe haven, would be both the humane and the proper thing to do."

"Of course no one wishes to see those poor people suffer any further trauma." For the first time, Teschendorff's expression and manner softened noticeably. "In fact, Commander, allow me to say that the one clearly mitigating circumstance of this entire disgraceful situation is that those slaves, and the civilian victims here aboard this platform, were saved from still further suffering and death. I don't suggest for a moment that that outcome justifies your decisions and actions, but, as you say, under the circumstances, allowing those liberated slaves to depart aboard your other vessel—the *Rapunzel*, did you say?—is clearly the proper course of action. Assuming, of course, that they desire to leave."

He regarded her stonily for several more seconds, then cleared his throat.

"Is that all you have to say, Commander?"

"Yes, Sir."

"No protests of innocence, no attempts to justify your actions?"

"Sir, I stand by the content of the reports you've apparently already seen. I will, of course, provide you with copies of those reports from my own computer files, as well, in . . . the interest of completeness. I acted as seemed required by my judgment in light of the information available to me. If that judgment and those actions have provoked, as you say, a potential interstellar incident, I naturally deeply regret that outcome."

He waited, as if expecting her to say something more, but she simply stood there respectfully, gazing back at him. Finally, he gave himself a little shake.

"Very well, Commander. I want you, your vessel, and . . . *Rapunzel* underway out of Casimir within six hours. Is that understood?"

"Yes, sir. Of course."

"Then this interview is terminated."

Teschendorff nodded brusquely to his flag captain, and the other officer pressed a stud on the console in front of him. There was a moment of silence, and then Teschendorff stood, his expression quite different, and extended his hand across the briefing table to Honor.

"Commander," he said, in a voice which had inexplicably lost its stern anger, as she gripped his hand firmly, "I hadn't quite expected my luncheon invitation to lead you into such deep water. For that, I apologize. It's unfortunately true that there are sometimes . . . problems which can only be addressed by stepping outside the normal avenues, as it were."

"Yes, Sir. I understand."

She held his eyes levelly, and Nimitz made a soft sound of agreement from her shoulder.

"Good, Commander." His grip on her hand tightened for a moment, then he released her, stepped back, and gave her a deep, respectful nod. "It's been a pleasure to make your acquaintance. I'd like to think that someday I'll have the opportunity to spend some time with you and Nimitz again. Over a meal, I mean, of course."

"Of course, Sir." She smiled at him. "And now, with your permission, Commodore, if I'm going to meet your timetable, I think I'd better be getting back to my ship."

* * *

"Admiral Webster will see you now, Commander."

"Thank you, Senior Chief," Honor Harrington said as the Admiralty House yeoman courteously pressed the button that opened the door to First Space Lord James Bowie Webster's inner office.

She stood, gathered Nimitz in her arms and waited until he'd settled himself on her shoulder, then marched as calmly as she could through the waiting door.

The better part of a complete T-month had passed since *Hawkwing's* return to the Manticore binary system. Obviously, she hadn't been expected, since her deployment was scheduled to last six more T-months, and her early return had provoked just as many questions as Honor had known it would.

She'd transmitted her own reports immediately to the Admiralty, along with the sealed official dispatch from Commodore

Teschendorff which he had insisted she take along. Given the nature of the "official conversation" with her which he'd recorded in Casimir, she didn't really expect his official dispatch to say anything exculpatory. He couldn't, after all. He'd already risked making entirely too many powerful enemies of his own, especially given Sector Governor Charnowska's obvious involvement, to do anything of the sort. Honor knew that, and she didn't blame him for a single thing that had happened. Whatever the ultimate consequences for her—and the fact that it had taken the first space lord this long to call her in looked like being a pretty bad sign—she understood exactly why Teschendorff had done what he'd done. And however much she expected it to hurt, she'd also come to the conclusion that throwing away her career was actually a bargain price for saving so many lives.

As soon as her reports had been received, the orders had come down quick and fast. *Hawkwing* was handed over to Her Majesty's Space Station *Hephaestus* for a long scheduled and well-deserved (but mysteriously expedited) major overhaul. The destroyer's crew was sent off on a three-week leave, as well, but only after every member of her complement had been informed in no uncertain terms that the events of her truncated deployment were to be considered classified. They were not to discuss them in any way with anyone—and, very specifically, not with the media—until the Navy had completed its own investigation.

The same points had been made with quiet emphasis to Honor by a senior-grade captain from the Judge Advocate General's office before *she* was sent home "on leave," as well. No one had brought up any words like "possible charges" or "boards of inquiry," but she'd heard them hovering unspoken in the background, and the JAG captain's general demeanor had been unpromising, to say the very least.

At first, she'd tried to pretend to her parents—and possibly to herself, for that matter—that everything would be just fine once it had all been sorted out. The fact that she'd been instructed to keep her mouth shut precluded any possibility of discussing her concerns with them, but she knew her mother and—especially— her ex-Navy father hadn't experienced any great difficulty guessing something was wrong. Dr. Alfred Harrington had spent enough time in the service to know deployments weren't cut short on a whim, and that a starship's scheduled overhaul period wasn't normally moved forward by almost a full T-year without some sort of significant engineering problem. Yet despite what had to be a burning sense of curiosity—and concern—he and Honor's mother had painstakingly avoided asking the questions they'd quickly realized she wasn't going to be permitted to answer.

Their silent support had been welcome, but as the days dragged by, and as they turned into weeks, still without any word from the Admiralty, Honor's heart had gradually sunk. Anyone who'd ever served aboard a Queen's ship had learned about waiting for news, but that was usually because simply transmitting messages across light-years of distance took a long time. It wasn't because they were sitting around at home, trying to distract themselves with things like long hikes, hang gliders, and sailboats, while they waited for the sword of Damocles to fall. Worse, as the wait stretched out farther and farther, her initial hope that what *Hawkwing* had achieved might somehow mitigate the consequences of her actions had grown dimmer and dimmer.

And then, the day before yesterday, had come the summons to report to Admiralty House in person. And not to just anyone—to the First Space Lord, the most senior uniformed member of the Royal Manticoran Navy. Honor had never met Sir James Bowie Webster in person, although he'd addressed her class at Saganami Island when she'd been a midshipwoman. He had a reputation for integrity and fairness, but he enjoyed a matching reputation for hammering those he felt had been derelict in their duty or in meeting their responsibilities as Queen's officers. She'd heard stories about other officers—most of them far senior to herself—who had been summoned to his office for personal meetings. Most of those stories had...ended badly for the officers in question, and despite her painfully maintained calm expression, her stomach felt as if she were stepping into microgravity rather than a luxuriously furnished office whose enormous window looked out over downtown Landing.

The large room was paneled in light-toned native woods, which wasn't the extravagance it would have been on one of the Solarian League's long-settled planets, and there was a fireplace in one corner. It was functional, not merely ornamental, and that *was* an extravagance. The Admiralty Building was over a Manticoran century-and-a-half old and little more than a hundred stories tall, but that fireplace's chimney bored up through thirty-odd stories of

air shafts and ventilation ducting. Which seemed just a bit much
to Honor, given that the capital's climate was far more likely to
require air-conditioning than the toasty warmth of an open fire.

The rest of the office—and especially the models of starships
and old-fashioned oil and acrylic portraits of ships, admirals, and
famous battles scattered about it—made it perfectly clear who it
belonged to, and there was no one else in it, she noted as she
crossed the carpet to Webster's immense desk. Just the two of
them...that didn't strike her as a good sign, either.

She reached the desk and came to attention, painfully aware
of the white beret tucked under her epaulet. She was still entitled
to that badge of a starship commander, and she wondered if that
would be true an hour from now.

"Commander Harrington, My Lord," she said quietly but crisply.
"Reporting as directed."

"So I see."

Webster leaned back in his chair behind the desk and contemplated her, his expression stony. He was a large man, although
probably a bit shorter than Honor herself, with the unmistakable
Webster chin. At the moment, he didn't seem precisely delighted
to see her.

"Stand easy," he said after a wait just long enough to make the
point that, starship commander or not, she was a very junior officer
reporting to her service's head under less than ideal circumstances.

She obeyed the command, dropping into an at-ease posture
she hadn't used very much over the last couple of T-years, and
he let her stand that way for several more seconds.

"So, Commander," he said finally, with more than a hint of a
bite, "I assume you have at least some vague idea of why you're
here. Would that be a correct assumption on my part?"

"I believe so, My Lord." Honor kept her own voice level, as
steady as her eyes as she met his gaze.

"And why do you think you are?"

"My Lord, I expect I was ordered to report to you because of
my actions and decisions in Silesia."

It was harder than she'd expected to maintain her calm expression and keep her inner tension out of her tone. In another way,
though, it was actually *easier,* as if the relief of finally being here,
knowing she was finally about to learn the price of her actions,
was a huge relief.

Or, she realized, as if being here, on the brink of learning that price, had burned away the last month's growing uncertainty and left her as certain as she'd been the day she launched the attack on Casimir.

"Well, as it happens, you're entirely correct about that," Webster told her coldly. "It's not every day a mere commander finds herself the focus of a cabinet-level exchange of notes between star nations, Commander Harrington. Indeed, I can't remember the last time it happened... assuming it ever did. Before, at least."

He showed a flash of white teeth in what no one would ever have mistaken for a smile.

"I'm aware, Commander, that certain of Her Majesty's officers are of the opinion that the Confederacy Navy consists solely of grafters, bunglers, and incompetents. I'm also aware that certain of Her Majesty's officers feel nothing but contempt for that navy, and that, on the basis of that contempt, they routinely denigrate both it and its officers. For that matter, I'm aware that certain of Her Majesty's officers see no reason to pay that navy the least heed, or seek to cooperate with it even in its own sovereign space."

He paused, his nostrils flaring.

"That is not, Commander Harrington, an attitude which I or Her Majesty's Navy are prepared to tolerate. Is that understood?"

"Yes, Sir," Honor replied quietly.

"Secondly, Commander, it is the position of Her Majesty's Navy that a Queen's officer obeys the orders he—or *she*—is given. In particular, I draw your attention to the portion of your own recent orders which stressed the necessity of cooperating with and supporting Sector Governor Charnowska. I believe it was made clear to you at your predeployment briefing that the Sector Governor's pro-Manticore attitude made it particularly important for us to avoid any incidents in the sector for which she is responsible. Am I mistaken in that belief?"

"No, Sir."

"I thought not."

He tipped his chair a bit farther back, regarding her in bleak silence for entirely too many heartbeats, then inhaled deeply.

"I am not, of course, privy to your innermost thoughts, Commander," he said then. "However, speaking from my necessarily limited vantage point on what may or may not have passed through your brain before you opted to ally Her Majesty's Navy with an avowedly terrorist organization before embarking upon a totally unauthorized raid on the sovereign territory of one of the Star Kingdom's most important trading partners, it would seem to me to be difficult to... reconcile, shall we say, your subsequent actions with those orders. Would you care to take this opportunity to expound your no doubt tortuous logic paths to me?"

"No, Sir," Honor said levelly, and one of his eyebrows rose. "I made my conclusions and reasoning as clear as I could in my reports, Sir," she continued in response to that elevated eyebrow. "I don't believe I could profitably expand on what I wrote and recorded at that time."

And I'll be damned *if I'm going to start trying to whine and beg for any sort of special consideration at this late date,* she added mentally.

"So you have nothing at all to add to those reports?"

"No, Sir."

"I see."

Once again, he contemplated her for several seconds in silence, then shrugged and let his chair come a bit more upright.

"Let me tell you a little bit about the correspondence which has passed between the Foreign Office and the Silesian ambassador here in Landing," he said then. "The Confederacy has denounced your actions in the strongest possible language, Commander. They've lodged a formal complaint over your violation of their territory and their sovereignty. They've made it clear that they totally reject your authority to act as you did, and I've been informed that their high court is most likely going to conclude that any so-called evidence of wrongdoing you may have turned up subsequent to your attack on Casimir will be inadmissible in any Silesian legal proceedings. In other words, whatever misconduct on the part of individuals beyond the Elsbietá platform might otherwise have been uncovered and prosecuted will *not,* because of the nature of your operations there, be prosecutable, after all."

Honor kept her face expressionless, but inside, her heart fell. If Obermeyer—and, especially, Charnowska—had managed to get all her evidence thrown out, then none of it would have any effect at all on cleaning up the cesspool of the Confederacy's political corruption. The possibility that it *would* have had any effect might always have been slim, but now she knew it wouldn't. And that the very people responsible for making the Casimir Depot possible were going to use her actions to protect themselves from any consequences for their own deeds.

"The ambassador," Webster continued mercilessly, "has specifically pointed out that the Navy's total failure to approach this matter through the proper channels has thus had a significant negative impact on the ability of Confederacy law enforcement agencies to do their jobs. In fact, Her Majesty's Government has been informed that your intrusion into the Casimir System has completely negated an ongoing investigation. That criminals—*Silesian* criminals, not just foreign nationals—who would otherwise have faced trial will now be untouchable because of your contamination of the investigation and evidence against them."

Honor felt her gorge trying to rise. If she'd thought for a moment anyone actually had been investigating the situation in Casimir, no doubt she would have felt like weeping, she thought bitterly. As it was, she found it entirely too easy to imagine the smile on Charnowska's face as that particular bit was inserted into the diplomatic correspondence.

"I doubt very much, Commander, that it would be possible for me to adequately express to you the severity with which the Foreign Office, Prime Minister Cromarty, First Lord Janacek, and the Navy view these events. The fact that we cannot dispute a single factual element of the Silesian condemnation of your actions does not, to say the least, make any of us one bit happier. I wish you to understand, clearly and without ambiguity, that it is not the part of a single junior starship's commander to negate the Star Kingdom's foreign policy. Nor would Her Majesty's Government be able, even if it so desired, to receive such a strongly worded protest from a foreign star nation without regarding it most seriously and without taking action upon it."

Honor said nothing, waiting, wrapped around an inner, singing hollowness.

"It may surprise you to learn this, Commander," Webster said in a marginally gentler voice, "but Her Majesty's Government is neither unaware nor unappreciative of the lives you and your people saved and the slaves you liberated. No one in the Star Kingdom has the least quibble with your desire to save those lives and liberate those slaves. Were it not for the fashion in which you did so, and the interstellar political ramifications of your actions, I feel confident you would find yourself being commended rather than censured. Nor, apparently, is the government of Silesia unaware of that fact. Accordingly, the Confederacy has agreed that if we will take appropriate action in your case, the entire incident will be allowed to pass without *public* condemnation of your actions. Neither the Confederacy nor the Star Kingdom will make any public reference to or have any official comment upon anything that happened in Casimir. As far as our two governments are concerned, it will never have happened. Is that understood, Commander?"

"Yes, sir."

This time, she couldn't quite keep the bitterness out of her voice. Of course the Confederacy was "magnanimously" willing to eschew any public discussion! It would scarcely be in Charnowska's interests for all this dirty linen to be publicly aired, now would it? The cockroaches were scurrying back into the shadows, and aside from the individual slaves and brutalized civilians she might have freed, nothing would change at all. Deep inside, she'd always known it wouldn't, but having it confirmed—hearing how sanctimoniously the Confederacy was *flaunting* the fact that it wouldn't—bit harder and deeper than she'd ever expected it might.

"I must also inform you, however, Commander Harrington," Webster went on, "that Sector Governor Charnowska, in particular, is adamant that actions such as yours cannot be allowed to pass without penalty. That the Confederacy's willingness not to publicly condemn them cannot be treated as some sort of excuse on the Star Kingdom's part to avoid the unpleasant necessity of making it abundantly clear how extremely seriously we regard this entire situation. Accordingly, you are relieved immediately of command of *Hawkwing*."

Despite all she could do, Honor's face tightened. She'd told herself she was prepared for this possibility; now she knew she'd been wrong. Knew that whatever she might have recognized intellectually, she'd never even guessed how deep the emotional hurt would be.

"It is the opinion of the Admiralty, in which Prime Minister Cromarty has concurred, that no action will be taken against any of the officers or enlisted personnel involved in this operation," Webster continued. "There will be no boards of inquiry, no courts-martial. Partly, of course, that will be because of the desire on the part of both star nations to minimize the public fallout of this entire episode. More important, frankly, however, is the extent to which your own reports make it abundantly clear that the officers and crew of the starship then under your command simply followed the legal orders of their commanding officer. Their actions were entirely proper—indeed, highly commendable—under those circumstances, and their service records will so reflect."

At least she'd managed that much, she thought bitterly.

"It gives me no pleasure to relieve a starship captain under such circumstances," the first space lord told her. "Speaking for myself, I find it impossible to condemn your motives. Nor, for that matter, do I think for a moment that you acted as you did without the full awareness that it could produce these consequences. For whatever it may be worth, I believe the *intent* of your actions, and the *consequence* of your actions—for others, at least—were in keeping with the highest traditions of the Royal Navy. That may seem like cold comfort at this moment, Commander Harrington. I hope though that, at some time in the future, you may remember I feel that way. And that there are a great many other people in Her Majesty's Navy who would almost certainly feel the same way, if they were ever to learn of your actions."

"Thank you, Sir," she managed to say, and was astounded by how calm her own voice sounded.

"There will be no official letter of reprimand in your file, Commander. Your relief will be treated as a simple administrative move in keeping with *Hawkwing*'s expedited overhaul schedule. When you leave my office, you will report promptly to the Bureau of Personnel, where you will be given your official end-of-commission leave and your name will be placed in the pool of officers awaiting reassignment."

"Yes, Sir."

They really were going to make it all go away, as if it had never happened, she thought bitterly. Not even a letter of reprimand to explain why she'd been stripped of command—explain why she would spend the rest of whatever Navy career she might have beached on half-pay like any number of other officers who'd been found wanting in their Queen's service.

"That will be all, then, Commander."

"Yes, Sir."

She braced to attention again, then turned mechanically towards the door through which she'd entered the office. She'd taken a single step when Webster spoke again.

"Just a moment, Commander."

"Sir?"

She turned back towards him, and he frowned.

"I believe Admiral Courvoisier was one of your instructors at the Academy?"

"Yes, Sir. He was."

Honor wondered if her puzzlement showed, and Webster grimaced.

"I'm afraid Admiral Courvoisier is one of the officers who's been fully informed on this unfortunate affair," he told her. "Given the outcome, you may find this difficult to believe, but before deciding how to respond to the Confederacy's protests, I instructed my staff to interview as many senior officers with personal acquaintance with you as possible. It was my hope that by doing so I might form a better understanding of your motives . . . and, perhaps, be helped in reaching a decision in your case which would combine at least some elements of fairness with consideration of the needs of the Service."

Honor's jaw tightened. She didn't even want to imagine how her old mentor had reacted to the news of her utter disgrace.

"The reason I mention this to you, Commander," Webster told her, "is that in the course of my personal conversation with Admiral Courvoisier, he informed me that he was extremely saddened to hear about all of the trouble in which you'd landed yourself. I thought you might perhaps like to know that he argued quite passionately in your defense. That, in his opinion, you have never demonstrated less than total dedication to your profession, to the men and women under your command, to the Service, and to the honor of the Star Kingdom of Manticore. Nor does he feel that anything which has emerged out of your actions in Casimir alters his opinion one millimeter in that regard."

"Thank—thank you, Sir."

To her horror, Honor's voice came out husky, almost cracked, and her eyes burned with the unshed tears the loss of her career had been unable to shake free. At least the admiral knew. At least he *understood,* and she hugged that knowledge to her.

"I hope that under similar circumstances, someone would have informed me of that, as well, Commander Harrington."

There was frank compassion in Webster's voice this time, and Honor looked at him. Silence stretched out between them, and then, finally, Webster let his chair come fully upright at last.

"There's one last thing, Commander," he said.

"Sir?" Honor asked when he paused again.

"As I say, I spoke personally to Admiral Courvoisier about your case. In fact, I'm afraid that when I screened him, I interrupted him. He was in conference with the senior instructors at the ATC facility."

Honor nodded. She'd been delighted when Courvoisier finally received his long overdue promotion to flag rank and was given the Advanced Tactical Course—otherwise known as "the Crusher." ATC was the final step towards senior starship command. A handful of officers might have received light hyper-capable commands without surviving the Crusher, as Honor herself had with *Hawkwing,* but no one who hadn't passed ATC could ever hope to command anything heavier or more prestigious than that outdated destroyer. She could think of no one in the entire Navy better suited than Courvoisier to run the Crusher, and the fact that the Navy at large had finally recognized that had filled her with deep pleasure.

"As I've also already mentioned," Webster continued, "the admiral was extremely distressed when I informed him that I saw no option but to relieve you of your command. He protested quite strongly, although, in the end, I believe he came to the view that it was the best decision all around."

Honor flinched. She couldn't help it. Her eyes darted in disbelief to Webster's face, but to her mingled horror and disbelief, he was actually *smiling* at her!

"I believe that the reason he came to that view, Commander," the First Space Lord of the Royal Manticoran Navy continued, "is that ATC is beginning a new training cycle next month. If we hadn't expedited the paperwork to get you out of command of *Hawkwing,* it would have been impossible for us to fit you into that cycle, and you would have had to wait another six T-months before you could attend it."

For a moment, it simply didn't register. And then, suddenly, it did, and Honor's eyes went huge.

"Don't think for a minute that we're not all dead serious about the extraordinarily dim view we take of officers who blithely disregard their orders," Webster said, his voice momentarily grim once again. "And don't even *begin* to think about getting into the habit of doing so! But this time, Commander—just this *once*—the

Service is prepared to overlook this little faux pas on your part. Of course," he smiled nastily, "if we can satisfy Sector Governor Charnowska and her allies by relieving you of command, so much the better. By the time they figure out what we've really done, the moment for them to press for something more... significant will have passed. But one of the reasons I just spent the last ten minutes scaring the hell out of you, Commander Harrington, is because you are *not* going to get away with something like this the next time. And you'd better be aware that you've just finished making yourself some *significant* enemies in places like Saginaw and Mesa. I doubt they'd even noticed you before, but, trust me—they'll be keeping an eye on you from now on."

"Yes, Sir. I understand."

"Good... even if I find it difficult to believe you really do, given the smile you can't quite keep off your face," Webster said dryly. "Now go."

"Yes, Sir!"

❈   ❈   ❈

"So, dear, are you ready to talk about it now?" Allison Harrington asked calmly as she and Honor helped Alfred Harrington load supper's dishes into the dishwasher.

"About what?" Honor asked.

"About whatever it is you haven't been talking about for the last month," her mother explained with exaggerated patience. Nimitz bleeked in amusement from his high chair at the table, and Allison glared at him. "You stay out of this, you furry little monster!"

Nimitz only bleeked louder, and Allison chuckled, then sobered—a bit, at least—as she turned back to her daughter.

"I'm serious. Are you ready to talk about it?"

"Alley—" Alfred Harrington said warningly, and she made a face at him.

"Oh, pooh, Alfred!" she said. "I've put up with you and Honor and all of that 'do the right thing' Navy crap ever since she came dragging home with her tail between her legs. Now I just want to know what it's all been about."

"Mother, I'm sorry," Honor said, "but I still can't tell you. They told me not to talk about it, and no one's told me that's changed. But, if it'll make you happier, I think I can honestly say my meeting with Admiral Webster went enormously better than I ever expected. In fact, everything is going to be just fine."

"You're sure about that?" Allison Harrington studied her daughter's expression with unusual intensity, her own eyes far more anxious than she would normally ever have allowed them to be.

"Positive," Honor said firmly, and her mother's taut shoulders relaxed.

"Good," she said softly, reaching up to pat her far taller daughter's shoulder gently. "Good."

"Yes," Honor replied, putting her arm around her and hugging her gently. "Yes, I think it really is—good, I mean."

The two of them stood that way for several seconds, and then Allison gave herself a shake and looked up at Honor with something much more like her normal grin.

"Now that you've told me that much, though," she said, "I suppose I should ask you if all of that stuff you're not supposed to talk to me about has anything to do with that little unauthorized attack you made on the Casimir System in company with the Ballroom?"

Honor blinked in astonishment, and Allison snorted.

"Honor, Beowulf is just on the other side of the Wormhole. Where do you think all those liberated slaves went? And what makes you think a 'merchantship' crewed almost exclusively by people with last names like 'X' could land a thousand liberated slaves on Beowulf without my family knowing about it? I got Jacques' first letter less than a week after you got home from Silesia! But since it was obvious to your father"—she glowered at Alfred—"that you'd been ordered not to talk about it, I didn't press you for any details. Now that you've been to talk to the Admiralty, though, I'm not feeling quite so charitable. So, tell me. Did Jacques get the details right?"

"Since I don't know exactly what he told you, I can't say," Honor said. Although, she reflected, her mother's older brother almost certainly had gotten "the details right." In fact, given his role in the Anti-Slavery League, she strongly suspected that he'd gotten the "details" directly from Samson X and Henri Christophe. "I'd say it's likely he did, though," she added out loud.

"And did you really come as close as he thinks you did to throwing your career away to do it?" Allison asked much more quietly.

"I don't know—" Honor began, but then she met her mother's gaze and knew it wasn't a time for brushing things aside.

"Yes, Mother," she said instead, her own voice quiet. "I did."

"Oh, Honor!" Allison half whispered, reaching up to take her daughter's face between her hands. She held her there, looking deep into Honor's eyes, and her own brimmed with tears.

"Jacques told me what you did," she said. "He told me he didn't think there was another officer anywhere—even in the Manticoran Navy—who would've done what you did with the *Ballroom,* of all people. He was so *proud* of you, Honor! But all *I* could think was to wonder why you'd done it. Was it my fault? I know how much the Navy means to you, love—did you come that close to throwing it all away because you know how *I* feel about genetic slavery?"

Honor looked back at her, knowing her mother wanted the truth, even if, until this very moment, Honor hadn't known exactly what that truth was, herself. And then, finally, she shook her head slightly.

"Mother, it wasn't your fault," she said. "Oh, I *do* know how you feel about Manpower, and Mesa, and genetic slavery. I won't pretend that how *I* feel about them isn't of reflection of what you—and Daddy—taught me to feel, either. But when the Ballroom came to me about this, I didn't decide because of you, or because of Daddy. I decided because of *me*—because of who I am, and what *I* believe, and what my conscience demands of me. I couldn't just walk away, knowing what I knew. That was the bottom line, Mother—not sitting on your lap when I was a kid and listening to you and Uncle Jacques talking about the ASL and the Ballroom. It was knowing that if I did something I might actually save at least a few lives from that sort of living hell . . . and that if I *didn't* do something, no one else could."

She looked down into her mother's eyes.

"I couldn't let that happen. I just . . . couldn't."

Allison Harrington looked up at her towering daughter for endless seconds, and then, slowly, she shook her own head.

"You're wrong, you know," she said softly, "it *is* my fault—mine and your father's. After all," she smiled hugely through a haze of tears, "we're the ones who named you Honor."

An Introduction to Modern Starship Armor Design

Mr. Hegel DiLutorio, CAPT, RMN, ret.
HMSS *Hephaestus*, 1906 PD

Author's Note: The author developed a healthy respect for and interest in armor systems during thirty odd years spent cursing the stuff while trying to get at some component or other. He is greatly indebted to friends at BuShips and various design yards across the Manticore System and beyond for their patience and willingness to provide (always strictly unclassified) information. They are too numerous to name here but their contributions made this article possible. All his dates are Post Diaspora (PD), and all his errors are his own.

The last century of dramatic development in naval weaponry has driven constant co-evolution in starship passive protection systems. A starship's main defenses might consist of electronic countermeasures, countermissiles, point defense laser clusters, and powerful gravitic sidewalls, but all too often the last line of defense between the spacer and vacuum is armor. Modern armor designs are able to protect vital components from beam attacks carrying energy enough to convert solid matter into plasma very much like that at the heart of a sun. How is this possible? The present work begins with a history of weapon threats to starships, goes on to examine the laser head armed impeller drive missile threat now emerging as a significant factor in armor design, and concludes with a description of the design process. The *Star Knight*-class heavy cruiser's armor system is used as a practical example.

Deep Space Warfare from 1246 to the Present: A Short History of the Threat

The threats to starships are often classified by origin—natural or artificial. Spacers have been familiar with many of these threats since the first primitive chemical flights left Earth in the centuries before the Diaspora. The natural threats are meteorites of various kinds and radiation from various sources. The artificial ones that come most readily to mind are weapons but also include debris from human activity—a constant concern even after two thousand years of spaceflight and made more serious by the high relative velocities generated by impeller drives. A collision with even small debris at today's relative velocities can produce catastrophic results quite as deadly as weapons fire unless proper safeguards are in place. Indeed, it was protection from the natural threats of micrometeorite impact, debris, and radiation that drove initial research into early spacecraft armors. Every threat has unique aspects and a proper treatment of armor design would examine their influence in detail. Bandwidth and the patience of editors constrain us here to pick just one threat whose influence has been growing in modern armor design.

It can safely be said that the impeller drive missile armed with laser heads is emerging as a significant anti-ship threat as the twentieth century of the Diaspora begins. The last few decades have certainly borne this out, though the ship-mounted graser and laser still reign supreme in short range combat. No single weapon type has ever been the central object of a longer arms race than the impeller missile. The laser head is merely the latest in a long line of developments. The thrusts and parries of the offensive and defensive schools within starship design circles are intimately connected with this amazing and terrible engine of destruction.

The impeller drive missile dates back to shortly after the introduction of the impeller drive itself in 1246 PD. The first small automated impeller test spacecraft were essentially missiles in all but intent. A single impeller ring, a short lived power supply, a guidance package, and a telemetry system were all mounted in a sturdy spaceframe which could withstand the notoriously unpredictable accelerations of these first generation drives. These early prototypes, massing thousands of tons, were uneconomical as weapons, but their test results spurred investment in the new technology. Widespread experimentation by several groups, notably Beowulf in the still young Solarian League, soon produced smaller more practical drives. The galaxy's militaries were quick to recognize the possibilities of weaponization. The age of the impeller drive missile had begun.

The early missiles were large and expensive. Only a few could be carried on the largest ships, but a hit was essentially guaranteed to completely destroy the target. These weapons had no warhead. Rather, the missile sought to slip between the planes of the target's wedge and ram its own wedge into the target directly. Then as now, no known spacecraft building material could survive contact with an impeller wedge. This lasted for roughly a decade and spurred several star nations research programs into producing the first generation gravitic sidewall generators. These were artificial gravity waves powerful enough to burn out an attacking missile's drives, vaporize the debris, and prevent damage to a ship.

The defense was not perfect. It was soon learned that only the side aspects of the wedge could be closed with sidewalls. The bow and stern aspects remained undefended, permitting the oft mentioned "down-the-throat" and "up-the-kilt" shots. Nevertheless the sidewall inspired missile designers to find alternate means of damaging a target. The reappearance of large multimegaton nuclear warheads on missiles dates from this period. These first attempts tried to use the missile to move a payload close to an enemy starship rather than killing the ship with the missile's wedge. These early impeller drive space-to-space nuclear weapons were mostly ineffective. The open ends of the wedge presented too small a target to incoming missiles, and the weapons were not maneuverable enough to drive around an imposed wedge or sidewall and detonate inside the perimeter. Tacticians also tried precisely timing the detonation of the weapon some distance ahead of the target in such a way that the ship flew into the radiation and debris from the explosion. The target's own wedge would then act something like a funnel to direct the blast onto the ship. These early nuclear "standoff" weapons were hindered by their low yield fission-fusion warheads, but did provide valuable lessons on precision timing in high crossing velocity missile engagements.

The gods that govern arms races abhor imbalance, and the sidewall's impenetrability did not last long. In 1298, research yielded the first practical sidewall penetrator. The term actually describes a bewildering array of different methods and technologies of getting an attack through a sidewall. Early devices took many forms and it is not entirely clear even today which type came first. Research has uncovered at least seven unique "inventors" of the sidewall penetrator. Whoever invented it, the consensus among historians is that the first widely employed devices used a precisely timed reshaping of the missile's own impeller wedge in the fraction of a second before contact to temporarily "flicker" the target's sidewall and allow the weapon to pass through unimpeded. This approach had the downside of destroying the attacking missile's own drive (and much of its afterbody) rendering it both unable to maneuver inside the target's wedge and removing its primary means of killing the target. The answer was to merge the standoff nuclear weapon with the sidewall penetrator and use the inert missile front end to carry a nuclear charge into the sidewall perimeter. Careful control of the missile's impeller power curve, proper construction of the afterbody, and a powerful pressor field which threw the payload clear prior to the impeller ring's vaporization allowed the warhead portion to survive long enough to detonate within the target's sidewall. Aside from the obvious improvements in understanding of gravitics, considerable advances in computing were also required to ensure that the nuclear explosive would properly detonate after the warhead was through the first sidewall and before the inert missile body was shredded by the intact opposite sidewall. It was not uncommon in this period for these "sidewall contacting nuclear weapons" or "contact nukes" (as they came to be known) to detonate on the opposite side of the target from the sidewall that they pierced.[1] Weapons that detonated prematurely outside the sidewall still had a chance to overload the generators by the sheer amount of energy dumped into the sidewall by the explosion. This had the happy effect (for the attacker) of weakening the sidewall for follow

---

1   A missile closing at high relative velocities (such as 30% light speed) crosses the ten or twenty kilometers between a target's sidewalls in a fraction of a millisecond. The interposed sidewall blocked sensors, and, for the first time, the missile could not track the target. These factors conspired to make the timing of the nuclear detonation a matter of some delicacy for the early contact nukes.

on attacks. The invulnerability of the sidewall had lasted less than fifty years and was ended forever.

Spacecraft designers responded with vigorous innovation in defensive measures. Early research in electromagnetic and gravitic deception and countermeasures renewed the importance of the ancient and archaically named art of "electronic" countermeasures. Navies turned to mass driver technology for point defense. The point defense autocannon found in some third rate navies today, and even on truly ancient reserve Battle Fleet vessels in the Solarian Navy, are direct descendents of weapons developed in this period as a response to the early contact nuke.

The stage was now set for an arms development race that has continued for the last seven hundred years. Military spacecraft designers devised increasingly effective ways to deceive, destroy, or block the attacking missiles. Weapon designers invented increasingly effective seekers, sidewall penetrators, and warheads. The evolutionary development over the period between about 1300 and 1800 was sometimes punctuated by bursts of revolutionary activity that introduced competing technologies on both sides of the offensive/defensive divide. The development of the inertial compensator in 1412 allowed larger starships which could carry more massive multilayered armor on their outer skins. The new armor reduced attacking energy in stages and was the first practical scheme capable of withstanding the detonation of contact nukes within several hundred meters of the hull. The damage from near misses was still enormous but the core of the ship protected vital systems and spaces from the worst effects and allowed it to continue to fight. Weapon designers responded by steadily increasing warhead yields until they reached the limit of the age old fission, fission-fusion, and fission-fusion-fission nuclear device technologies.

Further change hinged on many years of work on practical miniaturization of gravitic generators in the commercial sector. Their introduction made possible the long sought after pure fusion warhead in the 1650s. This was a nuclear bomb whose only fuels were relatively common light elements like hydrogen and its isotopes. Cheap gravitic implosion made it economical to fit devices with previously unheard of yields into a missile body. The pure fuel made it possible to predict the output radiation of the bomb explosion precisely and ultimately control (to a small degree) the spectrum and duration of the explosion's radiation.

Since most nuclear weapon damage to space targets is caused by X-ray radiation from the explosion, the ability to tune that radiation, even slightly, made the defender's problem significantly more difficult. Missile warhead yields of hundreds of megatons became commonplace in this time period and heavy weapons in the gigaton range were not unheard of. Ship to ship actions once again became brutally short. Warhead designers quickly realized that they could change the compression pattern and sequence of the new gravitic imploders to somewhat shape the resulting release of radiation. In 1669, a series of tests by several navies quietly confirmed the ability of the new warheads compressing fuel in different patterns to produce modest increases in stand-off ranges for impeller missiles in some cases. The necessary software to sequence the imploders and optimize the blast pattern at the moment of detonation appeared in routine upgrades all over known space, because essentially no new hardware was required. Little remarked at the time, these early nuclear directed energy weapons (NDEW) portended more lethal technologies to come.

The defense was not at all idle during this period. Advances in gravitic deception technologies raced neck-and-neck with seeker improvements. Sidewall systems largely took the lead in thwarting penetrator improvements and improved materials and designs kept the defense almost in step as missile warheads grew. The pure fusion warhead might have had more disruptive consequences if the impeller drive countermissile had not appeared on scene in 1701. Essentially a smaller version of the shipkiller, this weapon destroyed incoming missiles by wedge to wedge interaction. This added a new depth to the missile defense problem which allowed nearby ships to defend each other cooperatively as never before. The countermissile dramatically reduced the effectiveness of shipkillers. This was followed some eighty years later by the widespread introduction of numerous small point defense laser weapons. The new active defenses ensured that even a weapon whose seeker was not decoyed by the target's ECM would be stopped short of the sidewall. The point defense laser cluster created the final layer of light speed defense that resulted in the now familiar geometrically increased chance of the missile being destroyed in the last 50,000 to 60,000 km of its run. Hits against intact defenses became rare. This relegated the impeller drive missile to a counter sidewall role in which the best that could typically be achieved was a close aboard detonation of a multiple missile salvo to burn out sidewall generators and soften the target up for an energy range attack. Sidewall burning was in fact the end to which the largest pure fusion weapons were built.

That most navies kept building dual mode (sidewall burning and contact nuke) impeller missiles after this point surprises some. Dual mode weapons provided tactical flexibility. Opportunities occasionally arose in large counter-sidewall salvos to get a contact nuke through. Under those conditions, the ability to have a dual mode weapon capable of performing both as a contact nuke and in an anti-sidewall role gave a chance for a decisive strike at the slight cost of the space and mass of sidewall penetrating equipment and extra software. The RMN chose to retain the dual mode capability, and it is became known colloquially to old spacers (such as the author) as "boom" or "burn" presets. Other navies followed the same logic to the same capability.

Though retained, "boom" settings were rarely useful, so missile designers seeking ways to increase sidewall burning effectiveness kept trying for longer standoff range. The development of another generation of powerful practical micronized grav generators marked the next evolutionary step in missile warfare in 1806 with the introduction of the first nuclear gravitically directed energy weapon (NGDEW). The key components were grav lens arrays derived from those that had dramatically increased shipboard laser/graser effectiveness roughly fifty years earlier. The very first of these arrays was called a "plate array" and simply reflected the bomb's energy off a flat artificial grav wave similar to an impeller or sidewall behind the warhead. Research continually tightened the focus of the grav arrays as impeller missile standoff ranges grew from tens of hundreds to tens of thousands of kilometers over the ensuing decades. The early grav lens arrays were quite large, however, and frequently displaced the sidewall penetrators until further refinements could reduce their sizes. By 1826, a state of the art RMN impeller drive nuclear armed missile could boast a standoff range of 8,000 to 10,000 kilometers in sidewall burning mode.

That same year, a small Solarian defense contractor, Aberu and Harmon, developed the unique combination of a state of the art grav lens array with a series of multiple submunitions carrying rods that emitted short wavelength X-ray laser light when exposed to the broadband X-ray pulse from a nuclear explosion.

The idea was that these rods would produce intense laser beams which would impact on a target whose sidewall was weakened by the portion of the blast front that did not impact the rods. The slight delay produced by the lasing process ensured that the bomb energy which missed the rods would hit and weaken the target sidewall before the laser beams arrived. Initially called a laser enhanced nuclear gravitically directed energy weapon (LENG-DEW), the device quickly earned the handier title of "laser head." It promised to end the stalemate in missile arms and net the first star nation adopting it serious advantages over those which did not. Aberu and Harmon leveraged heavily to develop the laser rods, specialized submunitions to carry them, and telemetry links that allowed the main missile body and its deployed warheads to operate in concert. The Solarian League Navy, however, was less than enthusiastic about the effect of a potentially destabilizing weapon on its unchallenged naval supremacy. Strong Aberu family influence within the SLN and the lure of being first eventually won modest funding for a short series of live tests in 1833.

The tests proved embarrassing failures. Characterized by one Solarian League Battle Fleet observer as "anemic," the system's submunitions proved difficult to position accurately, focusing was much harder than predicted, and the beam output itself was too low to make an effective weapon. Some of these problems were easy to solve, but others could not be overcome with the technology of the day. The lasing process in the rods, in particular, was significantly less efficient than predicted. Recriminations, accusations of falsified data, and scandal ensued. The resulting media attention brought word of the laser head briefly into the public eye where it came to the attention of Astral Energetics, Ltd. Sensing an opportunity, the company bought out Aberu and Harmon, collected all existing research materials, and began a long term incremental development program. Astral's huge sales of gravitic and nuclear physics pack-ages for military, mining, and scientific uses meant a steady flow of resources to their extensive project team located amidst the sprawling industry of the 70 Virginis system. Their work took over thirty years, but it produced the first complete laser-head-armed impeller-drive anti-ship missile system in 1866. The key advance that made the laser head practical was the perfection of a gravitic lens array with a much tighter focus than previous units. This new array increased the bomb power fed to the laser rods and resulted in increased laser output. It also had the happy side effect of directing much more of the bomb output energy that missed the laser rods into a narrower cone. This dramatically increased standoff range and made the weapon significantly more effective against targets protected by active defenses.[2]

Once they had a product, however, Astral found that they could no longer interest their intended buyer. Time and negative political repercussions from the Aberu and Harmon tests had solidified the SLN's habitual disinterest in destabilizing technology into an abiding disdain for anything that altered the status quo. Convinced that the weapon was nothing more than a passing novelty, the SLN rejected the best efforts of Astral's sales department and lobbyists for years. Desperate, Astral eventually began advertising the weapon for export. The Imperial Andermani Navy was their first official buyer in early 1872. Successful, though infrequent, use of laser heads against pirates in Silesia over the ensuing decade encouraged the People's Republic to begin acquiring laser heads and the capability to produce them in the early 1880s in the midst of its forcible expansion into much of the Haven sector.

The Star Kingdom of Manticore pursued an independent path to laser head armament. Always admirably well informed on galaxy-wide research trends due to command of the Manticore Wormhole Junction, the Bureau of Weapons (BuWeaps) presumably learned of the laser head concept when it first became public knowledge in the late 1830s. Thus began a low-level development effort which confirmed the validity of the basic physics without developing a functional weapon. Even Manticore's vaunted research and development establishment struggled with the complex problems of gravitic technology miniaturization, timing, and nuclear processes for many years. Manticoran work paid off in 1870 with the introduction of their first laser head capable missile—the Mark-19 capital ship missile.

The advent of the laser-head armed impeller drive missile put a premium on keeping enemy missiles far away from one's ships and

---

2   Indeed, some authors classify the narrow conical blast pattern from these weapons as a "sidewall penetrator" because it weakens the opposing sidewall and increases the effectiveness of the laser beams which follow. This is understandable, though still regrettable, butchery of language because the term "sidewall penetrator" is properly reserved for devices that use gravitic fields to flicker or open a hole in an opposing sidewall. Sadly, such usage is rather common in the literature.

forced defensive system designers to make dramatic improvements in countermissiles, point defense laser clusters, gravitic sidewall strength, and armor. Armor and structural designers in particular were challenged as it became clear that a laser head strike, even against an intact sidewall, could penetrate dozens of meters into a target. Against an open impeller throat or stern the new weapons could literally punch straight through meters of even capital ship grade heavy armor. Warship armor experienced a general thickening in this period and much greater emphasis was placed on bow and stern hammerhead active defenses and armor design. It also became slightly more common to see dorsal and ventral armor during this period to protect against freak hits from laser-head armed missiles.

State of the Art in Laser Head Armed Impeller Drive Missiles: The Mark-13 Anti-Ship Missile

Armor design is based on the expected threat. BuShips would use intelligence estimates of Havenite weaponry to model the threat but such information is somewhat scarce in the public domain. This article will instead use the Royal Manticoran Navy's standard heavy cruiser/battlecruiser (CA/BC) weight anti-ship missile, the Mark-13. Even here, though more information is available, specifics are usually classified. The reader will soon see, however, that publicly available information gives us a good appreciation of the Mark-13's capabilities and the basics of the armor design problem.

Design and Construction

BuWeaps began the Mark-13 design in 1879 intending to produce the first RMN CA/BC weight anti-ship missile designed from the start to use laser heads. Previous RMN laser-head equipped weapons had required gravitic lens arrays too massive to fit into the smaller missiles fired by heavy cruisers and battlecruisers. Since operational experience with the laser head was relatively scarce, BuWeaps decided that flexibility would be the central feature of the design. It was felt important to support all attack modes into a single weapon. Proposals had been circulating for several years within BuWeaps speculating on the possibility of a multifunction gravitational lens array (MGLA) and fusion warhead combination small enough for use in a CA/BC weight missile, yet flexible enough to support laser-head attack, detonate in a counter-sidewall role, or act as a contact nuke as the situation demanded. BuWeaps began work on the Mark-86 general purpose fusion warhead and the Mark-13 program was initiated to carry it.

The Mark-13 impeller drive anti-ship missile bus is a 12 meter long, 78 ton weapon capable of a maximum 88,000 gee acceleration and carrying the 15 megaton Mark-86 pure hydrogen fusion warhead with six Mark-73 three meter independently targetable laser submunition vehicles. It was designed to be fired from the even then venerable Mod-7 series launcher. Development of the necessary components took over three years with major difficulties encountered in the miniaturization of the MGLA and synchronization of all of the different parts of the system. Towards the end of that period when the first prototypes were nearly complete, information indicating that the Republic of Haven had somehow acquired laser-head technology began to flow out of Haven sector. While the RMN had little operational experience with the laser head, it paid very close attention to the experience that the Havenites were getting with it as they annexed their neighbors. Additional lessons learned regarding Republican electronic countermeasures delayed the roll out of the final Mark-13 design by almost another full year. Its final release in 1883 is considered to have been worth the wait.

Figure 1 (see appendix) shows the general internal arrangement of the Mark-13 bus configured for the anti-ship role. The schematic shows the features typical of most of the galaxy's shipkilling missiles. The Mark-13 consists of four component groups. The foremost, called the "nosecone group," holds the warhead and MGLA. Its outer skin also carries sensors for target acquisition and tracking. The two-meter effective diameter of the nosecone group does not give the seeker much sensitivity, so the primary guidance during most of its flight is provided by the launching unit. Behind the nosecone group is the payload group. It contains the six Mark-73 laser submunitions, ejectable payload bay doors, and short range high bandwidth laser telemetry transceivers for communication with the submunitions immediately before detonation. Comprising most of the rest of the weapon, the propulsion and power group contains a single impeller ring with eight nodes and the superconducting capacitor storage rings that power the weapon's flight. This group also includes the missile's thrust vector control systems and control moment gyroscopes for rapid, fine, low vibration pointing. Finally, the tailcone group contains the weapon's telemetry transceiver and guidance package. The system consists of no fewer than five independent molycirc computer systems with cross checking routines to avoid the radiation induced upsets common during a space nuclear exchange. The computers are heavily radiation and electromagnetic pulse shielded to further reduce the chance of guidance failure.

Factors Affecting Performance

A variety of design factors control how effective a laser head will be. In simple terms, the laser head will be most effective when it puts the most energy into the smallest possible sized spot on the surface of the target. Other important characteristics include the wavelength of the photons in the beam and the rate of total energy flow (beam power). The discussion here ignores the weapon's function in a pure counter-sidewall or contact nuke role to focus entirely on its performance as a sidewall piercing anti-ship weapon.

NUCLEAR DEVICE YIELD

Increased device yield tends to increase beam power up to a point whose exact practical limit is a matter of intense debate in some circles. Above a certain device yield, the laser head's efficiency begins to drop off, indicating a maximum limit to possible laser output for a given system. The physics of this are beyond the scope of the present work but numerous schemes have been proposed in the open literature and on public boards to find ways around this fact. What BuWeaps is doing about it they decline to say.

GRAVITIC LENS ARRAY AMPLIFICATION

Generally, the more tightly focused the grav lens array pattern is, the more intense the resulting laser beam becomes. Increased grav lens amplification also directs more of the bomb energy that does not go into energizing the laser rods onto the target's sidewall. Beyond a certain point, however, more grav lens amplification doesn't mean a more powerful laser beam. Just as with increased device yield, laser efficiency starts to fall off as the radiation bombarding the laser rod gets too intense.

LASING MATERIAL

The laser material in the Mark-73 remains classified and the composition of the laser rods is known only as Special Laser Material or Special Lasant outside of BuWeaps. Sources cognizant of the relevant physics speculate that the lasant is a high atomic number material with favorable quantum structure such as tungsten or hafnium but are quick to point out that many materials could potentially be used. The lasant not only determines the wavelength of the X-ray laser beams but also influences how long the weapon will operate and what sort of focusing will be possible.

SPOT SIZE

The focusing length and diameter of the lasing rods, any X-ray optics built into them, and the standoff distance between the rod and the target at the time of detonation all conspire to fix the beam spot size on target. Smaller spots mean that the weapon's power is focused on a smaller area to burn through the target. Smaller is always better for the weapon because the target's sidewalls will defocus and spread out the beam. The importance of spot size becomes clear once one realizes that the better part of a kiloton of energy can be flowing into that spot. Indeed, one Grayson Navy officer of the author's acquaintance, upon his first introduction to the Mark-13, proclaimed it "the Tester's Own Cutting Torch."

ROD JITTER

In an ideal engagement, the weapon would deposit all of its energy into a single spot on the target. The real world of space combat is typically devoid of this idyllic situation. Not only is there a large closure velocity between the missiles and the target but the laser rods must eject from the missile bus, reach their appointed positions, and slew to face a target with a nearly microscopic visible spot size in a very short period of time. The forces required to get a laser rod into position and rapidly point it are considerable and the laser submunitions are long and relatively thin. Vibration is common in this environment, and stabilization is a non-trivial engineering challenge. If the rod is still in motion or if it is oscillating as its thrusters and control gyroscopes steady it, then the laser spot on the target can move a great deal, smearing the beam across the target's surface, or causing it to miss entirely. Any geometry that forces the missile bus to deploy its laser rods later than normal or the submunitions to slew a great deal will induce more jitter and tend to do less damage.

Weapon Effects and Armor: How Does a Weapon Damage the Target?

The most important thing from the armor designer's perspective is what the beam does to the target. One might define a modern space-to-space weapon as a device which deliberately changes the material properties of a distant spacecraft in a way undesirable to that spacecraft's owners. Most every anti-ship weapon damages a target by focusing some type of photon beam onto it. Beams disrupt spacecraft systems by breaking up the molecular structure of those systems so that they no longer perform as designed. When these beams consist of light of a single color, they fall under the archaic heading of "laser" beams. This term was originally an acronym standing for Light Amplification by Stimulated Emission of Radiation. Only some classes of modern beams rely upon the "stimulated emission" principle and the bomb-pumped laser is one of them. Understanding how these beams damage targets requires detailed knowledge of how the individual photons interact with atoms in the target. Only a cursory summary can be made of this rich field. Interested readers should consult an introductory radiation hydrodynamics course for more detail. Contact the author for several excellent resources.

Three factors conspire to predict beam behavior in a target: the wavelength of the beam photons, total beam energy delivered by all those photons to the target, and the rate at which that energy is deposited. Combined, these allow one to predict how deeply the beam will penetrate different materials, how much of the target's molecular structure will be disrupted, and what kind of shock waves will result.

The author begins with the photon wavelength. One might as well use frequency or energy because they are all mathematically equivalent but weapons designers fairly consistently use wavelength. Early space energy weapons used photons in the ultraviolet, visible, infrared, and even the radio range. These wavelengths are impractical to focus at contemporary combat ranges so modern weapons use shorter wavelength photons in the X-ray to gamma ray range. Indeed, modern space weapon lasers are so commonly X-ray lasers that the term "laser" is generally synonymous with "xraser" in naval parlance. Their rarer gamma emitting cousins are called "grasers." Both of these words have their obvious origin with the ancient "laser" though the fact that many such weapons do not operate on the principle of "stimulated emission" is generally forgotten. Confusion sometimes results because different scientific and engineering communities have different definitions of exactly what constitutes the cutoff between X and gamma rays. An astronomer's X-ray might be a particle beam engineer's gamma ray and so on. There appears little hope at this writing of ever clearing this up completely. This article uses the terminology of the Interstellar Association of Astronautical Engineers that a photon with a wavelength greater than one picometer (10^{-12} meters) is an X-ray and light with a wavelength shorter than that is a gamma ray. This value was chosen because one pm is a good cutoff point when discussing armor and weapons effects. This is because light begins to exhibit deep penetrating characteristics in common spacecraft materials for wavelengths shorter than this so that a graser cannon operating at 0.1 picometers damages a target in different ways than a laser at 10 picometers.[3]

Weapons designers prefer shorter wavelength photons because they are (up to a point) easier to focus at the ranges of modern beam weapons. Shorter wavelength photons also tend to penetrate more deeply into armor and deposit into denser spacecraft structures like impeller nodes, fusion reactors, and weapon mounts. If preferred, the reader can imagine the shorter wavelength packets of energy in a graser beam "slipping" in between atoms in less dense materials to penetrate more deeply into the target and hitting the more closely packed atoms of more dense materials. Shorter wavelength photons also (again up to a point) deposit more energy and thus do more damage to any structure they hit. Needless to say, any characteristics which make short wavelength photons the friends of weapon designers do not to endear them to armor designers. The downside to shorter wavelength photons is that they tend to be harder to efficiently produce than their

---

3 The reader is cautioned to always check sources carefully for actual wavelength figures. Just because a source says that a weapon emits in the gamma ray range does not mean that the beam necessarily will behave like a graser beam does.

longer wavelength siblings. That means less energy on target for a given amount of input energy from the fusion reactors for ship mounted weapons or the nuclear device for bomb-pumped ones. This is one fundamental physical reason why graser mounts are usually best practically mounted only on heavy cruisers or larger.

Wavelength is a microscopic property of the beam. We now turn from the microscopic to the macroscopic beam properties. Each of the countless photons possesses a tiny quantity of energy and all beam photons flow together at the speed of light to their target. Adding up all of the energy of each photon in the laser beam gives us the delivered energy to target (DETT). Dividing that energy by the amount of time that the beam pulse lasts gives the total beam power. A full treatment of how these combine with beam spot size on target, pulse time, and a variety of other factors to do damage requires much more time and space than we have here. Two useful generalizations can be made without extensive simulation. The first and most obvious is that high DETT does more damage because it vaporizes, atomizes, and then ionizes more of the target. The second and less intuitive fact is that very high-power beams (tens of billions of gigawatts or more) begin to produce unique shock effects in solid matter. Hence, in general, it is best for a weapon designer to deposit as much energy as possible into the target in as little time as possible.

Returning to our Mark-13 anti-ship missile example for specifics we discover that precise numbers are hard to come by without a security clearance. Publically available statements indicate that the Mark-13 uses one Mark-86 general purpose fusion warhead with a yield of 15 megatons pumping six Mark-73 laser rods to produce X-ray beams. This last is unsurprising since all practical bomb-pumped laser beams are in the X-ray range.[4] The exact wavelength of the Mark-73's Special Laser Material output is classified. Weapon characteristics are classified to frustrate enemy countermeasures, but they also frustrate attempts to understand and predict performance. What can be stated with some certainty from known physics is that the Mark-73's beams probably have a wavelength around ten

---

4   As already mentioned, bomb-pumped laser weapons are not particularly efficient to begin with, and beam generation tends to get less efficient as the photon wavelength gets shorter. This has historically made bomb-pumped gamma ray lasers completely impractical and physics appears intractable with our current understanding.

picometers. Total energy on target and laser power figures are not even hinted at in public and useful speculation is nearly impossible. Public speculation has these weapons depositing terajoules or petajoules into their targets at powers in the petawatt to exawatt or possibly higher range. Detailed computer simulations are required to fully describe laser penetration profiles and these simulations require a great deal of information about the beam and the target for accuracy. The best such simulations are, of course, classified. The author's speculations are enough, however, to give a hint of what happens when a Mark-73's laser beam strikes a target.

1. Ten-picometer photons are energetic enough to fully and completely ionize most common spacecraft materials. This means that all of the atoms in the area illuminated by the beam have all of their chemical bonds broken as their electrons are all stripped off. This is of particular importance for two competing reasons. First, ionizations generally consume massive amounts of beam energy without doing much further damage to the target. The material is ionized. Any structure made from it is destroyed after the first ionization, but the beam goes right on stripping electrons from the ionized matter as it rapidly expands away from the rest of the ship. Hence, materials which can soak up the most beam energy in ionizations usually make excellent armor. However, continuing to pour energy into the ionized cloud of target atoms can be useful from the weapon's perspective. It happens that, once a target is completely ionized by the first photons in a short wavelength beam, it can become largely transparent to the rest of that beam. Called "bleaching,"[5] this phenomenon means that if one puts enough short wavelength photons into the target material, one continues to burn through it.[6]

---

5   The author is indebted to Dr. Luke Campbell for his patient and insightful explanation of this and other high energy beam phenomenon.

6   This is a different effect than the so-called "high energy" cutting lasers familiar to many readers. Those longer wavelength devices lack the energy to fully and completely ionize their targets—producing only partially ionized plasma through heating effects. This plasma expands away from the surface of the target rapidly but keeps absorbing energy as it goes because the cloud of electrons continues to interact with the beam.

2. Most spacecraft materials are opaque to 10 picometer photons. That means that the X-ray photons in these laser beams will be absorbed within a short distance (perhaps one millimeter) of the target's surface.[7]

3. The massive terajoule or petajoule DETT of the Mark-73 renders the weapon capable of completely disintegrating huge amounts of the target. Perhaps the following reflection will supply perspective: one source close to the author mentioned test firings of Mark-73 laser heads which punched holes clear through stony iron asteroids dozens of meters across.

4. Couple the above-mentioned high energy with petawatt to exawatt power and one gets beams that convert any matter into plasma that resembles stellar core material. Nonintuitive things happen here—solid matter flows and expands like a gas, thermal radiation from the superheated matter pushes radiation shock waves through the material at the local speed of light, and mechanical shock waves travel long distances carrying tremendous energy of their own. While none of these shocks carry as much energy as the original beam they often carry more than enough to shatter the target's structure into splinters many meters away from the original impact site.

5. Ten-picometer photons are not energetic enough to penetrate the nuclei of target atoms. This means that the target does not, in addition to worrying about being ionized or torn apart by shock waves, need to worry about having its elements transmuted into something radioactive to complicate damage control or repair efforts.

7   While Mark-73 beams are generally similar to those produced by an anti-ship laser cannon, if much more powerful, the difference between these beams and a graser cannon's deserve mention. Bomb-pumped lasers consist of X-ray photons that, as already mentioned, are nearly totally absorbed in the outer layers of whatever they hit. Gamma rays fired by shipboard graser weapons, on the other hand, are well known to pass in significant numbers clear through centimeters of even the densest materials. Grasers beams can thus deposit energy through an armor system that is not specifically designed to defeat them.

A picture of the Mark-73's interaction with a target's armor now emerges. The first photons in the beam atomize and then fully and completely ionize a thin outer layer of armor and bleach the resulting plasma. This takes a few billionths of a second and it clears a path for the photons that follow to repeat the process on the newly exposed material deeper inside the armor. Later photons repeat this cycle and the beam "burns through" a target very much like an incredibly high-speed cutting torch. The whole laser pulse takes roughly a tenth of a microsecond or so. The huge total energies possible in bomb-pumped beams can propagate this process to tremendous depths. Thermal and mechanical shock waves race out from the nearly instantaneously ionized column or cone of material, inducing tremendous stresses in the target and often shattering it.

Armor Function: How Does Armor Work?

How does armor stop that process? The easy answer is that it typically doesn't.

Practical starship armor systems usually cannot prevent a beam attack from doing some damage. The popular Preston of the Spaceways image has the hero's ship charging withering enemy fire, shrugging off direct hits, and "coming right at 'em." It is possible to equip spacecraft with such a huge mass of armor that they can "shrug off" enemy fire. These spacecraft are common enough to have their own special name. It is "fort."

Real starship protection systems are layered affairs relying on sidewall, radiation shielding, and particle screen to defocus the incoming beam and spread the attack energy over a larger hull area so that the armor can handle the lower intensity beam that results.

Figure 2 (see appendix) shows a notational schematic of starship passive defenses: sidewall, radiation screens, outer hull armor, and core hull armor showing effect on incoming beam. Not to scale, of course.

This article will not treat these gravitic layers in detail but a brief overview helps clarify the underlying armor design. The sidewall has been mentioned in our history and consists of artificial grav waves generated between the wedges of a starship to protect its sides. These walls are less gravitically intense than an impeller wedge and suitably powerful beam weapons on opposing ships of the same class can shoot through them at ranges within energy beam range.[8] This range is highly variable depending on the ships engaged. The sidewalls are typically generated ten kilometers or so away from the hull. The space between the sidewall and the hull is filled with particle and radiation shielding to deal with natural space hazards. These shields plow debris and radiation out of the ship's path using a weaker gravitic field. Instead of the sidewall's small localized region of incredibly high acceleration, these shields are more gradual. They typically work on particles for longer periods, pushing their trajectories away from the vessel's hull. Specially mounted detection systems and the ship's energy weapon projectors vaporize the rare piece of debris too large or fast for the particle shields to deflect by themselves. High grade systems render normal space speeds of 80% lightspeed relative safe under most conditions. These shields also provide a slight defocusing capability against incoming beams.

It is reasonable to question use of physical armor given the existence of gravitic protective fields. The reason that armor still has a place in modern warship design lies mostly in the power, reliability, and maintenance costs of the sidewall. It is true that a sidewall generator takes up less mass to provide the same protection than a given mass of armor. However, it consumes the ship's power and may even require mounting more massive reactors. Sidewall generators also consume too much power to run off a warship's distributed storage banks for any useful length of time. Combat experience from the last several centuries of space warfare has shown that ships often lose sidewalls in combat either due to generator failure or loss of supporting power system components. Armor, while incapable of completely preventing damage, can at least preserve vital systems long enough to get a ship out of danger. Finally sidewall generators require more maintenance than armor. Some navies have the resources to do that maintenance and some do not. For all these reasons navies have historically relied on heavy gravitic shielding backed up by carefully designed material armor systems.

---

8 Effective energy beam range depends very much on the ships engaged, their armaments, and their sidewalls but is typically anywhere from 100,000 to 800,000 km.

The actual process of stopping a beam once it has been defocused by the sidewalls and rad screens has been described as "a glorified radiation shielding problem" by one shipbuilder of the author's acquaintance. In theory it is quite simple: place enough matter between the protected system and the attacking beam that the beam's intensity is reduced to a safe level by the time it reaches the back face of the armor. Modern weapon characteristics make it in some ways simple to choose armor materials. The many solid matter properties such as strength, heat capacity, thermal conductivity, and toughness that play an important role in our everyday lives depend on chemical bonds between atoms. Modern beam weapons tend to break all these bonds as they ionize the armor. Simply put, the armor's strengths in its solid form are irrelevant when the beam converts it to plasma. Recall that a beam can lose a great deal of energy ionizing a target without large increases in damage. Hence, armor designers look for materials with as many electrons per nucleus as possible to maximize the ionization energy pulled out of the opposing beam. The more mundane solid material properties like strength and thermal conductivity do play an important secondary role, however, because the job is not over once the armor has absorbed the beam. It must still dissipate the huge thermal and mechanical energies of the strike so that as little as possible gets through to the protected structures. This is where heat capacity, thermal conductivity, toughness, strength, and elasticity play their secondary but no less crucial role in an armor system.

A single homogeneous layer of material typically cannot accomplish all of these tasks. Hence composites of many materials are frequently used. Armor, like many other familiar structures in modern life, is formed, worked, and machined at the scale of individual atoms and molecules and so these are most properly called nanocomposites. Cross sections often reveal microscopic and macroscopic variations, some gradual and some sharp, within an apparently homogenous armor plate. Each of these layers is designed with a different function in mind, though all layers absorb beam energy in addition to their other functions. Refer to the right-hand side of Figure 2. Boundary layers at the surface and inside the plate provide structural support, the density to quickly absorb large amounts of energy, and also a path for heat and shock to quickly dissipate from nearby impacts thus limiting the extent of damage to surrounding armor. Boundary layers that are directly exposed to vacuum at the skin of the ship frequently receive special surface treatments to improve their ability to radiate the heat from nearby beam impacts into space quickly. Sandwiched between boundary layers, one finds scattering layers. Also called "refractory" layers, these typically have lower densities and absorb less energy directly than boundary layers. Their primary purpose is to further spread and diffuse an incoming beam. These layers tend to occupy the majority of the volume in a cross section of armor while thinner but denser boundary layers contain most of the mass. Finally, while all layers contribute to the structural strength and kinetic impact resistance of the armor, one sometimes sees dedicated structural layers. These layers stiffen and reinforce the armor and also attach it to the underlying battlesteel of the ship's primary load-bearing structures. While these interfaces usually do not figure directly in protecting against an incoming beam they play an important role in the armor's tertiary function by providing outer hull structural integrity under impeller drive. A ship whose outer hull armor is badly mangled must be very careful with its acceleration.

Literally hundreds of different armor nanoconstruction techniques can be used to form and machine the different layers, but one deserves particular mention. Designers sometimes use special structures within the armor surface to attempt to reflect a portion of the incident beam back out towards space. Most often used near the surface and called "face-mirroring" these tiny X-ray mirrors are formed by spacing highly absorbing layers of boundary material separated by precisely machined transparent spacers that are one beam wavelength in thickness. That this is only possible when the weapon wavelength is known precisely is the major reason that wavelength and any other information useful in deriving it (such as laser rod composition) is classified. The technique becomes progressively less useful as wavelengths get shorter and even under the best of circumstances does not reflect much beam energy. The precision machining required is time consuming and the materials used are typically expensive. However, it still finds application, particularly where there is risk of direct strike against bare hull as on hammerheads. Every reflected photon helps in these situations. Face-mirrored armor designed for the wrong wavelength means that the design wastes mass and construction effort for no improvement in protection.

Armor Materials

Armor materials are classified by their function in the armor system as described above: boundary, scattering, and structural. It is economics that determines which materials *are* used after the physical characteristics dictate which *could* be used. Cost-benefit tradeoffs are a grim necessity in war and it does a navy no good to design armor systems that it cannot afford to build. Even in an age of counter-grav spacelift it is expensive to mine planets for millions of tons of heavy elements and lift them to orbital construction yards for use as disposable armor for a fleet. Armor and other bulk space construction materials consist largely of alloys and composites of elements common in asteroids. This makes silicon, carbon, aluminum, titanium, iron, and so on particularly common in bulk armor substrates. That is not to say that rarer elements are not found in armor—just that they do not typically make up its bulk.

BOUNDARY MATERIALS

Boundary layers need high total ionization energies, density, structural strength, and good thermal properties. These properties can usually be achieved with a variety of available space resources. The most common boundary layers are ceramics such as silicon carbide and titanium carbide. These materials are sometimes combined with heavier elements in composites to provide greater mass and particle density at critical areas.[9] Iron, being abundant, is the most commonly used element for this purpose but rarer and more expensive elements can and have been used. These elements most often allow thinner layers to produce the same effect as a given thickness of iron and can result in significant mass savings.

SCATTERING MATERIALS

While these layers do soak up some beam energy to ionizations, their main function is to scatter the incoming beam by releasing as many electrons as possible when ionized by it. The more electrons that lie in the beam's path, the more scattered and diffuse it becomes. This requires materials delivering the most electrons at the highest total ionization energies in the lowest possible density.

---

9 This also serves to stop shorter wavelength weapons like grasers.

It is here that spacecraft structural gels are most often used. They are nanocomposite materials with very porous microstructures. The term derives from the old word "aerogel" and referred to the original process of replacing the liquid component of a gel with a gas (typically air) to produce low density materials with various useful properties. Modern spacecraft structural gels are made through a variety of different processes but retain many of the characteristics of their ancient predecessors: high strength for low density and low thermal conductivity. They commonly include foams of silicon, carbon, titanium, and aluminum as well as other rarer elements or compounds. It is very common for foams of light common elements to be doped or filled with quantities of other elements with more electrons per atom to increase the scattering effect. The great volume occupied by the scattering materials (sometimes a meter or more) means that they also play an important role in slowing down fragments and stopping heat transfer from nearby beam strikes.

STRUCTURAL MATERIALS

Battlesteel is the single most common spacecraft structural material in known space. It is the universally accepted term for a whole family of carbon-based nanocomposite materials used to build starship hulls and supports. While battlesteel is not used as armor, it is used to form structural elements within armor systems. Battlesteel comes in a bewildering number of varieties and an entire branch of modern material science exists to document new forms. The general advantages of all forms of battlesteel are extremely high tensile strength for a given mass, the ability to withstand great amounts of heat without changing physical properties, and an affinity for nanoalloying. The benefits are offset to some extent by low strength in compression and the amount of industrial infrastructure required for working battlesteel. The carbon that forms the raw feedstock for battlesteel production is almost universally obtained from the asteroid belts. Battlesteel has such low density that it is relatively transparent to the short wavelength radiation used in modern weapons, making it less than ideal as an armor component. A much greater thickness of battlesteel is required to stop a given intensity beam than with higher density materials found in armor.

LIQUID MATERIALS

While not technically armor, many liquids stored aboard starships have a role in the armor system. Liquid hydrogen and water are most commonly seen in this role. Tankage for these fluids can frequently be found wrapped around vital components. These liquid barriers, not as effective as dedicated armor materials, tend to be meters in depth and act both to absorb residual beam energy that gets past the outer armor and to stop splinters of shattered outer hull components from reaching deeper into the ship. The design and subdivision of these specialized tanks includes fast acting one way valves leading to vacuum filled flash expansion tanks to prevent overpressure rupture.

Overall Armor System Design

Viewed locally at the exact place where a beam strikes the ship, armor design seems a simple affair. The problem is that one never knows where a beam will strike and using the same thickness of armor everywhere is not practical. Armor designers, like all others, have to fit their system within the available mass and volume and armoring everything is simply impossible because of the mass cost. This means the designer must choose which areas will be protected...and which will not. Four principles guide this decisions process.[10]

1. Armor cannot do all the work. It has already been mentioned that armor works in concert with gravitic sidewall and radiation screen generators. Without these screens operating at design levels, some damage will typically occur to a target which is engaged by a ship of its own class once missiles begin to detonate or the enemy gets within energy range. Notable exceptions to this principle are the hammerheads which are more likely to be hit on bare hull (i.e. without the benefit of sidewalls).

---

10 The author is indebted to his longtime friend Dr. Nate Nuko at BuShips for sharing these lessons learned from his over-forty-year career in the employ of the Third Space Lord.

2. Armor cannot protect everything. Armor designers have experienced this problem for thousands of years: something (usually speed or firepower) is sacrificed to add greater protection. On an impeller drive starship, the problem arises because of limits to the mass and volume that a given propulsion system can economically move. This imposes limits on how much mass can be allocated to each system and armor is no exception.

3. Combat starships are designed to fight their equals or inferiors—not their betters. A heavy cruiser's armor scheme is perfectly adequate for fighting other heavy cruisers or lighter craft. Yet a battlecruiser would likely shatter it beyond recognition.[11] It is the ancient wisdom, "quantity has a quality all its own," which drives this practice. It would be desirable for every warship to be able to withstand a super-dreadnought's fire but that would effectively mean that every ship was a superdreadnought. While this would be good for crews, the Royal Manticoran Navy could not afford enough ships to be all of the places that it is required to be at once.

4. Armor's job is to limit damage—not stop it. The job of armor is to minimize damage, contain it to the maximum possible extent, and channel it away from vital areas. Of course, there are exceptional situations. One example might be a desperate light cruiser or destroyer engaging a dread-nought. The DN's sidewalls and armor in this case might very well be heavy enough that the lighter ship would find it effectively impossible to do meaningful damage. This should not be thought of as complete invulnerability for the heavier unit but rather as the lighter ship's chance of doing any serious damage to the heavier being so small that a sane captain just wouldn't try.

Armor design therefore requires study of the ship to separate that which is vital from the merely critical or nonessential systems

---

11 The author here declines comment on what sort of fool would take a heavy cruiser into an engagement with a battlecruiser in the first place. This is why heavy cruisers are designed to be able to outrun battlecruisers.

and to identify those components which cannot be practically armored. These decisions are subjective and each navy has detailed definitions backed up by ship modeling, mission analysis, probabilistic risk vs. threat simulation, trade studies, and so on. The definitions below are sufficient for the present purpose.

VITAL

Systems or volumes whose loss will result in loss of the ship or inability to accomplish a primary mission. The RMN includes returning safely to base as part of the primary mission and armors components accordingly. Examples include fusion reactors, hyper generators, impeller rooms, some structural members, control spaces, and at least a portion of the life support system.

CRITICAL

Systems or volumes whose loss will result in significant risk to the ship or primary mission accomplishment. Examples include individual power conduits, weapon mounts, and gun-crew capsules.

NONESSENTIAL

Systems or volumes whose loss results in minimal or no risk to mission accomplishment. Examples include the captain's day cabin, viewing galleries, and some storerooms.

UNARMORABLE

Systems which, by their nature, cannot be armored, regardless of their importance to ship safety or mission accomplishment. Typical examples include impeller nodes, sensor emplacements, communications arrays, and other surface features.

Distinctions like these govern the design of almost every warship built today and govern what goes into the core hull and what does not. The core hull layout puts as many vital systems and spaces as possible in the smallest practical volume at the center of the ship, puts an armor envelope around it, and then wraps this round with other critical, nonessential, or unarmorable systems and more armor. The nonvital systems effectively provide extra layers of armor by stopping damage that would otherwise reach vital components in the core hull. This layout maximizes the protection of a given armor mass because that mass offers greater protection when applied over a smaller volume. This is an almost universal warship design feature, with battlecruisers and higher having complete core hull armor systems. It is increasingly common to see extensive core hull armoring on new construction heavy and even some light cruisers. The notion is evident also in destroyers where fuel bunkerage and water tankage are often wrapped around vital spaces on ships with no true armor at all.

State of the Art in Heavy Cruiser Armor: The Star Knight class

BuShips began working on the *Star Knight*-class heavy cruiser in the late 1880s. The threat from laser heads was more or less fully understood from reports of the People's Navy's battles against Haven's neighbors at that time. *Star Knight* was in fact the first Manticoran heavy cruiser built with laser heads in mind. This had a major and not entirely happy effect. While widely thought to be the best protected ship of her type in known space, many actually criticize the vessel as having too much mass devoted to defense and not enough to offense. Be that as it may, a study of the armor system's salient features provides much insight into laser-head era protective system design.

The general arrangement of a *Star Knight*'s systems is shown in Figure 3 (see appendix) with the author's interpretation of which systems might be labeled vital or critical indicated. Exact internal details are not available to the public, but the plans BuShips has released and a basic knowledge of her missions are sufficient to draw conclusions about system criticality. Manticoran heavy cruisers' primary peacetime missions are commerce protection and long duration system pickets, while they are given additional commerce raiding tasking in wartime, as well as screening duties. They are designed to stand up to other heavy cruisers, crush lighter units in action, and conduct merchant interdiction. These mission sets emphasize mobility and long-range endurance before combat power and might lead to the following system classifications under the general definitions described above.

More than their larger battlecruiser brethren, heavy cruisers must have propulsion at all times. For this reason, the hyperdrive, impeller, and fusion reactors are certainly vital on the *Star Knight*.

Also vital to maximum propulsion capability are key structural members which take the load from the impeller rings. Other vital systems included in the core hull are life support and all of the ship's maintenance shops. The life support systems obviously might be called upon to support a crew on a long journey to a friendly base after suffering damage during a raid or convoy action. Less intuitively, the maintenance shops, spare parts, and damage control remote storage are protected inside the core hull to ensure that the ship, which is often the largest hyper-capable warship in a convoy, has abundant repair capability. The offensive and defensive armament constitutes the bulk of the critical protection priority systems and is concentrated on the gun decks and in the hammerheads. A desire for redundancy may be why the designers have chosen to carry more defensive launchers and emitters than strictly required on a ship of this size at the expense of fewer offensive mounts. If this were indeed the case, one might expect the design team to have downgraded the defensive weapon suite to critical rank in the armor priority scheme to save mass. A final critical component would be sidewall generators—they are necessary for defense but this ship carries more than she needs. These are, as discussed below, probably another case where increased redundancy would seem to justify reduced protection priority.

Protective Features

After determining what needs protecting, the designer looks at how to protect it. Significant laser-head influence appears before even looking at the armor. Atypically for RMN heavy cruisers before her class, *Star Knight* is reported to carry a 20% redundancy in her sidewall generators, meaning that she carries enough extra generating capacity to retain her rated strength even if 20% of her generators are out of action. This is an unprecedented level of redundancy for a heavy cruiser. It is indeed higher than that of some older battlecruisers. It represents recognition of the ultimate impracticality of stopping a bomb-pumped beam with material armor. The wealth of highly educated recruits and trained gravtechs which Manticoran society produces allows this. By contrast, Haven is short on technicians, and places more faith (and mass budgets) into armor.

A related ship design choice gave the *Star Knight* a truly astonishing second redundant fusion reactor above the normal one. Each reactor is alone capable of carrying the full combat load of the ship and the addition of a second spare at considerable cost in mass is a good indication that the design team was dedicated to ensuring that the sidewall generators continued to receive power no matter what. Ongoing criticism of the design's defensive emphasis cast doubt on the utility of this particular innovation.

The *Star Knight*'s armor scheme shows features common in heavy cruisers and quite a few borrowed from battlecruiser and capital class units. A general declassified arrangement of the armor system appears in Figure 4 (see appendix) as available on public datanets and enhanced by the author. Key armor system features are described below.

GENERAL OUTER HULL ARMOR

The skin of the *Star Knight*'s outer hull on the broadside has an armor system probably consisting of scattering layers of structural gels sandwiched between ceramic boundary layers. Due to the massive area covered by the general armor, it is likely built on a cheap abundant silicon substrate which means silicon carbide would be the ceramic of choice for boundary layers. The outer hull is generally fifteen or twenty meters from the vital systems in the core hull. Hence, a beam scattered on impact with the outer hull armor has fifteen to twenty meters to spread out before contacting the core armor. Public sources estimate that the outer hull is armored to a thickness of some half a meter or more. Localized specialized protection such as the impeller room belts tends to be grown or layered on top of the general outer hull armor substrate.

HAMMERHEAD ARMOR

Without benefit of sidewalls, the hammerheads are usually the single most heavily armored portion of a warship's exterior hull. Unofficial estimates from Jane's and other open source intelligence indicate that over half of a *Star Knight*'s armor mass might go to hammerhead armor. External holo inspection indicates an armor depth upwards of a meter in some places, though the sloping portions probably have less thickness than the vertical faces. Some sources report the use of a heavy metal additive as a boundary layer absorption enhancer in the outer surface hammerhead armor. The most common material for this purpose would be silicon or carbon based nanocomposite weave loaded with high concentrations of iron. Research papers by firms known to have been employed by BuShips while *Star Knight* class was being designed, however, described experiments doping silicon structural gels with tungsten, lead, and osmium. These have led to speculation that these materials may have been used in *Star Knight*'s armor. Such additives, if used, were probably a mass saving measure though they would also provide modest increases in graser resistance in thicknesses above a few centimeters. Another oft-commented feature is the bow hammerhead's longer and more angular shape compared to the stern's. This is due to key structural members which must run from the impeller rings forward to brace them under acceleration. The longer, sloping portion of the bow hammerhead armor envelope encloses the forward set of structures while those at the stern are covered by the impeller room belts.

CORE ARMOR

When the core hull of a starship has at least one dedicated protective anti-beam or kinetic layer, it is said to have core armor. Core armor is a universal feature on anything larger than a battlecruiser but less common on smaller ships. The *Star Knight*'s core armor encloses all vital systems that can fit within its envelope, including the vast majority of crewed spaces, power rooms, control spaces, and virtually the entire life support complex. The composition is probably similar to the hammerhead armors. The core hull itself is of course difficult to see in most imagery so the thickness of its armor is uncertain, but it probably at least half a meter. Given the location of external fueling and venting ports, it is likely that the fusion reactors are surrounded by layers of compartmentalized hydrogen bunkerage for extra protection.

IMPELLER ROOM BELTS

While the hammerhead armor provides some protection to the impeller room from raking shots, broadside protection is also necessary. These belts are the second most common armor feature after hammerhead armor and are known galaxywide by designers and damage controlmen alike as "the fore and after belts." They consist of thick armor just below the outer skin of the ship and extend aft/forward from the associated bow/stern hammerhead. The lack of any visible penetrations, airlocks, seams, or ports from the impeller rings forward and aft to a point about halfway along the taper of the hull probably gives a good indication of the length of these belts. There are no external seams which might give a rough estimate of the depth of the belts at these points, but they are probably thinner than the hammerhead armor given that they are protected by a sidewall and rad screens. A total depth of roughly three quarters of a meter is probably close. This belt is likely dense with absorption enhancers in the outer surfaces and possibly even face mirroring.

GENERAL ENGINEERING BELTS

Also known as "fusion belts" these are broad area armor over vital machinery in way of the fusion reactors. This armor is in the bow and stern tapers and provides protection for the fusion reactors and other nonpropulsion engineering auxiliaries such as heat exchangers, coolant transfer lines, damage control remotes, and secondary power systems. These belts are usually about the same diameter as the impeller belt. Figure 4 shows both how the belts sit some distance inside the outer hull envelope and how they are centered on two of the three fusion reactors. The space between the engineering belt and the hull leaves room for non-essential spaces such as the captain's day cabin, whose windows are visible on the starboard side of the after hull taper in some file holos. The redundant third reactor and the placement of all reactors within the core armor probably mean that the engineering belts are thinner than the impeller belts to save mass.

GUNDECK BELTS

Frequently called simply "the gun belts," these armor layers sit on the outer skin of the ship on the upper and lower curves of the hull and act to limit damage to the offensive and defensive armament, magazines, and sidewall generators. These belts would be rated successful if a hit by an opposing beam destroyed only the weapon directly behind the armor and not others. Extensive mount by mount compartmentalization is required behind the armor to ensure this. The gundeck belts are laid over the basic outer hull armor matrix and likely consist of additional high density boundary layer materials grown onto silicon carbide substrate. This additional material appears to thicken the belt by roughly ten centimeters.

Conclusion

This concludes our introduction to modern starship armor design. This area is still sadly misunderstood even among naval enthusiasts. It is hoped that this article provided the reader with insight into how combat starships are built so that their operations might be better understood. The available time and space meant that fundamental concepts such as compartmentalization, relativistic effects, lateral armored bulkhead placement, and control run protective features had to be omitted. The author intends to continue his research, exploring these subjects as well as finalizing armor and laser interaction codes of his own design. It is hoped that these codes, derived entirely from open source high energy density physics research, will appear in subsequent issues of this periodical and be useful tools to his fellows.

Appendix:
Armor Design
Figures

FIGURE 1: MK-13 GENERAL ARRANGEMENT

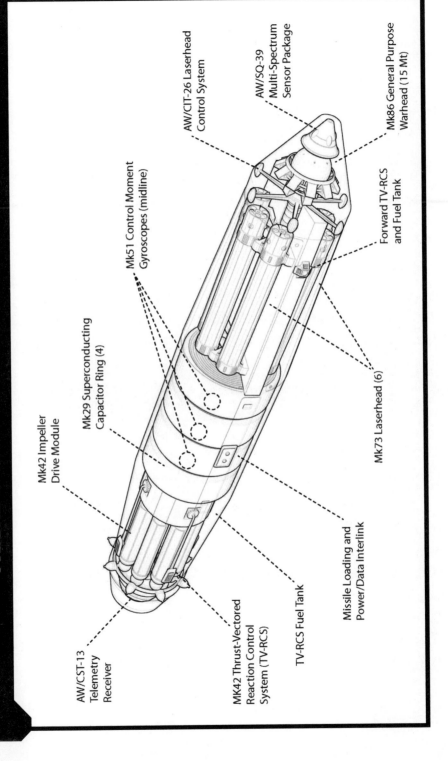

AW/CIT-26 Laserhead Control System

AW/SQ-39 Multi-Spectrum Sensor Package

Mk86 General Purpose Warhead (15 Mt)

Mk51 Control Moment Gyroscopes (midline)

Mk29 Superconducting Capacitor Ring (4)

Mk42 Impeller Drive Module

Forward TV-RCS and Fuel Tank

Mk73 Laserhead (6)

AW/CST-13 Telemetry Receiver

MK42 Thrust-Vectored Reaction Control System (TV-RCS)

TV-RCS Fuel Tank

Missile Loading and Power/Data Interlink

FIGURE 2: STARSHIP PASSIVE DEFENSES

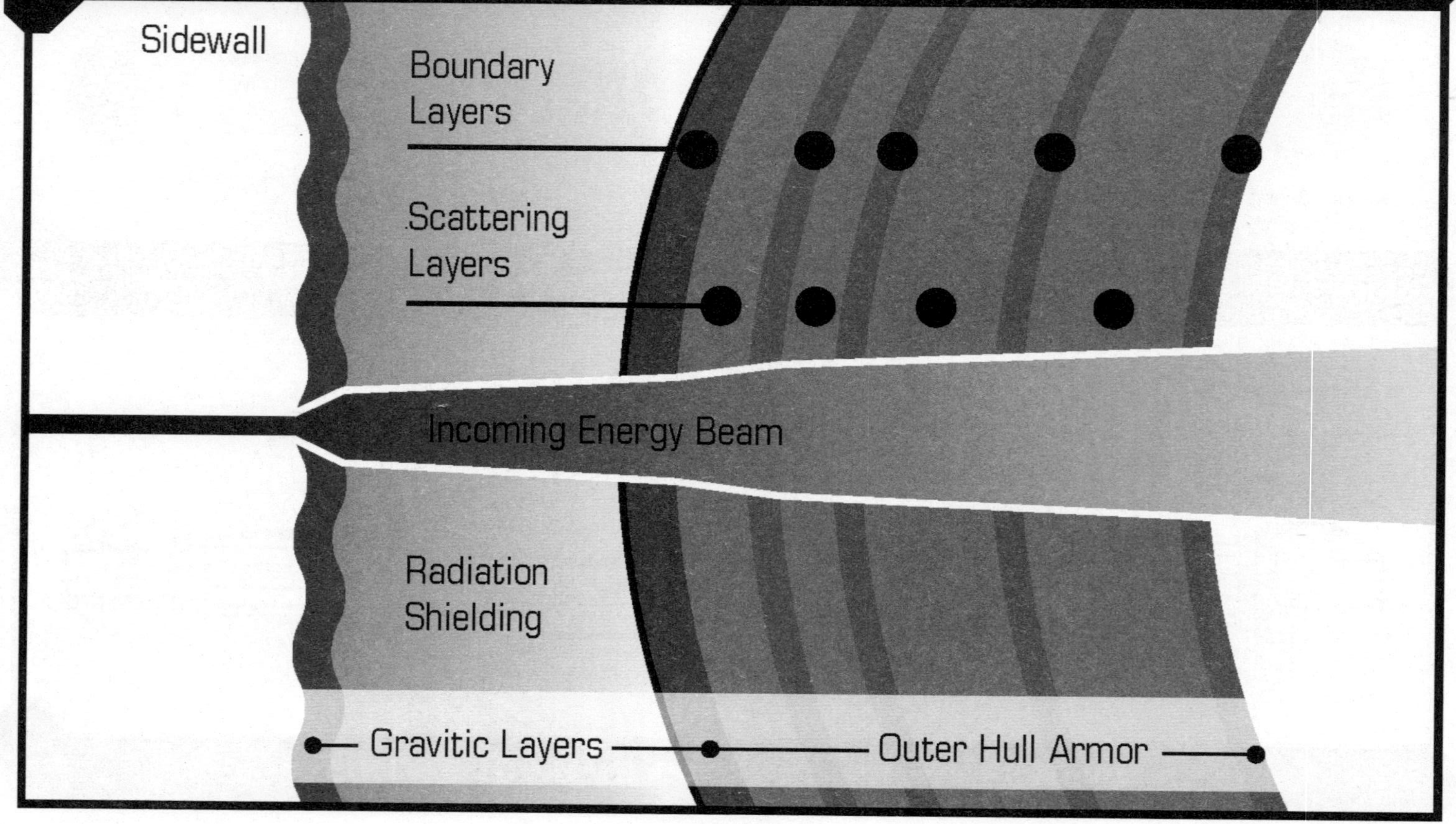

Sidewall

Boundary Layers

Scattering Layers

Incoming Energy Beam

Radiation Shielding

Gravitic Layers

Outer Hull Armor

FIGURE 3: STAR KNIGHT GENERAL ARRANGEMENT

Bow Chasers

Fore Impellers

Fusion 1

Offensive Gun Deck

Core Hull (bridge, CIC, life support)

Fusion 2 and Hyperdrive

Defensive Gun Deck

Fusion 3

Aft Impellers

Stern Chasers

FIGURE 4: STAR KNIGHT ARMOR ARRANGEMENT

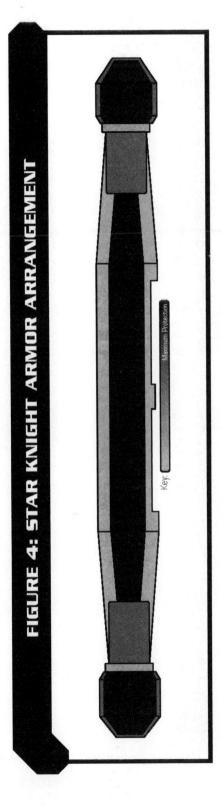

Key:

Maximum Protection